48 BROAD

STORIES

TOM LADY

CONTENTS

Joan(ne) and Frank wouldn't exist without two very special people. This book is dedicated to them.

1

BARRY

BED-WETTING BARRY AND WRONG-EYE ROGGEBUSCH

In the sky-blue room on the third floor of the three-story, squash-yellow Queen Anne on 48 Broad Street in Mount Holly, New Jersey, the same room haunted by a violin prodigy who was racking her ethereal noodle about what to play for her long-since-passed recital, a pudgy nine-year-old bed wetter named Bawrence Barney Roggebusch—Barry to his friends, of which he had none—the left side of his face all but drooping off courtesy of an illness that nearly killed him, was racking his own very corporeal noodle about how in the name of all that was deformed was he supposed to collect the new series of Garbage Pail Kids.

If you never thought you'd see all that stuffed into one sentence, that doesn't change the fact that our half-faced, dime-bladdered Barry was confronted with a very real issue here. He'd only just finished collecting all the pairings of GPK series one and two. Do you have any idea how many Schizo Frans he'd gone through before finally scoring her counterpart, Double Heather? It took a baker's dozen Phony Lisas before he landed her twin, Mona Loser, and twenty-two Dizzy Daves before he completed that pair. Where have you been all my life, Oliver Twisted? Even in 1986, a weekly allowance of five dollars could be stretched only so far, certainly not as far as Patty Putty could stretch her maw (eleven of that gorgeous freakazoid before he nabbed Muggin' Megan). It took weeks, during which he nearly bought out the entire GPK stock of the Mount Holly Pharmacy, before he matched Mark Bark with Kennel Kenny. At this point, Barry could walk from 48 Broad to the pharmacy backward in his sleep with all the GPK-tinged glory of King-Size Kevin (eighteen of those before he scored a Hugh Mungous), preferring the alley next to the garage that led to High Street via the parking lot of that huge church whose bells tolled the top and bottom of every hour.

Indeed, the bells were chiming six at this very moment while Barry shuffled through his GPK threes in the old Converse sneaker box Dan had given him back when GPK two came out. It was as obvious as the gaping hole in Gored Gordon / No Way Jose (he had neither of those... yet!) that the sky-blue shag carpet would be lost from view forever if some organization wasn't implemented, stat.

"Bawrence!"

Hard to believe it had barely been a year since this cardboard bubblegum madness began, almost a year since his allowance found purpose in this ghastly pop-cultural phenomenon that exploded across the complacent mire of the Reaganomic landscape like so many Adam Bombs and Blasted Billys (among the first pairs Barry completed from GPK one).

"Bawrence Barney!"

Was she yelling at him because his clock radio had gone from "Don't Dream, It's Over" to the synthtastic "Take on Me," which never failed to make him think of Misty and her bright blond hair that was somehow a million times more adorable when she had it in a pony-tail? Or was it Quiet Riot blasting from Jonathan's room across the hall that was twisting her phantom undergarments into a phantom knot?

"If I were a Garbage Pail Kid, I'd be Bed-Wetting Barry and One-Eye Roggebusch."

He slapped the protruding sides of the duplicate pile to straighten it into a rough-hewn column, a twisted tower of the most twisted children this side of Dickens. Barry shoved the Converse box across the carpet toward the toy shelves so he wouldn't trip over it this time. Now it was time to continue the never-ending dual between Optimus Prime and Megatron. "Hey, Bunny, where's Jazz?"

"So you *can* hear me. Marvelous. Because if I'm lost to you..."

Barry grabbed the leader of the Autobots and his Decepticons counterpart and bumped them together repeatedly. Having a half-dead face meant having a mouth that drooped on one side in a permanent semipout, but on the plus side, it allowed him to produce some pretty impressive explosion noises.

"Could you switch on the lamp please, Bawrence? I can barely read the score. Oh heavens, Sissy has been moody today."

You and I might be freaked out at the idea of sharing our bedroom with a ghost, but after three and a half years, Bunny was just as much a part of this room as the poster for *Rambo: First Blood Part II*. Besides, she'd been here way, way longer than Barry. He switched on the "lamp," as Bunny called it, the bare bulb in the protruding fixture by the Buttonwood Street windows.

"She liked Bruch today. But I wonder if she's just doing that to avoid Tchaikovsky."

What if the Decepticons won? Would that be so bad?

"Why One-Eye Roggebusch? Both eyes still work, do they not?"

"But this one hangs really low. I know you notice it. And no one says it to me at school, but they just don't want to hurt my feelings. But I heard them talk about it at lunch on pizza Friday."

"All schools have mean-tempered children, Bawrence. You take this school, for instance. I'm better than all of them, and they hate me. Not the younger ones though. I mentor them."

"It's not a school anymore, Bunny. It's a house. How many times do I have to tell you? Cut the crap."

"Language, Bawrence!"

"Jesus, Bunny, how am I supposed to get the new Garbage Pail Kids? I'm nowhere *near* finishing up the last series. God damn it!" He snatched one of the duplicate Fowl Raouls from the shoebox, peeled off the sticker, and slapped it on the wall next to Graffiti Petey. In five minutes, he was bored with the fantasy future of the Transformers and switched gears to the fantasy past of He-Man.

While Bunny showed off her Beethoven for the next hour, the clock radio did the same with INXS, Pet Shop Boys, the Cars, and Doug E. Fresh. Barry became increasingly distressed over the GPK issue. Something had to be done, no matter how drastic it might seem to others. What would the Goonies do?

At seven came the distant ding-a-ling of the kitchen bell.

His tummy a windblown cavern, Barry dropped Man-at-Arms and Beast Man and thumped out of his room and smack into the freckled, hairy, stinking arms of Jonathan, who promptly wrestled him to the ground and began grinding his scalp with his knuckles. I'm being literal when I say stinking. Jonathan always seemed enshrouded in what ranked on Barry's list of god-awful smells as the number one foulest stench his beleaguered nostrils had ever had the terrible luck of taking in.

"What up, *punk*! How about this time you be André the Giant and I'll be Big John Studd and wipe the carpet with your fat ass!"

Faith was spitting orders somewhere below.

It was truly remarkable how rank Jonathan could get. While closing his eyes and willing himself not to puke, Barry pictured green vapors twisting around him, like that one time when Wily E. Coyote tried taking out Road Runner with the poisonous gas.

"Nah, your ugly ass can be the Missing Link. I'll be the Piper. Hoo-yah!" Jonathan picked him up like the kid was any featherweight barbell, got down on one knee, and simulated breaking Barry's back across his thigh. That is to say, it was mostly a mock move. He didn't bend Barry enough to break anything, but it was more than enough to cause ungodly agony.

"Stop! God, you stink!"

"What the hell is going on up there?" Faith thumped up the stairs and stopped halfway to glare at her two stepsons through the balustrade. The Death Star's planet-destroying laser cannon couldn't hold a candle to those twin death rays.

"I told Barry it was time for dinner, but he wanted to wrestle instead."

Somewhere down the hall, Dan hung up the phone.

"God *damn* it, Bawrence!"

"You causing trouble, Double?" Dan was at the head of the stairs, his look as soft as Faith's was granite. He knew the game. Shit, even Bunny knew it at this point.

On their way down, Barry said, "If you were a Garbage Pail Kid, you'd be Jerky Jonathan and Double Trouble."

"They already call me Double Trouble in real life. Think of something else."

"Raging Roggebusch."

"Not bad, squirt." He rubbed Barry's head.

"Alexan-*dor!*"

The welcome redolence of lemon-peppered Cornish game hens hugged Barry on the way down the last set of stairs to the first floor. His father enunciated each person's name as he served them. Alexander was typically the first served because he was typically the first seated.

Okay, that wasn't quite accurate if you wanted to count Gorbachev, the family Lhasa apso. The Soviet premier had been all over the news the previous summer when they got the dog. With no other names to go on, Faith threw out Gorbachev. It stuck. Frank said Gorbachev. The kids said Gorbie. Faith, for reasons no one could figure out, frenchified it to Gorbacher (pronounced Gorbashay). No matter, Barry was quite familiar with the Soviet Union after having watched *Rocky IV* millions of times with his brothers, enjoying both the film itself as well as the sight of Louis yelling at the TV whenever the Stallion was having a tough time against the giant scary Russian guy.

Gorbie wasn't as hairy as he could've been. A Lhasa apso's natural appearance is that of a mop. Faith kept the hair cropped short to ensure no one would be wise to the pooch's being a purebred and therefore tempted to snatch him. This meant Gorbie sort of resembled a poodle mix, complete with a hilarious underbite that never got old. While Gorbie's parents had been champion show dogs in Canada, the champion gene seemed to have skipped his generation, if intellect were any measure. Obtuse though he may have been, Gorbie's appetite could hold its own against any of his ball-licking race. Exhibit A: When dinner was ready, he bolted under that fortress of a kitchen table. With seven kids and two adults feasting above, one or more was bound to share, intentionally or not.

"Ste-*van*, would you like to start us off with Good Thing Bad Thing New Thing?"

Seated at the head of the table with hands forming a cathedral, Frank Roggebusch, economics professor, consultant to his former employer, the Department of Energy, sometime jazz pianist, scotch connoisseur, and lifelong Washington Redskins fan, wore the look of a scholar even now, thanks mainly to his big square bifocals and in spite of the faded Redskins tee. With his salt-and-pepper hair neatly combed, that dark red mustache added a pinch of erudite spice.

Here's something you should know about Frank's firstborn before I let him share his Good Thing Bad Thing New Thing: Both psychologically and for the most part physically, Stephen Roggebusch was cut from Frank's cloth, even down to the square glasses. I say for the most part physically because he didn't have Frank's gut. He used to, and he would again, but for now, as a high school senior, he was pretty trim, almost as skinny as Dan. Like his father, his weight would be a lifelong roller coaster.

"Good Thing?" Stephen thumbed his glasses up his nose before using that same hand to grip the crook of his elbow in a subtle "fuck you" in Barry's direction that Barry was pretty sure he was the only one who noticed. "I'm forty-six days from being finished with high school forever. Bad Thing? I have forty-six more days to put up with my US History teacher, who's a Liberal Communist bastard traitor who should be taken out and shot. And New Thing? Let's see. Well, this could also be a Good Thing, but today I saw my first Chuck Mangione video. It was for 'Piña Colada.'"

"For heaven's sake," Frank said the way he did when he was pleasantly surprised. "And this was where?"

"MTV. Which I thought only played the racket Jonathan likes and that other racket Louis likes. But they've got class, it turns out."

"How 'bout that?"

"And!" Stephen jabbed a finger in the air, again just like his father. "Chuck Mangione has a new album, which I plan to get. So that's a dual New Thing."

"You also have a dual Bad Thing," Dan said. "Besides having an arch enemy history teacher, we're eating Cornish game hens. So we can't offer you any fat."

"Barry's got plenty of fat he can offer," Jonathan said. Alexander cracked up.

"Jona-*than*?"

"Good thing: Golf team's going to make state again."

"Thanks to you, obviously," his father said.

"I try."

"He's being modest." Faith beamed and blushed. Barry's queasiness from Jonathan's weed-y aroma nearly made him sit up and hurl right then and there. He covered it with a fake yawn.

"Bad Thing? My algebra teacher called me Jon again. You'd think after correcting her all year, she'd get it through her wrinkled old head."

"I am so not ready for high school," said the eleven-year-old John, Barry's stepbrother and the closest to him in age.

"And New Thing? I'll be fifteen at the end of the month."

"Have you thought about what you'd like to do?" Faith said.

"Springfield maybe?"

"Of course you go to Springfield all the time," Frank said.

"How about Great Adventure?"

"Yeah!" Barry perked up. Finally something he could relate to.

"We'll take thought. Alexan-*dor*?"

Alexander's spurt of giggling at Barry's expense was an anomaly for this bespectacled, long-black-feather-haired aspiring bassist. The vast majority of the time, which included his current rendition of Good Thing Bad Thing New Thing, he cracked nary a trace of emotion across that countenance. "Good Thing: I'm getting better at bass. Because I practice every day. Bad Thing: I have to practice every day. Practicing sucks. New Thing: I'm nearly done junior high. Which is scary. Not junior high ending. But high school beginning. High school scares me."

"You're gonna get creamed, bitch," Jonathan said.

"Double New Thing: I saved enough of my allowance to get a Walkman. In fact, just now? Before supper? I was listening to Night Ranger. On the Walkman. It's rad. I mean really rad. I think I'll sleep with it on. The Walkman, that is."

"Technology's amazing," Frank said. "Just think: We're talking here right now. And if you get on a plane, in just a few hours, you'll be at your father's in Los Angeles. Boggles the mind."

"Oh yeah," Alexander said. "Double Good Thing. I guess. John and I will visit our dad this summer. Or is that a New Thing? No, it's not new. We do that every summer. It's old."

"Baw-*rence*."

The very planet seemed to stop rotating the moment eight pairs of eyes zapped Barry.

"How about moving to your mother's?" Frank offered.

Oh yeah! Just like that, Barry's heart grew wings. "I'm going to live with my mom next year. I will live with her for fifth grade and sixth grade. I'll be going to Ephesus Elementary, which is right down the street from my mom's apartment. She lives in the Colony Lake Apartments on Ephesus Church Road."

"Fascinating," Jonathan said.

"It sounds like you have everything well planned, Bawrence. Bad Thing?"

Bad Thing was always a piece of cake for our Barry. So much to choose from, starting with having to sit at this very table.

"I don't know. The new set of Garbage Pail Kids came out last week. But I'm not finished with the set from before. And the weather's getting hotter. And since there's no air conditioning on the third floor and I don't have a fan, it gets really hot up there. That's going to suck a lot."

"Language," Faith said.

"My allowance is only five dollars. That's bad, especially with the new set of Garbage Pail Kids. I wish I could get a Walkman, but I can't, so that's bad. I like a girl at school, but she doesn't like me."

"You only get one Bad Thing, manure-for-brains," Louis said.

"New Thing?"

"I don't know."

"Do this." Frank raised his eyebrows up and down.

As always, only Barry's right eyebrow obeyed.

"And this." Frank smiled.

Barry half smiled, because that's all his face could do. Again, as usual.

Frank brushed his fingers along his mustache, rubbed his nose, and gave the 'stache a repeat feel before saying, "Well. Slowly but surely. We'll keep at it."

"Hey, Barry!" Stephen sat forward with a giddy smile and thumbed his glasses. "I remember when your mom took us to see *Star Wars*. You were only a year old, so you had to stay home with that Indian babysitter. And before the movie started, your mom got so pissed at us for being loud." The more Stephen got into the story, the wider his smile spread. "Your mom got so pissed, man. She said if we didn't quiet down, she'd take us home." His giggling face reddened.

"Were you there, Daddy?"

"Hell no!" Stephen said before Frank could answer. "Dad's not stupid enough to take a bunch of kids to the movies!"

Before Barry could fully process the fact that someone who wasn't his brother on his mother's side just insulted his mother, Frank prompted John for his Good Thing Bad Thing New Thing.

Barry, meantime, drifted back to his GPK predicament. He caught bits and pieces of everyone else's Good Thing Bad Thing New Thing while he banged his ruffled head against the GPK wall for a solution. It was impossible to say what exactly triggered it—John's Bad Thing of having a tough time with pre-algebra? Louis's Bad Thing of having his white friends give him a hard time for having a black girlfriend? Faith's Bad Thing of finding Gorbie's shit in the music room? Dan's New Thing of having gotten a new shirt from Veronica? Frank's Good

Thing of having seen *Bridge over the River Kwai* on TV the other day?
—but at some point the solution smacked him upside that same
ruffled head.

Barry knew what he had to do, and he wouldn't waste a single
second. That is to say, he'd do it tomorrow as soon as he got home
from staring at Misty from the back of class and from across the
blacktop during recess. And after watching *Goonies* and enjoying
some Reese's peanut butter cups chased down with a Coke Classic.
And then he'd do it. He wouldn't hesitate.

GPK series four would be his, and the Mount Holly Pharmacy
would have no idea what hit it.

Did Misty collect GPK? And why hadn't he wondered about that
until now?

"Baw-*rence!*"

"Yo! Quasimodo! Dad's talking to you!" Jonathan and the rest of
his brothers stared down at him with that special blend of pubescent
rage and the teen sense of indestructibility. Just like that, Barry was
faced with a white-hot marriage of *The Brady Bunch* and *The Star
Chamber*.

"Baw-*rence*, as you may have noticed on the chalkboard"—Frank
nodded at the roughly hewn nine-columned grid propped up on the
radiator behind Faith—"I moved your laundry day to Thursday. Is
that acceptable?"

"Yes."

"You're not emptying the trash every day," Faith said. "Is there a
specific reason for that?"

"I don't know."

"Earn your allowance for a change," Jonathan said. "Fat
lazy punk."

"You look like one of Jerry's Kids," Barry said. He didn't know
what that meant, but other kids at school said it because apparently it
was a real bazooka of an insult.

Jonathan, naturally, out-Rambo'd him with: "You *are* one of Jerry's
Kids."

"Enough!" Faith's eyes bore down on Barry with the full weight of tomorrow.

"Check out Hogg," Dan said, nodding at the window. They all turned to see their bald, elderly, rotund neighbor munching on something in his kitchen. The night they moved to 48 Broad, Dan and Barry had been up in the second-floor room that started out as a rec room but had since turned into Frank's office. They ambled over to the windows and looked down to see a man in his kitchen, the same man who was in the same kitchen right now. Dan immediately dubbed him Boss Hogg due to his uncanny resemblance to the character from *The Dukes of Hazzard,* which along with *The Incredible Hulk,* used to be one of Barry's favorite Friday night shows. To this day, no one knew the neighbor's real name, partly because no one in this house had exchanged a single syllable with him, even though he lumbered by every day, hunched over, walking his sickly, balding mutt that looked like a four-crooked-legged bed of pink fleshy soil that had sprouted a smattering of black malnourished weeds. One day last summer, Louis and Jonathan had snuck into Hogg's house when he was away and discovered that the Hogg moniker was more deserved than they could have ever imagined: shit from his innumerable cats was all over the place.

"What's Hogg up to?" Jonathan stood up to get a look.

Frank craned his neck. "Looks like Hogg keeps the same dinner schedule we do."

Alexander leaned over. "Are those cheese slices?"

Hogg chucked a slice at one of his cats.

"What's that on his head?"

"Liver spot." Jonathan cracked up. "That's nasty!"

Barry leaned his chair back to see past John. He cracked up too. "That's ugly!"

"Being ugly doesn't mean you can't be nice." Faith's eyes knocked the wind out of him.

"Faith," Frank said. "Calm."

Barry set his chair back down and nearly fell off at the sound of Gorbie's deafening squawk. The well-fed purebred scratched his paws in place until successfully yanking his tail out from under the leg of Barry's chair.

Jonathan turned to him in what seemed like slow motion with eyes weighed down by weed. "What the fuck, dude?"

Faith jumped to her feet. "What the hell did you do?"

"Bawrence Barney!" Stephen yelled in mock indignation, displaying that special skill he possessed in ridiculing both Barry as well as the way Barry's mom used to yell at him.

Barry wanted to assure them it was an accident, but Faith's tone sucked the spine right out of him.

She shot Frank a glare that lasted forever. "This is what I meant when I said his being in AP last year was a complete mistake."

At least it was Thursday night, hands down the best TV night of the week, what with *The Cosby Show*, *Family Ties*, *Cheers*, and *Night Court*, back to back from eight to ten. *Cheers* was the best, no contest. From the opening ballads about a place where everybody knows your name, and better yet, they're always glad you came, to the closing warmth of those fireside-yellow credits. Favorite character? Norm, obviously. He was overweight just like Barry, but no one ever picked on him. They were always glad he came, as evidenced by the ecstatic "NORM!" every single time he strolled in for a pint. Didn't matter who was there. "NORM!" Barry shouted it too on the off-chance the big guy could hear him.

"And we get to watch all this in stereo," Frank liked to say. "Isn't technology wonderful? Makes you wonder how ordinary people can survive."

Barry, like Norm, had his favorite seat, the rocking chair in the living room next to the broad doorway opposite the music room where tonight Faith punished that piano with classical songs Barry once in a while recognized from commercials. Besides Frank, Barry was the only one who watched all four shows every Thursday night without fail. In his father's case, though, it didn't really matter what was on. That recliner over by the huge floor-to-ceiling bookcase that spanned that side of the room was his permanent seat after dinner until bedtime, whether to read, watch TV or a movie, or some combination thereof. Thursdays at ten was some cop show called *Hill Street Blues* that just didn't do it for Barry. Besides, at that point his dad would usually be sitting on the floor in front of Faith's chair so she could rub his head. No thanks.

Honestly, it didn't matter who came and went during the magical two hours on Thursday night. No one existed for Barry except those amazing families and friends who, despite the quibbling, always got over their differences.

"Previously on *Cheers*," Carla said to kick things off.

Courtesy of such heavy-duty stress like his being madly in love with Misty, having nary a dime for GPK four and having to deal with everyone under this Queen Anne's roof, Barry had completely forgotten that tonight was a To Be Continued.

"NORM!" Barry shouted when the man came in for a much-needed thirst quencher.

Barry knew he'd never be Sam Malone, but if he could be Norm, then he could at least share the aura of someone like Sam. He could give advice to Sam whenever Sam was dating some weird, formal politician woman who tried to get everyone to vote so she could keep her job. Barry-as-Norm could enjoy cracking jokes with his pals when this politician woman tried to get Diane fired because she felt threatened by her. Barry-as-Norm could take comfort in the fact that if someone like Sam Malone had problems with girls, anyone could.

"NORM!"

"QUIET!"

Barry jumped in his chair and spun around only for the split second it took to register Faith in the high-backed, blue leather chair, rubbing Frank's head and making him even more incoherent than he'd already been rendered by the scotch. Barry's being nine and a bed wetter didn't impair that part of his noodle that spotted patterns. One pattern that stood out like a GPK sticker on a white wall was his dad's penchant for scotch after dinner. Want to have a coherent conversation with Frank? Hit him up before eight, otherwise you were screwed.

"Uhn... ugh..."

Hear that? A whole bunch of scotch followed by Faith rubbing his head had rendered Pater Roggebusch about as useful as the bowl of peas Faith loved to scarf.

"Baw-*rence*... Baw..."

"Oh no!" Barry said when *Cheers* ended yet again with a To Be Continued.

"Next week must be the last one," Faith said.

"Your mother mad at me?"

"Last one?"

"Then there won't be any episodes until the fall. So rather than whine about having to wait a week for a new episode, why not be grateful they're still making new episodes at all?"

"Baw... ren..."

As they were lining up to go inside the next morning, Barry spotted Misty easily thanks to her bright blond hair. On this fine morning she had it tied back in the most adorable ponytail you ever saw. The fourth graders, being the oldest at Folwell, lined up in their own special courtyard on the other side of the building from where the K through third graders assembled in the main courtyard by Jacksonville Road. Barry had waited so long, forever really, for fourth grade, and the exclusivity and superiority that came with it. Even if his chances with Misty were less than that of collecting GPK four, he could at least revel in the lofty rank he shared with her. And then next year he'd be living with his mom in North Carolina. Not only was it incredibly cool to be moving so far away, but the way schools worked in North Carolina meant fifth grade was still part of elementary school. It wasn't the bottom of middle school like it was here. No, elementary school down there was K through six, so Barry would get to enjoy a couple more years of being among the most senior and, by default, among the coolest. Even if he did have to go back to the lowest rung in seventh grade, he'd be so old by then it wouldn't matter.

"Hey, Barry!"

Patricia was waiting in line next to him. Patricia, whose crush on Barry was far more naked than Barry's on Misty, was an aspiring ballerina who carried about the same amount of extra tonnage as Barry, which was precisely why Barry wasn't interested in her in the slightest. He didn't hate her or anything. Not at all. Barry would happily yap with Patricia whenever she spoke to him. For the most part anyway. Sometimes, though, like, say, now, he had too much on his mind.

"Want to do homework after school and stuff?"

Did she really think she had any greater chance of achieving even a shadow of success in ballet than he did in getting Misty to go with him to Lumberton Plaza for a movie followed by dinner next door at King of Pizza? Honestly, it was embarrassing. Barry had no hope of succeeding in, say, the Olympics, like that Olympics video game he and his brothers played on the Commodore 64 in the poolroom, or in Wiffle ball. But at least he knew that, right? He didn't have the heart to direct her to a mirror.

"And we can watch a James Bond movie. Or *Goonies*!"

Good Christ, if she kept shooting with so much accuracy, not even Bunny Stringfellow would be able to save him.

Oh just look at Misty. Look at how she smiled and giggled and jerked her head at her two girlfriends who sat on either side of her in class. They sat in alphabetical order by last name, so you might think it pure luck Misty would happen to have two of her closest girlfriends next to her. That's not how it started though. They didn't know each other at the beginning of the year. Now look at them. What else would you expect from such a sweet gal like Misty?

"I hate *Goonies*."

"Bawrence! You could recite that whole entire movie from beginning to end and you *know* it! You *are* Captain Chunk!"

And Captain Chunk says let's get the hell out of here.

"You retarded or something?" sneered Kyle, the evil paper boy with the spiked blond hair, after skidding to a halt in front of Barry while Barry was heading home with "Goonies never say die!" on the brain. Only three blocks of Broad Street separated Folwell from the Queen Anne. That might seem like a walk in the park to you and me, and it almost was in a literal sense, what with these huge, ancient trees draping their canopies over these equally huge, ancient houses and their mostly untended, forestlike lawns. To Barry, however, these three blocks may as well have been infinity. Every single day the walks to and from Folwell brought the threat of Kyle and his dirt bike gang. The only reason they didn't pound on Barry every single day was because they had other shy, fat, ugly kids to pick on, although Barry could guarantee you none of the other victims wet the bed or had half-dead faces. What made the beatdown smart even more was that Barry knew he'd never in his whole entire life be able to afford a cool dirt bike like Kyle's. He could barely keep up with GPK as it was. Kyle was so much better than him in every way. All the cute girls loved him. It had to be the spiked hair and the fact that he could smile with both sides of his mouth and that his voice carried hints of Alex P. Keaton from *Family Ties*. "Smile. I said SMILE!"

What else could Barry do? So he smiled.

They all groaned in disgust. "What is *wrong* with you, man? You're like one of Jerry's Kids."

"I hear he wets the bed."

"That true, Jerry's Kid? You piss your sheets every night? What, you don't know how to use the toilet?"

"What a retard!"

"Don't look at me like that, retard!"

"That's the scariest look I've ever seen."

"Why's your eye like that?"

How in the name of Sloth could Kyle have heard about the bed-wetting? One of Barry's brothers must've spilled the urinated beans when Kyle came by to collect. But who? Jonathan came to mind. Of all his brothers, he was the most like Kyle in his evil and meanness. Their evil smiles were remarkably similar as well.

"I asked you a question, 'tard!"

"Ew, look at him!"

"I said do you wet the bed!"

"No, YOU do!"

"What?" Kyle hopped off his bike and let it fall to the ground, he was so steamed. He punched Barry in the shoulder with the might of Oddjob.

"Stop it, asshole!"

One of the other kids laughed the way the Emperor laughs at the end of *Jedi* when he's zapping Luke. "Hey, Kyle, he just told you what to do! HAWHAWHAWHAW!"

With each exclamation came another lightning strike from Kyle's fist. "Don't! EVER! Tell me! What to do! AGAIN! RETARD!"

At this bruised juncture, the pain that played tag across Barry's arm rendered him too weak to stay on his feet when Kyle and gang shoved him. Of course, it didn't help having ancient roots from ancient trees punching through the earth like so many gnarled knuckles. You guessed it. Barry stumbled on one of the roots hidden under the growth and, with no strength, let alone will, to maintain his balance, plopped flat onto the ground. The impact of his ass on another root would've hurt more had he not so much padding back there.

Just as Kyle and gang proceeded to pound on him, Barry caught sight of the adorable Misty and her adorable ponytail and her adorable friends with their adorable ponytails, including that one girl Stephanie, whose smile was the only smile that could hold a candle to Misty's. They traipsed and giggled across the street and pointed and giggled in that horrible, spine-tingling way only adorable girls can do.

"Get off my lawn!"

When he heard the cowl, his eyes squeezed shut to wait out the dizziness, Barry took solace in Kyle and gang getting a piece of an adult's mind. Only, when he cracked open his good eye and beheld the stringy-haired woman in the stained nightgown, her abominable, yellow-toothed visage, ancient as the trees, baring straight down on him, did Barry realize that the gang had already high-tailed it out of there. "Me?"

"Go! Now! Or I'm callin' the cops on yas!" She jutted a crooked talon at the spot between his eyes.

Barry got up and slung on his backpack and hobbled away with a "Get off my ass!" that came out in a higher pitch than he'd intended.

"The hell ya just say to me? Ya li'l SHIT!"

Yes, one of the perks of living in a house full of older kids, several of them in high school, was that Barry was learning the language of profane shootdowns at a faster clip than his peers. He figured in two to three years he'd have the entire lexicon down pat, and a good thing too, since words were all he would ever have.

Barry shrugged it off when he got home. Kyle was tough, but his fists didn't measure up to Jonathan's. Or Louis's. Or the daggers that flew out of Stephen's mouth.

He fetched a Coke Classic from one of the laundry room fridges, a four-pack of Reese's peanut butter cups he bought from one of the neighborhood kids who was raising money for Little League, some Soft Batch cookies from the R2-D2 cookie jar, and plopped himself on the rocking chair in the living room to watch *Goonies* for the fifty trillionth time. Gorbie was out for the count on Faith's high-backed chair.

The Roggebusches never needed to buy videos. Frank had bought a Beta machine back when Beta was the format to have. But then VHS snuck in, and Frank bought a machine to support that format. With two machines, the way it usually worked was they'd rent stuff on VHS and record it onto Beta. They'd recorded tons of movies this way, all the James Bond movies, for instance, and many of Barry's favorite all-time classics such as *Goonies*, *Better off Dead*, and *Ghostbusters*.

At the moment, Barry was going through a *Goonies* kick. Not every day, but, say, three school days out of five, he'd pretend he was Captain Chunk. And Data. Data was a 007 fan like him. The first time his brothers saw that 007 scene, they went nuts because they knew Barry would think that scene was incredible. Sometimes he'd even dare to pretend he was Mouth because Mouth's hair and clothes were perfect, even when he was drenched at the end from falling off One-Eyed Willy's ship. The only character Barry didn't like was Stef. If you asked him, he'd have no idea why. Maybe it was the big glasses. Or her short hair. Or maybe that voice. Yeah, the voice. It wasn't really a girl's voice or a boy's. Look at her name even. Stef. She was more of an it than a she or he. Barry knew that was a mean thing to think, but he also knew exactly how she felt.

Someone walked in and said hey to Gorbie. Was that...?

"Jesus Christ! Again? How many times...?" It was the scene when Sloth and Chunk are passing through all those pipes below that public restroom, and Sloth forces the pipes up so they stop shaking, and you can hear a car crash soon after. "Uh. Oh." At least that's how the scene would've gone had Barry been able to hear it. He played it out in his noodle while John shouted and stomped down the hall and out the door.

When *Goonies* was over and Barry came to from his sugar nap, John was still gone, and none of his other brothers had gotten home yet. This was the best thing about not playing sports and not having a girlfriend or friends in general. Because everyone else did and had all those, it meant Barry sometimes had this entire huge house all to his GPK-loving lonesome. His father was teaching, and Faith was making robots. Barry left his empty soda can and Reese's wrapper on the little table beside the rocking chair and didn't feel guilty about doing so because Karen the cleaning lady would deal with it come Wednesday.

The second floor was made of wooden floorboards that were in dire need of refinishing, which they never would be. If this were the middle of the night and everyone was home and asleep, Barry's footsteps would've sounded loud as hell. But in broad daylight with no one around, his footfalls didn't sound like much of anything.

Far louder was Baltimore, the black and orange finch in his father's office that pipped and squeaked as Barry walked by. Baltimore had his own three-story Queen Anne of sorts. It wouldn't've been big to you or me, but it would've been awesome if you were a finch. Or a Garbage Pail Kid. And yes, it had a 48 Broad style of architecture to it. Gorbie was Faith's, but Baltimore belonged to Frank, and Frank liked consistency and structure. Baltimore's racket didn't faze Barry at the moment, but Barry knew Boss Hogg's cats were going absolutely bonkers, just as Barry would have if a Reese's peanut butter cup or an Entenmann's chocolate donut started making noise from a place that was so close and yet so far away. No, the only time Baltimore pissed off Barry was early in the morning on school days when, before Barry's alarm had a chance to do its alarming, he'd wake up to his father's "Good morning, Baltimore!" followed by the finch's squeaks as Frank switched on his office light on his way downstairs to grind his Peet's coffee and whip up two slices of toast with eggs over easy, cut into quarters so it always seemed like he was having eight little breakfasts, the best use of math Barry had seen to date. Barry absolutely hated the whole "Good morning, Baltimore!" routine with a hot-blooded passion, you have no idea. And that says a lot since Frank's office was down one floor and toward the other side of the house from Barry's room.

Barry squished aside the wood-patterned plastic accordion door that separated the master "suite" from the rest of the second floor. Dead ahead was the bathroom, diagonal to the right was the bedroom, and to the immediate right were the back stairs leading down to the kitchen. Bunny told him those stairs were the servants' stairs. Barry tried to explain that they were no longer servants' stairs since servants weren't around anymore. It was just a quick and easy way for his dad and stepmom to get to and from the kitchen. Especially his dad. Frank used these stairs more than the main set.

He knew it didn't make sense, but Barry felt it was necessary to step quietly to the bedroom doorway. This one time, he'd been wandering around the house, bored out of his skull but also trying to stay out of his bedroom so he wouldn't have to deal with Bunny. She'd said something irritating that kicked off an argument. Whatever it was about, she won (as she always did), and Barry needed the day to sulk. At one point he heard a repetitive creaking sound from the master suite. He crept down the hall, squished aside the accordion ever so gently, and tiptoed up to the door. This being an ancient Queen Anne, the doors had those old-fashioned keyholes you usually only see in cartoons. And yes, they were the perfect peepholes. Barry peeped, didn't quite understand what he saw, but understood that whatever it was, it was making the bed produce the constant creaking back and forth.

As he stepped into the room now, the knobs on his father's dresser seemed like eyes. From the other side of the bed they considered Barry with an oaken indifference. Over to the left was that little nook that Frank referred to as Faith's thinking nook. With a quartet of windows overlooking the backyard, Faith's nook, if you could see it from outside the way Barry could whenever he and the other boys played Wiffle ball, stuck way out into the air, farther out than the third floor. If you could climb out the window the way Barry hadn't done but which Jonathan did once, you'd be on this tiny roof over the backyard porch where Gorbie slept sometimes if Frank and Faith were pissed off at him for going number two in the house.

Nothing was physically preventing Barry from going into the nook, but he wouldn't dare poke a single toe of his Velcro sneakers into that space. Not a chance lest he was in the mood to be Doomed Barry and Screwed Roggebusch. Faith would never know Barry had been here so long as he stayed the hell out of that damned nook.

Which brought him back to his father's dresser and its infinite number of knob eyes and their inscrutable judgments and the answer, at last, to his GPK dilemma. Right there in the top drawer.

For the rest of his life, Barry would always remember his very first day, or rather, night, at 48 Broad Street in Mount Holly, New Jersey: Sunday, January 30, 1983. That afternoon, he'd watched his mother and father embrace at the foot of the driveway on Soward Drive in Kensington, Maryland, where Barry had spent the first six and a half years of his life. His mother's eyes were red and drenched. It was the first time he'd ever seen her cry and, with any luck, the last. His mom and dad hugged for what seemed like forever before Frank, who shed a few tears himself, and the boys, tearless for not quite grasping what was happening, packed themselves into the white Ford van. Frank drove them out of the cul-de-sac, which had hitherto been their whole lives, for the last time.

When they arrived that night at 48 Broad, Faith, Alexander, and John were already there, as was the ancient George Taylor. Barry had no idea who George Taylor was, only that he was incredibly nice, never made fun of him and, most important, bore bags of Burger King goodness. That night the newly merged family feasted on Whoppers as the inaugural meal of their new lives. George Taylor had a bunch of card tables set up in the room on the first floor that soon became known as the poolroom. Barry and George Taylor sat at the same card table.

"You and I should be pals," George Taylor said with the last remaining bit of that Whopper with cheese clenched between his arced, ancient, thickly veined hand. Barry had only ever seen veins like that in cartoons. It was wild. "Would you like to be my pal?"

What else could Barry do but nod? Barely an hour into his new life and he'd made his first friend. Only later did he learn from his father that George Taylor had been married to the daughter of Mr. and Mrs. Saft, 48 Broad's previous owners. Mrs. Taylor was gone now, and George Taylor had picked out the spot where he would lie next to her when it was his turn to be gone. Meantime, he became the Roggebusch clan's always reliable and ever indestructible handyman and all-purpose problem solver. The reason he'd been there that first night was to help Frank and Faith make the place at least somewhat livable before the real sweaty restoration work began.

Super Bowl XVII was on that night. After the Whoppers became a memory and George Taylor went home, the nine of them sat their stuffed selves in the first-floor hallway on that giant red-orange pillow which they all couldn't've possibly fit on in real life but for some reason always did in Barry's memory. All except Barry. Both in real life and in his memory, Barry sat over near the bathroom and the stairs. Dan had lent him his Walkman. It framed Barry's head with a soundtrack of "Down Under" by Men at Work and "I Can't Go for That (No Can Do)" by Hall and Oats. Barry had no interest at all in football, but everyone else did apparently, judging by how they went ape shit at the TV.

When your team wins such an important game, you forget about anyone there who doesn't care. That's why no one noticed Barry getting up to use the bathroom or how long he'd been gone or how his face was a brighter shade of pale when he stumbled back out. Not one person out of the eight who jumped up and screamed as Riggo made that historical run—not his father Frank, not his brand spanking (pun intended) new stepmother Faith, not his six half and stepbrothers—noticed Barry barely able to stand on his own two feet and fumble with the Walkman. He himself didn't possess the where-withal to notice how lopsided the earphones were, with the right earpiece coming to rest against his chubby cheek while the left got lost in his scruffy hair.

Barry Roggebusch, on his first night in his new home, collapsed in a heap like so many Dolphins standing in the way of Redskins destiny.

"Hail to the Redskins! / Hail vic-tor-y! / Braves on the warpath! / Fight! / For old! / DC! / Run or pass or score, we want a lot more, etc."

Barry came down with Bell's palsy inflamed by a near-fatal virus. The facial nerves and muscles responsible for the left side of his face had gone colder than the third-floor radiators. That half of his face essentially died. Whenever he smiled, whenever he could scrounge up a reason to do so, it would look more like a twisted grimace. Frank took his youngest to the doctor no less than half a dozen times in the two weeks Barry was otherwise bedridden. And then there was that trip to the hospital for the CAT scan, which would go down as one of the most scarring experiences of Barry's life. Are you kidding? When you're six and a half, the whole idea of being strapped to a mechanical gurney with an iodine needle jabbed into your arm and a machine peering into your head... With the mercury topping one-oh-seven nearly every day, which theoretically is the point at which your brain shuts down and dies, Frank and Dan made it a daily ritual of dunking him into an ice-cold bath.

Sunday, January 30, 1983. It added up to the same number of hours as any other day. Except if you were Bawrence Barney Roggebusch.

Barry yanked open the top drawer, grabbed the thick wad of cash, and hurried out. The knobs watched while Baltimore pipped and piped.

That night at dinner, Barry held his breath during his father's Good Thing Bad Thing New Thing. The obvious window of opportunity was Bad Thing, but even at the age of nine, Barry was already familiar enough with his father's large-view, philosophical (whatever that meant) nature, that he sort of expected the old man to make it his New Thing.

Instead, Frank made it his nothing. He never said a word about missing money. In the back of Barry's mind, he'd wondered—hoped—his father possessed such vast sums of money that he wouldn't notice a few bucks missing from his sock drawer. Again, though, even at nine, Barry was a realist.

It being Friday night, everyone but Barry had plans. Dan was out with Veronica, Louis was at Tanisha's, Jonathan was out with his pals living up to the Double moniker, John was at his pal Donald's, Alexander was in the music room rocking the bass, Stephen was in the poolroom playing a football game on the Commodore 64, and Frank and Faith were watching dull-as-dirt nature documentaries on PBS. Or was it a history documentary tonight? Who cared?

Barry, like most bored chubby kids, wound up in the kitchen. He dragged one of the pedestals from the island to the counter with the little black-and-white TV and made the cable box his own personal instrument, pressing and flipping and clicking. He hopped back and forth across the networks—three, six, and ten—with the occasional check-in with Prism (seventeen) and HBO (twenty). Eventually he settled on ten when *Miami Vice* came on.

At one point he caught sight of Boss Hogg across the way. Was he feeding his cats or himself? Impossible to tell, his kitchen window was too grimy. Grimy Gary and Bald Hogg.

After Crockett and Tubbs saved the day yet again, he headed to the living room to find his father out for the count in his recliner. Faith was nowhere to be found.

Barry turned to head upstairs. He was bushed. What a day. Hell, what a week. He could use Bunny's soft string strumming right about now.

"Baw-*rence!*" Frank poured the last bit of seltzer water into his scotch. "C'mere a minute. Do this... now this... and this..."

"It's not getting better."

"We have to keep practicing. The doctors said it would take time. Now. Let me ask you a question." He folded his hands on his belly and turned thoughtful looking through his grogginess. "How's your mother doing?"

"Fine."

"You talk to her?"

"Yes."

"Every Sunday?"

"Yes."

"And she's normal okay?"

"I don't know."

"She's not mad at me, is she?"

"I don't know."

"You could always ask her."

"Night-night."

Whenever Barry was this tired, his bad eye hung nearly shut. Frank was the only person who never pointed that out. Alexander was up in his room listening to Mötley Crüe's "Home Sweet Home."

When Barry woke the next morning, Don Henley's "All She Wants to Do Is Dance" was playing on his clock radio. He was drenched, his tighty-whities and his sheets. Bunny wasn't there. As always when he wet the bed, she made herself scarce, making him feel the self-refuting emotions of gratitude and embarrassment.

The rest of the house was still asleep. Don Henley made way for the Thompson Twins' "Hold Me Now," which pissed Barry off for some reason. He slapped the radio off and headed downstairs. Gorbie was curled up asleep on this side of the accordion door, scene of yesterday's crime. Had he really done that? Poochie didn't care.

George Taylor was outside on the side lawn, watering the grass and flower beds. Barry came this close to pushing the door open to say hey to his pal before remembering the piss-soaked underwear.

Even the sound of the spraying water slapping the vegetation pissed him off.

Grabbing one of the steak knives from the wooden block in the kitchen and imagining all the Garbage Pail Kids he'd soon have, Barry headed into the poolroom, homed in on the basketball in Jonathan's cubby, got on his haunches, and rammed the knife in right up to the hilt.

He should get cleaned up and say hey to his pal.

Basketball-Killing Barry slid the knife back into the block before Ball-Murdering Roggebusch huffed and stomped back up to the third floor.

Bunny was back, strumming something strong and sweet.

2

FRANK

JAZZ SPAZZ AND HOP SCOTCH

On the southwest corner of Broad and Buttonwood in Mount Holly, New Jersey, there loomed a three-story Queen Anne that had apparently swallowed whole five hundred dollars cash. The base of the house was ringed with bricks painted beet red, interspersed with windows staring with dusty faces at the freshly lain mulch. The columns supporting the wraparound front porch as well as the smaller side porch were carrot orange and spinach green. The first two stories of the façade were squash yellow while the third story featured more carrot.

In short, the house at 48 Broad Street was a colossal hybrid of all the vegetables you hate.

Those third-story windows were framed by eaves so steep they should've been against the law. On the roof proper, a trio of bony chimneys jutted like arthritic fingers from those lethal slopes, accusing the leaden sky. When you spotted those chimneys from the sidewalk, it almost seemed like they defied physics. Even if they did, it wouldn't've made a difference, for all three led down to bogus fireplaces, big square spaces of plastic brick.

If you were wondering if there existed a physical manifestation of obstinacy, mischief, and salad, 48 Broad was it, with the square footage to match.

A leafy tree stood squarely in front of the house and towered just a tad higher than the highest eave. But the house couldn't've cared less. First of all, the tree's colors actually complemented the house's complexion in the fall. And in the winter, while the tree lost its personality, the house endured. The house knew that when it was time for one of them to go, it would be the tree. You see, this tree used to have a twin on the Buttonwood side. And then, on an otherwise sleepy August Sunday, a hurricane blew through with such howling, gusting ferocity, the tree toppled into the street. The house? You guessed it.

By now I'm sure you're dying to know what it was like inside this place. Well, that's where you and Frank Roggebusch were different. Upon first laying his bespectacled eyes upon the conservation-starved place in '82, after he and then mistress now third wife Faith Roggebusch, formerly Peterson, née Drummond, had decided to settle in Mount Holly because they heard the schools were better relative to other parts of Burlington County, all he could think of was a salad with rotten ingredients. And he hated salad even if the ingredients were farm fresh. Seriously, you should've seen this place the day he and Faith were taken on a dust-blanketed, musty, moldy walk-through with George Taylor, the septuagenarian son-in-law of the previous owners, Mr. and Mrs. Saft. To have called it a shell would've been an insult to shells everywhere. Everything clandestine in his life at that point—meeting Faith at that math conference at UC Boulder two years earlier, the trysts, the camping trip with Barry, Faith, and her two kids to that one place with the fields of snake grass where the snakes would leave you alone so long as you held your hands high, under arrest style, his decision to divorce Joanne, which he still hadn't informed Joanne of by the time of the house tour, all of it—suddenly and sickeningly felt like a blunder as massive and permanent as this house.

The feeling passed—or did he just bury it for it to reemerge at some future unspecified time?—when he saw Faith's eyes, with their brand-new contact lenses so she'd no longer have to wear those Coke bottles, light up the room that would become the poolroom the way gaslights must've lit up the place a hundred years ago when it was a music school. And the deeper and higher they explored, from the smothering, earthen basement on up to the rickety second floor, and farther up to the Neanderthal's paradise that was the third floor, the more in love Faith fell. She grew so giddy about the prospect of living at 48 Broad she organized another tour with Alexander and John. Her older boy snapped a photo of Frank and Faith sitting on the front steps with John loitering on the porch, framed by columns.

Frank and Faith bought 48 Broad for ninety thousand. And then they and all seven kids fixed it up.

The thrill of seeing Faith's thrill had long gone cold by the time Frank pulled up along the Buttonwood side where they usually parked, avoiding the jutting curb just enough to spare his Dodge Caravan's passenger-side tires. The back of the Caravan was bursting with Super Fresh grocery bags chock-full of mostly junk food for the kids. We're talking a good two hundred bucks' worth that would be completely consumed this time next week, including two packages of Soft Batch that would go from the belly of R2-D2 to that of Bawrence Barney.

He'd planned to pay in cash, but when he went to grab some from the sock drawer, all he found were his credit cards and checkbook. Frank didn't use a wallet, never had. He preferred his currency hard and loose. His whole life, going back to when his father started giving him an allowance at the age of five (hey, those Saturday serials cost money), Frank had used his sock drawer as his safe, and he'd never once had a single penny stolen from him, which was why he didn't think anything had been stolen now.

No, Frank was sure Faith had needed it for some emergency or other. Whatever the case, he needed that money for Karen. A hundred bucks was her weekly rate for single-handedly tackling this three-story wildebeest, but Frank had promised her a four-hundred-dollar tip so she could take her dog Shadow to the vet for those worms or whatever the hell was plaguing him and, by extension,

Frank. In the meantime, on his way back from Super Fresh he'd stopped by Mount Holly State Bank to cash a check for a hundred just to tide him over.

As sometimes happened, random jazz tunes (right now it was Oscar Peterson's live 1956 Stratford Shakespeare Festival recording of "Gypsy in My Soul") floated across the ether from Frank's past life while he hauled in the double-bagged groceries. How had Peterson done it?

Frank had a shitload of oil price forecasting to tackle for the Department of Energy, his former employer for whom he now consulted while holding down an associate professorship at Temple University. We're talking a good quarter-century's worth of numbers that carried at least moderate dependence on the weather. But that could wait. His fingers had an itch.

After storing all the beef and fowl and the tubs of ice cream in the laundry room freezer chest, all the soda in one of the laundry room fridges, the Soft Batch cookies in R2-D2, and the more healthful stuff like milk, OJ, and vegetables, which were mainly for Faith, in the kitchen fridge, Frank poured himself a Johnnie Red and soda and made a beeline for the music room.

Something thudded directly above. Was that Barry wailing "No! It wasn't me!" on the other side of Jonathan's growling and snarling? Frank and his kid sister had had their spats growing up. They turned out okay, right?

"Gonna play one of your masterpieces, Frank?" Louis said from the living room, one arm around Tanisha, the other holding a Coke Classic. Two of his buddies were sprawled on the floor, propped on their elbows, enraptured by the TV.

Frank sipped his nectar while using the index of his free hand to mimic a bobbing baton. "Enjoying a midafternoon refreshment while getting back in touch with my halcyon youth. I assume you have everything under control?"

Louis and Tanisha laughed. One of the buddies clicked the cable box.

Frank slid the huge, cumbersome door shut, or rather, as close to

shut as he could. None of these huge sliding doors on the first floor—
the music, living, and poolrooms all had them—closed all the way,
courtesy of time-warped wood.

Frank started out with his personal theme, a hybrid of "Blue
Moon" and his own original composition. He always began and
ended what now passed for jam sessions with this tune. Before he got
too far into it, Barry heaved open the door with chubby-pawed persis-
tence and marched up with half-faced purpose. Frank tapped out a
few more notes before stopping to take a pull from Johnnie.

"Daddy, can I have next week's allowance now?"

Frank belted out a quick ditty, the same ditty he always played
when he didn't have time for anything else but was feeling too great
otherwise. "Baw-*rence*!"

"Daddy..." Barry couldn't help giggling. "Can I have it... Can I
have it now?"

"You wish to deprive your poor, struggling father?"

"I just need my allowance for next week so I can get the new
Garbage Pail Kids."

"The which?"

"The Garbage Pail Kids, I told you!"

Frank turned on the stool to face his youngest square on. "Do
this." The eyebrows. "And this." Blinking. That wasn't so bad. "And..."
The smile. This killed Frank because it was the starkest reminder of
almost losing his son. Never before had he lived in such frozen terror.
When it was over, he phoned up Joanne to pick her noodle about
how he could better spot bugs in his (and their) kids before it got too
bad. Her advice was basically to open his eyes and ears. Dr. Buck had
assured him that, while the muscle tone would never fully recover, it
would eventually recover enough, certainly by the time Barry got to
college, for his smile to be close to normal and his left eyelid to be not
quite so droopy. As for that other thing... "You wet the bed last
night?" His boy's half look was all the answer he needed. He took
another pull from Johnnie. Had he budgeted for a new mattress?

His firstborn appeared at the door. "Girls."

"Ste-*van*!"

Frank dug into his sweatpants and clutched the wad of a hundred he'd cashed on the way home, peeled and stretched a bill from it with more gravitas than necessary considering it was just a five, gripped it between thumb and forefinger like it was radioactive, and dropped it into his boy's palms. "Here's to more Garbage Cans!"

"Garbage Pail Kids!"

Frank went back to playing.

Barry hurried out.

"Hey, Bawrence Barney, did you hear? The Mount Holly Pharmacy is having this massive sale on Garbage Pail Kids. Buy one pack, get three free. Today only!"

If Frank hadn't been buzzed, he'd've thought the dead half of Barry's face just managed to twitch while the other half lit up in that kind of glee-fueled awe Frank used to demonstrate at the sight of butterscotch ice cream and nowadays at the sight, or even the thought, of Lagavulin single malt.

"JUST KIDDING!" Stephen doubled over. "Bawrence Barney, don't you know better by now? I got to create a small spark of hope and then CRUSH IT!"

"Asshole!" Barry ran away and thumped upstairs. His big brother slapped his bicep and folded up that same arm while sliding his hand down.

Stephen wore the grin of a general who had just mopped up the enemy with superior schadenfreude. "Father!"

"Son!"

"I seek capital."

"Naturally."

"An investment that will pay interest, if not dividends, some of which may even be passed back to you."

"Oh well then..." Frank tickled a few more keys in mock excitement before pulling out more cash. "May I inquire as to the nature of this novel venture, of which I assume I will be the primary venture capitalist?"

"I have decided to take advantage of compact disc players entering the mainstream..."

"Ah yes!"

"...by not purchasing a compact disc player."

"That does sound novel."

"That is, I do plan on buying a compact disc player at some point in the not-so-distant future."

"Or CD player, as those in the know call it."

"That sounds too weird to say, so in the meantime, compact. Disc. Player. Mine will be strictly for playing compact discs for personal pleasure. Hopefully Chuck Mangione will release his future albums on the compact disc medium."

"Back to the not insignificant sum of money I am handing you now..."

Stephen stood on his tiptoes and pronounced with his index finger, the baton in this symphony of prophetic pronouncements. "I will purchase a boom box with dual cassette players!"

Maybe it was the scotch, but Frank had no inkling of why he should care. He turned back and tapped out a few more notes.

"Right after cassettes showed up, you could sell eight-track players for hundreds of dollars, thousands even. Not long from now, compact disc players will dominate the market, cassette players will be scrapped from the market, and visionaries like myself will be the only ones on the planet who have them. But I won't sell it right away. It's a dual cassette player. It will appreciate that much more, but I'll bide my time. Plus I want to enjoy *Fun and Games* a little while longer."

"I'm sure *Fun and Games* will be on compact disc."

Stephen's baton turned to four batons curled around a wad of dead presidents. "You shall behold what separates me from all those mental midgets."

"Stephen."

"Sir."

Frank turned to face him. "Have you looked into Temple's marching band? I'm sure they could always use a trumpet player of your technical acumen and natural ear for rhythm and harmony."

"I am prepared to dumb myself down if it means being accepted amongst the ordinary folk."

"Go Owls!" Frank took another sip. He nearly got through another song before Faith thumped in. Louis was making Tanisha laugh. They seemed so far away.

"Barry's card collecting habit isn't healthy," she said with hands pressed to her hips.

As was often the case when he didn't understand a word being said, Frank kept playing.

"Your son collects far too many of those butt-ugly cards, and it's going to have major consequences on his mental health and his ability to relate to and engage with society."

In their six years together (including the two and a half that were in secret), Frank had learned that the only way to get Faith off her high horse was to: A. Agree with her but only if he really agreed and never for the sake of shutting her up because he wasn't like that; B. If he disagreed, throw at her some incontrovertible data that would instantly and forever refute her thesis du jour; C. If he disagreed but only had his opinions sans data, argue with her until she stopped, not because he'd win but because, by definition of "du jour," the thesis wouldn't be that interesting tomorrow; D. If he only kind of disagreed but his ego was feeling especially tender, argue until he was blue in the face and introduce utterly irrelevant data if he had to, preferably something arcane and obscure to make his intellect seem that much more formidable so that she'd stop not because she lost but because she'd recognize she was up against someone who could dig deep for some pretty obscure shit when he really wanted to.

Point being, if it wasn't a matter of data but simply differing opinions, the spat could go any number of ways if you add up the above as well as the corresponding options on Faith's side, which really didn't correspond as neatly as all that, hence the shouting matches they could have, have had, and would continue to have over subjects you and I would probably find pretty innocuous, like whether or not to keep the foot on the gas when driving through a green light (Frank thought you should ease off so that it'd be easier to brake if a car or pedestrian sped into your path, while Faith thought the foot should remain firmly on the gas to take advantage of catching a green light, which in her perceived experience was a rare and precious thing).

On the topic of the Garbage Pail Kids' influence on his youngest son, which Frank hadn't realized until this moment was a topic at all, no data could be cited or disputed. To achieve closure, he'd have to tread the path of A, C, or D. He'd never be able to decide if he agreed with Faith until she articulated how she arrived at this thesis.

He tapered off the music as he said, "You're referring to the Garbage Cans or whatever the hell they're called."

"Those freaks will ruin him, Frank. He'll become a recluse. Sexually frustrated. Utterly unable and, worse yet, unwilling to engage with society. A sociopath."

"Bawrence has friends. They have sleepovers here; he has sleepovers there."

"He has slept over at someone's house once, and luckily he didn't piss himself. Why do you think he still wets the bed?"

"You're saying it's the Garbage Cans' fault?"

"It's exacerbating the condition, which will last his entire life if he keeps up these emotionally destructive habits."

"When I was in summer camp, one of the kids had a bed-wetting problem. The Garbage Cans didn't exist back then, of course."

Faith whipped out a stack of cards that would've taken Frank's nose clean off had he been sitting an inch closer. The images of these mutant babies reminded him of *Mad*, which in turn made him feel like a complete idiot, not for the first time, for throwing away the first issue. Yes, Frank was at one time the proud owner of the very first *Mad* Magazine which came out right after his thirteenth birthday. Fifteen years later, when he was packing up to move to Houston for the Rice University job, he threw it out. His gut had advised him to keep it, but at that point, fresh off getting his PhD in economics from Johns Hopkins, Frank fancied himself too intellectual to be bothered with gut feelings, not to speak of Alfred E. Newman.

He skimmed the cards: Jelly Kelly, Creamed Keith, Dinah Saur, Glooey Gabe, Wriggley Rene... If there were a level below frivolous, these would be that. But he couldn't say that out loud, not with his wife already so invested. Luckily for both of them, Frank's ego was fat and happy today, not to speak of lubricated. Perhaps he could pull off an A-C combo.

As if sensing his train of thought, Faith dialed it down a bit. "He's a stupid kid, Frank. But I don't think he's stupid enough to think he could imitate any of these pictures. What I'm worried about is that: A. They show images that are too graphic for kids his age. I wouldn't let John look at these; and B. The more time he spends with these, the less time he spends on schoolwork. Someone of his very limited intellectual capacity can't afford to be diverted from his studies even a little bit."

Frank exaggerated the slurp from his scotch to drown out the sound of his wife insulting his love baby. He took another, admittedly desperate, slurp in case the ice had anything left to surrender. A-C combo it was. "Well. These images, if taken a certain way, could be thought of as disturbing."

"Deformed babies doing destructive things and having destructive things happen to them. Louis's ghastly rap music is more preferable."

"I'm not so sure it'll stunt Bawrence. After all, I was into *Mad* Magazine for years, and they used caricatures that could be thought of as grotesque."

"You yourself have said many times that you were a late bloomer as a student, only thriving after you discarded your *Mad* habit, pun intended."

Damn! He'd told his *Mad* anecdote, pun intended, many times to multiple people but had never made the correlation between the habit's tapering off and his grades picking up. Frank knew, and he suspected Faith did too, that the real reason he finally blossomed into a straight-A scholar was probably more complicated than discontinuing his *Mad* subscription, but for the sake of the current argument, his A-C combo plan was kaput. It would be, perhaps appropriately, straight A from here on out.

He slurped in vain before setting the glass down with the same finality he mustered to say: "I shall speak to Bawrence about the hazards of collecting Garbage Cans."

Faith thumped out with commensurate finality. Louis, Tanisha, et al. were close again.

Frank improvised his next jazzy jam for about a minute before stopping cold. Faith hadn't said anything about the missing five hundred dollars. He was absolutely sure, and as a once-in-a-Venus-transit Atlantic City craps shooter, would've bet the house at 48 Broad that, had Faith removed a sum of that size from his sock drawer, she would've told him about it. Sure, she was volatile, but the flipside of her volatility was sandpaper-edged candor. She not only would've told him about it, she'd've done so with nary a trace of contrition, a matter-of-fact update delivered in Dan Rather / Peter Jennings / Tom Brokaw style.

He couldn't ask her about it lest he risk letting her know what he'd been planning to do with the money. Sure, he could spin a white lie. "Why, I was going to buy a surprise random gift for you!" seemed like the obvious option, but the third side of Faith's volatility coin—and yes, Faith was the kind of person whose coin had more than two sides—was X-ray vision that afforded her a bullshit quotient of flat zero.

Frank reached for the tumbler before remembering it was barren.

"Yo Frank."

"Lou-*is*!"

Louis was standing at the door in all his disheveled, scruffy-haired, perpetually sleepy, sleeveless Redskins-shirted glory. He spit juice from his Copenhagen chew into a plastic Phillies cup. "I'm sure you can hear the thumping up there."

Frank considered the glass again. Was Faith really that upset about those silly cards? "You and Tanisha are normal okay? All your friends...?" He craned his neck but couldn't see anything past his adopted son. The living room once again seemed a light-year away.

"Yo Frank. Would you be mad if I took Barry's allowance to protect him against Jonathan? If he offered it to me?"

Frank banged out a few notes with one hand and executed the

finger baton with the other. "Let me understand. Bawrence is taking the five dollars a week that I give him, and he gives it to you?"

"Yup."

"Because..."

Louis pointed above at the sounds of thuds and grunts and squeaky-voiced protests.

"Louis." Frank turned to face him. "If someone offers you money for a service, and you perform the service to the best of your ability and in good faith, then I see absolutely no reason why you should say no. In fact, if you said no, I'd be concerned you were developmentally disabled which, incidentally, Faith posits about Bawrence all the time."

"I'm going to repeat freshman year."

"Year's not over yet."

"Double calls Barry one of Jerry's Kids."

"I have no idea what that means."

"I made fifteen bucks this week. I won't feel like a douchebag about it."

"Want to play some poker?"

Louis laughed that special kind of laugh he inherited from Woody. It didn't bother Frank nearly as much as it used to. Louis turned to go.

"Louis."

"Yo."

The old man folded his hands. "How's your mother doing?"

"Hmm..."

"She mad at me?"

"Hmm..."

"I haven't done anything, so I don't know why she would be."

"Dan might know. Or Barry. He talks to her every Sunday."

"Mmmm."

Louis spat in his cup and headed back across the hall.

Once again Frank was slow to digest it all. It took another minute or so of reliving his glory days, that summer playing gigs on that cruise ship with the Panamanian flag so the cruise company could elude taxes, before his noodle alerted him to the real pot roast of what Louis had just said: Barry had given Louis three times his weekly allowance in the past week. So that's why Barry had asked for an advance. While this bolstered Faith's hypothesis that Bawrence was a cylinder short of a V8, Frank focused on the positive. "Baw-*rence!*" Any concern over his son's addiction to those goddamn cards was rendered moot. No one had as rock solid a grasp on the trials and tribulations of budgeting the way Frank did—it was the primary reason he'd divorced Bawrence's mother, after all, or so he told himself and anyone who'd listen—and Bawrence's budget was prohibiting him from realizing his stepmother's anxiety. Problem solved.

Frank waved a finger baton on his way down the hall for a refill. He'd just defeated Faith in a battle that could've dragged on who knew how long. Surely he deserved another wee nip before heading back up to do Energy's bidding.

He sat back down and started banging out a piano cover of Charlie Parker's "Hot House" when he stopped abruptly. What exactly did Bawrence talk about with Joanne inside that big second-floor closet that was used by Faith for her formal wear and everyone else for crap they didn't want?

"Hey. Hello. Hi, Frank."

"Alexan-*dor!*" Frank waved his finger baton before using the same hand to take a healthy pull from his refreshed scotch and Red, all the while keeping the other hand busy on the ivories.

Just as he always did when having a talk with Frank in the music room, Alexander took the stool from his mother's baby grand and hauled it over to the chunk of empty rug between Frank and the door.

While he circled back to his "Blue Moon," Frank said, "What is your report?"

"What if someone stole money from you, but you couldn't tell anyone? Because in doing so, you'd be giving up a secret."

Frank wasn't sure if his spinning noggin was caused by Johnnie or... Now he was using both hands to launch into another jazz ditty, this one part of the set he used to play every Friday at that Navy SEAL bar in Indian Head. Was this kid messing with him?

"Have you heard of Cliff Burton? He's this bass player for a group called Metallica. And do you know Paul McCartney? From the Beatles?"

"Never listened to the Beatles. Couldn't stand it. An affront to my senses, made me feel sick."

"Well, Paul McCartney's pretty famous. And so is Roger Waters from Pink Floyd. Another brick in the wall. And all that jazz. Actually, it's not jazz. But you get the point. So anyway. I was saving my allowance to buy bass tabs. With all their songs. And lots of others too. Songs, that is. It's expensive. But not prohibitively expensive."

"Nice use of prohibitively."

"Mom doesn't want me to buy more than one tab a year. She says I don't need tabs to practice bass. Which is true. Technically. But I also figure, you know, what better way to learn? Than from those who are masters of their craft."

"Nice phraseology with masters of their craft. Yes indeed, you are wise to... *emulate*... those who came before you, those who found and achieved success not simply because they worked their asses off, but because they possessed a genius for the... *musical idiom*... that, while educational from your perspective, cannot be entirely understood by virtue of their genius."

Alexander's deadpan face lasted another moment before he cracked it with a titter. "So I figured, you know, if it's my money, and I save it up and buy all these tabs with my own allowance and don't borrow, then that should be okay. Right?"

"You make a large expenditure without incurring debt. The definition of fiscally prudent."

"Mom should be okay with that."

Frank took a slurp and almost felt sorry for the kid. "Alexander. I haven't known your mother as long as you obviously have, but at the very least, I feel confident saying I know her quite well when it comes to—how shall I say?—*pecuniary* issues. Due to multiple factors, some known and understood, others known but not so understood, and nearly all stemming from her childhood, your mother possesses a somewhat rigid and delineated point of view when it comes to money, how it's made, how it should be made but isn't all the time made, and what should be done with it once it is made, however it's made." Another slurp. "For example, she has decreed that your allowance, which you earn ostensibly by performing your portion of the household chores as spelled out on the kitchen chalkboard, may not be used by you at your discretion to purchase whatever goods and services you so choose."

"But isn't that what it's for?"

"Depends who you ask."

Alexander looked at Frank with nary a speck of comprehension.

"Ask me? I say do what you want. Within reason, of course. Don't buy cocaine, for example."

"Or Double's pot?"

"Your mother has a, shall we say... specific... point of view which, due to the complex dynamics of domestic relations, I choose not to disturb."

"I guess my main point is, the money I've been saving? For the tabs? It's gone. I kept it in my sock drawer. And someone took it. I asked John. He swears he didn't do it. If I ask more people, I'll have to say what the money was for. And Mom'll get pissed. So. I guess. I'm in a conundrum. As they say. Is that a good use of the word conundrum?"

"Your verbiage, Alexander, both in this instance and throughout this discussion, has been impeccable. My advice? Opt for discretion. I don't always tell your mother about every problem I'm having. Besides. She has her own laundry list of things to worry about. Long commute to Princeton. A father she's trying to get along with in spite of his having beat the shit out of her on a routine basis when she was a child. Enough without me burdening her with all my problems, if that makes any sense."

"So Frank. You're saying I should conduct my own... internal... investigation? Of who stole my three months of allowance?"

Frank consulted Johnnie. "It would help you curtail any unnecessary domestic upheaval while sparing your mother a layer of domestic stress she doesn't necessarily... *just exactly...* need at this very moment."

"You know something, Frank? You're smart. Anyone ever tell you that?"

Frank folded his hands on his belly. "Occasionally I have had an audience so overcome with my advice, which some have ventured to label as sage."

"Dude. As they say in the Valley."

"Around the time Stephen was born, and I figured, quite rightly as it turns out, that I'd be having more children down the line, some biological, others not so, but all equally dependent, I made it my mission in life to know all known things."

"Are we playing Oh Hell! tonight?"

Frank slurped and swallowed with great care as he studied the liquid patterns on the tumbler. "It's been too long since I taught Oh Hell!"

Alexander shook Frank's hand and walked out with rigid purpose.

Gorbie trotted in with an earnest expression compromised by the adorableness of his underbite.

"Gorba-*chev!*" Frank belted out one of his jams while Gorbie performed the obligatory sniff along the carpet toward the old man's sneakers before hopping up on his lap. Frank was feeling far too 1960s groovy to stop now. He made mincemeat of the ivories for another minute or so before stopping to give the pooch a thoughtful reflection. "Gorbachev. What the hell am I going to do about the money?" The pooch hopped down and started licking his nuts. "My thoughts exactly." Frank stuck his tongue through the ice to collect what nectar he could while listening to Louis and the Gardens crowd laugh at the TV.

Eventually Frank made it back to his office, but the damage was done. He didn't accomplish a single thing, didn't fill in a single cell on a single spreadsheet, or forecast a single price of a single drop of oil. He chatted with Baltimore, who always flitted around his three-story cage whenever Frank became philosophical. Peering down through the cage, Frank's eyes adjusted their focus until he was looking past Baltimore at Boss Hogg in his kitchen sharing a cheese slice with one of his cats.

That night he whipped up Dan's favorite: pork chops and beans. Frank never failed to point out how nice it was they were having pork chops and beans specifically because Dan found so much favor with this particular entrée. The one practical benefit of this was that it inspired Dan, who usually did the dishes regardless, to get the dishes done with even more gusto and expediency so Oh Hell! could begin that much sooner.

Oh Hell! is a card game unique in the fact that it never fails to live up to its name for everyone who plays it, every single time. Frank had introduced it to the newly merged Roggebusch clan soon after they settled at 48 Broad. It was a Saturday night just like tonight. Not much was on TV, which of course has been the case with Saturday nights since time immemorial. So Frank suggested they all convene in the kitchen for a card game he wanted to show them. In no time flat, Oh Hell! became by far and away the favorite pastime of the 48 Broad brood.

I'll channel Frank to explain the game to you. Each player is dealt a certain number of cards. Let's say ten, a nice round number. 'Course that mandated the Roggebusches play with two decks since one deck only has fifty-two cards. After each player has been dealt their ten, they each have to declare how many hands they think they'll win. This is called their bid. Frank then uses his soft-tip pen (black, blue, red, or green) to record the bids on his yellow legal pad, on which he has sketched a grid with everyone's names on the left. After all ten hands have been played, Frank records each person's score next to their bid. If the player wins the number of hands they bid, they get that number plus ten. If they don't win their bid, their score is reduced by the difference between the number of hands they did win and their bid. The only exception is if that loser has the most points, in which case their score drops by that same difference multiplied by five. Okay? So for example, let's say you're the (un)lucky schmo with

the highest score, and then on the next round, you predict you're
going to collect three tricks. But then your luck goes to shit and you
win five. Instead of your score being reduced by two points, it's
reduced by ten points. Frank, with wet-lipped glee, then carves, not
writes, your new and much reduced score into the yellow legal pad in
tortuous, meticulous fashion. No one should enjoy keeping score so
much. Oh Hell!

Now about the bidding: Everyone can bid whatever they want...
except for the dealer. Let's say you're the dealer and this round sees
everyone get nine cards. The first person to bid is the person to your
left. And then we go around the table until we arrive at you. If you're
at the Roggebusch table, that means eight other people get to bid
before you. Let's say each person has bid one. That means eight tricks
have been accounted for. Let's say you, the dealer, would like to bid
one. Too bad. You can't. That would add up to the number of cards
dealt, and that's not allowed to happen. Oh Hell!, am I right? The
total number of tricks bid must not equal the number of cards dealt
to each person. Now if the other eight Roggebusches bid an aggregate
number of tricks higher than the number of cards dealt, you the
dealer can bid whatever you want.

Now comes the crucial question: How, for the love of trumps, do
you win a hand at Oh Hell!? After you've dealt the cards, you put the
remaining deck next to you and turn over the top card. Let's say it's a
three of diamonds. That means diamonds are trump for that round.
So if someone is dominating a trick with an ace of clubs or something, and it's your turn and you throw out a two of diamonds, you
beat that ace, and if no one throws out a higher diamond, you win
that trick. As with bidding, the first person to start the first trick is to
the dealer's left. That person can throw out whatever they want. So
let's say, to kick things off, the person to your left throws out a seven
of clubs into the middle of the table. The next person must now
throw out a club. If it's higher or lower than a seven depends on if
that person wishes to win that hand. If that person has no clubs, they
can toss out whatever. After all nine people have tossed out a card,
then whoever has the highest club wins the trick. But again, if

someone chucks out an ace of clubs, and then someone else who has no clubs throws down a whatever of diamonds, the diamond wins because it's trump. Whoever wins that hand will be the first person to start the next trick. That's the way it proceeds until all tricks have been played, at which time Frank takes up his soft-tip and records the results. After that, the next person to the left deals each person one card less than the previous round, and a new trump is declared.

See where this is going? Eventually we get to the point where each person is dealt one measly card. That's always fun (not!), because most everyone will bid zero, which means the dealer won't be allowed to bid one (or if one person has bid one, the dealer can't bid zero). After that round, everyone gets two cards. We now work our way back to ten.

Frank shuffled both decks and prepared to deal the first round of ten cards. Before he did so, he slid both shuffled decks to his right, where Alexander stared at him with a face as blank as the jack's. "Alexan-*dor*. Cut the deck, if you please."

And so the long-haired, bespectacled, aspiring bassist dug out his new Swiss Army knife, unfolded the parent blade, and prepared to sink it into the cards.

John cracked up at the same time Frank said, "Like so." He demonstrated with the first deck. Alexander followed suit with the second. "All right, team! Are we rea-*dy*?" He dealt out ten cards each and knew, with just a cursory glance at his own hand, that he wanted to bid three. Frank set his cards down and took advantage of everyone else pondering their hands by indulging in another proud Oh Hell! tradition: sketching World War II planes in the margins of the yellow legal pad. Indeed, he was sketching a particularly accurate B-52 bomber when Jonathan dropped a bomb of his own.

"Someone killed my basketball." He looked at his father and Faith before dropping his glare on Barry. "Stabbed it. To death."

"Were you really going to use your knife?" John was barely able to suppress his laughter.

Alexander betrayed nary a tick. "He said cut the deck. So I was going to cut the deck."

Frank sipped his Johnnie Red and seltzer and vaguely noticed Barry focusing extra hard on his cards under the weight of his brother's eyes. A memory popped into his head, a scene from about five years ago in the old homestead in Kensington on Soward Drive. He had purchased a vacuum cleaner at Sears and assembled it in the living room while Joanne and Bawrence kept him company. Joanne—yes, she was going by Joan these days, but that didn't make sense to Frank so he still thought of her as Joanne and always would—was wearing that white shirt with the tiny pink roses on it that were so tiny you could barely discern they were roses at all if you were across the room. But on this day she was plenty close enough, sitting on the carpet in front of her husband, who was sitting in the chair that was *the* chair before he graduated to the recliner. Frank adored how Joanne tried to be useful by reading the pictorial manual and handing him parts even if he would've been fine on his own. Barry sat on the carpet next to his mother and played with the *Star Wars* figures he would eventually flush down the toilet.

Frank didn't realize he was smiling until he noticed Faith's glare. He offered a shit-eating grin.

"Bawrence Barney!" Stephen said with mock righteousness. "Are you killing basketballs?"

Bawrence scooted back, bopping Gorbie's noggin in the process, and got up to fetch some cookies from R2.

Frank doodled a Focker and willed his face straight.

By the time the first trick started, yanking Frank back to 1986, Daniel and Faith were discussing a PBS animal documentary by *National Geographic*.

"That's a boring magazine," Barry said between sips of Mountain Dew.

"Yeah, Barry!" Jonathan gave him a high five.

Louis sniggered. "Dan write for *National Geographic*?"

Studying his cards, Dan's furrowed brow furrowed all the more. "That's a great magazine. I'd love to write for them."

Louis snuck a "bullshit!" into his mock sneeze.

John burst out laughing and shook his head at Alexander. "Dude, are you high?"

Stephen ended up winning with a score of 174. Faith came in second with 162, Frank a distant third with 140. This royally pissed off the patriarch even though he couldn't put his Johnnie-buzzed finger on exactly why. No matter, it was time for the traditional post-Oh Hell! round of dumbed-down seven card stud. "Everyone have a dollar?"

While they each dug in their pockets for a single, Jonathan pulled out a thick wad of dough but kept it below the table. Faith spotted it at the same time Frank did and reiterated her glare at her husband. Stephen said something about Jonathan being very successful at growing herbage and selling it to the townsfolk. That made no sense to Frank because Jonathan's math skills were horrible, he couldn't possibly be successful at anything involving a numbers-based trans-action. Which left the question of how he came by all that cash on an allowance of ten dollars a week, some of which he spent on things like Marlboros and Slurpees and Now and Laters.

As always, Frank provided commentary as he dealt the faceup cards. "Might have something therrrrre... Not a whole lot there... Alexan-*dor* has a pair of sixes, that's nice... Baw-*rence*, you'll be in fat city if the three is wild... Pair of gorick for Ste-*vannnnn*..."

The mystery wild card turned out to be a nine, which gave Alexander three kings. The bassist made a show of raking in the singles.

"Fucking figures, ya moron," John said.

"Hey!" Faith snapped.

"Will geeks inherit the Earth? Or retards?"

"Or Jerry's Kids?" Jonathan grinned at Barry with a spot-on Bela Lugosi impersonation.

"Or in Alexander's case, retards *and* geeks?" John said.

"I thought geeks were supposed to be smart," Alexander said.

"You're so fucking stupid."

"John Peterson!"

Alexander's stone face cracked a small smile, enough to assure his kid brother they were hunky and dory but not enough to deviate from deadpan as he said: "I. Will kick. Your ass. At G.I. Joe."

"You're on."

Faith's two kids scooted out, one of them bumping Gorbie in the head with the chair, and took their sodas to the poolroom to play the Commodore 64.

Up in the master bedroom, Frank stripped to his tighty-whities, torn at certain parts under the band courtesy of his expanding waistline, and whacked his pud to the memory of when he first met Joanne. Faith was reading something over in her nook, out of sight and mentally far enough away that Frank felt perfectly safe traveling back to New Year's Eve 1971. He and Mary had attended the party at Kenwood Country Club in Bethesda, where Frank's parents were members and where he and his kid sister were now lifelong members as well. Also in attendance was the couple from down the street, Joanne and Marcus "Woody" Woods. Frank couldn't remember who asked whom, but at one point he and Joanne were dancing together.

"You're cute," she said.

For the rest of his life, that was the only sentence out of her mouth Frank would remember from that night.

On most nights he could come with minimal effort before getting through the whole of that memory, and the whole of twenty-six-year-old Joanne. On this night, however, his thoughts kept reverting to Jonathan and all that dough. It didn't help matters that when he had started sleeping with Joanne, Jonathan was all of seven months. Thoughts of the money led him to Karen and the conundrum of how and when he should break it to her that he wouldn't be able to pay Shadow's way at the vet. Perhaps he should hold out another day or two. Big as this house was, the money had to be somewhere, right?

Karen was closer to his frontal lobe at this point, so he started having sex with her. Frank did this now and again during a moment of lucidity when he could accept the fact that he would never go back in time and that if he ever did manage to score with a woman who wasn't Faith, he'd have a far better chance with today's Karen than yesteryear's Joanne. Since Frank had never had sex with Karen, he had no sex memories he could exaggerate or gussy up. So he turned G-rated memories into X-rated ones, like the time Karen had to clean up the popcorn Bawrence spilled with impunity while watching TV in the kitchen. Upon Karen's protest, Bawrence pointed out, not without some merit, Frank thought, that she shouldn't complain about having to clean up the popcorn due to her getting paid to be the cleaning lady. The silver lining was Karen's getting on her hands and knees to pick up the mess with her ass aimed squarely—or rather, roundly—at the back stairs as Frank came down for his jog decked out in his faded Redskins windbreaker and other loose garb that camouflaged his hard-on. Picturing that ass was all he needed.

"Frank?"

"Alexan-*dor*!" Thank Christ he preferred paper towels over tissues for blowing his nose. They were that much better at mopping up semen. In less than a minute, Frank was mopped and robed. "Sir!"

Alexander strolled in, Tab in hand, as if showing up in his mom and stepdad's room toward midnight on a Saturday was perfectly normal. "So. I won the nine dollars tonight."

"I recall."

"Pretty rad. Oh wait. Mom? I'm still up." He waited for an answer that never came. "Sorry. If you're mad. About my being up. John and I were playing the Commodore. Which I know you hate. But, well, G.I. Joe is an awesome game. And so, you know, the Olympics. I always beat John at that. Which is fun. Beating him. Neither of us can figure out how to get high scores. I just always do."

"A savant."

Faith said something too faint to understand.

"This is a delicate topic because it involves your firstborn," Alexander said. "And his behavior toward me tonight."

"Stephen's behavior?"

"After I won the money. And went to the poolroom with John. Stephen came in. And he asked for money. At first I thought it was a general question. To the room. I mean, I was there. And John. And Gorbie. Performing oral sex on himself. Not that he would ask Gorbie for money. But he could have. Because stranger things have happened. As they say. But no. He was talking to me. He wanted to know if he could take my nine dollars."

"Take it?"

"To invest. In something. What, I can't remember. I just remember thinking it was weird. Most of the time he doesn't talk to me. Or if he does, he says something kind of snippy." He giggled. "It's okay. I just thought it was, you know, different for him. To talk to me in a semi-constructive way."

"Alexander? I have something profound to tell you. Are you ready?" Frank lifted his head a notch and lowered his voice commensurately. "Money changes people. The sooner you understand this, the sooner you'll understand the human race more than most. A person's behavior can utterly and completely change when you give them money, or even mention that you might give them money someday. I witnessed this a lot, as it turns out, when I adopted Daniel, Louis, and Peggy. Have I told you about that?"

"You were the only one who didn't profit from that transaction."

"And *they* all did! Every single one of those assholes. Their father, Joanne, Bawrence. All of them."

Faith said something else as she turned the page.

"The moral of the story? When it comes to money and people? Never be surprised. Understand that and you are golden."

They shook hands. Alexander walked out and closed the accordion door behind him.

Frank was settled back in bed with a World War II photography book focusing on the Pacific theater when Faith emerged from her nook in her pj's and Coke-bottle glasses. "Jonathan killed his own basketball," she said as she climbed in bed with a medieval fantasy novel. "He used one of the steak knives."

"Should I talk to him?"

"He's not happy, Frank. He's not happy. He's trying to say something. Classic passive aggression."

"I'll talk to him." But what would he say? Absent proof?

"You might talk to him about the drugs while you're at it."

"I know nothing about that."

"I'd happily talk to your kids, but they won't listen to me because they don't like me."

"I know nothing about that either. They spoke to you at dinner. They spoke to you during Oh Hell!"

"Have you spoken to Bawrence? Frank!"

Frank jolted awake and let the book slip off his lap. A yelp that wasn't Faith came from the other direction. He peered over to see Gorbachev shaking off the book's blow to his little noggin. While poochie recovered almost instantly and reverted to his entreating-to-jump-up stare, Faith was only just getting started. She exploded into Niagara Falls. Catching her breath, she was able to gasp, barely above a whisper. "Talk to Bawrence. Please. Talk to Bawrence."

"Bawrence?"

"Please, Frank."

Gorbie jumped onto the bed, plopped down between Frank and Faith, and started polishing those nuts with gusto.

Frank sat up and put a hand on his wife's arm. It felt so pathetic, but dazed from having nodded off, he didn't know what else to do.

"He hates me." She wiped the tears jerkily. "He never talks to me. Whenever he looks at me, it's a scowl. It's an ugly, ugly fucking scowl. I try to be nice. Do you think I'm evil? Am I an evil cunt?"

Frank struggled to find the words. He was so goddamned tired, but Faith seemed to be hanging on his response. "Faith. He's nine. And his face is fucked up. He wets the bed. He eats too much junk food and will probably suffer the weight problems I've had my entire life."

"That's why I worry about him. And he talks to himself. When he's in his room. I've heard him carry on entire conversations. Frank, he might be insane."

"Doesn't he play with those robot toys? The Translators or whatever they're called? It's all bullshit anyway."

"What about Louis? I'm sure he doesn't like me. He never has anything nice to say."

"Louis is what's called a teenager."

"Does he think he's black? It seems like he's only nice to the black kids from the Gardens."

Frank exaggerated a yawn and pondered Karen's ass.

"Good morning, Baltimore!"

Sundays at 48 Broad were like post-Oh Hell! stud: It would be a good day for one of the brood, but you wouldn't know who until the day was out.

Frank sat in his office and stared at the green-and-black screen of his Radio Shack TRS-80 until lunch. The house was empty. Did that make him the stud winner? After munching on eight quarter slices of bread with peanut butter in the living room to the soundtrack of Haydn, chased down with a can of soda water followed by a second can that he took with him back up to his office, he discovered Baltimore looking exceptionally unstressed. Beyond the mellow finch, through the window, he spied Hogg walking his balding dog along the space between the houses. Poor pooch was apparently too weak for a walk around the block.

This gave him the courage to call Karen and tell her about the lack of funds for Shadow. She took it surprisingly well but then broke the news that her mother was very sick, in the hospital, may not live, and so she wouldn't be able to clean up 48 Broad indefinitely. She'd call next week to give him a status update.

In the middle of the afternoon, and for reasons Frank would never fathom for the rest of his life, he hyperventilated. It lasted about a minute but seemed far longer. What really did take a good long while, indeed the rest of the day, was his processing of it. On a Sunday in May of 1986, Franklin Monroe Roggebusch, age forty-six, became aware of his mortality for the first time in his life.

Also a first, Frank didn't have much to say at dinner. He skimped his Good Thing Bad Thing New Thing. No one seemed to care. What would Joanne say if she had to do Good Thing Bad Thing New Thing? Or Karen?

He tried watching something intelligent after dinner but couldn't focus. When Faith changed it to Prism to watch the Phillies, he took a gander at the Civil War book he was in the middle of, this one focusing on the food favored in the field by the blue and the gray. Again, any intellectual fulfillment eluded him.

When he heard some of the kids wrestling in the hallway, followed by more thumping and shouting upstairs, Frank decided he simply didn't have the stamina for this house right now. After refreshing his Johnnie Red and soda, he flicked off the porch light and parked himself in the snug darkness of the side porch steps and mapped out an alternate timeline. If he hadn't dumped Joanne and they'd stayed together in Kensington, what would they be doing right now? On this very night?

Someone walked out and inadvertently kicked Johnnie down the steps. The tumbler broke on the sidewalk with a dull thud.

By the time he stood up and beheld Bawrence, the naked disgust had already carved itself into his visage. "Thanks a lot."

Faith cried again that night, but this time Frank didn't have the energy to offer words of consolation. He tried making up captions for the World War II photographs. No good. He couldn't focus. The only solution was to apologize to Bawrence.

Walking from the master suite to the stairs leading up to the third floor meant walking the full length of the house from back to front. Past his office and Faith's wardrobe closet, where Bawrence had spoken to Joanne a few hours ago like he did every Sunday, most likely telling her what an asshole his evil father was, were the other two bedrooms on this floor. Music of starkly contrasting styles hummed from down here. That metal racket Alexander preferred came from the room he shared with John, who was giving his older brother the third degree at the moment, perhaps about the music. From the room at the foot of the stairs, which Stephen shared with Louis, came the more modern jazz that Stephen couldn't get enough of. Louis, whose passion was the modern music made by the blacks, was laughing his ass off. After a few seconds, Frank realized Louis was on the phone. Perhaps with Woody.

The third floor saw less music because Dan's room was up here, down toward the same end as the master suite below, right by the bathroom. Over on the north side, Jonathan blasted music similar to

Alexander's. His room emanated a smell so rank it made Frank's stomach churn.

Approaching Bawrence's room, he heard his youngest talking and assumed he was playing with his robot or army toys. But when he put his ear to the door, what he heard instead was a passionate discussion about something else entirely. "But the violin is faster there! I like it when it's fast!" Since when did this kid listen to music that involved the violin? And that's when Frank heard it. It was extremely faint, like a radio turned way down on the other side of a large room: the third and final movement, allegro energico, of Bruch's Violin Concerto No. 1 in G minor (opus 26).

3

JONATHAN

POT A LOT AND GOLFING GRUMPY

For as long as anyone could remember, Jonathan's nickname had been Double because of all the mayhem and mischief he caused or was otherwise connected to. "Because he always gets into double trouble," was the official explanation. In fact, it was none other than Joan Purvis, formerly Joanne Roggebusch, formerly Woods, née Barney, Frank Roggebusch's second wife and Jonathan's first stepmother, who had devised the moniker on the fly during a summer in the seventies. Jonathan, fresh out of the operation room for a hernia, ripped up the flowers from Joanne's meticulously tended flower beds, then decided to swing a bottle of merlot at Stephen's head. The bottle shattered against the wall and soaked the cream carpet in deep red. It looked like a crime scene. As I said, Double.

You take now, for instance. Just days away from his fifteenth birthday and wrapping up his freshman year at Rancocas Valley, Jonathan had, in the barely more than three years since arriving in the Garden State, ascended to the peak of Mount Holly's pot dealer pyramid. He harnessed that same caliber of skill and acumen used to grow and cultivate the finest herbage an allowance could buy and parlayed it into growing and cultivating the most productive network of dealers and suppliers no allowance could buy. Jonathan may have sucked at math, he may have skimped English and ignored history altogether, but he was a natural with people. A smile splitting his freckled face—he was the only one at 48 Broad with an appreciable amount of freckles, inherited from his mother—could light up a room full of joints, as well as the joints themselves. At first he resented his father's strong-arming him into ROTC under threat of reduced allowance so the black sheep could experience some semblance of structure. In no time flat, though, Jonathan discovered a whole new customer base, and many of his fellow cadets introduced him to yet more customers. Jonathan looked so dashing in uniform, it never occurred to anyone, from RV to 48 Broad to Springfield Golf Course and all the street corners in between, that this modern-day Cary Grant was a deadbeat-cum-kingpin. He also looked poster ready on the basketball court and golf course. That these two extracurricular activities provided yet more avenues for his operation was just the icing on the pot brownie.

Yes, like Rocky and boxing, you couldn't talk about Jonathan without mentioning golf. Perhaps it was because of all the green the sport entailed, or perhaps, more likely, it was the genetics that hopped from his paternal grandfather, clear over Frank's head and square onto Jonathan's bright blond pate. Whatever the reason, golf was the one passion Jonathan pursued with more fervor and very accurate club-swinging vigor than anything else. Yes, even more than those other green acres.

Exhibit A: He looked forward to going to work at the Springfield links on Jacksonville Road, where he'd held a part-time gig for nearly a year now. Driving the cart around to collect balls may not sound like *Star Wars* to you and me, but that just means we don't know how to drive a golf cart like Jonathan. Ask some of his brothers, especially the ones he wasn't related to by blood, the same ones he could stand hanging out with, like Louis or Alexander. He didn't take them cruising in the cart after hours so much as flying in it.

Exhibit B: Even as a freshman, Jonathan was a key weapon on RV's varsity golf team and, as we speak, was leading the team to the

New Jersey state finals. They wouldn't win, but just getting there was thrilling enough. It would be their first such appearance since before Jonathan's kid brother Barry was born.

Yes, like Rocky and a punching bag, you couldn't talk about Jonathan without mentioning Barry. The mere sight of that chubby little bed wetter pissed off Jonathan to no end. That half-dead face. That chunky, Spanky-esque physique. The bed-wetting. The sight of him eating those goddamn chocolate Entenmann's donuts in the morning. That especially drove Jonathan up the wall. Being a pot kingpin was stressful work. Shit, just being a teenager was stressful. Now combine the two. Double had to de-stress somehow, right? Beating up Barry allowed him to do just that in addition to venting his inscrutable dislike for the kid.

Jonathan's stress was about to take a sharp left, and little did he know that Barry was the driver by virtue of pilfering five hundred smackers from their father's sock drawer. Frank was going to use that money to help Karen pay for an operation for her dog Shadow. Or so he thought. Jonathan knew that was bullshit because he knew Karen better than anyone else at 48 Broad. How, you ask?

Because they were sleeping together.

Jonathan was a mature about-to-turn fifteen. It sounds far-fetched when you hear about a teenager sleeping with an adult, but it isn't really. That's why you keep hearing about it. Jonathan and Karen didn't sleep together often, mind you, but enough to feel comfortable confiding The Secrets of Their Respective Worlds. Among Karen's secrets was her Mount Everest of credit card debt. Jonathan wasn't clear on all the details—he wasn't exactly Joe Awesome Listener, especially after sex—but besides Shadow's healthcare, Karen had a much older relative to take care of. Or something like that. And other stuff. Again, he wasn't clear on everything. All he knew was that the gal sure had a lot of drama for someone so hot.

As a grower, Jonathan always had a baggie or two, or three, of the green stuff lying around his bedroom. When Karen showed up to give 48 Broad the once-over on Wednesdays, she was always good about collecting the stray baggies and storing them in Jonathan's sock drawer, perhaps pinching a little as a gratuity. Christ knows she needed the roach's almighty hit more than Jonathan did. They'd agreed it was totally cool.

Jonathan had golf practice on Wednesdays. As they did now and again, he and his teammates had a postpractice powwow at King of Pizza in Lumberton Plaza, a few doors down from the Super Fresh where his father overflowed two carts at two hundred a throw a week. It was after nine when he got home and ran upstairs expecting to see a spick-and-span bedroom. It may have been spick-and-span of pot, but that was it. Most telling was yesterday's pair of socks, crumpled and crisscrossed precisely where Jonathan had tossed them this morning (he slept in his socks sometimes).

Before he assumed the little shit across the hall had stolen the goods, he needed to confirm that Karen had not, in fact, cleaned the house today. From the poolroom he heard Dan and Louis laughing their asses off while poor John was going ballistic. Someone was getting their ass wiped at the Olympics. Meantime in the music room, Stephen was doing his best Chuck Mangione on the trumpet. Someone was watching the little black-and-white in the kitchen down yonder.

And there in the living room, Frank, the man Jonathan sometimes woke up despising, other times woke up sympathizing with, and still other times woke up finding absolutely inscrutable, sat on the floor in front of Faith's high-backed blue leather chair while she one-third read her fantasy novel, a third watched a seventies movie on Prism, and a third snaked her pale fingers through Frank's scalp. The old man nodded in and out of consciousness.

Stephen stopped playing and stepped out to use the bathroom. "Hey, pussy!"

Jonathan didn't have time for that right now. "Karen come over or...?"

Frank mumbled something that mumbologists would decipher as a greeting.

"No," Faith said.

"Uhhhh... mmmm...?"

"Your son wants to know if Karen cleaned up his shit."

Frank mumbled something that might've been to the effect of Karen couldn't make it.

"She sick?"

Faith turned to Jonathan with eyes that he could've sworn were pitch-black, like that girl from *The Exorcist*. "It is no concern of yours where she is. Someday you won't have a cleaning lady to put your socks in the hamper."

Jonathan laughed. Ninety-nine point nine percent of the time, that grin could've melted anything. Faith was that point one percent.

"The only question you should be asking is how or why you could be so fucking dependent on Karen."

"I bet you'd like me to do more chores, huh?"

"Not until you stop stabbing basketballs."

"That doesn't make any sense."

"Since when was making sense a prerequisite?"

"Always have to cop an attitude. Can't answer a simple fucking question."

His father was trying in vain to contribute to the conversation. "Mmm... ummm..." He fingered his mustache and nostrils for good measure.

"Hey, pussy!"

Faith creased a smile that could've formed icicles on the porch overhangs. "I agree that an attitude exists in this room at present, but I disagree as to your alleged source."

"Coulda gone so fuckin' easy. I ask, you answer."

Faith went back to her book.

"Am I too dumb for you? You think I'm a retard like Barry?"

"If this is how you communicate with your pot gang, it's a wonder they haven't mutinied."

"What the fuck?"

"Faith..." Frank finally achieved coherence after swatting Faith's hand off his scalp. "Jonathan." He cleared his throat and crossed his hands and smiled through heavy lids. With his hair disheveled, he looked positively absurd. "While you were out leading RV's golf team to glory, Karen phoned to say she was indisposed and wouldn't be able to make her regularly scheduled appointment to perform the duties she typically performs on Wednesdays. Unfortunately, this includes the straightening and vacuuming of your third-floor abode. Now. Some people might call her unfortunate when she does, in fact, clean your room, but never mind that."

"She okay?"

"She sounded okay when I spoke to her. However, I believe her mother is not okay. That may even be the reason for her being indisposed."

Jonathan double-stepped the stairs back up to the third floor and marched into Barry's room. Jesus Christ, did it stink in here or what? The soiled underwear, the filthy socks he wore days in a row, the sheets, the unwashed hair, the yellow teeth, the abominable breath, it all came together to form the perfect stench from hell. "Think it's funny sneaking into my room? You don't even know what weed is, you fat little shit."

"You're a pain in my ass!"

"Cut the shit. I know it was you."

"You're an asshole!"

With Barry sitting on the carpet with his Transformers, all Jonathan had to do was collapse on him like the Hulkster on a lame Iron Sheik. "Listen, douche!" He started giving him a noogie. "You better fucking give me anything that doesn't belong to you. You read me?" Jonathan could only tolerate the stink for so long before pushing him away.

"There," Barry said after catching his breath. He pointed at something over by the door.

"What?"

"The Big Gulp and Zero wrapper. You said anything that doesn't belong to me. Your girlfriend Karen was supposed to pick those up, but she was too busy with Stephen."

"The fuck you just say?" He got the little porker in a full nelson à la Superfly Snuka on Rowdy Roddy Piper. The kid still wouldn't back down. Somewhere in the back of his mind, Jonathan felt a tickle of respect.

"Louis said you can't be in here!"

"Damn, you stink! God!"

"Stop it!"

Jonathan let go and jumped up. "I find out you took my stuff, no one will be able to protect you. Not Louis. Not Dad. No one. You read me, you ugly fuck?" Barry remained lying on his back and seemed to be studying the ceiling. He started picking his nose. "And why do you talk to yourself so much, man? Fucking creepy."

"She's a rad girl named Bunny. She plays the violin, and she's much nicer than you."

"Choke on a chocolate donut, asshole."

Enjoyable as that was, Jonathan still hadn't found the pot thief. Who then? Who would have the balls to walk into his room and just take it?

"Gorbie!" John called from below. "Gorbie! Hey, little guy!"

That's when the truth bodychecked him like André the Giant on Big John Studd.

That dumb little mop who couldn't even sit on command, who shat on the carpet with impunity, and who occasionally flirted with death by swallowing the odd staple, had traipsed into Jonathan's room and scarfed his weed. "You find him?"

John came into view in the thin gap between the staircase and balustrade and shrugged before continuing to call for the son of award-winning Canadian show dogs.

Jonathan checked his father's office. No go. Ditto under the couch in the poolroom. As far as he knew, Gorbie had never eaten pot, so perhaps the logic of being high should've inspired him to check a place where Gorbie would otherwise never go sober.

There he was, out for the count in the master bathroom tub.

"Hey, Jim! Hey, man. You know a place I can take a dog that's OD'd? ... Figuratively? The fuck does that mean? ... No, it's not a figure of speech. It's my fuckin' dog, man. You've seen him. Gorbie...Yeah, yeah, yeah.

Dumb little shit ate my pot and now I think he's dying. ... Yeah, we have a vet, but I don't have a fucking clue who it is. ... It's my stepmom's dog. Man, if he croaks, Faith will eat my nuts for breakfast and my dick for dessert."

Jim was Officer James Douglas of the Mount Holly Police Department. He and Double had met cute late on a school night when our young truant here was selling some weed behind RV. What Jonathan wouldn't know until after he graduated was that Officer Douglas had originally gone there to meet up with a junior with whom he was flinging. Officer Douglas took Jonathan and his customer in but let them off with a warning. I suppose he was hoping the whole process of riding in the back of a cop car and seeing the inside of a police station would be enough to scare those kids straight. Obviously he didn't know Double.

Since that night, Jonathan and Officer Douglas met up once or twice a month or so. Jonathan never made a sale in the same place twice, and while he was never caught again, Officer Douglas made a point of making his presence known. Sometimes he'd be there after school and stroll the three blocks with Jonathan back to 48 Broad. Or he'd shoot the shit with the frosh outside the Seven Heaven down on Mill. Now and again the small talk would veer into confiding. Officer Douglas became sort of an ersatz therapist. He was in his forties, divorced with two sons as well as a daughter who was dating Jonathan's stepbrother John.

After the vet made Gorbie barf up the weed, Jonathan and Officer Douglas walked the little pooch to the Wawa a couple of blocks down the main drag. Gorbie padded along all hunky-dory like nothing had happened. The cop and the kid each filled a large cup of the steaming-hot black stuff before stepping back outside to tap their packs against their palms. Jonathan tied Gorbie's leash to the fender of a rusty station wagon that didn't look like it'd be going anywhere anytime soon.

Officer Douglas tittered as he exhaled a puff of smoke. "You're an idiot."

"What are you doing up so late, man?"

"Got a date tomorrow. Can't sleep."

They puffed from one cigarette to the next while Gorbie sated himself with some beef jerky Officer Douglas had bought him.

"No customers tonight?" the cop said at one point, but Jonathan was thinking about tomorrow. What the hell was he going to tell those kids from Shawnee? He puffed and asked Officer Douglas if he'd grown up with a bitch stepmother. "My dad never remarried after my mom left him. I was eight."

"I was barely a year when it happened."

"Barry's mom, right?"

"They had an affair at Watergate or something."

"You're shitting me." They lit up again. "I'm kind of glad your dog almost died. Saved me having to arrest your dumb ass."

Jonathan threw his trademark punch to the shoulder and guffawed. "You're full of shit."

He skipped school the next day and spent the meat of the day on the pay phone at Lumberton Plaza trying to scare up someone, anyone, who could lend him the pot he needed for tonight's peace talks with his Medford rival, a senior at Shawnee and a veteran of this racket who would never go for a canceled invitation without coming to Mount Holly to get the score.

A distressing number of Jonathan's friends actually bothered to go to school today. How was that possible? How could they possibly focus on algebra or earth science or *Of Mice and Men* on such an important day? No matter, not a single one of those knuckleheads knew how to score more product.

His last resort—and he really didn't want to do this the way a moth really doesn't want to dive into the flame—was to phone up his oh-so-spicy flavor of the month, Fiona. Fiona's father and brother broke into homes and stole refrigerators to resell. By virtue of their so-called enterprise, they knew no shortage of scumbags in the Burlington County underworld who could score Jonathan some product as easily as they could scratch their filthy balls. But Fiona wouldn't have it. She was skipping school to lend dear old Dad a hand with offloading some of those black market iceboxes and could easily have just handed the phone to the old man. Unfortunately for

Double, he had completely forgotten the double trouble he'd gotten into the last time they made out because he tried to finger her while she was having her period. How was he to know? He wasn't a mind reader. She hung up.

Jonathan was, in a word, fucked. That night, staring at his freckled, peach-fuzzed visage in the third-floor bathroom mirror, the Jacuzzi tub and steam room shower mocking him with their temptation while Alexander's metal, Louis's rap, and Stephen's jazz floated in at various decibel levels, Jonathan resolved to face his own music. Losing all that pot was one thing, but he was discerning enough to know that flaking out on a meeting of marijuana minds would be far worse.

Cheers was on. On his way out, he heard Barry's "NORM!" and felt a pang of jealousy.

While cutting down the alley, he reminded himself that he needed to hit up Gregory's at some point to see what the next generation telescope cost. He could just barely, if the night were super clear, clearer than tonight, catch a faint dusting of the Pleiades, the elusive Seven Sisters. They'd resolve so much better with just a slightly bigger lens.

The alley led clear across the block, from the Roggebusch garage on Buttonwood to the parking lot behind the High Street church where Jonathan and his pals played street hockey. Three of those same pals were waiting in an idling Ford pickup across High.

The powwow with his Shawnee High counterpart, Sean Kenzler, was scheduled to take place in the food court of the Moorestown Mall, a quick shot down Route 38. Sean was already there with three of his own self-important underclassmen. Watching Jonathan and Sean shake hands in that fist-forming kind of way teens have always done throughout time, you'd think they were meeting to talk about last night's Phillies game. They grabbed one of the tables and told their crews to hit up the arcade.

In spite of himself and everything else, Jonathan flashed back three years ago this month to the Sunday when the entire brood came here, right over there, to see *Return of the Jedi*. The line sucked.

Barry bawled his eyes out. Jonathan and Dan and everyone else tried desperately to show him how many people were behind them, that in the big scheme of things, they weren't so bad off. That just made it worse. Only now did it occur to Jonathan that Barry had probably thought they were patronizing him. Sean said something. "What?"

"Tab. That your drink?"

"It's all right."

"You on a diet, faggot?"

Jonathan was about to meet that barb head on when his father's voice butted into his brain and told him to be philosophical. "Know what's messed up? I only started drinking this because my brother said he hated it. I just wanted to piss him off. He was right; it's fucking disgusting. But I can't tell him that."

"And now you like it."

"Yeahhhhhhh!" They shared a chuckle between sips of their pop. Brilliant! The Tao of Frank!

"And you like that, huh? Cherry Coke?" How was he supposed to broach the topic of the vanishing pot without it feeling forced and potentially betraying his nauseous dread?

"Dr. Pepper. Been drinking this stuff since I was a kid. Rumor has it Dr. Pepper was my first word."

"Words."

"What's that?"

"Man, that's rad!" No, it wasn't. What the hell was he doing?

Sean sucked down some more pop and took sidelong glances as if looking for his cronies.

Jonathan kept his eyes locked on his counterpart's in as cordial a manner as he could muster. Whether he admitted it or not, he had Faith to thank for teaching him this little-valued tactic.

"Like hockey, man? You watch the Flyers?"

Sean stopped sucking but kept his mouth on the straw.

"You play?"

This time his opposite number gave a slight head tilt.

Jonathan now had his cue to get to the point. As he feared, he tripped and stumbled all over the food court with "So, uhs..." and

"Wells..." and all manner of nonentity verbiage before finally getting out something that vaguely resembled, "I don't have the pot because my dumb dog ate it and he was this close to dying."

Sean finished sucking down his Dr. Pepper until it turned to slurping for what seemed like all night. "Just let me know who to hurt," he finally said. "In your family. It has to be in your family. And don't worry, I won't do it in that stank-ass house."

He knew where Jonathan lived? Jonathan must've wondered this out loud because Sean's next words were:

"Everyone knows where you live, man. You live in the butt-ugliest house in Burlington County." He slammed his cup down and locked eyes for the first time.

Jonathan blurted out a name and then promptly forgot the name he blurted.

Their peoples showed back up as if on cue. Jonathan ran and did not walk to the pickup and ignored his friends when they drilled him for the score. Instead of the church, he told them to drop him off at the Seven Heaven. He half hoped Officer Douglas would be there but then was glad when he wasn't. He needed some alone time. During the walk home, he spun his brain in manic circles trying to remember the sacrifice he'd offered. Which name made sense? Who wouldn't he mind getting his ass kicked up and down Mount Holly?

Barry, of course.

Jonathan's first reaction was to crack his first smile in hours. Like goodwill from a teacher, though, the feeling didn't last. Within a few blocks, not only was the thought not putting sunshine on those freckles, the idea of having done such a thing to such a helpless, defenseless bed wetter made him barf in the bushes on Cherry Street.

As soon as he got home, he withdrew to the telescope in his room to consider the stars. Aldebaran had been front and center during the walk down the alley what seemed like a couple of trips to Mars ago, but now he couldn't find the red planet. Still, the Big Dipper never got old. Nor did Jupiter, which at the moment was enjoying a conjunction with the waning crescent moon. Jonathan tried like the bastard he was to enjoy their companionship, but the stress proved too hot.

"Fuck!"

He jumped up and stomped around, blasting AC/DC and not giving a shit who had a problem with it.

What would Sean ultimately do?

Jonathan slept for shit that night. Worse, the next day was Friday, ROTC dress-up day. What the fuck was the point? He took advantage of the insomnia and snagged a rare early start, which he sort of needed anyway to don the uniform. Decked out like the proper cadet he most certainly wasn't, he headed down to the kitchen hoping to accomplish another rarity on a school day: cereal and toast.

His breakfast hopes were dashed like so many eggs when he came upon Barry stuffing those Entenmann's chocolate donuts down his gullet. Tough bastard though he was, Jonathan simply did not have the stamina to listen to that porker eat. While dousing hastily prepared Peanut Butter Crunch with Faith's skim milk (the only milk he could find), he took advantage of Barry's having his back to him by making fuck-you gestures. Jonathan was an innovator par excellence with those two words without ever having to utter either one of them.

"Get the fuck out," he mumbled to Gorbie when he hurried into the living room to crunch his Crunch in peace. Gorbie didn't budge. Jonathan slammed his bowl down, sending Crunch balls skyward, and threw the pooch into the hall. The little guy skidded and slammed into the wall. He quickly rebounded and darted up the stairs and down the hall to the master suite.

Jonathan barely had time to shovel the Crunch into his mouth before Barry's pudgy little silhouette appeared. "Fuck do you want?"

"I wanna watch *Goonies*."

"Go to school."

"I don't have to be there until seven forty."

"Fuck off, punk." As Barry stomped up the stairs, Jonathan decided to spite him by flipping on MTV. He'd never been so happy to see Twisted Sister belt out "We're Not Gonna Take It."

The only thing that saved Friday from sucking was that it was Friday. Fiona ignored him in algebra, but by lunchtime, as they kicked up a leg at the smoker's wall, she finally confessed to wanting to go to the Pine Barrens this weekend. By the end of eighth period, her period seemed truly over. She bussed him deep and wet and said she'd see him tomorrow.

If he wasn't so anxious about what Sean would do, the walk home would've been light-footed. Jonathan felt yet heavier when he spotted the broken pickets in the backyard fence, like someone had taken a bat or a sledgehammer and went to town. And it must've been a drive-by, for the pickets in question were all along the Buttonwood side.

He was fetching a Tab from one of the laundry room fridges when a fist collided with his shoulder. Jonathan barely had time to register Stephen's beat-to-a-pulp visage—did Sean break his glasses too? He wasn't wearing them, and Jesus, was he crying?—when his brother punched him again and pushed him against the dryer. "Think it's funny?"

"The fuck is your problem?"

"Gotta send your goons after me, asshole? Don't have the balls to fight me yourself?"

"You're full of shit."

"Pussy!" The shoves were relentless. Who knew the trumpeter was this strong?

"I didn't do anything!"

"They broke my trumpet, you FUCK!"

"HEY!" Faith was stomping down the back stairs.

"THEY BROKE MY FUCKING TRUMPET!"

"Okay!"

"I hope the pot business is going well because you're buying me a new one. Asshole!"

"HEY!"

Stephen huffed away.

Jonathan followed him into the kitchen. "You're out of your fucking mind."

Stephen spun back around and got in his little brother's face. He looked completely different without his big square glasses, a Hyde to the usual doctor. Jonathan was three years younger, a lot of years when you're a teenager, but everyone agreed he was stronger. He wanted to feel some relief that Barry was safe, but he'd have to take a rain check until this bomb was defused. Faith was keeping her distance on the far side of the table.

Stephen jabbed a finger into Jonathan's chest. "You think that fucking uniform fools anyone? It makes you the fucking joke of the house."

"Cut it out!" Faith's usual gravitas had been rendered light gravy no one wanted.

"You're the joke, dude." Jonathan tittered. "Look at your fucked-up face."

Stephen pushed him. "Afraid to fight me yourself, you fucking PUSSY?" And another push. And another.

"FUCK you, man," the would-be cadet said with a robust shove of his own that nearly robbed Stephen of his balance.

BAM!

THUD.

Jonathan's head jerked sideways as if clobbered simultaneously by both the bolt and the clap. The pain didn't start right away, but it soon made up for the delay with an intensity that banged gongs in an echo-prone cavern. He winced as he turned to his stepmother. Faith was panting as if she'd done something strenuous. And that's when he spotted it at his feet, one of the innumerable cans of Del Monte peas that never seemed to run out in the cupboard above R2.

A few hours later, head still throbbing, Jonathan took advantage of Faith's punishing the ivories in the music room to approach his father in the living room. Frank was watching the news, nursing his customary predinner scotch and soda, and dipping his fingers into his customary predinner Planters peanuts.

"Jona-*than!*" The old man slurped and chomped and stared and waited. Then he stopped everything and flashed a perfunctory smile.

"I talk to you a sec, Dad? About Faith?"

"What kind of faith?"

Jonathan gestured over his shoulder.

Frank's eyes wandered over the bookcases and TV before arriving back at his second born. Clearing his throat and folding his hands on his belly, he asked, "This have anything to do with why Stephen came to see me?"

"I have no idea."

The old man thumb-scratched his scalp. "Your brother told me, not without some eloquence, as is his nature, that Faith is an insane bitch, and he demanded to know why I married her."

For the first time since the can of peas, Jonathan laughed. "What'd you say?"

"To the insane bitch part or the marriage part? Well, the insane bitch part did not warrant a cogent answer since the question was, as phrased, a nonsensical one. In spite of his insisting on it as an extent problem, by the way, which bordered on being out of line. As for why I married her, the simple answer is I love her. However, marriage is a complicated topic, as both you and Stephen will realize in due time, and most likely sooner than either of you appreciate. And that makes the question rhetorical."

"I guess the marriage question depends on your agreeing with him about Faith being a lunatic."

"I guess." Frank thumb-scratched his scalp again. "Uhhhh, but since I don't agree with that claim, that renders the marriage question forfeit altogether."

"You know why he said that?"

"That?"

"She threw a can of peas at my head, Pop. A can of peas. And I'm not talking underhanded, like a softball throw. More like Steve Carlton or Jim Palmer. It still hurts. I could have a concussion."

"I question the concussion claim. But let me ask you." Frank sat up and crossed his bare feet on the recliner's foldout stool. "Did she throw it unprovoked?"

Jonathan stared at the old man. The throb only seemed to pound harder.

"Other words, did she just show up and throw a can of peas at you for no reason? Or might she have had a reason?"

"Stephen thought I sent someone after him to beat him up and break his trumpet."

"And did you?"

"No."

"Do you know who did?"

"If I wanted to kick his ass and break his trumpet, I'd do it myself."

"That doesn't answer my question."

"You didn't answer my question."

"Which was?"

"Faith threw a fuckin' can of peas at my head."

"Let's consider this from Faith's point of view. There you and your brother are. Shouting at each other, pushing each other, causing a stir. Each of you is twice her size. It's like if you or I came across two Big Foots having a bad day. You've got to defend yourself, right?"

"We weren't threatening her."

Frank thumbed his scalp and considered his books. "Faith came across an explosive situation involving two much larger males, and she defused the situation the best way she knew how. Now. Does that make her an insane bitch? I don't think so. A touch overreactive? Perhaps. But with any lasting damage? I predict you will survive. She'll survive. We all will. Except for Stephen's trumpet, the cause of whose demise is, I suppose, a mystery. Like your basketball." The old man took a nip and turned back to Dan Rather. "Everything is wonderful."

Up in his room, Jonathan was about to blast Zeppelin before deciding against it. Dinner would be ready soon, and he didn't want anyone pounding on his door because he hadn't heard the dinner bell. So he played it low while getting Fiona on the horn to give her the third degree. Jonathan had to get pissed at someone, or he'd combust. At first he pretended that he needed to reconfirm one more time that she would be coming to the Pine Barrens tomorrow. She said of course and that he was a moron for having forgotten already. Her attitude only gave him an excuse to turn up the burner. Barely thirty seconds into the call and the lovebirds were spatting. This was just the therapy Jonathan needed. Indeed, he felt so much better after slamming the phone down while Fiona was midsentence, he celebrated by turning up Zeppelin just a bit.

Unfortunately it was a bit too much.

"JOHHHHHHHN...!"

"WHAT?"

"...athan."

Jonathan yanked open his door to find Alexander on the stairs. "The fuck do you want?"

"Hey, man. Hey. We rang the bell. But not everyone answered. So I'm going around to find those who didn't answer. Which is most of you. Except Faith. Everyone's playing music."

"What about me?" John said from below.

"Don't know. What about you?"

"I can't eat?"

"A fair question."

Stephen's Good Thing was that his glasses were broken, which meant he couldn't see far enough to make out Barry's hideousness. His Bad Thing was his trumpet getting destroyed, and his New Thing was seeing Jonathan getting de-brained by a can of peas, which he was sure he'd never see again, not because he didn't want to, but because he wasn't that lucky. Faith's Bad Thing concerned the damage to the fence, about which she expressed confidence that Jonathan was connected in some way, shape, form, or baseball bat. Her New Thing was agreeing with Stephen's assertion that Jonathan was behind the attack on him and his trumpet, New because she couldn't remember the last time she agreed with Stephen on anything. Her Good Thing was her ability to break up the Jonathan-Stephen kerfuffle without their father's intervention or assistance. This made her smile with that trademark shit-eating grin she and Frank were wont to exchange during dinner. As if on cue, Frank lit up.

"So my Good Thing is that I finally got around to my annual spring cleaning."

"I didn't realize you practiced an annual spring cleaning, Alexander," Frank said.

"He doesn't," Faith spat between bites.

"You should've used the past tense, Mom. I didn't. But now I do. This was my first. Spring cleaning, that is. My room is much cleaner. But I still miss Karen. I hope she comes back. And soon. Because I'm messy."

"Your poor closet."

"Now see, Mom. You're being cynical. I did not just stuff my closet. I went through that as well. I found all this old crap. Old crap that's been there since we moved here. And when we were in LA? John and I? It was in the closet there as well. From one closet to the next. But no more. And you know what? It took me three hours." He forked three fingers. "And that's okay. You know why, Frank? Because I took your advice."

"Then naturally you found success."

"When I was sitting up in your office. Baltimore was going bonkers because he was out of food. And I was complaining about bass practice."

"Ah yes. The investment of practice time and the eventual payoff."

"You say it so much better. So I kept thinking of that. And that's when I thought of cleaning all the shit. Out of my room."

"Quit your goddamned cussing."

"And how much time it would take to clean it. But then I thought, well, it's an investment of time that will pay off later. Because if I continued postponing it, who knew how long it would take before, you know, I finally did it? And the garbage kept piling up? And up? And up?"

"A wise man once said, 'That's a shitload of garbage,'" Frank said.

"It's also bad for you," Faith said. "Living with trash has long-term health effects. So the investment's much more valuable than you think."

"I also had it perfectly timed," Alexander said.

"Alexander, I've noticed your timing with most things tends to be impeccable."

"What's your point?" Stephen asked.

Alexander gave him a blank look.

Stephen guffawed. "Where are you going with this?"

Alexander jabbed a finger in the direction of the laundry room. "I timed this project for the day before trash collection. You know, so that it wouldn't have to sit there. And the raccoons wouldn't get it. And, you know, we have six bins. So I figured, you know, there'd still be some space. In the bins. For my shit."

His mother gave him a look.

"But there wasn't any space. For the first time ever, all six bins were overflowing. I had nowhere to put my doo-doo. But I was careful. I arranged it all to the side. Nice and neat. At least nice and neat considering that it is, you know, doo-doo."

"But then the garbage wasn't taken out," Stephen said. Jonathan hated how Stephen always used the napkin-clutching hand to point at people, the way he was jabbing said index at Jonathan right now.

"And you saw a raccoon, right?"

"Three." Alexander forked three fingers. "They attacked when I was taking out the last bag. Gorbie was there. Poor little guy. They almost got him."

So not fucking fair. After the week he'd just had, Jonathan figured he deserved a free pass on taking out the trash. Looking at Barry chew his food crookedly, with the dead side of his mouth dropping open with each chomp, he was more convinced than ever that his baby brother murdered his basketball. Fucking trash, were they serious?

Faith didn't drop her fork so much as body-slam it. Her eyes lasered holes through Jonathan's skull. "If Gorbashay had died, his death would've been on your head. Is your brain capable of grasping that? That you came this goddamned close to being a dog killer?"

"I'm sorry I couldn't take part in your capitalist exploitation." He couldn't blame Faith for cracking up. His mom made it sound much more convincing. Besides Mary Miller, though, he was also Frank Roggebusch's son, and that meant he stuck to his guns. "You're benefiting from free labor. You exploit us when you make us do things like empty your trash and clean up after you."

"Karen cleans up after us! And I know you appreciate her. More than most." She glared at him. "I just hope that doesn't result in your father and me having to clean up after the baby that results from your not paying attention to WHAT THE FUCK YOU ARE DOING!"

"Faith...," Frank began, and ended.

Jonathan was the worst planner, so the fact that the Saturday jaunt to the Pine Barrens came when he needed it the most was a complete fluke. He was so desperate for his own kind he even invited Sean "Dr. Pepper" Kenzler to tag along, as a show of good faith and no hard feelings. The same pals who'd taken Jonathan to the Moorestown Mall picked him up in that same Ford pickup. Before picking up Fiona, they hit up the 7-Eleven to grab some smokes and a couple of cases of Schlitz, Jonathan's preferred poison since discovering it in the Springfield storeroom. As they were pulling out, that same homeless boozer who seemed to live at the Seven Heaven was pointing a filthy finger at the back of the truck and laughing his drunk hairy ass off.

"How much do you need to drink before you start hallucinating and junk?" one of Jonathan's pals asked.

With everyone aboard, Jonathan and Fiona and one of the pals sat in the back while Sean joined the other two in the cab. "You think we'll see the Jersey Devil?" He didn't buy into any of that bullshit, but he knew Fiona did. Some of his pals did too even if they never admitted it.

"Fuck you," Fiona said.

"Dude, what kind of stuff you bring?"

"It'll be rad, dude. I'm probably more desperate than the rest of you assholes to get high."

"How'd that delivery go the other night? Heard that cop is getting the hots for you. We's just getting started with that new Hainesport strain and junk. He gonna fuck that up?"

"It cool if we don't talk business, man?"

"And the blacks in the Gardens are making some pretty potent shit. Tell him to go ride their asses."

"Don't worry about Jim, man. He's cool. Now shut the fuck up. I hope we do see the Jersey Devil, it'll take my mind off all this bullshit."

"Stop that!" Fiona slapped his arm.

They wouldn't see the Jersey Devil that day, but Jonathan still should've been careful what he wished for. No sooner did they pull up to their usual niche of open space deep in the Barrens than the deformed, droopy-faced, devilish visage of Barry emerged from under the tarp in the back of the truck. Jonathan's pal scooted away with a "whoa!" while Fiona yelped and squealed the way she did when they watched *A Nightmare on Elm Street*.

At first Jonathan didn't know what to say, he was so dumbstruck. It wasn't until Barry brought a Cherry Coke Slurpee to his cherry-red lips and gave it a suck that he finally found the wherewithal to mumble, "What the fuck?"

The others got out of the cab. "Bodyguard?" Sean chuckled.

"Isn't this your little brother and junk? Fuckin' A. Vince, pass the smokes."

"Barry, dude..."

Barry spat out rapid fire, "I went to 7-Eleven to get a Slurpee a Cherry and Coke mixture, and then you showed up, and when you came out I went under here, and when that smelly guy laughed, I thought you'd find me but you didn't, so would it be okay if I stayed here with you?"

One of Jonathan's pals contorted his face and got in Barry's. "The Jersey Devil's going to eat you, you fat little shit!"

Another pal growled, "He loves fat kids."

"What the fuck, Bawrence Barney?"

"That really his name?" Fiona laughed.

"I hate Faith; she's stupid."

Jonathan and Barry exchanged a long, unblinking look of experience only veterans of war could understand.

"Jon! Weed!"

"It's Jonathan!" Barry said in a voice so terribly puny in this forest of pines and ruffians Jonathan couldn't help smiling.

"That's right." He ruffled his kid brother's hair.

After divvying up the herbage, Jonathan took Fiona's hand and led her into the woods so they could make out. This would be just the tonic he needed. As they removed their tops, though, his mind started swirling in a head-splitting spiral around the image of that damned house. What's more, the dead pine needles were killing his back.

"What the fuck is your problem?"

"My head is killing me."

"Why didn't you say so?" She dug through her purse.

"Don't worry about it. You can't cure a can of peas to the head anyway."

"Fucking Sean!"

"He had nothing to do with it."

"Stephen, that prick!"

"Warmer."

"I'll kill her."

"Now that's something I'd pay to see."

"I've got an idea." She climbed off him and went down.

The blow job worked wonders for the first minute or so. It took the pain away at least. But Jonathan's thoughts, free of the peas, sailed over to Karen. The more he thought about her no-show on Wednesday, the more convinced he became that it had nothing to do with her mother.

"Ow, what the fuck?"

"Pay attention or I'll bite it off."

When they arrived back at the clearing, Barry was hacking his lungs out while Sean rolled on his ass with a burning roach between his fingers. Jonathan was about to cuss out his frenemy, but Fiona's cackling made him think better of it. Everything with Sean was going so well today. Now wasn't the time to snap the olive branch in two, certainly not over Barry.

"Tell him how you feel, Bawrence Barney Roggebusch!" Sean was barely able to get out. Jonathan's pals guffawed and rolled around with their Js.

The poor kid could only keep hacking.

Jonathan made for the cooler to get a bottle of water, but Fiona clutched his arm to prevent her hysterics from knocking her over.

Fortunately for Jonathan, or rather, for Barry, Sean had a conscience too and threw his water at him. The bottle smacked the kid in the head.

Jonathan fetched a couple of Schlitzes for Fiona and himself. It only took one more hit from Sean's joint before the fourth grader puked his guts out. And then the sidesplitting ass rolling really began. Jonathan felt obligated to be part of the hysterics. Barry would hate him for it, but it was either this or compromise his business. He glanced sidelong at Fiona. Monday he'd call her and break up.

On the way back to Mount Holly, Jonathan told his pals to drop him and Barry off at the Seven Heaven. "Hockey later, right?"

Sean took him aside. "Thanks a lot, man. This was awesome. My nana's got a rad place in Medford Lakes. Hot tub and shit."

"Oh yeah?"

"Dude, she's never there. So. You and your buds can come over and hang. And bring that fat little shit, he is goddamned hilarious. The way his one eye just hangs?"

"Hey, sure."

"Hey, man. This was a big move on your part. After I kicked the shit out of your dorky brother and that bugle horn. That thing looked so queer I had to fuck it up."

"Hey, man. Stephen can drop dead for all I give a shit. Now touch a hair on Barry? And it'd be a different story. You know, I'd have to fuck you up."

"You and what army?"

"Mount Holly Police, man. They're in my pocket. And you know they've got cop friends in Medford."

"You're bluffing, bitch."

"Look into my eyes. But hey, your nana's Jacuzzi. That sounds rad."

"Cool." They clasped hands.

Jonathan ruffled Barry's hair on the way into the store. "We need to get some food in you, squirt." He treated the kid to a scrumptious meal that included a Zero, Whatchamacallit, Now and Laters, Nerds, and Charleston Chews, chased down by an orange soda Slurpee. For himself he got some beef jerky and a sixteen-ounce Schlitz (in a brown paper bag, of course).

"You have the great American adventure?" the homeless guy bellowed.

With mock anger and a mock rigid finger, Jonathan said, "Up your ass, Sinatra!"

Coupled with the junk food, Jonathan knew the walk home would do wonders for Barry. While at first his kid brother's chewing was languid and uneven, it was downright determined by the time they turned onto Buttonwood.

"Wait!" Barry ducked behind one of the colossal ancient trees.

Jonathan looked toward the house and spotted that little blond kid collecting for the *Burlington County Times*. He collected twice a week, one more than he was supposed to but not in any obvious way. He'd jilt Frank, show up only once the following week and perhaps once the week after, and then hit him up an extra day the week after that, all the while jilting other houses in a similar off-and-on pattern. Jonathan had caught on to him months ago but hadn't brought it up only because he had so many other fish to sauté. "You're afraid of the paperboy?"

"He's an asshole. Beat him up! Him and his friends! They're assholes!" Barry sucked down that slushy orange masterpiece with renewed fervor.

Jonathan chuckled. "Can't take you by himself, huh? Know what we call someone like that at RV? A pussy. Not worth your time, man." He made to continue onward.

"Wait."

"Dude, he's leaving."

"You just want me to get beat up!"

Jonathan grabbed Barry by the shoulders and forced him out into the open. They watched Kyle speed walk up Buttonwood and swing a right onto Ridgeway.

Jonathan had about an hour before he had to meet his pals at the church parking lot down the alley. He spent the whole time, plus a few more minutes, trying to call Karen. She never picked up. He'd let it ring for about five or so interminable minutes, hang up, do some perfunctory look-sees through his telescope, dream about getting that bigger and better one at Gregory's, then go back to the phone.

Jonathan might've missed the hockey match altogether if Louis hadn't snapped him out of it with a "JOHHHHHHHN... [John's hurried footsteps] ...athan."

"What the FUCK?" he roared from the third-floor balustrade.

"Maybe you could answer like a normal person," Stephen said from somewhere below.

"Fuck you!"

Louis double-hopped up to the second floor and appeared in view before giving in to that trademark chuckle he inherited from Woody. "Need your golf clubs, yosie."

Jonathan snorted.

"I'm going to the Gardens."

"Take the nine iron."

"Peace!" Louis flashed two fingers and disappeared.

The walk down the alley only gave Jonathan more time to stew over Karen. She hadn't missed a single Wednesday in three years. He brought his one blue ball while one of his pals brought a couple more. It was just as well. Barely ten minutes into the game and Jonathan, reaching a boil, slap shot the ball clear across the lot and into a gutter on Garden Street. Later in the match, his team up by eight, he slap shot the ball square into the cheek of one of his opponents. While his pals stopped the opponent's boil just short of an overflow, they weren't so successful when Jonathan bodychecked someone else. The grilling and pushing and headlocks lasted a good ten or fifteen minutes before they all shook it off, slapped themselves on the back, and carried on.

This was just the ventilation Jonathan needed. Collected and refocused, he racked up twelve more goals, taking the match somewhere beyond a rout. Afterward, kicking a leg up against the back of the church and sharing a J, his pals gave him heaps of shit for showing up with his asshole face on. The playful bellicosity mixed with the well-manicured greenage to bring lazy smiles to their peach-fuzzed mugs.

Jonathan gave Karen one more try that night. No dice. The only diversion for his righteous indignation now was a long hard peer at Ursa Major.

Two things happened when he had to use the can. Or rather, after he used it. On his way back to his room, Barry emerged from his, having just woken up, clad in bed head and yellow-stained tighty-whities. And then Frank, thoroughly sauced on Johnnie, thumped up the stairs with a tired, incoherent yet sincere look on his face.

"Team! I'm coming up here to check that all is well and no one is mad at me. At least not at this moment. Baw-*rence!*" He stopped himself as he took in his youngest. "Looking stylish and fashionable as always. You are doing normal okay?"

Even when he was wide awake, Barry's left eye hung lower than the other. At this hour it was all but cemented shut. That whole side of his face practically hung off his skull like a wet sweater on a clothesline. It infuriated Jonathan. "Speak up, Jerry's Kid!"

Frank teetered at the top of the stairs. "Bawrence? Are you mad?"

"I don't know." Barry squirmed past Jonathan.

"Jona-*than!* Are you mad at me?"

"Mad as in Stephen batshit crazy or mad as in Faith pissed off?"

Frank squinted and stroked his chin and gave the walls and slanted ceiling a thoughtful gander. He shrugged. "Either."

"I wasn't just a moment ago."

"Ah." And then it sunk in, faster than Jonathan predicted. "So you ARE mad?"

Jonathan flashed his trademark smile. "Good night, Dad."

"Wait!"

"I just wanted to take a leak. And then you show up. And I have to look at Barry."

"So you're mad at me AND Bawrence?"

When Barry came back, Jonathan stuck an arm out to block his passage. "If I have to deal with him, so do you."

"Move!" Barry tried to squirm past.

All Jonathan meant to do was push him back. Instead, Barry tripped over his own two feet and plopped onto the hard carpet like freshly caught trout.

With a lightning flash of sober, and sobering, strength, Frank gave his second oldest a shove that would've sent Jonathan on his ass if not for the balustrade, both because it was so unexpected (this was the first time his father had shoved him) and because Frank used the heels of his palms to punch him at the same time.

Barry took full advantage of the opportunity and disappeared into his room and started babbling to himself.

"And now you have a real reason to be mad at me." Frank stuck his hands through his shorts' back waistband like he typically did late at night when he was buzzed and invested in the conversation.

The adrenaline burned Jonathan's chest until he couldn't breathe. He could've easily taken his father if not for the fact that it was his father.

"How's your financial situation?"

Was that a trick question? "Fine."

Frank nodded at his room. "Mind if I take a look?"

"What do you mean?"

Frank charged past him. Jonathan stood by his telescope and held it with one hand like a security blanket.

"Well." Frank came to a stop in front of the Mötley Crüe bumper sticker. "I don't see a wad of five hundred bucks floating around."

"What?"

Frank walked out and gave the opposite door a "Good night, Bawrence!" before taking his time back down the stairs.

Jonathan spent the next hour staring at the Big Dipper. He wanted to contemplate other asterisms, but first he needed to recapture that same state of calm he'd achieved before his father and brother demolished it. Unfortunately, they really did demolish it. By the time he resigned himself to this, it was already too close to Sunday morning, and his shift at Springfield, to make catching z's worth it.

Mount Holly's very own golf heaven, Springfield was just a couple of miles past RV and Folwell on Jacksonville Road. Normally Jonathan rode his dirt bike, but on this morning he opted to walk.

Springfield offered courses for all levels, including fantasy-themed miniature golf as well as putt-putt. Jonathan went for the full eighteen, for both work and play. First came the work. He got there at five thirty and polished the clubs and got the buckets ready for the driving range. Then came driving the cart across the range and the eighteen to collect the balls still out there from yesterday. No matter the time and no matter the day, you'd always find those little white suckers dotting the landscape like so many forlorn Easter eggs. And with no one around, Jonathan could floor it. Not only was the adrenaline rush a drug second only to weed, it would help vent any pent-up stress. Most of the time. On this early spring morning, wonderful as it felt to zip around the vast manicured expanse, it didn't come close to helping him vent it all out.

That's why, when his shift ended at one, Jonathan decided to stay, rent a set of clubs (his boss waived the fee), and play a full eighteen.

Only after that, after taking his father's push-punch and cryptic room inspection and spinning it around his skull for all those hours and flooring the cart from hole to hole and back again, did the boil finally start to simmer down. He was drenched in sweat by the time he tripped into the clubhouse.

Jonathan didn't mean to give the nineteenth hole such a wistful look, but he'd never been so thirsty in his life. His boss wasn't a complete moron. He knew the kid could handle the odd pint. He let him nurse a cold one with the peace of mind that Jonathan had a very convincing fake ID in case anyone had any qualms. No one ever did. Jonathan was a man, DOBs be damned.

The walk home was pure bliss.

He didn't mean to call Karen, but when he got back up to his room, his phone was the first thing he saw.

She answered. Her voice seemed a light-year away when she told him she was pregnant and needed him to help pay for her to get rid of it. Jonathan couldn't remember much of what she said after that.

This being May, it was taking longer for the sun to get out of his telescope's way, but tonight he didn't care. Besides, the waning crescent moon was already visible.

"JOHHHHHHHN..."

You never think about it, but our moon has a sky. Earth rises and sets in it every day.

"...athan."

Jonathan never got tired of thinking about that.

4

JOHN

CAFFEINE KAREEM AND CATCHER NATURAL

"**J**OHHHHHHN..."

John Peterson dropped his pencil in the crook of his pre-algebra book and darted out into the hallway.

"...athan."

Normally he was okay with this trick which, in spite of his being an honors student and one of only three sixth graders at Holbein Middle in pre-algebra, he always fell for. But when it happened while he was straining his noodle in that perfectly cube-shaped head, the same shape as his mother's but with his father's thick Swedish blond mane, it drove him so batty he had to resist the burning urge to throw his textbook through the window. John swallowed the fire and managed to squeeze out a laugh complete with a mock shake of his fist. "Damn you, Louis."

Louis laughed his trademark mischievous laugh. "Dinner, dude."

"You tell the real Jonathan?"

"Will the real Jonathan stand up?" Louis hollered on his way back downstairs.

John peered up between the stairs and balustrade. Jonathan's door was just out of sight. "Jonathan! This isn't a prank! Dinner!"

Jonathan never showed up for dinner that Sunday night, and even though everyone knew he was in his room, no one seemed particularly concerned. Except John. He'd felt like a complete sack of shit ever since feeding Gorbie all that pot. He wasn't catching more than three or four hours of winks a night.

After the game last Saturday, one of his Little League teammates on Lippencott Oil had offered to pay him a healthy hunk of moolah for weed (everyone on the team knew John's stepbrother ran the weed show in Mount Holly). Like everyone else at 48 Broad, except his mom and stepdad, John knew Karen always cleaned up the herbage while pinching a bit for herself. With her not around and Jonathan out with his gangsters or whoever, John had the perfect opportunity to solve the conundrum that had been driving him bonkers since first seeing that commercial on MTV last fall for the best bike in the world: How would he ever be able to afford that bike?

Before the bike, it was the mitt. John's old mitt, a tattered ribbon of cowhide that dated back to playing catch with his father in Colorado, hadn't been a real catcher's mitt. Last year, he resolved to stockpile his allowance, week after week, fighting the urge to spend it on those packs of Red Man bubble gum that came shredded like tobacco to make Little Leaguers feel like Big Leaguers. As slowly and surely as Barry ran the bases, John saved up enough for the awesome new catcher's mitt. The gravy? Lippencott Oil made it to the championship. That they lost didn't matter one jot. It had been John's best season yet.

Still, the mitt was one thing. The thought of stockpiling five bucks a week for that bike was simply unfathomable. That would mean living like a monk seemingly forever. How could he do that when he lived with six other kids who spent their allowances on awesome things as if awesome things were endangered? You couldn't imagine the pressure to be a consumer in an environment like that.

John chomped on his blue ranch-slathered salad while racking his noodle for his Good Thing Bad Thing New Thing. Somehow he had to tell them about the pooch and the pot without confessing. He had come really close twice last night, during dinner and then Oh

Hell! but chickened out in the end. Louis was just finishing up his New Thing, his new record for how far he'd hit the Wiffle ball.

"I'll play next weekend if you and Barry are on the same team," Stephen said, rubbing his palms together in front of his goblin-like smile.

"You're an asshole!"

"Bawrence!" Faith's face instantly sunburned.

"Hey, Stephen! Would you like my fat?"

Stephen's smile dissolved while Dan and Louis laughed themselves to the edges of their seats.

"Baw-*rence*." Frank folded his hands and gave his last born that trademark philosopher's look John lived for every morning over coffee. "Quit your goddamn cussing."

"Barry, you're stupid," Alexander said with nary a trace of emotion.

"John-n-n-n?" Frank used the 48 Broad way to accentuate the difference between John's name and Jonathan's.

"Two Good Things. The school year's over in a month, and then I get to visit my dad in LA and maybe see Alyssa Milano at the Sherman Oaks Galleria like last year."

"She ignored you," Alexander said.

"Stop pretending to like girls," Stephen said.

"And the second Good Thing is we killed Don's Barber Shop eleven to two."

"Aw yeah!" Louis slapped him a high five that stung and reverberated throughout John's forearm for the next several minutes.

"Bad Thing?" Now was the moment. His brain was a messy blankness, like the chalkboard after being hastily erased at the end of the day. "I accidentally hurt an animal. And my New Thing? I'm finally getting that awesome bike I've been saving up for."

Louis: "You step on a squirrel?"

Stephen: "Did you trip over Hogg's dog and give it a heart attack?"

Daniel: "Anyone seen Gorbie? Or Baltimore?"

Alexander in full deadpan mode: "Did its gizzard spew through its mouth when you stepped on it?"

And Barry: "Did you hit the baseball during the game and hit a raccoon?" He guffawed his half-faced guffaw.

John wanted to shoot back with a barb, but the sight of Barry's face melting back to that half-dead look made him laugh that contagious laugh that got Daniel and Louis splitting their sides as well.

"Baw-*rence*," Alexander said in a deadpan version of Frank. "You're an idiot."

"So what animal did you kill?"

"I didn't kill it."

"Then why is it your Bad Thing?"

"What was it?"

"Was Donald with you?"

"I was riding my bike."

"But you don't have a bike."

"I felt like riding my old bike, okay? God!"

"And you killed a dog?"

"I caught this cat right in the tail. And it was a black cat. It was crossing the street."

"If bad things happen to you, it's because of the choices you make, not because of some random bad-luck bullshit," Daniel said.

"Exactly," Faith said between crunches of salad. "And what's this about a bike?"

"It's at Gregory's. I've been saving up for it since September."

"Donald's got that bike." Stephen grinned. "So now you two can go away together."

After what was perhaps the worst Good Thing Bad Thing New Thing in the history of that tradition, John needed some loving, and he needed it now. Of course he'd been lying about riding his bike into a cat, but talking about that fossilized pair of wheels his father had gotten him a million Christmases ago made him want to try it out. He'd sworn never to ride another bike until he scored that amazing new one, but when you're eleven, what's an oath?

Tara Douglas lived in Eastampton, the neighborhood right behind Folwell and RV. It was surreal to see the schools this late on a Sunday night. He turned into Folwell's inner courtyard and flashed back to his first day of school here, the first week of February 1983. He'd been in third grade. Third graders lined up on the far side of the courtyard.

It might've been his imagination, but he could've sworn his bike chain's squeak and the brake's squawk suddenly grew louder when he turned onto Tara's dead-silent street. Tara's dad was a cop, her oldest brother was a wrestler at Rutgers, and her next oldest brother played football and shot put for RV and took jujitsu on the side. Knocking on the door and asking if their daughter/kid sister was available for a booty call simply wasn't an option. John parked the piece of shit, appropriately, by the overflowing garbage cans on the side of the house before speed tiptoeing around to the other side via the Amazonian rainforest of a backyard. Tara's desk light rendered her first-floor window the perfect golden box to wiggle through.

"Talk is cheap," he said just as Tara, adorable in her Spider-Man tee, tried to get the dirt on her boyfriend's newest beef with his amazing family.

They made out in her ergonomically correct (but only if you were one person) desk chair for a good half hour or so before John screwed up enough courage. He spilled the baked beans about feeding Gorbie the pot and the genuine mistake it had been and if Gorbie had died, a big part of John would've died with him. And all that contrite jazz, which was quite genuine. During the ride over here, though, John had convinced himself that Tara would never buy into it, would brand him a dog killer, and forever exile him to the Siberia of singledom.

"Oh my God, baby. I'm so sorry!"

How about that? Simply communicating his feelings bought him fifteen more minutes of make-out. Should he tell Phil Donahue to pass it on?

When they finally came up for air, John, as many of us would, felt overly cocky, pun mostly unintended. "I can't wait to tell Donald. He'll know what to do."

"Oh come on!"

"Your dad?"

"Can we go one night without you mentioning Donald?"

"I mean, he's a smart guy and junk. Couldn't hurt to ask. As Frank would say, the worst that can happen is he won't know."

They made out some more until they were lying atop the Cabbage Patch bedspread. Tara hadn't reacted well when he tried to remove her shirt last time, so this time John started with her clip-on Cabbage Patch earrings. He'd barely unclipped the first one when she jerked away and clipped it back on.

"Seriously?"

"I just wish you weren't so scared to ask me stuff once in a while. I'm smart too."

"What'd you get in math last marking period?"

"Frank you!"

He cracked up. That never got old.

Tara rolled over and took in the Rick Springfield poster on her ceiling. "God, your mom and stepdad are so weird. But why don't they have more rules in your house? My dad has so many stupid rules."

"We've got that stupid chalkboard."

"I've got it!" She sat up. "The Burlington Center has that rad pet store. Get Gorbie one of those toys or maybe a new bed or something. When you sell that pot to Rick, you'll have more than enough for the new bike and a present for Gorbie."

"That bike is super expensive though."

"Oh please. Both my brothers deal pot for your stepbrother. You can keep yourself out of it because you live in that huge house, but my brothers are impossible to avoid here. I have no choice but to be an expert on pot. If Rick pays you what that pot is worth? Like, oh my God. John. You will have. A lot of cash."

Logically, the idea was absurd. By the time John got around to going to the Burlington Center, Gorbie would have no memory of OD'ing on pot. How could he have known who was behind it? Or that anyone was behind it? Assuming he knew the stuff he'd eaten was potentially lethal in that dose, which was a stretch. Unfortunately for John, his guilty conscience was impervious to logic, which meant Tara's suggestion made perfect sense. If he had any hope of returning to restful slumber, he had to do something penitent for the pooch.

Yes, pooch penitence was on the noodle when Tara's dad swung open the door and, in so doing, swung John's heart up his throat. "Sweetie. The trash. Let's go."

"Later."

"Now."

"Dad!"

"It's been rad." John hopped to the window. "Enjoy the rest of your evening, Officer Douglas."

"The hell are you doing? Tara, are you making him climb through the window?"

John tapped the sill. "Golly shucks, I sure could use the exercise."

"Stop being weird." He waved John over. "Tara Douglas?"

"Gawd!" She jumped out of bed and flitted her lithe frame between them.

"I could take out the trash for you, Tara! I'm leaving anyway!"

"Don't even think it, Peterson."

"'Night, officer."

"Jim. But call me Jimmy and I kick your little ass." John was halfway down the hall when: "John-n-n-n?"

"Officer?" John turned back. "I mean Jimmy. I mean shit!"

"Say hi to Jonathan for me, will ya?"

This time John pedaled at a leisurely pace. The gentle wafts through his hair and across his face dissolved the gong in his head and the vise in his chest. As he turned onto Broad Street, not even the mosquitoes could obscure the waning crescent moon reclining on a pillow of deep violet.

"Good morning, John-n-n-n!" Frank poured them each a cup of Peet's at six o'clock the next morning. "Ready for another week of scholarly excitement and the wonders of learning?"

"I'm ready for that steaming cup of Arabica blend you've got going there." Nothing was cooler, figuratively speaking of course, than a cup of coffee that had begun life as whole beans delivered to your doorstep. Nothing came close in John's book of life, and he never admitted that to anyone. As they always did, he and Frank relished the bold aromatics and even bolder taste of steaming black unadulterated coffee.

Unadulterated. John's father had taught him that word when he was four. It had been one of those miserable, gray, freezing Colorado days that convinced you it would stay winter the rest of your life. Ford Peterson and his boy were standing in that mostly yellow kitchen with its soft lemon ice cream walls and yellow-patterned floor, sprinkled with bits of tangerine flourish. John couldn't remember why— he would always hypothesize it was that singular aroma—but something compelled him to ask for a sip of that hot stuff Dad was drinking. Ford's repeated warnings that this was most definitely not hot chocolate with melted marshmallows didn't faze our John here. In spite of that clumsy first attempt that spilled scalding liquid down his Batman shirt, it was love at first slurp.

Ford used the opportunity to espouse his Swedish heritage. John's paternal grandparents hailed from a country far away where it was cold and dark half the time... and where coffee was king. Every day for the rest of his life, John would recall that morning when he got his first taste, literally and figuratively, of who he was.

"This coffee is *très* superb. Like that use of French, Frank? Top her off, would you? Thanks, dude. I tell you, my head is just totally adulterated right now. I can't think straight. I have a wrong to right, but the person I wronged has no idea I wronged them. Righting the situation will change nothing for them, you know? It was an accident. And they'll never know. But I can't sleep."

Frank sipped, closed his eyes, and nodded. "Know what this reminds me of?"

John slurped and pondered. "When the Washington Senators moved to Texas and it was the second time they moved, the first time being to Minnesota? And you felt heartbroken and betrayed all over again and forever alienated from the sport of baseball?"

Frank sipped. "This coffee reminds me of a special blend I once bought in Colorado. It was around the time I met your mother. 'Bout six years ago."

"I thought you guys met when we went camping. That place with the snake grass."

Frank smacked his lips and kept his eyes in the general vicinity of Gorbie's food bowl and the basement door. "And this conundrum you've just described, while thankfully not a common occurrence, at least for me, does remind me of the time Peggy came up here to visit and gave me the address of where I should send the checks to finance her education. Have I told you about that?"

"About a thousand times."

"It was right after we moved here. She was finishing high school that spring and, quite understandably, chose to stay in Maryland so she could complete her education at the same high school. But of course she had to live somewhere. Her mother couldn't afford dependents, so she moved in with Woody. Even though she was still legally my daughter. I was—how shall I put it?—ambivalent about the arrangement. Even though I understood, or at least thought I understood, that the main point was so she could finish at the same high school. But after she graduated, she came up here for no other reason than to tell me that she was now claiming Woody as her legal father, she'd be attending college in Maryland, and by the way, here was her address so I knew where to send the checks."

"Barry was really excited about seeing his big sister. He didn't sleep the night before. And then when she got here, she was supposed to spend the night in Dan's room. She must've left super early because when Barry and I ran up to Dan's room the next morning, her sleeping bag was there but she was gone."

"John. If there's one nugget of wisdom you retain out of the infinite nuggets I pass down, make it this: nothing will make people you think you know behave in a way that will completely flabbergast and shock you... than money. Money changes people like nothing else. I take it back. I want you to remember two things. Second thing is, make sure that when the going gets tough, you do not turn a profit. In fact, if anything, make sure everyone else involved profits except you. I made absolutely sure I was the only one who did not profit from my divorcing Bawrence's mother. She profited, Peggy, Dan, Louis, even

Bawrence. Everyone profited from that transaction except me. This way, those assholes have nothing on me. They can get mad all they want, but in the bitter end, they profited. I didn't. If you hold on to that lesson for the rest of your fucking life, it will be the smartest thing you do, I guarantee it. Now." He took a long, loud sip, and bopped his teeth together as he savored and swallowed and moaned pleasurably. "An opportunity has presented itself for you to spend money in recompense for what you perceive as a past wrong. Based on the wisdom I've just shared, can you guess what my advice would be?"

John thought hard while taking very deliberate slurps.

"You need to make sure you don't profit from this situation. If I understand you correctly, you have the choice of doing something that will cost you money that will right the balance of things. Whether that other person knows you're doing it is immaterial. At least to me. And choosing not to spend your money based on such data means you are profiting from that person's ignorance of said data."

John's eyes lit up as he slurped. "Rad, dude. And thanks to my financial wisdom, which I also learned from you, I have the money not to profit from this situation even after I buy the awesome ten speed I've been saving up for. So that's perfect!"

"Can't beat perfect." They sipped and slurped.

"Donald's already got an awesome bike. It's really fast."

"He lives near the firehouse, right? You never seem to go there. He always seems to visit here. Not that I mind. Just something I've noticed."

When John got home that afternoon, Donald was with him. They had the Commodore 64's Olympic Games on the brain. During the four-hundred-meter hurdle relay, which John won handedly, he proposed a trip to the Burlington Center. At first Donald didn't say anything. They were two tries into pole vault when he finally fell into the question John was waiting for: How would they get there if John didn't have a bike? The only hitch was Donald's not asking it with much curiosity. In fact, his dead tone reminded John of HAL. "I'm going to Gregory's tomorrow. Then we can go to the mall on Wednesday. Sound rad or what?" He held out his hand for a high five. Donald ignored it and said yes the way a zombie would say yes to cremation.

John clenched his jaws as he turned back to the game. Time for the ten-meter platform dive. He chose to represent Romania as a way to get some distance from this maddening conversation. When Donald as the United States and the Commodore as Argentina scored the gold and silver, the simmer became a boil.

"JOHHHHHHHN..."

"WHAT?" John jumped up and body-slammed his joystick and stomped and huffed into the hallway and glared red-faced into the kitchen just in time to see Louis emerge from the laundry room.

"...athan."

John was about to spew a "FUCK YOU!" when he heard Tanisha's giggling. Apparently, her laughter was contagious, judging by how Donald tittered to himself while long-jumping against two Commodore-controlled players from the Eastern Bloc.

John walked back to the couch with a willed calm that went to shit when Louis and Tanisha laughed themselves into the room. Donald's face lit up like 48 Broad at night as he started gabbing with them while continuing to rack up medals. Donald and Tanisha had only met a couple of times and briefly at that, yet now they were bantering back and forth like two long-lost siblings. It appeared they knew the same people, and most of them were RV students. How did Donald know so many cool older kids?

John slammed his joystick again, this time at getting a bronze in the fifty-meter sprint. No one noticed.

Eventually Louis and Tanisha laughed their way down the hall to the living room to blast MTV. Just like that, Donald flicked his switch back to off. During the two-hundred-meter fly, John stopped playing and stared at Donald's stony countenance while his swimmer flailed helplessly on the screen. Would the staring or his swimmer's last-place performance make Donald look at him?

No.

Donald piped up a little when they switched to G.I. Joe. It almost seemed like he was returning to his normal chatty self when he called it quits and said he had to get home to help his mom with dinner and at least make an effort at his math homework.

Gregory's, like the Westwood pool and tennis courts, was over in Eastampton, so walking that-a-ways meant walking past Tara's house. John had developed monomania about the bike since the maddening Commodore session with Donald yesterday. He was bound and determined not to let Tara's feminine wiles divert him from his one and true path like some pubescent siren of the Garden State. Unfortunately for John, he too was pubescent. Doubly unfortunate was his love of coffee, as it was Tara's offer to come in for a cuppa hot black stuff that was the caffeinated nail in his Swedish coffin. Perhaps most unfortunate of all was Tara never having the intention of making him a cuppa anything. John was unshouldering his backpack and going on about how in Sweden, singles would put ads in the paper about meeting for coffee as code for going on a date. Tara cut him off with a kiss. Apparently she already knew about coffee invitations as code for nooky.

As they lay on her bed, John stared at her Rick Springfield poster and asked why she didn't want to make him coffee.

"I don't know how to make coffee, doofus!" she said with a kick.

John would've made a cup himself, but it was already past six. Besides, the Rutgers wrestler brother had gotten home and was parked in front of *Magnum PI* reruns with a package of Oreos. The other brother wouldn't be too far behind.

After all the buildup, planning, strategizing, saving money, breaking the law, and nearly killing the family dog, the act of buying the bike was as anticlimactic as you could get. John was worried the tough-looking twentysomething dudes behind the counter would get pissed at this eleventh-hour customer making a big purchase and asking them to assemble the bike for him. But no, they were nothing like his brothers. They not only put the bike together at no extra charge, they let him test it out on the gravel lot and adjusted the seat for him.

His feet met the pedals, but they could very well have been

making circles in the air, the equipment felt so light. The tinkle-crunch of gravel was pure poetry. The sky was that perfect, bifurcated light blue, dark blue you only get during a spring sunset. The whole thing would be a postcard in John's brain for the rest of his life, and he would forever view his life up to this point as leading to this very moment.

Wait until he showed Donald.

Three times the next day—at their lockers before homeroom, at lunch obviously, and once more for good measure via a folded note during social studies (damn the counties of New Jersey, Ms. Henderson, and in alphabetical order!)—John informed Donald of his amazing new wheels. Whatever bug had nested in Donald's ass had apparently, thankfully, completed its cocoon phase and taken flight. Taking in Donald's smile in profile as they took off like rocket ships down High Street, past the church as it chimed four o'clock, past the Acme and the bypass and Woodlane Road, at which point High became the more substantive—in asphalt and name—Burlington-Mount Holly Road, would be carved into his noodle for the rest of time, all the more so because of Donald's imminent disassociation with John and the Roggebusch clan.

Just as they were passing the Howard Johnson's, Donald started peddling like his very life depended on it. In less than a minute, he was a smudge against a horizon that had been clear at lunchtime but was now getting eaten alive by onyx spaceship clouds.

John rounded the turn onto the mall's access road without having to compromise his speed at all, having gotten plenty used to the feel of this masterpiece. When he came to the first choice of turns and considered the store names beside the arrows pointing left, right, and up, he was at a loss to guess which store Donald would've most likely picked.

His concentration wasn't blown up by just any car horn but by that of the pickup that belonged to one of Jonathan's friends/pot dealer accomplices. The truck growled and crawled forward as John got out of the way in an awkward sidestepping movement that nearly cost him his balance. A chorus of laughter rose from the back. Sure enough, Jonathan was among the throng. He and his new girlfriend, whom he'd started dating about two hours after dumping Fiona, and all their friends raised their cans of PBR in a toast.

"Have a nice time shopping, faggot!"

Jonathan leaped to his feet, sloshing some beer on his new woman's head. "How'd you save up for that so fast?"

"I've been saving since September."

Jonathan considered him while a particularly massive pent-up cloud formed a sort of halo of imminent violence over his fire-gold hair. He raised that skinny can like a scepter. "Don't let me see you in the mall. If I'm upstairs, you're downstairs, got it?"

The truck tore off with a screech and a holler. After passing one or two entrances, a cold, floppy sweat enveloped John's body. What if Donald had turned tail and gone home? As more mother ship clouds positioned themselves for landing, he pedaled around that mall for what seemed forever until coming upon Donald's bike outside Strawbridge's.

On the other side of the department store, he emerged into the mall proper, smack in front of the *Jungle Book* fountain. The boy astride the elephant was shielding his laughter from the water snorting from the elephant's trunk. John went up and down the aisles of Kay Bee Toys twice before moving on. Heading up the escalator to the food court, he scanned the tables and the lines and those with trays looking for a table. No Donald.

When he reached Sears at the other end of the mall, he checked both levels. No Donald.

John had been hungry on the way here, but now his appetite was getting choked by the knots in his gut. Sure, the mall was big, but it wasn't that big. It had nothing on the Cherry Hill Mall. He was on his way back to Strawbridge's when he stopped at a short corridor leading to the exit near where he'd run into Jonathan. On the left, the last store before the glass doors was that sportswear store Dan and Louis loved so much. Donald had never expressed much interest in sports, and yet...

"Hey, hey, hey!" Donald was trying on an Oakland A's jacket.

"You really took off like Jazz, dude!" When Donald just looked at him: "That one Transformer that turns into a Porsche."

"It was like the Olympics for real. I got a ten; you got a five."

"I ran into Jonathan. He'll kick our asses if he sees us."

"He'll kick YOUR ass. Ha ha!"

"What's with the jacket?"

"Pretty rad, right?" Donald held up a thick wad of cash inches from John's face. The teenage girl employee threw her head back and chuckled. "Ma hooked me up so I could feel like a bandit. Like Cobra Commander after raiding GI HQ." Donald's giggle was that special kind of rapid-fire giggle that was as impossible to resist as it was to imitate.

John could barely get his question out while laughing his face beet red. "Why Oakland?"

Donald ended up buying an Oakland A's cap and a Los Angeles Raiders shirt. After donning both, he smiled at John with his special Joker's grin that split his face in two. Then he straightened his face enough to say: "Come on, I'm hungry."

They made their way to the food court and agreed Chinese was in order. "By the way," John said as he and Donald dipped their egg rolls into their respective clear plastic cups, which were, as always, too small to admit the roll's full width. "In case you're interested, LA's like a five-hour drive from Oakland. My dad lives in the San Fernando Valley, and my mom's from Berkeley. They're like two different worlds."

Donald was halfway through his egg roll before he said, "But weren't the Raiders in Oakland first?"

They went downstairs to invade Kay Bee Toys where they scoped out the G.I. Joe figures, the Transformers, and the Commodore games. John was leaning heavily toward getting the Cobra jet when Donald said: "Weren't you supposed to get something for Gorbie?"

John dumped a slew of flea collars in the basket before loading up on milk bones, plastic bones, a blanket, and a nice little bed Gorbie would love far more than that improvised bed-in-a-laundry basket on the back porch. After arranging for shipment of the bed, he grabbed the bag of Gorbie goodies and speed walked past a sound effects-spouting Donald without acknowledging him. He walked up the escalator so he could reach the top faster and maintain enough distance so Donald wouldn't hear him mutter "Fuck you" repeatedly.

John and Donald had just gotten back on the Burlington-Mount Holly Road when the clouds, that armada of Star Destroyers, commenced their bombardment. This stretch of highway offered nowhere to take shelter. And even if it were bone dry, John couldn't've gone too fast thanks to the hefty shopping bag. When the Howard Johnson's came into view on the right behind sheets of downpour, he slowed a bit and gave serious thought to pedaling his drowning ass under one of the walkways. A truck that looked an awful lot like Jonathan's friend's barreled past with a roar and a holler and soaked John to his caffeinated bones.

He was another mile along when the obvious question hit him with the same force as these fat drops: Where the hell was Donald?

John pedaled through stubborn walls of water and lost count of how many times he got splashed by those blurred hunks of metal whipping by. One such whip, which looked vaguely like another pickup—was THAT Jonathan's friend's truck?—smashed him with enough water and wind to throw him into the weeds. As he regained his feet, which ached from all that pedaling, he was reminded of when he, his dad, and Alexander were walking through a blizzard. Where had they been going? And why hadn't their mom gone with them?

When he reached the Fairground Plaza, he got it into his head that Donald stopped out of pity and was waiting for him in one of the stores. Maybe the Acme. When he saw no sign of him through the windows, he gave the parking lot a cursory glance. The rain had thinned to a wavy curtain.

A quick check inside the Acme wouldn't hurt. He hopped off the bike and took it in with him and ignored the stares. An older fellow made some asinine joke that would've no doubt been hilarious fifty years ago. Eventually John reached the snack aisle on the other side of the store, fully expecting to find Donald browsing the wares, perhaps with a package of Double Stuffs already in hand. But no. All John found were a ravenous pack of Folwell-aged kids in front of Keebler. For the first time in his life, he felt old.

The thin curtain had reduced to a gossamer mist as dusk encroached through the dissipating clouds. John got back on the main road for another minute or two before swinging a left up Hillside Road. At the top, the road curved to the right and became Buttonwood. Forty-eight Broad was two blocks down that way.

On the left was the town's namesake Mount, where he and Barry and Donald and all their friends, and occasionally Alexander, would gather to play army. John hopped off his bike and entered the woods. The trail meandered gently upward before leveling out and guiding John along the main path in this cathedral of childhood memories for every kid in town. The main path, if you stayed on it, took you back toward the Acme. Reaching the Mount's center, John spotted that felled tree, which had already been prostrate his first time here three years ago, hollowed out by rot, where Barry had cleverly concealed himself and got Alexander good, that half a face lighting up with a mischievous half a smile through the hole in the deadwood.

If Donald was around here, it'd be easiest to spot him from the top. Because of its obvious strategic advantage, John always made it a point to summit the Mount during army, but it had never been so quiet. When he got up there, he dropped the pet store bag and lay the bike on the ground. "Donald?" The glistening leaves waved at him. The thing about silence so absolute was the open invitation to aural trickery. It only took one rogue gust or rustle of some herbage to convince him he wasn't alone.

John made meandering circuits around the top of the Mount but saw no sign of him. A bird chirped fitfully somewhere below, then stopped. When he reached the opposite side of the summit from the bike, he looked out and squinted through the murk.

Something rustled behind him, which John only half heard, so intent was he on figuring out the identity of that gray-black hulk down there. Was that another dead tree? Then came the unmistakable sound of all those canine goodies spilling out of the bag. "I knew you were up here, douchebag," he said, still squinting at the strange shape.

He probably never would've figured it out if the push hadn't come, sending him straight down the steep incline and into the ditch. "Yep," he thought just before the darkness came. "A dead tree."

The dream was a memory fragment. John and Donald lay on John's bed, reading Batman comics. This issue featured a very nimble looker of a Catwoman on the cover. They compared the characters to people at school. Commissioner Gordon looked like their science teacher. Robin's alter ego Dick Grayson was a spitting image of this one kid who sat at the next table at lunch. They moved on to other issues and continued comparing and giggling. The Penguin could've been the playground monitor's twin.

John woke up to the High Street church bells tolling against his skull.

He chucked the merchandise back into the bag and pedaled down Buttonwood through the peaceful night and past the historic Queen Annes and under and through the archways of ancient trees.

"John-n-n-n! London broil is on the menu for this evening."

"Join ush, join ush," Louis said in a pitch-perfect imitation of his biology teacher.

"Nice date at the mall?" Jonathan said.

Alexander said in his best deadpan: "Did you get beat up?"

"No means no, John Peterson," Stephen said.

John took a swig of milk. "Good Thing: My new bike rocks. I've already crashed it once, in the rain, and it's still good as new. Bad Thing: I rode home in the rain from the mall. New Thing?" He ran out to the hallway couch, grabbed the bag, hurried back in, and dropped it on the island. "I bought Gorbie a whole bunch of stuff. I also got him a new bed. It rocks."

"You hear that, Gorbashay?" Faith said, peering under the table.

John's head was still pounding the next morning, but do you think that crimped his coffee ritual with Frank? "I took your advice, Frank. Even though the person I made it up to will never know what I did wrong, I made it up to him, and better yet, I didn't profit from the transaction."

"Because knowing you're wrong and profiting from it at the same time makes it even more wrong. You did the right thing. I salute you." They sipped and slurped.

"It's also a great motivator for never doing something that stupid again. Spending all that money on stuff that wasn't for me wasn't fun."

Frank's eyes lit up through the java steam. "Wait until you have dependents."

John forgot the throbbing for a moment, but it stormed back when his brother walked in, his long black mane still wet and redolent of Pert. "Team."

"Alexan-*dor*! Are you ready for another day of scholastic rigor?"

"School sucks. I mean, it sucks bad. But you know what, Frank? I'm taking your approach. I'm being philosophical. You taught Baltimore how to be philosophical. What's my excuse? Poor bird lives next door to a house full of cats. What if one escapes? And sneaks into our house? And eats him?"

"Hey, Alex, you ever spent money on someone besides yourself?"

Alexander gave his kid brother a blank look before turning back to Frank. "I would say Gorbie is philosophical. But I don't think he's there yet. He still poops in the house. Sometimes I wonder if he's, you know, passive-aggressive."

"Or dumber than a box of cat hair," Frank said.

Alexander burst out laughing in that way only Frank seemed able to inspire.

"Alex, dude. You ever spent money on someone besides yourself? Animals count."

"Mom knows how to give a spanking," Alexander said. "To dogs. To Gorbie. One time, she hit Gorbie so hard? You could hear it from the third floor."

"Yo, Alex."

Alexander jabbed him with a finger and a "Maybe you should shut the hell up." For whatever reason, maybe it was Alexander's getting physical, which he almost never did, John felt a tingle of accomplishment that became a flame in his belly. It was his second physically combative encounter in barely more than twelve hours.

When he headed into the poolroom and grabbed his backpack from his cubby, he caught a fleeting glimpse of Gorbie underneath the couch. He tried to kick the pooch but instead smacked his shin against the wooden frame. "Fuck!"

You might think there'd be some awkwardness between John and Donald, but lunch was fun as ever, complete with chili con carne chased down by wholesome vitamin D milk in the little red carton. John, Donald, Tara, Rick, and the rest of the crew enjoyed a meaty discussion on the merits of *The Cosby Show* family versus the *Family Ties* family and how the Coz's family was doing better, and let's hear it for racial equality!

Lunch was the only time John wasn't fully conscious of the fire in his belly. By the time he parked himself front and center in pre-algebra, though, the flame had become a full-grown conflagration of spitting, licking tongues. He kicked himself for forgetting his bike. Walking home after school, John had just made the turn from High Street onto Broad when Donald whipped by on that awesome futuristic equipment, his windbreaker doing just that.

The house was quiet when he got home, mercifully. He could get the Commodore 64 to himself and vent his frustration on G.I. Joe. At least he thought he could. After fetching a soda from one of the back fridges, he heard Chunk doing the Truffle Shuffle in the living room. The sight of his little stepbrother giggling at *Goonies* while Gorbie gave himself a blow job on Frank's recliner was all it took.

"JESUS CHRIST! HOW MANY TIMES DO YOU HAVE TO WATCH THIS FUCKING MOVIE?" He sloshed soda on his shirt. "FUCK!"

He sat in the poolroom teaching Cobra a lesson while desperately trying to ignore the giggling voice in the next room going, "Johhhhh-hhn...athan. Ha ha! Johhhhhhhhn..." Barry's attempts to play the already-hackneyed prank sounded beyond pathetic. Any other day would've seen John shrug it off. When he jumped up and headed back to the living room, he found himself taking those measured steps Frank always took. If only the professor were here, maybe John wouldn't've done what he was about to do.

"...athan!" Barry said through a mouthful of Soft Batch cookies when John cast his shadow across the Mountain Dew.

"The only people who know how to play that joke are Dan and Louis. You fucking suck at it; everyone tells you that. When the fuck will it sink into your thick skull? And why the fuck do you keep watching this stupid fucking movie?"

He kicked Barry in the shins until the latter got up and retreated against his father's towering bookcases. The sight might've made John chuckle on a happier day. On this day, however, he proceeded to beat the living shit out of his stepbrother while Gorbie alternated between watching impassively and licking his nuts. When he grew tired of his own anatomy, the little mop helped himself to the rest of Barry's cookies and knocked over the Mountain Dew.

At dinner that night, Faith pilloried Barry for the spilled soda. Neither she nor Frank seemed concerned about the bruises on his face and arms. John had cooled down enough for a small part of him to feel like shit for his mom lighting into Barry for a crime he didn't commit. To make it up to him without letting him know he was, à la Gorbie and the pot, he took a break from the ranch dressing, Louis's favorite, in favor of Barry's all-time favorite, Thousand Island.

Toiling over his pre-algebra up in his room after dinner, John heard the sounds of the Thursday night sitcoms in the living room directly below him. He didn't get a single problem done during *The Cosby Show* and *Family Ties*, partly because he enjoyed listening to the shows but mainly because he wanted to hear Barry laugh. Just one of those goofy giggles would've told him his stepbrother had taken the first steps to getting over it. All through that hour, though, the only laughter belonged to his mom and Frank. And then at nine came *Cheers*. If Barry didn't laugh at this, you could forget about getting a wink of sleep. That's why it felt like an anvil being craned off his neck when he heard "NORM!" as clearly as if Barry were in the room with him.

John proceeded to tear through his homework and had all the problems wrapped up, including the extra credit ones, by ten, at which point he phoned Tara.

As soon as he got home from school the next day, he sequestered himself in his room and gave thanks that Alexander was going to be at band practice in his friend's garage until the wee hours of the morning. With Louis taking Tanisha to the movies at Lumberton Plaza, John fetched his older stepbrother's boom box and parked it on his desk. Steve Perry's "Oh Sherrie" reminded him of Tara. He phoned her up and immediately got the third degree for having walked out of gym too quickly or something. They got past that soon enough and ended up chatting for hours. At one point Officer Douglas poked his head in the room to say good night. "And a good night to you, Peterson! Say hey to Jonathan for me, would ya?"

Tara and her dad showed up at the game Saturday, as did her RV brother. He seemed less interested in the game than whatever John was doing. Fortunately, the position of catcher was quite a busy one, keeping John so occupied he sometimes forgot about the audience. During the fourth inning, though, when he peeked over the dugout, Tara's brother's mirror sunglasses were locked on him.

Rick was starting pitcher. Every couple of innings he and John would have a conference on the mound, during which Rick would mumble things like, "Pot's too weak," or, "I paid you too much," or, "Where's your bosom buddy from the ghetto?"

"I sold that stuff to you fair and square. It's a crop. Don't you know anything?"

"Keep your voice down, asswipe."

"How good a crop is depends on the weather and stuff. Try paying attention in class for a change."

"Yeah, well, it's weak."

Rick always chewed his bubble gum the way you see pro players chew their chew on TV, the wad permanently parked against one cheek. He was wadding and chewing grape right now, apparently oblivious to the deep purple it inflicted upon his lips. During a conference on the mound during the seventh inning, he said, "You don't want to cross me, John Peterson. I know people."

"There was this one time when Jonathan smoked pot, right? Whenever he does, the third floor reeks. I swear to God, dude. He was higher than a helium balloon for hours."

"So?"

"Dude, it was so strong it affected Barry. Know how Barry's room is across the hall?"

"Who gives a shit about that bed-wetting Porky Pig?"

"You're so full of shit. That was Jonathan's homegrown product. Worth every puff and you know it."

"Go run to your black bitch."

"How about you get down and slob my knob, Johnson?"

"Hey, girls, you done? We got a game going on here. Let's play ball!"

John was exhausted when he got home. The house was mostly empty. Even his mom and Frank had plans on this Saturday night. Only Stephen appeared to be around. He had taken over the music room to flex that fancy new electronic drum kit, complementing it with his trumpet and his father's synthesizer.

Before heading up to the Jacuzzi and steam room shower to purge Rick's grape-stained vitriol from his soul, John headed to the laundry room to grab a Cherry Coke. The open back door was letting in what was left of the day. The sun was out of sight, but its influence was still enough to turn the clouds into salmon. On the enclosed porch, in the new bed John had just gotten him, Gorbie was out for the count on his back. And there through the screen door, at the opposite end of the backyard, his back to the house, stood his little stepbrother.

As he stepped down to George Taylor's perfectly mown grass and past his mom's veggie garden, all the sound in the world seemed to get sucked out of the air. Barry was standing perfectly still which, combined with the absolute silence, made him seem unreal.

"Come on, feel the noise! / Girls ROCK your boys!" came the shrieks of Quiet Riot through the open window of a passing pickup. Keeping his eyes on Barry, John listened to the truck come to a rolling stop at the stop sign before swinging onto Broad with a roar from the engine and a screech from Kevin DuBrow.

By the time absolute silence returned, John had gotten within ten feet of Barry, and that's where he remained for who knew how long. His guts swirled with a feeling he couldn't name at the time but which he'd eventually recognize as that of being split down the middle, a perfect bifurcation born out of his paradoxical decision-making that now led to indecision. One half of him wanted to get back inside and up to that Jacuzzi. The other half kept him planted right here on this very spot, as rooted and full of future growth as those vegetables. What he would say if Barry turned around he had no idea. As it was, he convinced himself Barry didn't know anyone was behind him. That introduced yet another paradox: John was in the presence of someone who was by himself.

At some indeterminate time, after the sun had gone, John headed back inside. He stuck his Cherry Coke in the small fridge in the third-floor bathroom while he showered and baked in the steam and made every oily pore across his body open up and cry for mercy.

Dripping and dizzy, he retrieved the soda and, once fully ensconced in the bubbling tub, popped it open and downed half in a single pull. Whenever he used the Jacuzzi, John always thought of Eddie Murphy's line in *Trading Places* about farting in the tub. On those occasions when he farted in the Jacuzzi, like now, he'd burst out laughing.

He was a new man when he slapped on his Phillies pj's. Now that he didn't feel so wiped out, his senses could point out other things, like how famished he was. He went down to the kitchen, thinking he'd cobble something together from three fridges and a freezer chest, but Stephen had already ordered two pizzas from Sal's, one pepperoni, one sausage.

John was too hungry to give a shit about what was on the little black-and-white TV. He just needed some noise. He flicked on HBO, which was showing *Beverly Hills Cop*, and parked himself at the island with another Cherry Coke to chase down the pizza. One of his first dates with Tara had been to Lumberton Plaza to see this, followed by dinner at King of Pizza. She'd been wearing a cream turtleneck and smelled awesome. The turtleneck didn't really matter. Tara could wear a yak fur coat with checkered corduroy bell-bottoms and still be the most adorable creature on the gym-floor-turned-school-dance floor.

Now Barry? He represented the opposite end of the fashion spectrum. He could make a tailored, three-piece suit look positively hideous. Just look at him now, parked in the poolroom playing one of those Dungeons & Dragons games on the Commodore in those ugly-ass blue pants. No, not blue jeans. Not blue slacks or corduroys or any other recognizable material. Just a generic hunk of nameless fabric that had been shaped with legs and a waistband with zipper and button that positively suffocated against that expanding girth. John and Jonathan had laughed their asses off watching Frank and Dan struggle mightily to get those very same dreadful pants on Barry last fall when the weather had gotten too cold for his jams. However much they pulled and yanked and strained in so much vein-popping endeavor just to get the pants up around his waist, they had to redouble their efforts to marry the two halves of that damned button.

John found himself thinking about Barry quite a bit on Sunday. He didn't want to talk to his stepbrother or otherwise interact with him in any way, but he didn't want to let him off his radar either. And so for the whole day, wherever Barry went within the house, John would make it a point to stay within two rooms' distance, except of course when the entire brood went out back for some Wiffle ball. John enjoyed it all the more as he and Barry played on opposing teams. He could giggle with impunity whenever Louis gave his kid brother the third degree for being a scrub.

After the game, when he assumed Barry would park himself in the living room to take in some "Goonies never say die," John went up to his bedroom to be above him. Instead, Barry and his Mountain Dew also trekked up to the second floor and into Faith's wardrobe closet. How could John have forgotten about the one ritual his stepbrother practiced more consistently than any other? He kicked off his Velcro New Balance and tiptoed into the hallway.

"When I live there, can we go to South Square every weekend so I can play video games?"

"FUCK YOU, PUSSY!" was hurled at John in tandem with Louis's palms, still filthy from sliding in the dirt. He slammed John against the closet door, cutting Barry off midgiggle. "Next time we're going to kick your faggoty ass!"

John and Donald bantered with each other during lunch on Monday and then played the Commodore after school. While he was ripping shit up as Snake Eyes, Donald's eyes wandered over to the Dungeons & Dragons game and asked when they'd be able to give that a try. John said that when you sign up for something like that, you're in it for the long haul.

"How long we been playing this?" Donald nodded at Cobra Commander. "A year?"

"JOHN-N-N-N!" Even though he was only wearing that blue golf shirt with the orange bleach stain and a pair of Temple U jogging shorts, the usual garb for his work-from-home days, Frank carried that unmistakable whiff of authority as he marched into the pool-room with Jonathan in tow. "Question for you. And if you could tell Donald to turn off the game, I would appreciate it."

Donald paused Snake Eyes midpunch.

"Turn it off, I said."

John flicked off the TV but left the Commodore on with the floppy drive humming.

"Now. Question for both of you: Do either of you know anything about money that went missing from my room?"

Jonathan's steely freckle-framed squinting eyes clamped down with bolts on Donald's camouflage-green cap and the bill that hid his face. "Yo, John. Didn't you say when you went to the mall that Donald flashed you a wad of cash? Where could he get that kind of money if he's always over here? Playing our video games? Drinking our soda? Eating our food?" The room went still. Across the way, Hogg was feeding cheese to a kitty on his shoulder. "Dude, the fact that you didn't have any trouble going through my dad's underwear is fucking disgusting."

"My dad always says don't bite the hand that feeds you," John said.

"Historically, I haven't agreed with anything your father has said," Frank said. "Including his and his new wife's refusal to pay the child support they owe your mother. But on this particular topic, your father's keen insight comes to the fore." Everyone looked at Donald, whose face remained hidden under the bill. "While I have no objection to John's socializing with you in general, even if it betrays base morals on his part, I would appreciate it if you didn't socialize with him here."

"Daaaaaaamn!" Jonathan guffawed.

Donald rocked back and forth on the edge of the couch and mumbled something. After adjusting his cap, he got to his feet slowly, slid his backpack over one shoulder, and squeezed between Jonathan and the wall to leave the room.

John stared at the blank TV that showed Jonathan and Frank's reflections and, between and beyond them, distorted into a gaunt figure by the convex screen, Donald's silhouette disappearing through the door for the last time.

The floppy drive's hum was positively deafening.

5

BUNNY

SPOOKY SMART AND VIO LYNN

If you don't value your life, by all means, call her by her full name: Bunneficence.

Bunny Stringfellow, phantom virtuoso par excellence, was beating her bow through the allegro energico of Bruch's Violin Concerto No. 1 in G Minor when Barry stomped into the room, looking like a dejected heap of duplicate Garbage Pail Kids. This was partly because he was lugging a heap of duplicate Garbage Pail Kids.

Pilfering five hundred ducats from dear old Dad's undergarment drawer was supposed to have cured all ills, from here to North Carolina and all the ships at sea. But now he was saying that Bed-Wetting Barry and Wrong-Eye Roggebusch were starting to feel like Losing Faith and Dyin' Dinah. He added that, in all seriousness, he couldn't really know what they felt like since he'd yet to get either half of that pair. Was it possible that Topps—whoever this Mr. Topps was, Bunny couldn't fathom—had shipped a fixed set of pairings to the Mount Holly Pharmacy, forever dooming Barry from ever owning the whole of every series?

Bunny stabbed the air with her bow in Barry's direction the way a fencer cried en garde. "Don't you dare say anything about this Mount Holly silliness, Bawrence! It's Northampton!"

Barry plopped down on his bed and sprawled his chubby frame across the black comforter. "If I just call it a pharmacy, will you stop being a pain in my ass?"

Before I go any further, I should probably point out that Bunny Stringfellow was most definitely not a figment of Barry's imagination. Whatever his strengths may be, and at nine they were still mostly hidden, imagination was not one of them. Perhaps he could stretch it a bit when imagining blood-soaked skirmishes between his G.I. Joe or He-Man figures, or his Transformers actually transforming without the aid of his pudgy fingers, but that was it. Most of Barry's creative acumen still lay ahead of him. When he got there, and perhaps to make up for the lean years, his creativity would define him and his path.

Meantime, he wasn't there yet while Bunny, in stark contrast, had gotten there early. Good thing too, considering her fate. Bunny was that special kind of ethereal paradox we all hope to behold at least once before we become ether ourselves: a real ghost. She was the spirit of a thirteen-year-old violin prodigy who met the Big Stradivarius in the sky in 1913. Bunny couldn't remember a day in her life, not to speak of death, when she wasn't playing the violin. As far as she knew, she popped out of the womb with instrument in hand, strings already tuned, bow arm akimbo.

Her continuing to play beyond the grave was a purely practical matter. It had been spring when she passed. The school year was building toward its climactic recitals with all the unstoppable push of a Beethoven symphony. Speaking of Ludwig van, his Violin Concerto in D Major (opus 61) was one of the five pieces Bunny had been mulling for her recital. Each of the five concertos presented a monumental challenge for different reasons and with different sonic payoffs. All guaranteed the same heaven-high dosage of gratification and achievement to the successful pupil.

"I say, Bawrence. Whenever Leo used such language, my parents would cram a bar of soap in his mouth until he swore never to use such language again."

"Maybe that's why he ran away and never came back."

Ironic as it may seem, given she was dead, Bunny would none-theless have to catch her breath sometimes while talking to Barry. She sat up straight and took several deep breaths, during which the memory of the last time she saw her older brother flashed through her mind. Burgundy suitcase in hand and wearing the black Ascot cap Bunny had helped Mother pick out for his twelfth birthday the year before, Leo Stringfellow hadn't barged through the front door like Bunny had been expecting, like he'd done many times before after a family tiff. Instead, he stepped out quite calmly, as if leaving for another school day.

"I recall you watched the Summer Olympics a couple of years ago, Bawrence. I remember the Summer Olympics were taking place in Sweden when I was a student here. Those are practically children competing, Bawrence. Older than me but still very young. When you're young, having that kind of pressure on you is unspeakable. Father told me many times that what defines character isn't when things go easy, it's when things are tough."

Barry sat up and crossed his legs and, just like that, became inter-ested. It was like he was sitting at a campfire and she was telling—I swear no pun intended—a ghost story. "Wow. So you're saying your brother was a complete jerk who had no character."

Bunny sighed. "Once upon a time, I would've said you were right. But now I'm not so sure. Remember, he was named after our great-grandfather."

"Who was supposed to be super famous even though no one's heard of him. Even my dad's never heard of him, and he's heard of everyone."

"A dubious claim, but nevertheless, Leopold was all of nineteen years of age—nineteen, Bawrence—when he played Große Fuge, one of Beethoven's last string quartets, with Beethoven himself conduct-ing! Can you imagine?" She sighed again, but this time it was that other kind of sigh girls do.

"Mozart was better. Me and my dad have watched *Amadeus* a million times. How come your grandpa didn't play with Wolfie if he was such hot shit?"

"You've the mouth of Beelzebub. Anyway! Leopold, my *great*-grandfather, performed for aristocracy as far away as Berlin. And I've told you about his son, my Grandpa Ulee. Grandpa lost his right arm in the Civil War but taught himself to play with his mouth and left hand. He kept at it out of sheer love, Bawrence. Have you ever loved something so much?"

"I don't know."

"My point is that Leo inherited unspeakable pressure. So much is in a name. Look at you. Bawrence Barney Roggebusch. Poor child, you're ruined."

"Asshole."

"Mother were here, she'd shut you in... well, here!"

"Your mom was mean. My mom's nicer. That's why I'm going to live with her next year. You're mean."

"Compared to your brothers, I can honestly say I am the nicest to you of anyone in this household."

"I'm calling my mom. See ya."

No sooner did Barry plod into the hall than he got beaten up by that ogre who lived in the opposite room that used to be the boys' practice room. Bunny played Tchaikovsky as loud as she could, which she knew the Russian virtuoso didn't deserve, yet she had to balance propriety with her own sanity.

For reasons both she and Barry long ago gave up trying to understand, no one else at 48 Broad could see or hear her. For the most part.

MONDAY: Beethoven's Violin Concerto in D Major (opus 61)

"Like this!" were literally the only two words Bunny's father ever said when teaching her how to hold the bow and the instrument. That's all he needed to say. The technical basics felt as natural as breathing to Bunny. Just as Pa Stringfellow learned the Beethoven concerto at five, so too his baby girl. Soon enough, his "Like this!" had graduated to a full-throated "LIKE THIS!" with a dry finger and closed eyes.

To this day, whenever she played this concerto, Bunny recalled that dry finger and those closed eyes. That's why she was sometimes relieved beyond measure when Barry got home. He may not have been the most skilled conversationalist, but he could still distract her from ancient history.

Bunny tried not to smile at the sight of Barry emptying the little blue plastic wastebasket into the obscenely huge black plastic bag that always looked so unruly in his puny hands. That was Barry's contribution to the upkeep of the house, emptying every can in every room on every floor when he got home from school. Yes, Bunny had to hand it to this Frank Roggebusch fellow. He sure knew how to impose structure as well as anyone who ran the Broad Street Music Academy.

When he finished the remaining rooms and came back, she asked: "What is the update on Misty? Come now, I am fascinated."

Barry dove straight into playing with the figures he referred to collectively as He-Man.

"You were fairly nasty with me yesterday, Bawrence. In fact, as long as I've been both alive and dead, no one has ever used that tone or language with me."

"I'm sorry!"

"Oh Bawrence. You still can't deduce my sarcasm? Honestly."

"Misty wasn't there today. I had to stare at her empty seat all damned day. It sucked!"

"Well, take heart. The longer her absence, the more overjoyed you will be upon her return. Absence makes the heart, and all that."

Barry stopped abruptly and switched to the military figures scattered across the room that he collectively called G.I. Joe.

"And how fares your progress toward collecting those little cards? The so-called Garbage Children?"

"Stop calling them that! My dad calls them that. It pisses me off."

"I'm not far off though, now am I?"

Barry tired of his military figures and dug those trading cards out of that orange-and-white shoebox given to him by his brother Daniel, the one who had nursed Barry and all but saved him from joining

Bunny on the other side three and a half years ago. He took out the stack from the most recent series and, even though he'd organized them impeccably the last time (and the time before that and the time before that), went through what Bunny called the solitaire routine, laying them out carefully, pairing each one with its hideous twin. It smacked of a pointless exercise, but judging by how he smiled with that half smile of his and sometimes guffawed, Bunny surmised the real point was to relax and distract him. She grinned herself as the monsters multiplied across the sky-blue shag carpet.

Her grin vanished when she remembered how Barry had been able to afford all these. "Bawrence? When are you going to face up to what you have done to your father?"

He got up and switched on the electronic clock radio.

"When I was alive, five hundred dollars was a vast sum. I don't care how obtuse you fancy your father to be. Anyone who's doing well enough to purchase this establishment, marry three times, and convince a perfectly capable father to sign over his three children, must possess an appreciable intellect. By now he has no doubt figured out what happened."

"No one knows except you, and you're dead and he can't see you."

"Perhaps he's waiting to see who suddenly starts buying more than their allowance can afford. How will you explain it?"

Barry lay back on the bed to take in what passed for music these days. He started mumbling to himself and picking his nose.

"He may become so infuriated with you he won't let you live with your mother next year."

"Shut up."

"Then again, if you turn the logic around, if you infuriate him enough, he may be happy to get rid of you."

"I've got four Ashley Cans and not one Greta Garbage."

The dinner bell tolled.

"JOHHHHHHHN!"

"Too fucking hungry to fall for that bullshit tonight, yosie yo-yo," John said as he emerged from his room just below. His voice seemed to make Barry wince.

"Hey, dickhead."

Bunny and Barry started at the low, yet carrying, voice of Jonathan, the vapor of his nicotine-ranking breath snaking its way into Barry's domain.

"You gonna lie there on your fat ass and mumble like a retard, or are you coming down to dinner?"

"Team! Dinner!"

Bunny took up her violin. "Well, Sissy, it's just you and me." She began playing the Largetto (G major), at first tepidly, bracing for Jonathan's trademark violence.

"Bawrence Barney!"

"Yo, dickhead! You deaf?"

Barry giggled. "Sissy."

"The fuck you just call me?"

And so it began. Jonathan finally let up when Barry started crying.

"Shake it off. Be a man."

"Bawrence Barney! How do you expect to maintain your weight if you don't eat everything first?" Stephen cackled on his way down the stairs.

Daniel was standing outside Barry's room. Barry couldn't see him, but Bunny could. "Dad puts in all that effort to cook for everyone since his useless fucking wife won't do it, the least you can do is show some appreciation." And that's when Daniel did something Barry and his brothers did to each other quite often when the other wasn't looking or couldn't see them: the middle finger.

"He's doing it again, Bawrence."

"I don't care."

"Why don't you care?" Daniel said.

"Fuckin' idiot," Jonathan said. "Look at that, you even cry crooked."

Jonathan and Daniel laughed uproariously all the way down to the first floor.

Barry crawled back over to those ghastly children, the snot latching to his lips while more tears poured from the eye on the healthy side of his face. The eye on the dead side managed only a feeble drip, like an old faucet when it was turned off.

Testament to his experience in these big brother matters, Barry did indeed brush it off in impressively short order, wiped all the fluids on his Rocky tee, heaved himself up, and switched off the bulb.

"Bawrence!"

His chubby silhouette plodded toward the door with one shoe untied. "You're a ghost. You like the dark."

"A common misperception perpetuated by the ignorant practitioners of pop culture!"

He slammed the door and thumped down the stairs.

The church on High Street, which had been chiming the hour since before Bunny was born, chimed ten o'clock before Barry shuffled back upstairs, that one shoe still untied. Bunny was just wrapping up the rondo allegro. Perhaps because she wasn't alive, Barry felt no qualms about stripping down to his tighty-whities in front of her. He always came back after the holidays with a new pair of pajamas courtesy of his mom, but he never wore them.

"Beethoven wasn't very cooperative with me today, Bawrence," she said as Barry climbed into bed and flicked on the clock radio. "Many difficult memories held me back. Family memories." She could make out his chubby, lumpy form in the darkness, a giant cyst on the full-sized bed beneath the slanting ceiling. On Bunny's side of the room, by the window overlooking Broad Street, the ceiling slanted on either side of her, following the gables. The more confined space suited her. She could focus on the discipline. "We shouldn't let domestic hardships hold us back and define who we are, Bawrence. I don't mean to get preachy on you, but there it is."

"I made it to the next level on G.I. Joe."

"Your tone of voice suggests this is a good thing."

Barry sat up, crossed his legs, and started rocking. "My Bad Thing was that Misty was absent today. That'll be my Bad Thing tomorrow if she's still absent."

"And your Good Thing?"

"Shut up, it's my favorite song!"

In addition to the rocking, another bedtime ritual was that clock radio contraption playing this one song Barry had told her always reminded him of Misty. He said it was called "Take on Me" by a group of musicians known as a-ha. Bunny thought the name ludicrous at first but had come to appreciate its minimalism. The song itself didn't amount to much more than repetitive noise, but it always made Barry stop rocking and lie down close to the clock radio.

TUESDAY: **Mendelssohn's Violin Concerto in E Minor (opus 64)**

As she oozed with relish into the andante, Bunny recalled one particular Mendelssohn lesson with Ms. Strombach. With knuckles like salted boulders, Ms. Strombach clenched her fists even tighter than her false teeth. "Child! You need to EXPERIENCE the allegretto non troppo and the allegro molto vivace. Remember, it is nighttime when most people attend concerts. Many after the andante are feeling restless and expectant, like during foreplay. Some may have even fallen asleep, again, as can sometimes happen during foreplay. Now it is up to you to explode across the bridge and invade the allegretto to rouse their senses. You are the allegretto, child. Show me!"

Ms. Strombach's slightly German accent—her family had left Heidelberg for Hackensack when she was a tween—filled Bunny's phantom head as phantom drops of sweat coated her phantom forehead. Mendelssohn's climax never failed to enslave her. She squeezed her eyes shut and, in spite of her need for control, surrendered to the music coursing through her. You could easily make a case for this piece being tougher than yesterday's Beethoven, but Bunny didn't shoulder any family baggage with Mendelssohn. Playing Mendelssohn could make her feel like she was floating. Which, of course, she sometimes was.

"The fuck is that?"

She stopped and whipped around. Jonathan's muscular frame and invisible nicotine cloud filled the doorway. He was holding a phone to his ear with the cord leading back across the hall to his room. His dark, roaming eyes stopped when they met Bunny's. This couldn't possibly be, could it? "Well, Jonathan, I suppose you have a lot of questions. And I have more than a few for you, as for three and a half years now I have borne witness to the utter lack of civility and respect with which you've been behaving toward Bawrence. You know, as an older brother, your charter should be to protect—"

"Never mind," he said as he thumped back into his room. "Fucking room stinks. See what happens when you stop coming?"

Bunny took Felix from the top.

She sat before the fist-clenched Ms. Strombach in the recital room on the first floor, which Barry had told her was now, amazingly, the music room. In Bunny's day, the performer would sit over to the far left in that niche framed by the four windows looking out at Broad. The room seemed practically cavernous when it was just you and Ms. Strombach. She'd haul in one of those creaking wooden chairs and slam it on the opposite end of the room and drop onto it and close her eyes. That was your cue. That day, the only day when Bunny could say she truly nailed Mendelssohn, Ms. Strombach leaped to her arthritic feet, shaking both salted boulders. "JaWOHL! JaWOHL, MEINE SCHATZE! BRAVISSIMA!"

You don't understand. Ms. Strombach never said bravissima.

When she got home, Leo gave her grief for that stupid smile pasted on her face.

"What are you so goddamned happy about?" Barry said when he came in to empty the trash.

"Was Misty there?"

He walked out to empty the rest of the cans. A few minutes later, he thumped back in and flopped down on the bed stomach first.

"How did you and she get along?"

He flicked on the clock radio and let his unkempt head drop onto the pillow. Within seconds he was out for the count. Bunny proceeded to practice softly.

"Yo, shit-for-brains! Dinner! In case you forgot what the bell meant!"

Barry stirred with a moan. His normally droopy eye was now all but shut. Bunny knew his brothers would rain down a hurricane of ridicule. She attempted a smile of understanding that felt woefully inadequate.

"She didn't even look at me today. Not even when we were outside playing kickball and she was on my team and stuff." He hurried downstairs into the maelstrom of Louis's profanity.

Bunny was probably more familiar with Barry's patterns than Barry was. On Tuesdays he usually came back up around nine or nine thirty. She'd surmised that Tuesday, for whatever reason, was the day his brothers had the fewest extracurricular activities, meaning they were mostly all under this roof for Barry to avoid.

He almost never came back up at eight, hence the red flag as Bunny heard him lumber up the stairs at a few minutes past. He didn't sit on the floor so much as drop himself like a burlap sack of dejection. Stephen hollered up the stairs that he was trying to record music and would Barry not shake the house with his fat ass.

Instead of series four, Barry dug deeper into the shoebox for a random mishmash of two and three. Bunny had seen him do this before. It meant he was bored out of his mind and/or depressed. She tried to distract him by belting out those funny, clever, acrobatic ditties her father had taught her. It went over about as well as you'd expect.

"Hey, bro." John knocked on the door as he opened it. "Garbage Pail Kids!" He sat on the floor and took an immediate interest even if that interest didn't seem to Bunny a hundred percent sincere. Normally, she would have found his presence, especially this late on a school night, objectionable, but tonight she felt relief. Maybe he'd find more success distracting his stepbrother. "Which ones are these?"

"You take these ones. I'll take these."

John shuffled through them and giggled at the names. "Double Heather and Schizo Fran. Tommy Gun and Dead Fred. Jolly Roger and Pegleg Peter..." He and Barry were cracking up. "Gorgeous George and Dollar Bill. Ghastly Ashley and Acme Amy. Ugh Lee and... Wow, Ugh Lee is FAT!" He held the card up with a maniacal grin. "Super fat. They should've called the other one Super Fat Snuka."

"Put them on the floor like this."

"Those the new ones?"

"I don't have them all yet." Barry set to laying out the cards while John followed suit only haphazardly. "But I will. I've been saving my allowance."

John burst out laughing again. "How could you be saving when you've been spending it on this crap?"

"Shut up! Your bike is crap!"

"That bike is pure radness and you know it."

Barry jumped up and stomped over to his dresser.

"Don't let him push your buttons, Bawrence."

He yanked open the top drawer, pulled out the wad, and flashed it in John's face.

"Rad, dude!"

Barry looked at Bunny, whose stony look said all he needed to hear. He tossed the wad back in and retook his place on the floor. "Drew Blood and Bustin' Dustin. Bruised Lee and Karate Kate. Grim Jim and Beth Death. There's a girl in my class named Beth. She's much fatter than this. Distorted Dot and Mirror Imogene. What's Imogene?"

"Do you mean what or who is Imogene, Bawrence?"

"Is that a name?"

"Seriously?"

"Bawrence, honestly! It's a very common name for women."

"You ever heard of Imogene Coca? From *Vacation*? She was the evil aunt."

"Oh yeah!"

"It's a super old-fashioned name for the female species."

"I resent that utterly unnecessary remark," Bunny said.

Someone thumped up the stairs.

"Hey." John lowered his voice to a whisper. "Want to hear something fucked up? Know how Karen hasn't been cleaning? She usually cleans Jonathan's pot, but when she didn't show up, I went in and took it all."

"No way!"

John flashed another maniacal grin. "And then! I took it over to Tara's. We smoked some of it before we made out. When are you going to get a girlfriend, dude?"

"I don't know."

"You're still very young, Bawrence," Bunny said.

"You've at least kissed a girl, right?"

"Change the subject. Mention your Neanderthal brother talking to your housekeeper."

"Hey! Did you hear that Jonathan and Karen...? K-I-S-S-I-N-G?"

John cracked up. "Dude, everyone knows they go out. I bet they've fucked in his room."

"They have done no such thing, but he may be onto something, it pains me to say."

"She's not a housekeeper," Barry said.

"Yeah, your dad and my mom already have housekeepers. Us."

"Why don't you suggest that Stephen is also dating Karen and that he is the only one who is unaware of Jonathan's dalliances?"

Barry relayed the ghost's words in his own special Barry way.

"No fucking way!"

"Yaw-haw!"

They cracked up. Eventually John said, "Did you know Donald and I kissed once?"

"Gross!"

"It's just like kissing a girl. Want to try?"

"You're full of shit."

"It was on the Mount. It's no big deal."

Barry chuckled. "You were like Garbage Pail Kids."

"What would our names be?"

"Frenching John. John French!"

"We didn't french."

"Don Lip. Lippy Don!"

John leaned in and pecked Barry on the side of the mouth.

"Pecker John. Get it? Double meaning." He kissed Barry again and giggled. When he stood up, he said, "Tara's probably done her homework by now."

"I stole that money from my dad."

John giggled again on his way out.

WEDNESDAY: Brahms's Violin Concerto in D Major (opus 77)

Brahms was just the guy you wanted to hear on hump day, what with that latter part of the allegro non troppo picking itself up and resuming the celebratory gusto. Bunny beamed as she entered the first movement's final six minutes. She never wore this kind of glee in the presence of others, not even Barry, except at night when the lights were off and he bellyached about her criticism of eighties rock.

Bunny would never admit this to him, but the only other person she ever knew with a face as peculiar as his was Jared, the boy who had lived around the corner. A bit on the chubby side, Jared would often walk by with his mom and little sister, always wearing an agonized expression. Bunny developed the hypothesis that Jared wasn't really in agony, that his countenance looked that way naturally.

Bunny would never tell Barry about Jared because in those last months of her life, she had developed a Queen Anne-sized crush on him.

As he always did on days when he worked from home, Frank would luncheon in the living room to the soundtrack of music that Bunny actually considered music. She stood in the bedroom doorway and soaked it up. For whatever reason, Frank seemed partial to violin concertos, especially Mozart's, for his lunchtime listening.

A couple of hours later, Bunny was flying across the clear blue skies of Brahms's third movement, one of her all-time favorite pieces to play, allegro giocoso, ma non troppo vivace— poco più presto (D major), when two sets of footsteps stormed up the stairs.

"Gym class sucks anyway," Daniel was saying.

"I know, right?"

"I can't do pull-ups. I'll never be able to do pull-ups. What's the point?"

Veronica always struck Bunny with her classic beauty. Even today, with her plainer garb of lopsided, left-shoulder-revealing shirt, tight denim, and feathered hair bound in a large colorful plastic clip, she looked camera ready. Daniel couldn't keep his hands off her as they fiddled and fondled in the hallway. He whispered something that made her laugh.

They stumbled and laughed to the doorway of his room. Veronica froze. From where Bunny stood at the opposite end of the hallway, Daniel's room appeared to lead into darkness.

"Oh my God," Veronica whispered.

Daniel looked like he had a smile perched on the edge of his mouth but wasn't sure he should let it out. He took a deep breath. They laughed together.

Bunny's mouth fell open in spite of herself. Had she lived, would Jared have been her first? The last time she saw him walk by, he glanced at her. It was the first time he acknowledged her. Or had he even noticed her? When Bunny had gone to bed that night and started shivering, she couldn't tell if it was from an oncoming fever or a different sort of fever. If Jared had been her first, would it have been like this? Certainly they couldn't've gone to her house. Could you imagine? Perhaps the Mount.

Giggling spurted from under the door now and again, then tapered off. At one point Frank, back in his office, said something to Baltimore about deadlines. Eventually the house went still. The church on High Street chimed the bottom of the hour and snapped her out of it.

Bunny tore into Brahms like a glowing, hot blade through her mother's hand-churned cream butter. At some point she lost track. When she rounded the languid bend of the second movement into the third, she realized she'd just been here.

Barry bumped the doorknob on his way in to empty the trash.

"You gave me a fitful fright, Bawrence!"

"But you're the ghost, stupid."

She resumed the third movement.

Barry headed over to Jonathan's room. "Jesus Christ, it stinks in here!"

Bunny's breath stopped short at the sight of Barry plodding down the hall with that massive plastic bag. "Bawrence, wait!" She dropped Sissy.

Barry stepped into Daniel's room, emptied the trash, and reemerged like it was any other day. Just before closing the door, he ducked his head back in and asked his big brother if he wanted to play the Commodore. If Daniel answered, Bunny couldn't hear it. Barry closed the door and proceeded into the bathroom. He bumped the walls with the trash bag on his way back to the stairs.

"Was anyone in there?"

"Where?"

She nodded down the hall with wide eyes.

"Dan and Veronica are taking a nap. I think they fucked." He plodded down the stairs, gripping the bag by its unruly neck as it bopped along.

"Too much D major," Bunny said as she sat back down and collected Sissy.

She dawdled with the adagio (F major), the patient middle movement and the only one of the three not in D major. It was quiet enough that she heard everything Jonathan said when he got home and called Karen about money and drugs. They also talked about something else of even greater weight, and while Jonathan referred to this third topic as an "it," Bunny was fairly certain "he" or "she" would've been more appropriate.

Stephen stomped up the stairs two at a time and filled Jonathan's doorway, his arms jutted out ever so slightly, tense and straight, as if they were wings braced for takeoff. "Hey, asshole, if you could refrain from smoking your pot downstairs or anywhere else besides this godforsaken room, I'd appreciate it. It fucking smells, man."

"Hold on a sec. Hey fuck you, pussy! All right, I'm back."

Stephen walked across to Barry's room and looked at nothing in particular. He chuckled and kicked the shoebox before marching back into Jonathan's room and yanking something out of the wall.

Jonathan threw the phone at him. "What the fuck is your problem?"

Thus began the battle of shoves, something Bunny had seen these two wildebeests do more times than she could count simply by sitting here in this one spot.

"I didn't fucking smoke pot downstairs, dipshit. Someone else coulda done it."

"Coulda done it? I think the pot's already making you retarded."

"This isn't your property."

"You own the house now, fuck wad?"

"This is MY room! MY property!"

Stephen pushed back with enough force to send his brother off-balance. Jonathan recovered and charged. Stephen's laughing sapped some of his strength, allowing Jonathan to slam him into the balustrade. One of the wooden bars flew down the stairs, inciting more guffaws from Stephen.

Bunny didn't realize she'd broken her own rules until she already had. Despite it being Brahms Wednesday, she abruptly fled the soundscape of major Ds and Fs for that of the minor E of Mendelssohn. "Allegro molto appassionato, gentlemen!" And with that, she tore into the first movement. It matched the spectacle flawlessly.

"What the fuck?" Jonathan lifted his head toward Barry's room.

Stephen tore himself away in disdain, as if suddenly afraid mere contact with his brother would give him the plague. "So the pussy's afraid of some squirrels, huh?"

Bunny continued playing. That Jonathan had some inkling of her presence while Stephen didn't made no sense to her, but she'd mull that one later. For now, Felix provided the perfect balm.

Stephen grabbed a wad of cards from the shoebox and shoved them in Jonathan's face. "Check it out. Barry has your card."

"Go fuck yourself, faggot."

Stephen scattered the cards all over the floor. "Asshole. Everyone on this floor is an asshole." He scooped up another stack and flicked clusters out in random directions.

"Sorry about that," Jonathan said to the phone. "My dickhead brother unplugged the phone and tried to start a fight he couldn't win."

"Bawrence Barney's an asshole." Stephen flicked more cards. "Daniel's an asshole. I'll punch him out someday. And his mom. That is a life goal."

Jonathan slammed the door.

Stephen walked over and looked out at Buttonwood. He dropped the cards and walked out.

Bunny held up the violin. "Do you not agree, Sissy? Such an excess of D major, I feel I may plummet into a state of delirium." She surveyed the mass of cards and felt forlorn for Barry.

When he came back up, he was clutching a can of that sweet carbonated soda in one hand and several wrapped candies in the other, much larger and wrapped in brighter paper than anything from Bunny's day. He set the sweets down on one of his toy shelves before popping open the can to take a long pull. The sugar must have stimulated him immediately because he didn't set the can down so much as slam it before marching back out into the hall. "ASSHOLE!"

"Who's an asshole?" came Jonathan's voice from behind the door.

"ASSHOOOOOOOLE!"

"What?" said Frank from somewhere far away.

Barry marched back in and got on his hands and knees to clean up the cards. Bunny went back to Brahms. His adagio was just the right accompaniment for the scene before her.

Frank's measured footsteps announced his imminent arrival. He was dressed in what Bunny had come to know as his jogging garb: faded T-shirt (sometimes Redskins, today Temple University), shorts, and sneakers. "Baw-*rence*. All is well?"

Barry remained immersed in his cards.

Jonathan poked his head into the hall. "Careful, Pop, he's on a warpath."

"It appears your Garbage Cans are disheveled."

"Steve messed them up."

Stephen thumped up the stairs until his head was just visible through the balustrade. "Let it be known that my only intention in coming up to this wretched floor, which I generally avoid due to its wretchedness, was to persuade Jonathan to limit his illicit drug activities to this floor so the rest of us don't have to smell it."

"You just make shit up, right?" Jonathan chuckled. "Fuck you, man."

"Gentlemen. Calm. Stephen, if you can possibly help it, please cease and desist from rifling Bawrence's room."

"I'm afraid I can't make that promise."

"Because?"

"It would be like asking you to promise never to drink scotch again."

"I don't believe that analogy quite works."

"Or asking Jonathan never to do drugs again."

"That analogy might work even less."

"However, if it makes Quasimodo over there feel any better, since I hate the third floor and everyone on it more than anything I've ever hated in my life, I would say the chances are very high it will never happen again."

"Bawrence. Do those terms sound acceptable to you?"

At this point Bunny was on Brahms's third movement, the D major allegro giocoso, ma non troppo vivace, poco più presto, which she'd had the distinct privilege of playing to orchestral accompaniment in the parlor of Ms. Strombach's aunt, a century old if she'd been a day. That day marked a host of firsts: the first time she performed Brahms with an orchestra; the first time she performed in a private salon; the first time she performed for a relative of Ms. Strombach, whose Old World wealth afforded her a house with a salon big enough to accommodate an orchestra.

"You hear that?"

"What?"

"So long, girls!" Stephen headed back downstairs.

Jonathan scanned the room. "You hear the music too?"

"What music?"

"It's called drugs!" Stephen said.

"Team. I will now go run the steam room and take a shower and shave. Cornish game hens are on the menu for tonight, accompanied by scalloped potatoes and succotash. Dinner will be served at seven o'clock per the usual." Frank headed down the hall to the bathroom.

"Oh, Bawrence, you are soooooo lucky!"

"I'm going to the pharmacy." Barry grabbed a couple of bills from the stash in his drawer.

"The fuck you talkin' to?" Jonathan barked as Barry headed downstairs.

When Barry came back, he threw the door shut before dumping the new cards all over the floor.

"Series four, Bawrence?"

Barry beamed so widely that even the dead half of his face managed just a hint of a dimple. "You remembered it was series four!"

"They're such monstrosities. I do hope you have all of them now."

"I got some of the older ones too. I don't have all those either."

Bunny took Brahms from the top while Barry went to work on the cards. He took all the cards back out of the shoebox and stacked them by series before tearing open the new packs. Judging by his occasional outburst and half smile, he was making headway on plugging gaps. He was about halfway through the new cards when the High Street church chimed seven o'clock. The dinner bell sounded soon after.

"Be calm, Bawrence. Be in good cheer as you recite Good Thing Bad Thing New Thing."

Barry must've taken her advice to heart. When he came back up, he was joined by Jonathan, John, and Daniel. They turned off the hallway light and the lights in Barry's room and threw open the two windows overlooking Buttonwood. Before Bunny could take it all in, someone else thumped up the stairs.

Louis stepped into the room and closed the door quietly. In one arm he was cradling a bag of charcoal. "Shut the fuck up, yo. Wait." He set the charcoal down with all the delicacy of an antique dealer before opening the door a crack. Faith's unmistakable footsteps marched down the hall from the master suite. Nine times out of ten, those steps would've turned and headed down to the first floor. Not on this night.

She stopped at the foot of the stairs. Louis mouthed something to John.

"My room?"

Louis put a finger to his lips.

"Hello!"

Their faces went whiter than Bunny's.

"Bawrence. Bawrence! God damn it!" She started up the stairs.

Louis waved over Barry. Jonathan gave him a kick in the ass to speed him up.

"What do you want?" Barry said as he stepped out into the hall.

Faith stopped halfway up. "Did you not hear me calling you?"

"I don't know."

"John up here?"

"I don't know."

"Are you by yourself? Why are all the lights off?"

"I don't know."

"Would you stop acting like a FUCKING idiot?"

"Beast," Bunny whispered.

Jonathan jerked his head in Bunny's direction.

"It's not up here."

"It?"

"I mean..."

Bunny cupped a giggle while craning her neck to get a glimpse of Faith's pasty face. Her expression was granite, which made her dark eyes all the more chilling.

"He at Donald's?"

"He's not up here."

"That's not what I asked."

"I don't know."

Faith stomped back downstairs. "He fucking better not be or I will kick his ass. Frank!"

"They like to ride bikes together."

John smacked Barry in the head. "What the fuck, dude?"

Barry closed the door and dipped a hand into the bag of charcoal and came away with three or four pieces. The others did the same. "Get off my ass."

"Which way's yonder?" Daniel asked.

"To the right," Louis said.

"And left is over yonder," Jonathan said. "Barry Barney, get over here." He and Barry manned the left window while Daniel and Louis took the right with John, who kicked things off with an "Over yonder!" before hurling a piece of charcoal to the left at a car that was hopelessly out of range.

"Pathetic," Bunny hissed. "John is always eager to impress Daniel and Louis when they are not worth impressing and are never impressed with him besides."

"Yonder!" Daniel cracked himself up with an awful throw at nothing in particular.

"So what's Faith's deal with you and Donald?" Louis said.

"Over yonder!" Jonathan zinged charcoal at a car heading down Broad in the direction of the schools.

He nailed it. And hard too, judging by the metallic thud. He and Barry high-fived. The car screeched to a halt, idled, and drove off tentatively.

Before resuming Brahms's third movement, Bunny huffed. "Bawrence, if you must partake in this ridiculous ritual, please take care not to cause any serious damage, either to the vehicles themselves or those poor innocent people inside of them."

"Awesome hit, man," Louis said.

"He stole the old man's money," Daniel said.

"A thick-ass wad. Just snatched it from the drawer. But what else do you expect from someone like that?"

"Yonder!" Barry threw a piece of charcoal straight down at a car passing directly in front of the house. Bunny didn't hear any result.

"What the fuck are you doing?" Jonathan asked. "You're supposed to wait until the car's gone by and then throw. And hit it on the front so it's not obvious it came from behind."

"But you hit yours on the back, stupid."

"He didn't see me, did he?"

"Barry!" Daniel craned his neck out the window and looked left. "Yonder!"

"That's OVER yonder, Dummy Stupid Shut up!"

The car heading down Broad toward High was well out of sight by the time Daniel's charcoal smashed into powder in the middle of the intersection.

An inviting green-and-brown station wagon came rumbling down Buttonwood from the right. Louis shoved Daniel aside. "I'm taking all y'all to school."

Louis's usual scattered focus suddenly solidified and fixated like a hawk's. The station wagon idled at the stop sign, waited for a couple of cars to pass, and coughed up Buttonwood with a lurching clearing of the throat. "Over yonder!" With the sidearm throw of a professional pitcher, Louis whipped the charcoal clear through the humid nighttime air, up the length of Buttonwood. It arced over the station wagon and met the hood with a POP!

Everyone in Barry's room, including Bunny, who could just see the station wagon through the tree outside her window, erupted in awe and celebration, and they laughed at the driver searching for the culprit in all the wrong places. Louis squinted at the silhouette. "No way. Dan, you recognize him?"

"I think he's in my math class. Total dick."

"Double, Tanisha would kick your ass if she found out what you said about Donald," Louis said with his trademark chuckle.

"She has her gang, I have mine. We'll keep them where they belong."

"The more things change." Bunny sighed.

"Yonder yonder!" Barry cried.

Bunny gasped at the sound of the breaking window.

Everyone erupted in another round of hysterics.

"Everyone, be calm," Daniel said, sounding to Bunny exactly like

Frank whenever he came up to the third floor to investigate a fracas. She could hear the driver getting out.

"Oh fuck me," Jonathan said.

"Head to your rooms and pretend you've been doing homework or reading or whatever smart activity you can think of." Daniel put his arm around Barry and gave him a kiss on the cheek. "Love ya."

"Oh, Bawrence," was all Bunny could think of saying when they were alone. Barry switched on the wall bulb and his bedside lamp and started playing with his G.I. Joe figures. While listening to the voices of Frank and the indignant driver down below, Bunny set bow to string and made to launch into the adagio. The cautious F major would've been beyond apropos at the moment, but the adagio, like the toys, just didn't seem to be in the mood.

"Everyone downstairs!" Faith's voice rang off the walls. "Now!"

Barry dropped Snake Eyes and Cobra Commander and headed for the door with a pitch-perfect emulation of Jonathan when he said, "Oh fuck me."

Bunny stood in the doorway and picked up snatches of voices and the odd full sentence. If Faith was the herder, Frank was chief shepherd. True to his philosophical form, he never raised his voice. Eventually Jonathan and Louis mumbled something like a deadpan apology to the driver. This was followed by footsteps into the living room. Peering over the balustrade, bow in one hand and Sissy in the other, Bunny whispered a prayer that Barry would gain the wisdom of perspective sooner rather than later and without experiencing anything traumatic.

After the lecture, Faith could clearly be heard giving it to John in the poolroom, where Alexander and a friend were apparently playing the Commodore. Even though Alexander had had no involvement in the charcoal shenanigans, Faith reserved some vitriol for him, for playing video games instead of practicing his bass. Ms. Strombach's legacy was alive and well in this place.

When he plodded back upstairs, the side of Barry's face that worked looked just as dead as the dead half. He stared at his toys for a moment before heading back out and down the hall. Bunny's mouth fell open at the sound of him brushing his teeth. When was the last time he brushed before bed?

She hurried back to the chair and pretended to be mid-Brahms when he thumped back in. Instead of playing with his toys, he cleaned them up. "Bawrence..."

"You're weird, Bunny. Ghosts don't need to whisper."

"The suspense is positively killing me!"

"Be calm. All is well."

"Where are the others?"

Barry arranged the figures neatly along the shelves, the good-guy G.I. Joes in one cluster, the bad-guy Cobras in another, Autobots here, Decepticons there. Once his room was cleaner than Karen had ever made it, he sat up on the bed and switched on the clock radio and rocked back and forth.

"I can't fucking believe you didn't say anything. Fucking pussy." With a slow, measured pace that must've tortured Barry even more than it did Bunny, Jonathan walked over and started pounding. For some reason this otherwise routine scene chilled Bunny's blood. She didn't grasp why until Jonathan was on top of Barry, pinning him on his back. He grabbed one of the pillows and began smothering him. Barry flailed helplessly like a turtle, his pudgy arms and legs wobbling in the air.

"Ghosts don't need to whisper."

In less than a blink, Bunny was astride the bed, hollering at Jonathan to stop. He'd somehow heard her before, but this time her words didn't register. A full minute of having the pillow squashed on his face didn't stop Barry from shouting with all he had left. Now and then one of his feet would kick within a few inches of Jonathan's face. If he just kicked a bit more this way...

Bunny didn't realize she was reaching out until her hands found purchase on Barry's leg. She threw it. The sneaker caught Jonathan square in the jaw, sending him into the lamp and knocking over the clock radio, which incidentally was playing "Take on Me."

Barry threw the pillow aside and jumped to his feet with a felicity that took Bunny aback. There the two children stood, waiting for the next attack. Jonathan, on the other hand, had apparently exhausted his indignation. He headed for the door and laughed darkly. "Barry, man, if you shamelessly backstab people like that, how are you ever going to make friends?"

As he was walking out, Bunny floated over to him and whispered, "Don't ever come back."

Jonathan stopped cold. All the blood and bravado that usually added a touch of rouge to his freckled cheeks suddenly drained from the third floor.

Eventually he stepped across to his bedroom and closed the door with a whisper all his own.

Barry grabbed a couple of Transformers and sat in the center of the bed and turned one of them into a truck and the other into a plane.

Bunny reclaimed her seat and picked up Sissy. "To cheer you up, I will deviate from my usual repertoire and play a concerto by Mozart. Your father listens to this on occasion."

"Then I definitely don't want to hear it."

What with all the D and E she usually played, Bunny opted for the first of Mozart's five violin concertos, in B-flat major. Something about it was playful to her, although you didn't hear it so much as feel it by the end of the allegro moderato.

Toward the end of presto, Barry put his toys away and climbed under the covers. Within seconds of his turning off the light, Stephen leaped up the stairs two at a time and threw the door open. "Bawrence Barney!"

Barry turned up the radio.

He cackled. "I guess you thought that guy would suspect someone threw it from the other direction. Reverse psychology, I get it."

"Go away!"

"I mean, there's stupid, and then there's, well, your kind of stupid. The kind that takes stupid to another plane of stupidity. And includes wetting the bed. Now most people, by the time they reach, say, kindergarten, understand that wetting the bed is bad. How much you want to bet you'll be the only kid at Holbein who pisses in his sheets?"

Barry sat up. "I won't be here next year! Idiot!"

"That's right. You're going to be living with your mom in... Where is it? Russia?"

"North Carolina, stupid!"

"I'll bet I'm not as stupid as your mom. She fled to Hickville and left all you kids to rot under the same roof as Faith. I ever tell you how your mom got me in trouble for something I didn't do? Maybe you were the one who did it. I'm not sure. But someone pulled up a bunch of flowers in your mom's sad little flower bed. Pretty pathetic compared to what George Taylor does here, but I guess it was the best she could do. Someone thought so little of her handiwork they ripped it up. She assumed it was me and told Dad. He didn't say much, just, 'Don't touch the goddamned flowers,' or whatever. And went back to his scotch. I couldn't believe she did that, man. I guess it's in the blood. Thank God I'm not her son. I couldn't imagine being a coward and a retard and a bed wetter. Have a good night, buddy."

"Reprehensible human being." Bunny was about to take Mozart from the top when Barry made an odd nasal sound that sounded like an aborted snort. She didn't understand what was happening until the high-pitched wail filled the charcoal-black air. It was the most pathetic sound she'd ever heard. "Oh, Bawrence, please. They'll hear you." He mumbled something that the snot rendered incomprehensible. "Heavens, was that even English?"

"I want my mommy."

"Oh, Bawrence..."

"I don't want to be here anymore."

"School will be over soon, your brothers will fly away to faraway places to visit their other father or mother, and you'll get this nice big house to yourself. And then, just as those monsters return, you'll go to your mother."

"And escape this shit hole!"

"If you were at your mother's right now, what would you be doing?"

The slobbering ebbed until all that was left was the odd sniff. "I don't know."

"What does your mother make for supper? What's your favorite thing that she makes?"

"Macaroni and cheese with fish sticks."

"Oh how I wish I could eat again, you have no idea. What your father makes is wonderful."

"It sucks."

"And then after supper?"

"I don't know. Watch TV. Board games!" He sat up and started rocking. "She's got lots of board games! You ever hear of Monopoly? Or Clue?"

"I'm afraid not, but they sound fascinating, I must say."

"Or Sorry! Have you ever played Sorry?"

"There's a game called Sorry?"

"When you lose? And the other person knocks one of your pieces off? They do it really hard and say, 'SORRY!'" Barry cracked himself up. "But it sucks when it happens to you."

"I don't doubt it."

"And movies! My mom and I go all the time."

"Now Bawrence, you know what I want you to do?" Considering the little chubby shape, Bunny suddenly felt an ineffable pull across the room until she was sitting at the foot of the bed, where she and Barry could meet each other's eyes courtesy of the moonlight hitting the sky-blue shag. Barry rolled onto his back as he cracked up. "I want you to close your eyes and imagine being there. That's it. Close your eyes. Can you see your mother's house?"

"She lives in an apartment. It's kind of small."

"You're at the front door. She's waiting for you inside."

"Shouldn't she be outside with me if I just got there? She always picks me up at the airport."

"And you step in."

"Mommy's watching *Cheers*. Norm!"

"She prepares macaroni and cheese with crispy fish sticks. Oh, to

be able to eat again! And after supper, she makes you ice cream."
They giggled.

"My favorite flavor is coffee!"

"Repulsive!" She couldn't stop giggling.

THURSDAY: **Tchaikovsky's Violin Concerto in D Major (opus 35)**

Bunny was on a roll this week in her prediction of who would
skip school on which day. It was lunchtime when she heard two
voices thumping up the Buttonwood steps. She drifted to the
doorway as Gorbie started yapping.

"Knock it off, Gorb Man," Stephen said.

"Hey, little guy," Karen said while the pooch made those excited
sniff and snort noises. "Hey, little Gorbie! You miss me? I sure missed
you. Shadow misses you too."

Stephen leaped up the stairs two at a time while Karen took her
time and played with Gorbie. She was better dressed than Bunny was
used to seeing her. Her blouse was modest and tasteful, and those
denim trousers defined her figure well.

Stephen was wearing what he always wore: an open button shirt
with the sleeves rolled up over a plain undershirt. He checked his
watch, which looked exactly like his father's. "He teaches two classes
today. Gets home around five. Satan usually gets home around six."

"What about...?" She looked over at Jonathan's room.

"Golf practice. If he was here, you'd smell him."

She took a few steps toward the room to peek inside. "You sure?"

"Keep it up and he'll see you're stalling," Bunny said.

Karen sighed. "I don't know what else to say."

Stephen chuckled. "You haven't said anything yet."

"You were pretty tired and pissed off last night because Jonathan
beat you up."

"He barged into my room and threw charcoal at my head. I had
my headphones on. It was an ambush."

"Are you really going to make me say it again?"

"Jonathan's so stupid he probably thinks I was the one who threw the can of peas at his head."

"Charcoal. Peas. This house is so weird. What will the baby think?"

"That part I remember."

"Why were you pretending?"

"You claimed to have already finished the discussion before it even started. This discussion, not the one on the phone last night. I thought you were going to add something else."

"Sorry to disappoint you."

"Who else have you been fucking?"

"Beast," Bunny said.

"No one. Since you?"

"And before me?" She looked at him. Stephen cackled again. "I knew all that stuff about your mom was bullshit."

"She was pretty sick a few weeks ago. I had to drive down there every night. I wouldn't get home until fucking midnight. Not that you care. Look, you want to be a father or not?"

Jabbing the air with his index: "I'll give you two guesses."

"I don't have insurance."

"See? We do have something in common."

"But you have money."

"I get an allowance same as everyone else."

"Shit, Stephen."

"There are cheaper options."

"Let's just get a coat hanger from Jonathan's room."

"You must be watching those HBO after-school specials. There are legit doctors who do them out of sympathy. Like a pro bono lawyer."

"They're not real doctors. You want to have this kid, we're living together, and I don't think you could handle me."

"I couldn't agree more," Bunny said.

"As a rule, I avoid the doctor's office. Doctors don't know anything. It's all fraudulent as far as I'm concerned."

"You're such a douche."

"Tell you what I'll do to show you how much I'm willing to go out on a limb. I will go to my father and request a loan. We will work out an agreement whereby I will repay him in monthly installments with interest."

"He'd do that, wouldn't he? Interest."

"You'll help me pay it back."

Karen looked over at Jonathan's room again. "At the end of the day, Frank won't have to give me anything."

"I'll make something up. I need the money to visit my mother in Florida."

"He always calls her Dracula."

Once more with the index: "Now that's interesting. I didn't know you two have been conversing about my mother."

"She was really nasty to the poor guy."

"And I suppose he forgot to mention he cheated on her with Barry's mom."

She headed downstairs with a smirk. "Whatever reason you give, just make sure it's believable." Bunny heard her step into Stephen's room. "I leave for a couple of weeks and look at this sty. How long's this ice cream carton been here? It smells like cheese and popcorn."

"Leave my popcorn alone."

"These kernels are changing color. Why can't you take your shit downstairs?"

"I have a foolproof system. Want to hear it?"

Karen ran back up and gave him a playful shove. "Everyone's room smells. Here..." She led him into Jonathan's room and closed the door. "If I left you in here for a day or two?"

Stephen made exaggerated gagging noises.

Neither of them said anything after that. Bunny watched their foot shadows recede.

"Heavens to Betsy!"

"You hear something?" Karen asked.

Bunny marched over to Sissy and, after shaking out her arms and flexing her fingers, parked herself on the chair and started amping up the D major of the allegro moderato just as she heard Stephen yelping.

"It stinks, it stinks, it stinks, it STINKS, OH MY GOD..."

"Don't you dare come now!"

"...it stinks, it stinks, it stinks, it STINKS!"

The third movement, the D major finale, allegro vivacissimo, was much shorter than the allegro moderato, quicker and louder. It allowed Bunny to fill the air with the Russian's veloce joviality like her afterlife depended on it.

She was playing the finale for the third straight time when she was startled off her chair by a series of stomping feet. Daniel mumbled something that triggered Louis's trademark chuckle.

Before anyone knew what was going on, Daniel and Louis were standing at the now wide-open doorway of Jonathan's room. Never before had Bunny heard so much profanity spew from one mouth as she did now from Stephen and with a preternaturally high pitch that reminded her of the traveling chorus of 1909.

Bunny retook her seat, set her chin on Sissy, and began playing Tchaikovsky's second movement, the G Minor Canzonetta: Andante. This piece was the portrait of calm, quiet sweetness. Normally it would take about ten minutes to play this movement, but Bunny imagined the sweetness as viscous honey she could stretch out between her fingers.

"Be proud of yourself, Stephen Roggebusch!"

"I want your fat!" Daniel and Louis hurried back downstairs in hysterics.

"What is your fucking problem?" Karen threw on her blouse. "You're not married. I'm not married."

Bunny traipsed to the doorway in time to see a beet-faced and frothing Stephen killing the air with his finger. "I don't find *any* of this remotely humorous."

"If you haven't been caught fucking the cleaning lady, the porn movie is incomplete."

"This shows you the kind of people they are. They are the principal reason I resent having to live in this house, which is why I ultimately resent my father more than them."

"I thought Faith was your arch enemy."

"But I wouldn't have to deal with that cunt if my father hadn't married her. So IN THE END..."

"Don't use that word." Karen checked that the blouse's tag was under the collar and ran her fingers through her hair to fling it out. Just like that, with her hands on her hips, she was the adult addressing the child. "Everything will be fine."

"They're all my arch enemies! Death to them all!"

"Look, babe, I've got to run. Let me know how it goes with Frank tonight, yeah?" She put a stick of gum in her mouth and, her eyes passing over Barry's room, headed for the stairs.

"Douche," Stephen said.

"Sorry?"

"Jonathan uses that word."

Karen paused at the top of the stairs, then headed down.

Stephen turned and looked at nothing in particular in Jonathan's room for what seemed an eternity. He snapped out of it when a truck roared by with metal music blasting.

"Bawrence!" Bunny said when he stumbled in and nearly tripped over a very full trash bag. "Where have you been?"

He steadied the bag with one pudgy hand while using the other to cram down the garbage to create more room. "Ew!" He yanked his hand out and wiped it on his Hulk Hogan tee. When he came back after finishing with the trash, he said, "Ghosts should always be happy."

Bunny smiled at him preparing his G.I. Joe figures for battle while he munched on peanut butter cups. "And why, pray tell?"

"Because you're dead already. You don't have to worry about anything anymore. You'll never get beat up. You'll never worry about waking up in time to go to the bathroom."

"What inspires this lecture, Bawrence?"

"You're always mad at me."

"Am not!"

"I just think you should be happy all the time." He had the Joes and Cobras facing off in what would obviously be a draw. "Die, die, die! Look out! CRASH! KA-BOOM!"

She set bow to string and took the Russian master from the top.

"Get him! Get him! BOOM!"

Thursday was the one night a week Barry stayed downstairs after dinner for hours to watch his favorite shows. *Cheers*, Barry's synopsis of which had failed to convince Bunny of its appeal, came on at nine. Sure enough, right on cue, from two floors below: "NORM!"

Out of the blue, Faith and Alexander came up to the third floor. Faith flicked on the hallway light. "You can't go to music camp."

"But you said I could."

"I'm sorry."

Alexander stared at her like she was the ghost up here. "What the fuck, Mom?"

"You have every right to use profanity in this situation."

"We talked about this, we agreed. I have to go."

"Alexander..."

"I'll pay you back half out of my allowance. Like we said."

"Alexander."

"What the fuck?"

"We cannot pay for it because we do not have the money."

He stared some more. "Were you fired, Mom?"

"Someone has stolen a significant amount of money from Frank and me."

"That doesn't make any sense."

"Oh, Bawrence, what have you wrought?"

"I blame Frank. At least in part. Naturally I also reserve disgust for the thief. But Frank doesn't use a wallet. He keeps everything loose. Hundreds of dollars, Alexander."

"NORM!"

"Mom..."

"Some think John's black friend may have had something to do with it."

"Mom, I have to go to music camp."

"Stephen asked his father for several hundred dollars to have his room repainted. Which I know is bullshit, so now I have to wonder what Stephen is up to."

"Everyone else is going."

"Alexander."

"We planned it. I helped write the lyrics. We've rehearsed millions of times."

"Alexander."

"What the fuck, Mom?" His voice cracked.

"It's a lot of goddamned money for some glorified rock garage."

Alexander plodded down the stairs, his face concealed behind the black curtain of hair. He lumbered into his room and slammed the door.

"NORM!"

Faith marched through Bunny and into Barry's room. She kicked toys, dug through the shoebox full of cards, and snooped in the closet Barry used as a glorified toy archive. After rifling the nightstand drawers and spending an obscene amount of time digging under the clothes in each dresser drawer, she parked herself at the foot of the bed and began wringing her hands.

What Faith Roggebusch proceeded to do next was so bizarre, so utterly unexpected and, in a way, terrifying, our resident ghost could only hover with ethereal mouth agape. At some point, she dropped Sissy.

"Say what you want, Daddy, but I never peed in my bed. Barry's retarded. He looks just like that retarded boy who went to my school, the one who was in the same grade as Sarah. That useless little shit. When Barry smiles, I want to puke. His daddy lets him get away with everything. Everything! He's not a real daddy like you are. He doesn't teach discipline. His kids get away with everything." She craned her neck at the Buttonwood windows. "I CAN'T hit them! I've already had one husband try to get me arrested."

FRIDAY: Bruch's Violin Concerto No. 1 in G Minor (opus 26)

Mountain boots punished the steps outside: Jonathan was home.

Bunny took Bruch from the top. It was around lunchtime. Right on cue, Frank headed downstairs for his classical music luncheon, taking the back stairs to the kitchen while Jonathan ran up the hallway stairs to the second floor. If he came home early one day a week, it was usually Friday. The pattern had tapered off recently, though, thanks to RV golf's Friday match schedule.

Bunny interrupted Bruch when she heard Alexander and John's door open. Someone had stayed home all day. She floated to the door and peered down through the balustrade.

"Who stole money from Frank?" Alexander's ashen face hovered just outside the hallway light.

"Looks like it was John's bosom buddy."

"You know that for a fact?"

"You won't be seeing his dark face around here again."

"But how do you know he did it? Unless he admitted it?"

"You should have seen his face. He had guilt written all over it."

Alexander looked down, then back up for what seemed a very long time. "I have doubts."

"About your manhood?"

"I can't go to music camp with my band. So, you know. I'm sort of pissed."

"That's why Karen's not coming anymore. The old man can't pay her."

Their hushed voices became harder to make out when Mozart's third violin concerto started playing below them. Frank, as he always did, sighed pleasurably upon falling into his recliner.

"Her mom's sick."

Jonathan guffawed. "Her mom's in Delaware. I think she's fine."

"I don't think Donald stole the money."

"You should've seen how scared he looked."

"I'd be scared too if I was black in a house full of white people accusing me of stealing five hundred dollars."

"So what then? Someone just broke into the house?"

"It was someone here. I'd stake my allowance on it."

"John just bought that awesome bike. There ya go."

"You know something? I don't think I've ever been this pissed off. I have to find out who did it. If it's the last thing I do. You know, so I can beat the shit out of that person. For ruining my life."

"Damn, dude."

"I wrote the lyrics. It was all arranged." His voice started cracking again.

"Whoever it is, yo? We'll tag-team their ass, like the Hulkster and Sgt. Slaughter."

Alexander turned the doorknob a bunch of times.

"So is that why you're skipping school?"

"I'm not skipping school, asshole. I'm sick to my fucking stomach." He stopped fidgeting with the knob and shot a look up through the balustrade.

Bunny froze.

Jonathan guffawed. "No way, man. That fat fuck?"

"You can't live here and steal that much. And expect to get away with it."

"I stayed home sick once. Puking my guts out. Your mom got pissed at me."

"What about Louis's new boom box? That he draws graffiti on?"

"All his friends live in the Gardens. Maybe they helped him."

Alexander fidgeted with the knob again.

Jonathan looked up through the balustrade and lowered his voice. "Hey, man. You ever hear strange shit coming from Barry's room?"

"If I lose my friends over this... Be calm. Be philosophical. That's what Frank says. But how can you be philosophical? About losing your friends?"

Bunny didn't move.

"Whenever I go up there?" Alexander said. "I always see the most fucked up thing."

Jonathan looked at him.

"Barry."

They cracked up for a good long minute or so.

Bunny parked herself on the chair and took Bruch from the top. When she hadn't heard their voices for a while, she got back up and then froze stock-still when she met Jonathan's eyes. He was standing in the doorway, staring straight at her. "Can you see me?"

His eyes wandered to the carpet.

"You could be a role model, you know. You have a real opportunity with Bawrence. To help him in a way no one else could."

He stepped back across the hall into his room and closed the door delicately.

Bunny was about to head back to her chair when Jonathan stormed back out and marched across the hall through her. "Where's the money, faggot?" He went through Barry's dresser drawers and closet, all the places Faith had checked. At one point, after digging through a box in the closet, he emerged with a tattered blue dinosaur. "I remember this fucking thing." He walked it along the air and made horrible noises.

Alexander walked in and looked around. "Wow. It stinks. It stinks bad."

"He's still got all this old shit from Kensington."

Alexander picked up the shoebox and turned it over. Bunny gasped at the sight of several hundred Garbage Pail Kids raining onto the carpet in a torrent of paper-flapping freaks. He then snatched up a plastic bag from one of the shelves and dumped several hundred more GPKs plus several dozen unopened packs. He shook out the bag with a slap of the stale air. The three of them took in the huge pile. Alexander said in his monotone: "I like math. And I don't see how five dollars a week gets you all this." He headed downstairs and used the back stairs to the kitchen, presumably so Frank wouldn't hear him leave the house.

Jonathan marched back into his room and slammed the door.

Bunny parked herself on her chair and once again took Bruch from the top. "No more distractions, Sissy. What say you?"

Alexander returned before Barry got home from school. Jonathan was on the phone with Karen. Bunny smiled through the balustrade at the sight of Barry lugging the garbage. His stepbrother swung open the door before he could touch the knob. "Buy any Garbage Pail Kids today?"

"No."

"Why not?"

"I don't know." He tried to walk into the room, but Alexander wouldn't move. Barry shrugged and proceeded down the hall toward Stephen and Louis's room.

"Actually, wait. I do have something." Alexander disappeared into his room and returned with packages of Garbage Pail Kids.

"Where'd you get those?"

"Good old Mount Holly Pharmacy. I was going to throw them away since I'm pretty sure you already have these. Want to check to be sure?"

Bunny had a good idea where this was leading. Barry, of course, hadn't a clue. He ripped open the packs and thumbed through the cards with the dexterity of a Garbage Pail pro. "I don't have this one!"

Alexander's stone face betrayed a crack of surprise. "Crushed Shelly?"

"I've got a million Dale Snails but no Crushed Shellys. Can I keep this one? It's part of series four!"

"Keep all of them."

Barry stuffed the cards in his pocket. Lifted by the euphoria of completing another pair, he hobbled up the stairs with the giant garbage bag and a huge half grin. Only when he reached the top did Alexander decide to follow. "He's coming, Bawrence."

Barry's euphoria was crushed like so many Shellys when he came upon the countless spilled cards in his room. "Holy shit."

"Bawrence!"

"Jonathan's an asshole."

"Hey." Alexander appeared in the doorway. "Don't get mad at Jonathan. I mean, you can if you want."

"You people are assholes."

"Someone stole five hundred dollars from Frank. Everyone thinks it was Donald. I think it was someone who lives here. So I'm eliminating the possibilities. That means I have to do my research. On Garbage Pail Kids. Since you have hundreds and hundreds of them. I went to the Mount Holly Pharmacy. One pack costs thirty-five cents.

You get five cards in a pack. So for a dollar and five cents, you get three packs. If you spent your five-dollar allowance on nothing but Garbage Pail Kids, you'd get fourteen packs. That's seventy cards. And you'd have a dime left over. You could apply that to next week's allowance. Realistically speaking, do you spend every single penny of your allowance on Garbage Pail Kids every single week? I mean, realistically?"

Barry just stared at him.

"Watch yourself, Bawrence." Bunny retook her seat and played Bruch softly, an insult to the old master, but what could she do?

"How many packs have you bought this week?"

Barry continued staring.

Alexander tittered. "Today?"

Barry stared some more. Then he said, "Three." He pointed them out.

"That leaves you with four dollars. Well, actually, three dollars and ninety-five cents. What will you be spending that on? More cards?"

"I don't know. I already spent some of it."

"On?"

"A Slurpee. And a Zero."

"Zero?"

"Candy bar. It's the white one."

"How much did that cost? The Slurpee and the Zero?"

"I don't know."

"Know what might be better? Let's count them. The cards. All of them." Alexander sat down on the carpet. "This'll be fun. Let's see how many of these ugly suckers you own."

Without missing a beat with Bruch, Bunny said, "Do take caution, Bawrence. I simply cannot think what would happen if he finds out you've spent it all."

"I only spent a little."

"Bawrence!"

"A little?" Alexander said while pairing each card with its twin.

"I could positively strangle you!"

"A little of the money I have left. Three packs of GPKs. And then a Slurpee and a Zero. And then today a... a... Whatchamacallit. And that's it."

"Do you think you might spend the rest tomorrow? And do you think you might spend it all on GPKs? Don't you also sometimes buy a bag of those cheese-filled pretzel bites when you go to the pharmacy? And you love Mountain Dew. So let's say you go to the pharmacy tomorrow and get three more packs. That's a dollar five. That leaves you with enough for pretzel bites and a Mountain Dew. And that's Bawrence Barney's allowance for this week. Would you say that's fair?"

"I don't know."

"Six packs of GPKs would cost you two dollars and ten cents. That leaves you two dollars and ninety cents. To buy junk food. You're counting too, right?"

"Forty-six, forty-seven..."

"A hundred for me. And so much more. Let's keep it going. So does six packs a week sound like a good average?"

"I don't know."

"Keeping in mind it's an average. And when did you start collecting these freaky little beauties?"

"Ummmm..."

"Don't stop counting. You can think and count at the same time, right?"

"If memory serves," Bunny said, "this addiction began last December. Series two had already been released."

"That's right!"

"What's right?"

"Counting and remembering, it's easy." Barry did a terrible job suppressing a half smile.

Alexander chuckled. "Barry, man. Stephen's right. You're so stupid."

"And you're an asshole. Does that make us even now?"

"Bawrence, that will only make things worse."

Actually, it made things better. Alexander rolled on his ass. The atmosphere loosened considerably.

"I started in December. Series two came out in November. So I remember having to catch up. That's why there were some weeks when I bought more than six packs. I spent all my allowance on GPKs."

"And that would amount to fourteen packs, eight more than the average. How many weeks do you think you did that?"

"And your mother at Christmas, Bawrence."

"Yeah! When I flew down to North Carolina to see my mom for Christmas. She got me some too. Like five packs or something."

"I'm up to two hundred. You?"

Barry counted to himself for several more cards before announcing, "One hundred ten!"

"How many weeks do you think you spent your allowance on nothing but GPKs? Two weeks? Three? Five?"

"Maybe four. I did it last week too."

"Let's say four. Why last week?"

"Series four came out. And I still don't have all the other ones yet."

"So let's see. It's been five months since you started collecting Garbage Pail Kids. Four weeks in a month times five months equals twenty weeks. Six packs of cards is thirty cards. Thirty times twenty is six hundred." He surveyed the cuddly freaks. "I'd say you have more than six hundred, Bawrence Barney. Four of those weeks you got eight extra packs, which equals forty extra cards per week. Times four weeks is one hundred sixty. That gives you seven hundred sixty cards. Five more packs from Mommy equals twenty-five more cards. So that's now seven hundred eighty-five." He considered the cards again, then Barry. "Okay. Well. I'm pretty sure you have more. Than seven hundred eighty-five, that is. Let's keep counting."

Bunny couldn't remember ever being in a situation where she was rooting for both sides. She tried to eye count the remaining cards at the same pace as Bruch. Surely Barry had exceeded the six-pack weekly average more than four times.

Just as she finished the third movement, Alexander announced:

"Five hundred."

"Two hundred twenty!"

"That's seven hundred twenty. Sixty-five more and we'll have seven eighty-five. But you know what? You definitely have more than sixty-five cards there. Here."

"Not by too terribly much, I'll be bound. So long as you stop answering me in his presence, Bawrence, you may get out of this with your hide intact."

Alexander made short work of the remaining cards. "Eleven hundred forty-five." He looked over the stacks, impeccably arranged in columns by series, with nary a trace of emotion, while Barry hung on his next words with obvious anxiety. "That is a lot of fucking cards, dude. That's three hundred sixty cards more than what we predicted. So let's see. Three hundred sixty divided by five cards a pack equals what?" He did the math in a few short seconds. "Seventy-two packs. Times thirty-five cents a pack? Twenty-five dollars and twenty cents."

"Remarkable!" Bunny said.

"So. I guess. That's not a huge amount of money. It's a lot of cards though."

"But sometimes!" Barry bounced up and down on his bubble ass. "Sometimes my daddy buys me GPKs. Because they have them at the Acme. So when we're there, he might buy me a pack and stuff."

"Doesn't he go to Super Fresh?"

"Super Fresh doesn't have GPKs; they don't have them."

"Even allowing for Frank's rare trip to the Acme, and the even rarer instance of your being with him when he's there, you're still pretty off in terms of number of cards. Although not by dollar amount. Which is interesting. Very interesting. Not really. I'm just pretending it is. But why are you so off? Do you think?"

Bunny racked her brain for something Barry could say but was distracted by his slowly forming half smile.

"I guess I'm retarded." He giggled.

"Oh, Bawrence, I could kiss you!"

Alexander laughed, although this wasn't the contagious, ass-rolling laughter. This was more of a whispering laugh, the silent, stung humor of someone outwitted but who didn't want to appear like a sore loser. He stared at the cards for a while. Barry resumed yesterday's battle between the Autobots and Decepticons. Bunny took Bruch from the top with a smile. At some point Alexander said, "Life really sucks, Barry, you know that? I guess you don't. But you shouldn't. It's too soon. I wish I was nine. Elementary school was rad. Nothing to worry about. Just what's for lunch. Sloppy Joe? Corndogs? Pizza? Which kickball team am I on?" His trademark chuckle came back. He hopped up and walked out and sprinted downstairs.

While Barry was downstairs having dinner, Bunny gave serious consideration to Bruch as her capstone. It had so much going for it. For starters, as the shortest of the five, it would appeal not only to violin aficionados but to those like Leo who appreciated beautiful music in small doses. And it truly was sublime, even to the lay ear.

Bunny felt light as the ghost she was as she upped the volume at the conclusion of the allegro energico. Sissy filled the third floor with a sweet viscous pool of G minor honey. And then she floated back to the beginning to breaststroke the vorspiel with even more string-diving verve. She should've known Barry hadn't spent most of his father's money. In a way, she was as guilty as his stepbrother for underestimating him.

Barry ran back up after dinner and dug out all his G.I. Joe figures, including a pile of them on one of the lower shelves he usually never touched because they were older and therefore not as interesting as the ones his mother got him this past Christmas.

"Tomorrow we're playing army on the Mount."

"I know your mood changes between feeling like the hero versus the villain, which is fine when you're nine but not when you're twenty-nine. Heed these words."

"Okay."

"I trust army was your Good Thing at supper?"

The Cobras killed off a couple Joes before he said: "We didn't do Good Thing Bad Thing New Thing because no one was there because it was just me and John and Daddy and Faith."

"Well then. I suppose you'll get to watch your *Miami Vice* program in the poolroom."

That's when she heard it. Just as Barry announced Snake Eyes would be commencing a sneak attack against Cobra Commander, footsteps started a slow, weary climb to the third floor. They were footsteps she'd never heard before yet faintly recognized. The voice they belonged to didn't sound like anyone she knew, yet the cadence rang a bell. It was a decrepit yet hopeful voice, a voice that wanted to sound more cheerful but couldn't because it had seen too much. "Last time I walked up these old stairs, I could do two at a time, goddamn."

"What was this place like? I just can't imagine."

"Tell you the truth, it wasn't much different than now. At least this floor. Yep. Same musty old smell."

By the time the owner of the voice and the footsteps reached the top, Bunny realized what was tickling her brain. The gait favored one of the feet due to a leg being slightly longer than the other. She'd only known one person like that in her entire life and death, but it couldn't possibly be him.

"Baw-*rence*! We have a visitor who would like to see your room."

"Bawrence, pick up your toys!"

Even as the gray, hunched form stepped gingerly into the sky-blue bedroom, Bunny still refused to entertain the reality of who this was. She couldn't breathe.

"I would like to introduce you to... What'd you say your name was?"

"Leo!" Bunny shot up from her chair, Sissy and bow falling to her feet.

"Hey there, big guy. Name's Leo. Leo Stringfellow." He shuffled up to Barry with a yellow-brown-toothed smile and an outstretched knobby, chiseled-oak hand.

"I'm Bawrence, but you can call me Barry."

"You look like a Barry! You know, Barry, I got a great-grand-daughter round about your age. Name's Bunneficence. Everyone calls her Bunny." Leo took in the room. "Lordy. Sure wasn't blue the last time I was here. Not sure if I like it. You like it, Barry?"

"My favorite color is black. I really love black."

Leo laughed that deep-chested, phlegmatic laugh only old men can pull off. Bunny had never seen Barry smile this much. Even the dead side of his face budged a bit. "Oh my. Oh my, oh my, oh my. Bunny practiced in this very room. This used to be a school, you know."

"Your great-granddaughter?"

"No, his sister!"

"I knew this was the one." He peered through one of the windows overlooking Buttonwood. "Last time I looked through this window, Bunny was down there. She was with some of the other girls. The instructors let them all go to High Street for an ice cream break. I snuck up here to talk to Eunice. She studied here too. Oh I was mad about Eunice."

"EUNICE?" Bunny said.

Leo smiled a smile that squished his eyes shut. "Came here a lot of times, Barry. Yessir. Bunny... he-he. She thought I liked her music, bless 'er. But I didn't give no never mind about that. I just wanted to see Eunice. I always think I would've married her if I hadn't run away."

"And what about me? Your poor sister who died in her prime for heaven's sake?"

"Haven't thought about Eunice in a long, very long time. Nosir."

"What instrument did your sister play?" Frank asked.

"Violin!" Barry erupted. "I play piano!"

"That's wonderful."

Faith appeared. "Bawrence *should* play the piano. But his practicing schedule is horrendous."

"Yes, I would say Bawrence is a piano player in theory," Frank said.

"Take heart, Barry. No one likes to practice. My sister hated it."

"Not true," Bunny said.

"Our father always had to push her."

"For the record, I practiced every single day."

"Things you do for your baby sister. I almost got kicked out of the house when I covered for her. Bunny and Eunice and some of their friends took the streetcar to Burlington City. Shopping maybe? Who the hell knows? Told our folks she was having private lessons with that old German witch. Luck would have it, our mother ran into the old German at the market. Bunny had no choice but to confess the crime, and I had to confess I covered for her. You should've seen the look on our father's face." He nodded at Faith. "Kind of like the way she looks at you, Barry."

"Heavens to Betsy, I forgot all about that."

"All Bunny got was a stern talking to. When it was my turn? Daddy took me outside and doled out a whipping like you've never seen."

"Daddy would never!"

"My parents used to play violin," Frank said. "In fact, that's how they met. Middle school. At the end of the year they had to perform in a recital."

Bunny's eyes never left Leo. He was here, and yet he wasn't. The way he looked right now, his eyes resting on the baseboards, the way his lips parted just a bit as he forgot himself, and especially the way he used his right hand to rub the top of his left...

"I swear, that virus came out of nowhere. I reckon that's what it was."

"I had a virus too," Barry said. "See how this side of my face can't move? I almost died."

"I hope you tell your brothers you love them once in a while."

"I hate their guts."

Leo reared back and roared with laughter. "Oh my, oh my. Well, I reckon time changes a lot of things. But not everything."

"Remember the picnic, Leo? Playing chess? We were there for hours!"

Leo's laughter tapered off in tripping gradations while the wrinkles on his face went from a very burrowed and twisty network of passed time to a more organized system of tributaries. "Oh my. Oh my, oh my. I just thought of something I haven't thought of in... Picnic on the Mount. We skipped school, brought Daddy's chess set. I tried to get Eunice to come with us. Sweet girl was too honest for her own good. So it was just me and Bun."

"So that's why you were sulking," Bunny said. "You said you weren't feeling well."

"Didn't last long. She was just so devoted to that instrument." He chuckled. "Sissy, she called it. To make up for not having a baby sister."

"Did you beat her?" Barry asked.

"Ha! First game, I made the boneheaded decision to go easy on her. Big mistake. She cleaned my clock, let me tell ya. Then I beat her in every game after that."

"I beat you one more time. And you did not go easy on me."

"Jonathan hates losing," Barry said. "Whenever I beat him at the Olympics, he beats me up and pretends like he won."

Leo guffawed again. "You remind me of my great-granddaughter Bunny. Too wise for your own good. Oh my. Oh my, oh my. This other time we skipped school and went all the way to Philadelphia. Oh my. That was so far."

"Yes! That concert!"

"Jesus, Bunny sure skipped school a lot," Barry said.

"Quit your goddamned cussing," Frank said.

"I always made up for it with hours upon hours of practice."

Leo chuckled. "I didn't have the heart to tell her, only reason I could pay for any of it was the money I stole from Daddy."

"Leo, tell me that's not true!"

"Stealing from him was like taking candy from a blind kid. He didn't keep a wallet or anything like that. Just kept it all stashed in his sock drawer."

"Neat!" Barry said.

He looked down and seemed to get lost again. "I miss that girl."

"She sounds like a remarkable person," Faith said. "A superb violinist."

Leo's smile crept back, twisting the tributaries. After a while, he looked up at Frank. "Bunny also had to play a recital. She was almost there. Gonna be the hardest of her life, that's what she said, yessir."

He chuckled. "No one else her age was close to her. That cranky old Kraut gave her five different pieces to pick from. Bunny tried explaining what the differences were, but it was all mumbo jumbo. Oh, Bun." He chuckled and sniffed. "Don't mind me now. I haven't thought of my baby sister this much in so long." He knuckled away the tears. "It was an honor to meet you, big guy! You're okay with it and your folks don't mind, I'd love for you to meet my great-grand-daughter."

"That sounds rad."

Leo followed Frank and Faith out of the room.

"Wait! Leo!" Bunny headed to the door to watch her brother gingerly negotiate the stairs.

SUNDAY

Barry came back up after devouring one of his father's famous egg-and-bacon sandwiches and played with his He-Man toys. The forces of Skeletor launched their attack to a multi-composer soundtrack.

Bunny loved the weekend for its freeing her of the composer-a-day discipline. On this particular Sunday and for the first time in over a year, she played Haydn's Violin Concerto No. 3 in A Major. She was so tickled by how much she enjoyed it she played it twice more all the way through before taking on Paganini's Violin Concerto No. 2 in B Minor. True, she'd just played Paganini a month ago, but she never tired of the B minor fun. Dvořák's Violin Concerto in A Minor, Bach's Violin Concerto in D Minor, and Elgar's Violin Concerto in B Minor, which had been a recent hit in Bunny's day like Barry's "Take on Me," were also on today's program.

Around midday, Louis bounded up to the third floor and punched Barry's door open. He loomed in all his sleeveless glory, punctuating each sentence with a bicep flex. "Barry! What's up! Bawrence Barney! Suit up! You suck!"

"Let's go, pussy!" Jonathan called from below.

"Barry, you're the missing link," Alexander said.

"He certainly looks like the Missing Link," Stephen said.

"I don't feel good," Barry said. Evil-Lyn was locked in a duel with Battle Cat.

"You had one of Frank's awesome egg-and-bacon sandwiches, didn't you?"

"I don't know."

"Did the sandwich suck? Should I tell Frank he's a terrible cook and that he made you sick and that you might get that face disease all over again but on the other side so that you'll never smile again?" Louis let all that hot air stagnate between them before he burst out laughing. Daniel could be heard giggling in fits somewhere behind him.

"But all you do is yell at me."

"I won't yell this time. Promise. Come on, man. Right now it's uneven. You've got me, Stephen, and John against Alex, Dan, and Jonathan. That's two and a half against three. John's only half. And you're half. So suit the fuck up."

"Bawrence Barney!" Stephen yelled.

"Bawrence!" Jonathan roared. "This is Faith calling! Get your fat ass down here before I beat it pink like I do Gorbie's!"

"I think you mean Gorbacher," Stephen said.

Barry carefully set down the feline and villainess and left everything in place so he could resume the skirmish later. Louis hugged him close with one massive bicep and gave him a peck on the head. The rest of the gang mock cheered as Barry emerged from his sky-blue cave.

As Bunny expected, Louis's words turned out to be as hollow as his biceps were thick. Even from Barry's room on the opposite end of the house, she could easily make out every pissed-off word.

"Yeah I'm yelling at you 'cause you're SHITTY!"

Part of her wanted to feel sorry for Barry, but she simply didn't have the emotional availability right now. Her head was still spinning from Friday. The more she played Elgar, the more Leo's visit played out in her head like a filmstrip out of control. So many questions.

And that laugh. That wasn't at all how he laughed when they

were kids, when he had that quick-hit kind of giggle that felt like he was pelting her with candy pebbles. Now it was long, drawn out, and very warm, a milk-and-cookies kind of laugh.

"Shake it off, pussy, we won!"

Barry's footsteps were the only pair heading upstairs. "Soon I'll be living with my mom and I won't have to deal with any of you assholes EVER AGAIN!"

"Baw-*rence*. All is well?"

Barry slammed the door and dropped down on the carpet to resume the duel. This time Evil-Lyn didn't stand a chance. The green-furred feline pounced on the lithe, pale-skinned seductress and, judging by how Barry kept hammering Battle Cat's face against her midsection, ate out her guts.

Hopefully the sweet notes of Paganini would calm him down. "Bawrence, you're not supposed to open the door and invite mockery in for tea." She played a little more before saying, "Oh, Bawrence, do you think we'll really see Leo again?"

Apparently this was Battle Cat's day. After eviscerating Evil-Lyn, he moved on to Beast Man. The latter mounted a modest defense before it all went to Castle Grayshit as Barry tried to cram Beast Man's head into the cat's fixed plastic-fanged maw.

"And what if you do get to meet my namesake?" Bunny floated upward without meaning to. "I have so many questions my head could positively burst."

After Battle Cat disposed of Skeletor's forces, he turned on his master He-Man and his friends and made a short meal of them.

"Bawrence..." Bunny gaped as Barry, for the first time ever and to the soundtrack of Paganini, crossed franchises. Battle Cat was now on the prowl for fresh G.I. Joe meat. Eventually she recovered enough to say, "Leo likes you, Bawrence. He could become a sort of friend and confidante the way George Taylor has."

"I don't care about your stupid old brother or this stupid old house or the stupid old people in it!" Instead of having Battle Cat munch on the figures in any organized way, Barry swept the entire population of Joes off the shelf. Holding Battle Cat by the hind quarters, he proceeded to club the lot of them. Bunny wasn't sure, nor did she want to cut off Paganini to get a better look, but she thought she saw the arm of one poor Joe pop right off. When his indignation was fully spent, Barry sprawled across the bed and picked his nose.

"Yo dick!" Jonathan was right outside. "Tell that invisible girlfriend of yours that if she's looking for some real action, I'm right across the hall." He headed into his room and slammed the door and fired up the heavy metal.

As she waded into the second movement, a thought occurred to Bunny, a favor she could do for Barry that would win him back. "Bawrence, listen. There's something you should know, something I've learned through the mere act of sitting here. Karen is pregnant. And the baby belongs to either Stephen or Jonathan. She seems to be making each one believe he's the father so she can get more money. She wants to have the baby. Stephen does not. Jonathan is on the fence. Normally, when she comes on Wednesdays and cleans up that awful-smelling, grassy drug in Jonathan's room, she takes a bit for herself. But when she didn't show up the other week, John helped himself before Gorbie went in and ate the rest. Bawrence, are you listening? I know it may not seem like it, but in due time you will thank me for disclosing this."

Barry spoke to his mother that night, as he did every Sunday. And, as always, he was accosted on his way down to the wardrobe closet by a random mishmash of whichever brothers happened to be passing by.

"Bawrence Barney!" Stephen said. "Ask your mom about the time she wouldn't let me each lunch."

Louis giggled. "That time you would only eat soup, faggot?"

"Ask her why she moved to North Carolina!" Daniel called.

"Yeah!" Louis agreed.

Phone calls with his mother typically lasted an hour. When one hour became two, Bunny stopped Paganini and stood in the doorway. Usually she could make out Barry's voice, if not his words. Right now she couldn't hear anything. The wardrobe light was still on under the closed door with the phone cord pulled taut beneath it.

The silence became so complete that Bunny started at the distant plastic clunking sound of the phone being dropped on its cradle. The wardrobe light went out. But Barry didn't emerge. A few eternal minutes went by with nary a sound. A ghost and Mötley Crüe were the only signs of life at 48 Broad.

Barry opened the door and lumbered with limp arms to the table in the corner of the hallway to put the phone back. Instead of setting it down, he dropped it like a dead fish. The handset fell off the cradle and clunked onto the wooden floor while Barry's socked feet thumped up to the third floor. The healthy side of his face looked as dead as the dead half.

For the first time ever, Barry walked right through Bunny.

After throwing the door shut, he stepped on the toys en route to his bed. One poor Cobra trooper let out a crack. Barry crawled under the comforter, turned on the radio, and turned off the light.

Bunny floated over to the bed. "All is well, Bawrence? Your mother? She is well?" The only sounds coming from the lumpen shape were sniffs. "Whatever it is, please, you can tell me."

He sniffed some more and swallowed a few times. "I can't live with my mom."

"I don't understand. Form your words, Bawrence."

"She said she's not ready. She has school. After work she goes to classes. And she says she's not done yet. I have to wait another year."

"So you will still get to live with her, yes?"

"I'll never see her again." He sniffed and swallowed and let out the odd whimper.

Bunny floated around to the other side of the bed so that Barry's back was facing her. That "Take on Me" started playing as she did so was an obvious good omen. Lying on her side behind him, her head above his on the pillow, Bunny placed a hand on the part of his arm protruding from the comforter. "Can you feel that? Is it chilly?"

He sniffed and swallowed. "It's warm."

From a world away, Frank was ringing the kitchen bell for dinner.

6

DANIEL

ADOPT ED AND DUNK HUNK

Dan belched happily as he scrubbed the dishes. This Sunday night had seen Frank once again whip up a masterpiece of pork chops, baked beans, and apple sauce. Dan might've been biased since this was his favorite meal of all time, but no one could cook a chop the way Frank could.

"You think you can drive us, man?" Louis said, perched on one of the island pedestals with the black-and-white TV behind him humming with baseball highlights on ESPN.

"What's that?"

"Phillies game."

"Drive you to Philly? Get the fuck..."

Louis cracked up. "Get a ticket for yourself. Get a nosebleed."

"I go, Veronica'll want to go."

"Her dad could fucking buy Veterans Stadium."

"Gentlemen!" Scrubbing the congealed fat off the rack, Dan found a measure of comfort—or was it reassurance?—in Frank's postdinner getup of stained golf shirt and khaki shorts and bare feet that announced his approach. The pantry's soft carpet dampened the thumping for a beat before those same feet kissed the yellow-and-white tiles that Karen hadn't mopped in weeks. In his hand was the usual tumbler with melting ice. "I have a report. A very interesting report. Your mother called."

"She called you?" Louis asked.

"Among others. I assume she spoke to Bawrence. And most likely, among other topics they might've discussed, I assume they spoke about the topic she broached with me." He set the tumbler down, folded his hands behind his back, and spread his feet shoulder width. "Your mother's living arrangements, whatever else they may entail, include a salient limitation that means Bawrence will be unable to live with her next year as previously arranged."

"Where's he going to live?"

"With me. I don't know who else would support him since no one else has any money."

"So I won't get the blue room next year?" Louis said. "Fuck! I mean... sorry. God damn it! I'm sick of sharing rooms."

"When I relayed to Faith the results of my phone call with Joanne, she expressed, shall we say, acute concern. She refers to Bawrence, when she's in a good mood, as a bed-wetting Neanderthal whom I spoil too much and who, perhaps as a result of a combination of factors, should be placed in special education for the rest of his life."

"Like for retards?"

"Let us call it a program for children who require extra-special care and attention and whose academic accomplishments may not be bound by the same standards of rigor as the mainstream student body." He scooped up the tumbler and slurped a wee nip. "Do you think I spoil Bawrence?"

"I was raking leaves in Kensington when I was younger than him," Dan said.

"Stephen says I shelter him too much."

"Want to make him a man, you've got to treat him like a man," Louis said.

"And here I was thinking I'd only be spending a hundred dollars a week at Super Fresh instead of two. Ah well."

With the last plate in the dishwasher, Dan grabbed the Fantastik from beneath the sink and set to polishing the counters and stovetop.

"I'm just fucking bummed I won't get the blue room. Damn you, Bawrence Barney!"

"And Daniel, you may very well be here next year. Assuming Temple accepts you, and I don't see why they wouldn't. Your grades are above average, right?"

"Sure, if you don't count English. But they're okay."

"As previously discussed, you may live here for the first four years of your attendance. If you haven't graduated by then, you may need to seek other living arrangements."

"Don't be a moocher!" Louis said. "That's my job."

Dan hadn't been accepted by Temple University, where Frank taught and where his kids, if accepted, would get tuition remission, because he never applied. Months ago he applied to and was accepted by the University of Maryland. He opted for Maryland because of its proximity to his biological father. Before he graduated next month, Dan would have to have a sit-down with Frank about living with Woody. He had only been four when Frank adopted him, Louis, and Peggy. While he used to visit Woody regularly during the Kensington years, Dan didn't see him more than once or twice a year now. Perhaps it was age or the proclivity for deeper introspection or self-reflection that comes therefrom, but now that Dan had grown up with this man who was legally his father, he wanted to live with the man who really was his father. He wanted to get to know Woody on an adult level. Perhaps he'd gain insight into the mindset that led to his letting Frank adopt his children.

"I won't get into Temple," Louis said. "I already know I'm repeating ninth grade." He laughed that trademark contagious laugh he inherited from Woody. Hearing his father's laugh wasn't helping to distract Dan. Every time he tried to predict how Frank would react to the idea of his moving in with Woody, it went wildly in one direction or the other, depending on nothing else but Dan's state of mind.

Frank slurped and examined the glass. "I admit that flunking a grade may create a stain on your academic curriculum vitae. But take heart, Louis. You have three more grade levels to redeem yourself.

And if worse does come to worst, you could attend Burlington County College and then transfer."

Dan started feeling nauseous. Life after high school suddenly seemed extremely unpleasant. "Barry must be super bummed."

"Super bummed?" Frank said as if he couldn't believe what he'd just heard.

Dan gave the counter one more wipe. "He was really excited about living with Mom." He threw the soiled paper towel away while Louis started flipping channels.

Frank stabbed the air. "I will make a prediction. Bawrence will adapt to the idea of living in a house where he is paid a fixed weekly income for doing menial work that costs very little of his time. This is what's called an advantageous cost-to-return ratio. Advantageous to him, by the way, not to me. I have no money. Apparently, someone thinks it's okay to go into my room and help themselves."

"That's fucked up," Louis muttered, still flipping.

Dan had no idea who took Frank's money, but that didn't stop him from feeling awful about it. Since the theft, he'd been seeking part-time employment so the old man wouldn't have to pay him his twenty-five-dollar allowance.

When he headed upstairs, Dan fully intended to do his US History homework. As soon as he cracked open the text to the chapter on civil rights, though, he thought it'd be a better idea to check in with his big sister.

Peggy split her sides when he told her about the stolen money. "He still doesn't use a wallet?"

"He prefers everything loose."

"Does that mean he never wears underwear?"

"He never wears jeans either."

"I forgot about that! Jesus!"

"What are you laughing at? You're the one who can't go to bed without the TV on."

"And when was the last time you tried falling asleep without talk radio?"

"It's like having bedtime stories read to you. What's wrong with that?"

"Who do you think stole the money?"

"Jonathan. Or Louis, I guess. It'd be easier to figure out if we only had one criminal in the house."

"Louis may be failing his freshman year, and he may prefer to hang out with black people in the ghetto, but I don't buy that he'd steal all that money. I love the kid, but he's not smart enough to get away with it."

"I just feel like shit. Karen hasn't been here in a while." He settled on his back and rubbed his eyes. "He's really stressed about Barry living here next year."

"Selfish asshole. How do you think Barry feels?"

Dan continued rubbing his eyes before letting his hands fall to his sides. One landed on the history text. "Fuck! I haven't even started my homework."

"The alcoholic?"

"He also coaches football. Louis says he's always like, 'Give us a look!' He repeats his lectures. Frank repeats a lot of shit too. Like when he saw *The Thing* when he was six and it scared the shit out of him when he was delivering papers."

"Martinis still?"

"Scotch."

"Have you told him about your grand plans?"

He didn't say anything.

"Pussy."

"I'm going to get a job. Something part-time. I want to contribute. You waited tables your senior year. I could do that."

"Doesn't your alcoholic history teacher work part-time at a liquor store?"

"I think so."

"Liquor stores are shit holes that attract creeps, but in this case that works for you, right? They're always looking for someone willing to suffer shit holes and creeps."

"But how do I work a register?"

"Let's see, the same way old people with turbans who don't speak any English do it?"

"But wouldn't I have to be old enough to drink? It's twenty-one now. I'm worried about Barry." Dan's head felt as leaden as one of Louis's weights. And he still had that goddamned homework to do. "Frank won't let me leave, will he? But why wouldn't he?"

After they hung up, Dan reached over to his nightstand and turned on the Top 40 radio station. Duran Duran's "Hungry Like the Wolf" was playing, a song which carried the sole distinction of making him think he was hearing Louis say he hated him. He knew it was all in his head, yet it never failed. Every time they said "I'm on the hunt down, I'm after you," Dan would hear "I'm on the hunt, Dan, I hate you!" Most of the time he could play it off, but tonight it was sticking in his craw. What the hell was wrong with him? He was barely a month away from the end of high school forever. Every other senior he knew was basking in the sunny climes of senioritis, blowing off homework if they weren't skipping class altogether, biding their time until the shackles of study hall and gym class and x equals who gives a shit and five minutes to get to your next class sloughed off like so much dead hide. After the umpteenth "I'm on the hunt, Dan, I hate you," he practically jumped on his clock radio and switched to AM and fiddled with the dial until he found Philly sports talk.

Next thing he knew, that same clock radio was blaring the arrival of six in the a.m. Dan jolted awake with his face in the text, dried spittle on Rosa Parks.

"What the fuck is your damage?" Veronica and Dan were sitting out on RV's front lawn during lunch, as were oodles of other kids, most in couples or cliques yet more loners than you might think. This was high school, don't forget. Since it was May, the weather was plenty pleasant enough, and the school administrators were flexible enough, to permit outside luncheon to those who wanted some natural light. "Earth to Danny, this is your Houston calling."

"You think Barry's all right?" Dan scarfed his last tater tot and chased it down with chocolate milk.

"Want to walk over and ask him? Like, I bet he could really use our help."

"What are you talking about?"

"He's adorable. I love Barry to pieces, but babe, he's Quasimodo. Like, that's why they pick on him so much."

"No one picks on him. He's in fourth grade. That's like being a senior over there."

"Becka's little brother goes there, second grade. He says other second graders totally pick on Barry because of his face and his last name and because he wets the bed."

"He doesn't wet the bed anymore."

"Dan..."

"Why would Becka even give a shit?"

"I'm just saying. I feel bad, you know?"

"He can deal," Dan said. "How does that saying go? If it kills you? Or wait, if it fucks you up but doesn't kill you..."

"You're so cute." She pecked him on the cheek and started picking at her string beans.

"He didn't come to dinner last night. You don't understand. Barry always comes to dinner. He always eats. He stole my barbecue chips at the pool. Right in front of me."

Veronica giggled. "I still can't believe he just walked in on us. Right? I told Becka and she was, like, whoa."

Only Peggy knew Dan's relationship with Veronica would soon be over. Veronica had nary an inkling of Dan's designs on Maryland and living with Woody. Until he told her the whole truth and nothing but, he had to make her think they were still a couple. A show of confiding was one way to do that. "I'm getting a job."

"What's that?" She kept picking at the string beans.

"We can't afford Karen anymore. Faith can't afford to send Alex to rock star camp or whatever it's called."

"I'll see if Daddy's willing to part with some money. How much are we talking?"

"Ronnie. We're not poor."

"Five hundred, right?"

"Maybe Laz could get me a job at that liquor store."

"Ew!" She leaned in and smooched him on the ear. "I will not let you work in a place like that."

"Just for a couple months."

"Babe, I can get Daddy to give you money if you need money. And then after high school, we'll totally move to Philly and get our own place. Center City so we're, like, halfway between Penn and Temple. And then we can both get part-time jobs. Daddy says it's good to have gainful employment while you're in college so that when you graduate, you have some experience. Preferably something related to your major, but it doesn't have to be, he says. Just so you have some work ethics."

"Ethic."

"Silly, that's what I said."

"Does Daddy Dearest know he'll be paying for our apartment?"

"Town house, dumbbell! And I'm not taking his money. I'm just telling him how much the new Mustang costs."

"But you're going to tell him it costs much more than it does so you can pocket the rest. I can't believe he wouldn't check with the dealership."

"I'm his only child. Of course he trusts me."

"Frank thinks any of us could have stolen the money."

"Can you blame the man?"

"Houston."

"What's that?"

"This is Houston calling. Not YOUR Houston. Barry would know that."

US History II was the eighth and final class of the day. Don't be fooled by the flat-topped barrel-chested teamster look of Laz. You see that tattoo on his upper bicep? It might be hard to tell what that is because of its age and the bicep having gotten meatier over the decades. All you need to know is that it was a Special Forces tattoo. Laz was in 'Nam. He never told his students this, but he didn't need to. Every year without fail, he would choke up a bit when the class arrived at the Vietnam chapter. The kids would exchange looks and understand. While he was also the varsity football coach, Laz dialed down the rowdy coach knob in the classroom while dialing up the passionate scholar. Sure, he might repeat the occasional lecture now and again due to short-term beer memory, but he made up for it with superlative oratory skills.

After class on this fine May Monday, Dan stepped up to Laz and figured the best way to broach the topic was point blank. "Are they hiring at the liquor store?" A few overheard him and smirked. Someone snidely asked his pal if Veronica's money wasn't good enough.

"What are you talking about, son? I've got some kids coming in for ninth. Sit over there. We'll talk in a few." He snorted and nodded his block head at a seat in the row farthest from the door, next to the windows overlooking the baseball practice field. Dan figured he could tackle some trig and make note of which problems to ask Frank and Faith for help on, which would most likely be almost all of them.

He was making decent headway before someone punched his shoulder and asked with nicotine breath: "The fuck are you doing here?" Jonathan made the one-piece wooden desk chair look puny and insufficient.

How was Dan supposed to talk to Laz with Double sitting here with that evil grin? Where the hell was Laz anyway? He looked around until he heard the gravelly yuk-yuks of the old veteran out in the hall with a couple of cheerleaders. "Struggling with civil rights."

"That must be why you have your trig out." Jonathan guffawed as he cracked open Western Civ. "Cool, cool, cool." He flipped through random pages. "Laz and Dad are trying to keep me indoors. But I'll always have golf."

"Frank never goes to those PTA meetings. He says they're bullshit."

"I think he stops at the liquor store on the way home from Temple. They're like twins separated at birth. Laz went to Vietnam and got all big and buff. Dad avoided the draft by staying in school until he got his doctorate."

"And they love the sauce."

"Me and Dad ran into Laz once at Cherry Hill Mall. They were laughing and making fun of me and shit. Naw, man. They're up to something. I can smell it. So what the fuck are you doing here? Where's your bitch?"

"Faith thinks I'm an idiot, and this can only help. And at least this lets me avoid her."

"Yeah-heh-heaaaah!" They high-fived.

"Frank thinks I'm stupid too. He's just nicer about it. Sorry, man, I don't have your dad's smart genes."

"Fuck him, man."

"My real dad doesn't even know how to pay bills. He was dumb enough to let Frank adopt his kids. And then there's my mom."

"Your mom's nice."

"She's fucking stupid. You know, instead of going to college? She went to one of those schools that teaches girls how to be good wives or some shit."

"They have those? Should we send Faith there?"

"I'm just happy high school is almost over because things need to change. Right now." Dan tried in vain to rub the exhaustion off his face. Initially he had no intention of telling Jonathan the real reason he was here, but suddenly he didn't give a shit. "What would you think if I got a job?"

"I'd steal all your money."

"I want to have money that I've earned."

"Yeah, bitch." They high-fived again. "That's how you do it."

"You're probably the richest person at 48 Broad."

"Dude, running a business has expenses."

"Someone stole a shitload of dough from the old man. I'll have to get a job soon anyway. A lot of college students get jobs. Look at you, you're just a freshman, and you work."

"Awesome, man. Go for it. Then you and I could pop open a couple of beers on the porch and shoot the shit about how much we hate our jobs. I can't do that with Dad. He didn't work at all during high school or college."

"But he played piano in a jazz band."

"Which of course got him laid and free admission on cruises and shit. Dude, put it here." This time the hand clasp was somewhere between a high five and a traditional handshake. "Congrats on stepping up and being a man. Shit, you do good enough? Maybe Dad can hire Karen back. Fuck knows we need her. Barry's room smells like shit." He guffawed and lowered his voice. "Dude, you see what happened to Stephen? He and the other band geeks were walking to gym, right? And they're all carrying their instruments. So the xylophone guy, right? He's in front. And after they pass through the gate and start going down to the entrance? Muh'fucker trips. Dude trips and falls and smashes the xylophone, and all the metal bars go fucking flying. Then Stephen and the giant violin guy are right behind him? And they both go bam! Hawwwww! Right on top of him. Fuck yeah, dude! Three geeks and a pile of instruments. Right there in front of all the hot varsity cheerleaders. Everyone's laughing their fucking asses off. Stephen jumps up and forgets his trumpet and hurries into the locker room with his head down like this and shit." Jonathan jumped up and ran in place with his head down and his arms swinging wildly. His guffaw sharpened into a cackle.

"Roggebusch!" Like a cannon on the opposite hill whose boom shook the entire valley, Laz announced his presence from the doorway. "I recall correctly, you've got a chapter to read with questions to answer. By end of period. Not done by then? Happy to have you for double overtime."

"You can't do that."

When the bell rang, Laz charged Jonathan's desk and snatched up his answer sheet and snapped the air with it. With his reading glasses still on his desk, he held it out until that tree-trunk arm was perfectly straight. "Get out of here, bum. Without you, we'll never make state. Go!"

"Ciao, brutha." Jonathan slapped the top of the doorjamb on his way out.

Laz slumped down at his desk and made a show of catching his breath. "Can't believe you two are brothers."

"I'm adopted."

"I'd've said he's the adopted one, but whatever."

"How's the liquor business going?"

"Come again?"

"Are they hiring?"

Laz started to drift. Then he snapped out of it and cleared his throat and used his jaw to adjust his dentures. "I had a private bet with myself that Jonathan was going to blow the whole assignment and come back tomorrow. But he tore through it faster than most students could." He cleared his throat and tongued his dentures. "Frank's a nice guy. Can't be easy with someone like Jonathan. Not to speak of the rest of you. No offense."

"Frank's one of the smartest people in the world, but no one got the smart genes."

"Have you thought of studying more?"

"Peggy was adopted too. She's my sister. But then she un-adopted herself somehow. She stayed in Maryland to finish high school and moved in with our old man. Our real old man."

"Fucking fascinating."

"So the liquor store..."

Laz shook the classroom as he paced. He reached a meaty hand in a desk drawer and came away with a bottle of something in a brown paper bag and pulled a deep swig. "Jonathan's a goddamned Arnold Palmer in the making. And I'm happy for him." He took another pull before slamming the bottle down and splashing a few drops onto Jonathan's answer sheet. "Scuttlebutt on the street says you want to work where I work."

"I need money."

"The hell for?"

"I'm starting college next year, and..."

"Where?"

"Maryland."

"Thought Frank taught at Penn."

"Temple."

"Same thing, different ghetto. What's your last name? Your real one?"

"Mine?"

"No, the asshole taking out the garbage."

"Woods. My real dad's name—"

"Why are you bullshitting me? You're Frank's child legally. You could get a good, solid, four-year college education for free."

Dan clenched his jaws. "Sometimes when I see my real father or talk to him on the phone, I call him Woody instead of Dad." For a second, not even a second, the smallest subdivision of a second, a scalding-hot flame forked his insides with hatred for Frank.

Laz tongued his dentures. "Had a buddy killed in 'Nam. Wife remarried. This new stepdad, never met him. But he adopted their kid. My buddy's kid. So he could have a dad again. Never met the guy, but that sounds like a swell gesture. But what Frank did? Adopting a shitload of kids whose real dad is still alive and living practically down the street? All due respect to Frank, he's a great guy, but that shit's just crazy. And it fucks you kids up forever." He took another pull and wiped his mouth on his bushy arm. "Job's yours."

For his New Thing that night, announcing his new gig at the liquor store was at the tip of Dan's tongue. Jonathan kicked him and faked a cough that, intentionally or not, wafted a nicotine stench over Dan that killed the words in their tracks. So instead, he said he was looking forward to working with George Taylor this weekend, planting all the new flowers around the house as well as the vegetable seedlings in Faith's produce garden.

"Baw-*rence*?"

"I'm not living with my mom next year. That's my Bad Thing forever."

The liquor store was on Route 38, too far to walk from 48 Broad. Taking Frank's Dodge Caravan was no sweat. Practically every week since he started dating Veronica last year, Dan had asked Frank if he could borrow the Caravan to take her out. Tonight he said he was heading to Veronica's so they could tackle the trig monster together. This fib of course had the added benefit of showing Frank and Faith they were off the tutoring hook for the night.

"You're late, Woods!" Laz stood behind the counter with hands pressed on the glass in a protesting-customer pose. Only his flattop and mustache were the same. Not only was his getup different—a white tee instead of a golf shirt, jeans instead of slacks or khakis—but his eyes were somehow different. These weren't the eyes of someone who'd been drinking, droopy and glazed and faintly bloodshot. No, these eyes were wide and alert and all-seeing like an owl's.

"It's nine-oh-two," Dan said.

"Think I want to stand here on your schedule? Owner of this place is an old Marine buddy of mine. Thing about Marines is, we don't like late. Not by a second. People come in, they're going to be in a hurry. No one wants to be out late if they don't want to be, right? You need to be quick on your feet. They have a question, man, you need to have the answer coming out of your pie hole before they're done asking. A lot of them will be foreigners. Whites are trending toward the minority in this country. The census tells us this, look it up. And 7-Eleven is not the only place where this stark reality is reflected. Get it? Now let's go over a few things. Think selling booze is easy? Well, it is. Then again, lighting a Bunsen burner should be a cakewalk, and yet look how many of you knuckleheads screw that up. Am I right?" Laz led Dan up and down the cramped aisles and refrigerated cases and shouted a perfunctory CliffsNotes version of the Official Liquor Store Training Course. "Questions?"

"Ever been robbed?"

"All liquor stores get robbed, my friend. It's as sure as shit and death and taxes. Last time I got held up, I beat the living piss out of the runt. I was going toe-to-toe with Viet Cong when that shit stain was a squirming little tadpole in his one-balled dad's nut sack. As for you, Woods, I would advise against the Chuck Norris approach. Anyone comes in with a gun or a knife and wants something, you give it to them, man. Now. A quick test. Name a single malt from Islay."

"Lava grueling."

"The fuck you call me?"

"Lava... Lah..."

"Lah, lah. Act like that in front of customers, next thing you know, a little old Puerto Rican lady will be holding you up for everything this store is worth. Lagavulin, moron. Now. Wine... Actually, I don't know shit about wine. Customers who want wine already know their shit, so you're off the hook with that one. But beer? Give me a good Milwaukee beer."

"How about Pabst?"

"Okay you're ready. See you in class tomorrow."

One small detail Laz had neglected was how to use the cash register. Fortunately, it wasn't rocket science, and Dan, thanks in large part to Frank and Faith, was accustomed to being pushed into the deep end. It was Dan, after all, who had figured out how to steam the wallpaper on the third floor after they moved in.

Nearly an hour passed before a customer showed up, a very patient elderly Asian woman whose smile never wavered while Dan wrestled with the correct sequence of buttons. When he finally did figure out how to ring up her twelve-case of Schlitz, her smile vanished like the sun after homeroom. Toward midnight some Hispanic guy stormed in saying in broken English that the rest of the night belonged to him until the "first scary Marine" showed up at dawn.

Almost every weeknight saw Dan at the liquor store from nine to midnight. At first he was harboring serious doubts about the viability of this venture. When you were a senior in high school and had a girlfriend, a job in and of itself, how realistic would a real job be? But when Laz gave him that first paycheck, he knew he'd made the right decision.

This was how he laid it out for George Taylor that weekend when the old warrior recruited him for the latest horticultural project. "Sure you can keep all that up, big guy?" They'd just finished up the flower bed at the front of the house and made to start on the Buttonwood side. "Just seems prudent you ought to focus on your studies before you worry about gainful employment. 'Sides, I thought Frank gave you a weekly sum. All youse guys should be focusing on building up good grades and moral character."

"I just want to carry my weight," Dan said. "That's what my

physics teacher says. He breaks us out in groups during lab, and everyone has a specific task. The only way the experiment works is if everyone does their thing."

"And you reckon you've got a certain role here?"

"I'm the oldest. I'm older than Stephen by two months. And the oldest is supposed to set an example." Dan hit his knee on the grass a bit too hard when he kneeled, spilling some of the seeds. He clenched his jaws.

They started planting down the Buttonwood side. Stephen's trumpet sounded so clear those music room windows may as well not have been there. At this point all these flowers looked the same. Dan used his sleeve to wipe the sweat. How did George do it? Dan was in shorts and a tee, and the May sun still scorched him. George wore that same long-sleeve camo-green button shirt with khaki pants, black shoes, and thick black socks. And while his face, with its craggy lines, did glisten here and there, the man wasn't betraying the slightest exertion.

"Funny you talking about carrying your own weight. That's how it works in the Army. In your platoon. Don't carry your weight, you get everyone killed. I went into construction after the war. Same deal. But your situation is different. I don't think Frank expects you to bring in money."

"He tell you someone stole five hundred dollars out of his sock drawer? What if someone in the platoon did something that slowed everyone else down? Like, I don't know, stole all the weapons so you and your buddies had nothing to fight with against the Germans."

"Don't believe Frank mentioned it."

"It was one of my brothers."

"Talk about this with any of them?"

"I don't know, a couple."

"So it's possible you've been talking about the crime with the guilty party."

As they shifted down the flower bed, Dan once again bopped his knee against the earth.

They arrived at the section of flower bed just below the stained glass window of the first-floor bathroom. "Frank's a good boy. Can't imagine why anyone would do that. It's more than the money, it's the trust. The idea of Hortense stealing anything from her parents would've been beyond belief."

George almost never mentioned his late wife's name, which was why it made Dan jerk his head forward the same way as that one time back in Kensington when he stuck his pinky into the socket because he thought Barry somehow lost one of his *Star Wars* figures in there and he wanted to be the Han Solo who found it. "It's not really Frank I'm worried about," Dan said. "It's Veronica."

"Oh boy!" George beamed through stained false teeth. "That is one pretty bird."

"She hates that I have a job. Especially in a liquor store. Especially in Lumberton." They were nearly at the steps now. At this point, Dan was accustomed to the putrid smell of the mulch, although his eyes still watered. "She lied to her dad because he says Lumberton's full of punks."

"Meh. Punks everywhere. Remind me to show you Berlin sometime."

"She doesn't have to work because her dad's rich. And her friend Becka and all her other friends come from rich families. They make me feel like such a lowlife piece of shit."

George made that guttural laugh that sounded like Freddy Krueger on a good day. "Your pretty bird should be proud to have a man who can carry more than his own weight and still keep up the grades and the sports." The old warrior paused, rested one hand atop the hoe, wiped his brow with his battleship-gray cap, and considered the street in both directions. "Look here, big guy. Pick your battles. 'Kay? Not everything's worth it. Whew. The heat, am I right? Couples grow apart. One of you will change too much for the other to keep up with. Now, you were drinking age? I'd take you to a bar and tell it like it is. Let's keep it moving, we're making good time here."

When the pungent heat smacked Dan's face and stabbed his eyes, he resolved to clear the air with Veronica on Monday.

"What the hell is your damage, Dan? It's like, seriously, you know?"

"Why do you talk like that? You're not from Hollywood, you've never been to Hollywood. Talk like a normal fucking person."

They were lunching and lounging on RV's front lawn. On today's menu was chili con carne, which, in Dan's experience, was hit and miss. Today it was quite the hit while Veronica picked at her mother's famous fruit salad.

"Check this out and tell me you're still mad." He dug his paycheck out of his jean pocket and unwrinkled it right up in her face.

"Oh gawd, how insulting. Just, like, tear it up or something."

"I fucking earned this. And I still got my homework done and got a B on my English test. The one you bombed? I'm carrying my weight, and you know who says that's rad? George Taylor."

"I'm totally thrilled you've got this great bond with an old man or whatever. I love my grandpa and don't know what I'd do without him. But I mean, what if you get robbed and they shoot you?"

He kept the check there and just looked at her.

"I've told you a million times. You can work next year when we're living together."

"My family doesn't have endless amounts of oil. Why do you always make me feel like this?"

"Like, you and George should become detectives and find out who took the money. Then you can quit that stink hole."

Veronica's reasoning was sound, but that would've only mattered if Dan wasn't so proud. As it was, her protests hardened his resolve. When Laz asked him after class if he was sure he could keep it up, Dan gave an overkill affirmative that included slamming his fist on his desk.

"Now that's what I call giving us a look. Well done, Woods Roggebusch."

On his way down the hall toward the school's parking lot exit, Dan made an impromptu detour to the front entrance. This way he could avoid Veronica and her clique. In no time at all she'd lose her patience and take off and have a girls' afternoon at the Cherry Hill

Mall, not because it was an awesome mall (even though it was), but because it was far away, and any mall that required a sincere effort to reach must be amazing. Veronica would come home, have a wonderful meal cooked up by her housekeeper, and finally call Dan, claiming she'd been stressed this whole time about why he hadn't shown up. Luckily, he wouldn't be home tonight.

Until then, Dan needed to take his mind off things, and that's where Barry came in. Folwell let its students out at three-oh-eight. Dan walked across the street and stood in the courtyard with a bunch of waiting parents. This was the same courtyard where he and Frank would await Barry's emergence through that door that Mrs. Miller, that looker, would stand against to hold open. Dan harbored no illusions that she'd remember him. That's why his heart leaped when her face froze on his when she came out to hold the door open. After a pregnant ten seconds, Mrs. Miller finally smiled and waved. Several more seconds passed before Dan realized he was grinning like a goof-ball. Where the hell was Barry? As if reading his mind, Mrs. Miller pointed over her shoulder.

"Fuck." Dan clenched his jaws and hurried around to the back. He spotted Barry heading in this direction with a chubby girl yapping his ear off. When Barry spotted him, he froze. The girl stopped yapping.

"Hey, Barry." The girl tugged at Barry's sleeve without looking away from Dan. "Is this the one brother who beats the shit out of you all the time? Hi, I'm Patricia."

Dan shook her hand. It felt like a marshmallow. "And I'm not Jonathan. My name's Dan. The good brother who saved Barry's life."

"Rad. See ya, Barry." She pecked him on the cheek and wobbled down the hill and across the field.

"Yuck." Barry wiped his cheek just as Patricia turned back and waved.

"Don't do that, man. At least not when she can still see you."

"I don't even like her, and she talks to me all the time."

Dan waited until they were on Broad Street, out of the schools' shadows, before he gave into the urge to talk in an attempt to purge his brain of Veronica and her gum smacking and faux Valley-speak. "How was school?"

"Fine."

"How was recess?"

"Fine."

"You play kickball?"

"I don't know."

"How'd that go?"

"Fine."

"Who's your teacher again?"

"Ms. Johnson."

"She sexy?"

"She's the fat black lady, and she's the nicest teacher in fourth grade."

"What's the deal with Patricia?"

"She talks to me all the time, and I hate her."

"Dude, she's sweating your balls. Ask her out already."

"Ew! People say she's got cooties and had sex with her cousin."

"Her cousin hot?"

"Ewwwwwww!"

"She lives close enough, you could sneak out at night."

"She lives in Eastampton, but her parents are getting divorced just like my mommy and daddy."

"*Our* mom and dad."

"She's moving with her mom and brothers to Hainesport, so she'll be going there next year instead of Holbein. Her mom drives the school bus. Patricia wants to be a dancer, but she's too fat."

"You don't tell her that, do you?"

"Dancers are skinny, everyone knows that."

"You told a girl she's fat, and she still adores you. Dude, that's love."

"She doesn't like video games, and she makes fun of my Garbage Pail Kids."

"Ronnie hates sports and makes fun of how dumb I am at math. You don't have to have everything in common."

"She's not my girlfriend. Gross!"

"That's kind of cool, your being at separate schools next year. When Ronnie and I get into a fight, it sucks because we have to see each other the next day. It's awkward."

"What's awkward?"

"Wet the bed last night?"

"I don't know."

"The way you feel when you wake up in your own piss? That's how I feel when I see Ronnie at school after we've had a spat."

"What's a spat?"

"You still bummed about not living with Mom next year?"

"I don't know."

"She loves you very much. You know that, right?"

When they reached the house, Dan unclenched his jaws and looked up and down the flower beds with a satisfied smile. Barry huffed and puffed up the stairs, his WWF backpack bouncing up and down on his chubby ass and making the Velcro binder clonk against the lunchbox.

The solitude of the liquor store, starkly lighted though it was, was just the balm Dan needed. Who knew a fluorescent hum could sound so sublime? When he looked over at the glass doors, all he saw was the store repeated. During the lull after each passing car, he was the only living thing in the universe. That's why he stared at the Camaro pulling into the lot like it was an extraterrestrial.

For one bone-chilling moment when the woman was stepping out of the Camaro, Dan thought it was Mrs. Miller. His fears were allayed as she stepped into the fluorescence. No, of course it wasn't Mrs. Miller. She was too pure to go to the liquor store this late on a school night. This woman, stepping so lithely through the door the bells jingled only once, was more like Mrs. Miller from a parallel universe. She was about the same age and just as attractive, perhaps a touch more so, at least for now, because of the mystery. Her hair was the same light brown, only longer and less tamed. The final difference, small yet huge, was the absence of a wedding ring.

He clenched his jaws. With his luck, she'd ask him about a particular brand or product and make him trip over a bullshit answer. But this fear also turned out to be unfounded. She knew exactly where to get Sapphire gin and beef jerky. Even with the height advantage of the raised floor behind the counter, Dan was only an inch or two taller.

"Mind if I smoke?" Without waiting for an answer, she dug out a pack of Camels, the same brand Dan's mom smoked. Only after she'd taken a couple of puffs did he realize he hadn't scanned her items yet.

"Find everything you need? Ma'am?"

She continued puffing and exhaling and considering the specimen before her. The way she squinted, a kind of gaze Dan had never seen before, made him vacillate between thinking she was going to dare him to do something outrageous one moment and stamp out the cigarette on his eye the next. He was so lost in the smoke that he started at the otherwise soft sound of a crumpled bill dropped on the counter.

"Here's your change, ma'am. And thank you so much for shopping with us." Did he really just say that?

"Amanda. I usually don't tell child cashiers my name, but I'm so fucking desperate for you to stop calling me ma'am." She grabbed a pen from atop the register and scribbled something on the receipt. "Sorry about the girl trouble."

"It's not trouble, ma'am. Amanda."

"Girls are bitches. Why do you work here if you don't need to?"

"Have to carry my own weight, ma'am. 'Manda." Shit. He clenched his jaws.

She grabbed the bottle and beef and gave Dan an annoyed look before whipping her hair around and clapping her heels out the door (three chimes this time) with what he was sure was the same official gait she used at whatever important office she worked at doing whatever important job she had.

"Oh shit! Sorry! You want a bag? Amanda!" She roared away in her Camaro.

Of course, if he'd had a pair of stones twixt those thighs, he'd go to that address she'd scrawled on the receipt and ask her what she did for a living. And offer a proper apology for not offering to bag her purchase. And talk to her without ever addressing her as ma'am. And otherwise make up for all the fuckups littering the past two minutes. Laz had told him that drinking on the job was totally cool so long as he paid for it and didn't get caught. Dan laughed it off because he couldn't imagine actually doing that. Of course, that was before Amanda. As luck would have it, Frank gave him this week's allowance yesterday so he had more than enough to purchase a sixteen-ounce of Oranjeboom, a Dutch lager Laz had recommended to the point of nearly losing his dentures. Could Dan trust a beer he couldn't pronounce?

He'd barely slurped his way through half the can when the idea of paying Amanda a visit seemed the most natural thing in the world. Her address was in Hainesport, just a hop and skip down 38.

Thanks to there not being a single streetlight in this farm community-cum-subdevelopment in flux, Dan drove by the house twice before he figured out he was in the right place. "Never make a woman wait. That's the first rule." She was wearing a thick bathrobe that reminded him of what the mom wore in *A Christmas Story*. A smile crept at the corners of her lips.

Her house looked somewhat similar to 48 Broad, old and historic, only it was two stories instead of three. The bedside lamp upstairs provided the only light. By the time they reached her room, Dan's mouth was dry as George Taylor's scalp. Was he really here? He kept his hands in his pockets to mask the sweat and trembling.

"On or off?" Letting the robe collapse around her feet, she stood on a little island of *Christmas Story* plush. Her hips were wider than Veronica's, her tits sagged more, and in general she had more meat on her bones. Yet Dan was far more turned on by this woman than Veronica.

"I'm obviously on."

Another smile twitched her mouth. When she flicked off the lamp, the darkness seemed more pitch than outside. He didn't move an inch. She planted a kiss and proceeded to undress him. With her guidance combined with his proclivity for adaptive learning, he was a pro in no time.

He was not a pro, however, at endurance.

"First time eating pussy," she said.

"Uh-huh."

"I wasn't asking."

Dan felt like he was melting into the pillows. "I lost my virginity last week. My brother walked in on us. But I didn't get pissed like I sometimes do over stupid shit. I was just..."

"Terrified?"

"I guess. A bunch of things. And then Barry comes in and asks if I want to play the Commodore."

"You didn't even know what a Commodore was. Not at that moment."

Damn, this woman was good. Was it too soon to ask what she did for a living?

"Litigator."

What the hell...?

"Kind of lawyer who argues a lot."

"Rad."

"Was it her first time too?"

"She said it was."

"Go down on her, and you won't fight so much. You heard it here first."

"I have to break up with her. How should I do it?"

"I just want you to know this isn't *The Graduate*, okay?"

"Uh-huh."

"You even know what that means?" She lit a cigarette.

"That smells good. I think Frank's mentioned it. Sounds so fucking familiar."

"And Frank is...?"

"My dad."

"You address him by his name?"

"I'm adopted."

"Drink? I'll be right back."

Dan needed to get the hell out of here. He had homework, and then before homeroom tomorrow he was supposed to meet Ronnie and Becka and a few other friends in the library for a last-minute trig cram.

Even late at night and sipping Sapphire and tonic in her birthday suit, Amanda still walked with purpose. They got comfy against the pillows before she handed him a beer. Dan squinted at the logo through the darkness.

"Iron City. My ex drank it."

"So what do you argue about?"

"With my ex?"

"I have to go. I guess. Sorry."

"What happened to your real parents?"

"This one time when Frank was drunk, he told me he still loves my mom. Why would they get divorced then?"

"Money. I would surmise Frank adopted you guys thinking you'd conveniently forget your real father but that your real father would still help out somehow, pay child support. Which makes no fucking sense because once you were no longer legally his, he had a case to never pay a dime again. So Frank bleeds money. How to stanch the bleeding? Throw a stick of dynamite into the mechanism causing the bleeding—that would be the family—and blow it to bits. I'd give a lot of my own money to have a sit-down with your mom. Then I'd tell Frank he's got shit for brains."

Dan took a long pull from Iron City. He'd have to tell his buds about this. "Shit, man. You want to hear fucked up? He thinks I'm going to Temple next year. I never even applied. I'm going to Maryland. I'm moving in with my real dad. Frank has no idea."

"Why would he think you're going to Temple? No offense to Temple."

"It's where he teaches. Free tuition."

"And you said no to that? The fuck ate your brain?"

"If you lived in that house, you'd understand."

They continued sipping and staring into the void. "Frank drink? You said he was drunk."

"Scotch."

"It's simple. Wait till he's having scotch in his favorite chair. Then lay it out for him straight."

"I guess." He wanted to clench his jaws, but Iron City was liquefying him.

"It's all in the delivery. I do this for a living. Pad the shit out of it, tell him he's a rock star for adopting you, you're so grateful he's been there for you. All hail Frank."

He took another swig. God damn, she was a genius.

"Your stepmom, you get along with her?"

"Everyone fucking hates her."

"All the more reason to give her ass a little smoochie. Frank will appreciate that. Now let's fuck one more time, and then I need to get some sleep for a deposition at dawn's ass crack. Finished?"

Dan was wired when he pulled up to 48 Broad at three in the morning. His head was spinning with everything he needed to do over the next twenty-four hours, starting with the homework he had to do right now. If he wanted to talk with Frank tomorrow before going to the liquor store, it might be too early for the scotch.

He paced in front of the steps and imagined all the ways the conversation could go. Occasionally he'd stop to take in the stars. The night was remarkably clear. At one point he spotted someone, ever so briefly, looking down at him from Barry's room.

During the pre-homeroom trig cram, Dan was the definition of distracted. The only time he spoke was when he disagreed with Veronica about a particular problem that he knew how to solve thanks to a recent tutoring session with Faith. Veronica assured him she was right and moved on to the next problem, which only incensed him further. Faith's ironclad clarity rang in his ears when he raised his voice in the otherwise dead-quiet library.

This made lunch more stressful than necessary because he had to spend the bulk of the hour on RV's front lawn on this otherwise gorgeous day, putting on a show of contrition. That meant laughing at Veronica when she wasn't remotely funny.

During history class, Laz repeated the lecture from yesterday.

Usually this was just harmless fun for Dan. Not today. He simply didn't have the patience. Barely ten minutes in, when it became clear this would be the longest eighth period ever, he shot his hand up and didn't wait to be called on. "You said all this yesterday!"

Laz stopped pacing and smiled. Dan almost forgot those were dentures. "Think I'm drunk, don't you?"

"But you said all this! *Brown v. Board*, we get it!"

"Know why I do it, Hoss? We've got kids here who are slow. And since they're not in special ed, then these morons need all the help they can get. I know what you punks say behind my back. I don't drink during the day. Ninth period doesn't count. Do I like scotch? Guilty. As is the man playing your father. But that's all we're guilty of. We clear on this point, Woods Roggebusch? Everyone?"

Dan avoided the parking lot again and headed home alone. The only thing he thought of, the only thing he had the energy to think of, during the walk down Broad Street was Amanda's advice about Frank. Was that really wise? Talking to Frank on scotch was like not studying for a Spanish vocab quiz. No, he needed the old man sober.

Jonathan, Louis, and Tanisha were playing the Olympics on the Commodore 64 in the poolroom. John was parked on the pedestal in the kitchen, watching cartoons on the black-and-white. Alexander and one, perhaps two, of his friends were jamming in the music room. That electric bass reverberated across the entire first floor. Stephen was kicking back in Frank's recliner, chasing Soft Batch with Tab while taking in his umpteenth viewing of *Conan the Destroyer*. Gorbie was mopping his nuts in Faith's chair.

Dan eventually found his way to his desk in the third-floor hallway niche and gripped his head in his hands and gazed futilely at the inscrutable trig problems mocking him from those musty pages.

"Hello, Gorbachev!"

He craned his neck and saw Frank just back from his three-mile jog in his Temple tee and shorts. He always capped off the run with push-ups and sit-ups on the grass. Before he knew what he was doing, Dan was hurrying downstairs. The old man was gasping through the sit-ups when he stepped out on the side porch. Watching

Frank do sit-ups was agonizing. He never quite made it through the full motion of an actual sit-up because of his substantial midsection. Those last few weren't even semblances of sit-ups, just a sort of bizarre nonmoving movement that made Frank take the most tortured breaths Dan had ever heard. Not even Coach Masters breathed that hard after reading the riot act during basketball practice.

As he dragged himself to his feet, Frank emitted the human equivalent of a centuries-old door turning on hinges that hadn't turned in living memory. "Becoming the paradigm of blue twisted steel isn't easy, I'll say that."

"I need to talk to you about Maryland."

"Collecting!"

They both turned to see Kyle, the *Burlington County Times* paperboy with the spiked blond hair, hopping up onto the sidewalk with his little spiral notebook of lime-green cards.

"Ah yes," Frank said. "Tending to today's profit, I see."

"Two dollars."

Frank turned back to Dan. "Let me see to the child's profit. I wouldn't want him to starve to death and die because I neglected his entrepreneurship."

Dan sat on the porch while Kyle loitered on the sidewalk and looked up and down Buttonwood as if expecting someone. Frank eventually came back out with two ones plus a quarter for a tip. "That ought to tide you over with bubble gum until the next time."

Kyle darted down the street and around the corner with an ivory-toothed look of pure glee. For an instant Dan would've given anything to be that age again. And not adopted.

"Daniel. Before we have our discussion about your chosen topic, let me get a soda water and two slices of bread with peanut butter. Would you like a refreshment?"

"That's okay." As if matted pits weren't bad enough, all of a sudden he had to take a monster shit. He was willing that infernal turtle back inside when he was struck by the clarity that he should've talked to Frank weeks ago.

Barry's footsteps startled him. His little brother plodded up the steps without looking at him. "Barry." He turned to Dan with an exasperated look on half his face. "Sometimes I wonder if Double's right and you're completely fucked up."

"You're an asshole!"

"Baw-*rence!*" Frank emerged with two cans of soda water and a plate of peanut butter bread cut into quarters. "Quit your goddamned cussing."

As Barry disappeared into the house, Stephen could be heard calling out in mock anger: "Bawrence Barney! Stop eating all the cookies! Stop wetting the bed! Empty the garbage!"

The only thing keeping Dan together at this point was the thought of sex with Amanda. If she didn't show up tonight, he'd call her to tender his reward. Something had to go right today.

When Frank sat down, he dove into that peanut butter bread with a vengeance, chomping and smacking throughout the conversation.

Eventually the words started coming with gradually less effort. More than once Dan reiterated that he wasn't asking what Peggy had asked three years ago. More than that, if Frank wasn't okay with it, then he'd stay and go to Temple and only visit Woody when he had the time. If Frank was indeed okay with it, he'd be in no way, shape, or form obligated to provide financial support.

The old man shoved the last quarter of peanut butter bread into his mouth and chewed and chomped good and long. "That was a very thoughtful and well-thought-out proposal, Daniel. It's true, I'm still a little sore at your sister for asking me to support her college education even though she was, in essence, disowning herself from me. So I appreciate your sensitivity to that. This is a complex issue. And yet it's not. In the end, you just want to get to know your real father. Who doesn't understand that? Tell you what. I will give it some thought. Not in a bad way. But you know, you took the time, so I want to take the time. Fair enough?"

To say that Dan was positively steamed as he double-stepped up to the third floor wouldn't have done justice to his indignation. What the hell just happened? He parked himself at his desk and glared at his trig through wet, bloodshot eyes.

Faith pulled up in her VW Rabbit. Dan resented every tooth in that smile as Frank came down the steps and reciprocated her Rockwellian greeting.

And who the hell was Barry talking to in his room? Dan jumped up and strained his ears. His brother stopped talking as he emerged into the hallway. Dan met him at the stairs. "Dude, what's the problem?"

As Barry made to head down, Dan shot out a long, lanky arm and snagged a fold in the back of his Transformers tee and yanked him back up to the landing and let him fall onto his back. "Asshole!"

Dan squatted down and kept his voice low. "You need to shape the fuck up and learn how to behave. No one likes you because you're a dick."

Barry sat up and made to regain his feet. This only doused Dan's flame all the more. When he slapped Barry in the head, he knew he'd swung too hard, but it felt too goddamned good to care. That's why he did it again. And again. Barry ducked back to the ground and squealed something unintelligible.

One positive to come out of the kerfuffle was Dan's second wind. Now he had the energy to bite off a hunk of his trig by the time Veronica called. The second he picked up the phone, he decided he'd help Frank make dinner in addition to performing his regular dishwashing duty. This would assuage his guilt about Barry while also providing him an out from this call.

"Becka's dad's brother's in town and they're, like, having this big mega outing to the Phillies game Saturday. Becka says they've got two extra tickets and junk."

"Sure." It was the last thing he wanted to do, and that was a shame. Like Louis, Dan was a sports omnivore. Had almost anyone besides Veronica asked him to a Phillies game, he would've gushed forth with an unqualified affirmative. When he heard Frank thump downstairs, he jumped up and checked the digital clock in his room: five thirty. Frank, buffed and polished and redolent of Old Spice, would park himself in the living room with a scotch and soda to complement either peanuts or cheese and crackers. At six he'd head into the kitchen to watch Dan Rather on the black-and-white while making dinner. But Veronica wouldn't know any of that. She didn't need to. "Sorry, gotta go, gotta help with dinner."

Burgers and Tater Tots were on the menu tonight. No sooner did Dan start helping the old man shape the ground chuck than Faith stopped playing piano and marched down to the kitchen, ostensibly to fetch a can of V8. On her way out, she stopped abruptly and asked Dan about what he'd done on the third floor. At least she was keeping her voice casual. This helped him stay calm and not miss a beat with the patties. "He was being rude. It reminded me of what you said about how he should be nice even if he's ugly."

"And you hit him?"

"Not hit."

"On the head? How hard?"

"It wasn't a punch."

"Did you hit him pretty hard?"

"I mean, I wouldn't call it hitting. Maybe pushing. Nothing like what Jonathan does to him every day." The slimy coolness of the meat helped balance out the heat of that glare burning a hole in his peripheral vision.

Frank grabbed the two big bags of Tater Tots from the freezer chest in the laundry room and poured them out on an aluminum-foiled cookie sheet.

Faith abruptly retracted the glare and thumped back to the music room where she slid the door shut. Dan stayed in the kitchen and pretended to be interested in the news while questions bounced around his skull. How long did Frank need to think about it? Would he seek input from Faith? How could Dan end it peacefully with Veronica? How long would the affair last with the *Christmas Story* litigator? How long should he keep up the liquor store job?

If Frank said no, then what?

Dan knew the Tots were done when their heavenly carb smell

achieved just the right degree of thickness and warmth. Faith marched back into the kitchen while he was taking them out.

"Gorbachev went number two in the master bathroom today." She turned her glare on Dan. His peripheral vision exploded into smithereens. "I disciplined him. But I didn't hit him as hard as Dan hit Barry."

Dan was in the act of setting down the Tots when she said that. For reasons he never understood, her mentioning his hitting Barry as part of an otherwise unrelated topic, especially a topic that included her own brutal treatment of Gorbie, cooked his temper like one giant Tot, without the carb smell. "WHY DON'T YOU GO FUCKING CODDLE HIM LIKE A BABY?" And on "BABY" he slammed the Tots down on the stovetop and stormed out.

"Why don't you learn how to treat your brother?"

"Why don't you...!" What? He hadn't a clue. Best to get upstairs and as far away from her as quickly as his long legs could hop two steps at a time.

"You're sexy, Daniel!" someone called out from the poolroom.

He didn't realize he was out of breath until he reached his desk. His heart pounded his ears the way Faith's bare feet did the floor. One look at his trig and he decided to get the hell away from that too.

He ran through the rarely used two sets of double doors at the front of the house and jumped down the steps, leaving nothing but air between his Converse and the "48."

Dan walked and huffed for ten or fifteen minutes before he had any idea where he wanted to go. By the time he decided the liquor store would be the wisest destination, he was in Eastampton, on the other side of Mount Holly from Lumberton. It ate up nearly two hours to walk to work. He got there with just a few minutes left on Laz's shift. Those few minutes of shooting the shit with his history teacher were the best of Dan's day. Hell, month.

During the downtime, he called Amanda and willed with all his might to keep his voice even as he related his conversation with Frank and everything else. "It's driving me nuts, that fucking place."

"He wasn't expecting it. He's got a lot on his mind, okay?"

"Fuck you."

He looked around at all the booze—the cases, the six-packs, the single, standalone, robust cans and bottles—and lent serious consideration toward indulging. Then he turned around and considered the porn mags on the top rack. Laz had told him he was free to peruse so long as he was discreet about it (Laz always used one of the golf magazines as the "cover"). Dan spotted one particular pair of come-hither eyes looking right at him.

A Camaro roared to a stop on the other side of the glass. Not only did Amanda's abrupt appearance tie his tongue, so did her garb. Instead of business attire, tonight was all about supersexy casual, complete with a sleeveless top and a frilly skirt that barely reached her knees. She took her time perusing the aisles, affording him a full-on look several times over thanks to those round corner ceiling mirrors. The sleeveless top was also backless, so he could enjoy how that well-toned back gracefully met the curvature of her ass.

Eventually she ended up at the counter empty-handed. "Can't decide what I want. And I'm not in the mood for beef jerky. Any thoughts?"

"Maybe a Zero. Barry loves those."

Once again with a languid pace that belied her purpose, she walked around the counter. Her hand, with those freshly manicured nails, greeted his erection. She squatted down.

Dan focused on those come-hither eyes. No, that wasn't helping. How about the video game mag? No, that just reminded him of Barry and John on the Commodore. Christ, what then?

She bit him.

"What the fuck?"

"Focus."

When Veronica seemingly materialized out of thin air on the other side of the counter, Dan grew dizzy and fell over. When he came to, Amanda was standing next to his girlfriend with a hand on her shoulder. Veronica's eyes were bloodshot pools. Behind her stood Becka and several others, her clique, dolled up and feather-haired, smacking pink gum and smelling even better than that. Dan went from cold to numb to without limbs. He spotted that couple who'd been dating since Folwell. What were their names? The guy liked race cars.

"Let's go, sweetie." Amanda put her arm around Veronica and led her outside where her Camaro had been joined by a pride of other equally expensive and sporty cars.

A few of them went outside to help console Veronica. Of those who stayed, some perused the aisles while the rest hovered around the counter to study Dan. The race car guy and a couple of his buds chucked insults and expressions of disbelief.

"Dude, you're my new idol."

"You're fucking toast, Roggebusch."

"You were going to break up with her anyway, weren't you?" Becka blew a bubble. "Girls can tell these things." Her gum's watermelon smell wafted over Dan like a bracing breeze. However wrong it may have been to feel this way at this particular moment, Dan thought, for the first time ever, that Becka was kind of adorable.

"I don't know."

"Why are you working here anyways? So yucky."

"It's where party people come to get their party on, Becka." One of the guys was holding up a small keg.

"Put that down," Dan said. "Unless you intend to buy it."

"Or what?"

"Or Laz kicks your ass back into the Stone Age, fucko."

Fucko put the keg down.

Dan squinted through the glass and could just make out Amanda and Veronica's silhouettes where the parking lot met Route 38.

"I thought your dad was rich."

"He's not my dad. He fucked everything up."

"Wait. What?"

"I have to leave." He looked back at Becka and couldn't help smiling at her button-nosed cuteness. "You didn't take the money, did you?"

She slowed her gum chewing as she studied him. "Fly's down, Roggebusch." She flicked her hair.

Fucko appeared out of nowhere with a six-pack of wine coolers. "Yo, Becka, use your fake ID to get this."

"Fuck off."

The bells jingled as Amanda and Veronica walked back in. The former's hand was still on the latter's shoulder. Veronica's eyes, still red, were at least dry now. Mostly. When she opened her mouth and hesitated, Amanda whispered in her ear.

"It always made me feel weird when you, like, like, pretended to think I was funny and junk."

"I don't know."

"I'm not an idiot, Daniel. I was picking my battles."

"Pick your battles," he repeated. "My mom told me that once."

"The one who adopted you or the real one?" Becka asked.

"I won't miss your fake laugh. But I will miss other things."

"Breathe, just breathe," Amanda said.

"I mean if you're, like, totally into it, we could still do trig."

"That would be pretty rad."

"You're lucky your father is so smart at math."

"He's not his real father, Ronnie," Becka said. "Gawd, get a clue."

"I'm sorry, Ronnie. I'm really, really sorry."

It started drizzling while Amanda was driving him home. "That was your get-out-of-jail-free card."

"Yeah."

When they arrived at 48 Broad, she got out and stood beside him to take in the house and the sky. "Want to understand women? You need to understand this house. Houses like a little mystery. They like to leave you guessing."

Dan wasn't sure how long they'd been standing there when the stooped silhouette of Boss Hogg appeared, walking his dog up Buttonwood. Moving so slowly he wasn't sure what they were doing until they were halfway there, Hogg and his dog ambled out into the center of the intersection. The dog wasn't going to the bathroom or sniffing around or doing much of anything. Like his master, he just sort of looked around here and there, up Buttonwood, down Broad. If they saw Dan and Amanda, they made no show of it. Whenever the pooch did dip his schnozzle to the asphalt, Hogg nodded his own ancient face toward the ground.

Dan grabbed Amanda's arm. "I'm never coming back here."

The dog, no longer in sync with its master, peered up Buttonwood toward the Mount. It made the faintest murmur. Hogg's face was still angled downward. And then that bald creature toppled over on its side with a final, phlegmatic exhalation.

Dan passed out.

"Daniel!"

His eyes snapped open to Frank and Faith's faces hovering over him with that huge ancient tree surrounding their furrowed brows like a wreath. "I only got a job to earn money and help Frank." They helped him to his feet.

A pair of Mount Holly's finest were interviewing Hogg who, in the harsh glare of police lights, looked less sad and more confused. A sheet covered the dog. It had been about the same age as Dan.

"Sad," Frank said to no one in particular. "Heart just stopped beating. Your friend's gone home, by the way."

On his way to the front door, Dan caught the eye of one of the officers. "Say hi to Jonathan for me, would ya?" The cop cracked a smile and tipped his cap.

Dan headed up to his room and called Peggy and spilled everything.

"You could've at least waited until after prom."

"I'm not going." He cracked open his trig.

"Losers, nerds, and geeks don't go to the prom. Someone like you always goes."

"Are you going to marry that chiropractor and move to Florida?"

"Daniel..."

"Mom thinks you should drop him like a bad habit."

"And Mom's such an expert at marriages. That must be why she got dumped by not one but two different husbands."

"Dad didn't dump her. She left him for Frank."

"I was there when Dad came back from the Caribbean and left

Cathy's panties on the bed. On purpose. I was sitting right there with my dolls."

Four problems to go. Holy shit, would he do it? The only puzzle was why it was Amanda's voice, and not Frank or Faith's, urging him on.

"Know what you can do to seal the deal? Get Dad up there."

"Frank?"

"What?"

"Which dad?"

"Our dad. Dad."

"What are you talking about?"

"Get him up there. He can talk to Frank about why you should move."

"Sometimes I can't tell if you're joking." Two problems to go. "Drive three hours to talk to the guy who stole his wife and adopted his kids?"

Raccoons broke into a sprint above Dan's room in that gap between the ceiling and the roof. Their claws scraped and scratched from one side to the other. He remembered when that always used to startle him his first year here. Right now it only made his pencil scratch faster across the blue-lined, loose-leaf notebook.

While Peggy continued promoting the idea of an in-person meeting between Frank Roggebusch and Woody Woods, Dan proceeded to solve, no, coast through the final problem, at two in the morning, fresh off breaking up with his girlfriend after having gotten caught getting a blow job by an older woman in a liquor store. "HELL YES!"

He hung up and collapsed onto his back as the raccoons scratched and scrambled some more. As he was giving in to sleep, something or someone shuffled out in the hallway. A raccoon? Dan jumped out of bed and stuck his head out. Nothing. Barry and Jonathan's half of the hallway was dark.

Soon as he stepped back in and closed the door, the shuffling returned. Any second now he was expecting foot shadows to appear.

Instead, a trumpet blasted.

Dan sighed as he collected his trig and slid it back into his back-pack. "This fucking house."

By Saturday Frank still hadn't given him an answer. If George Taylor hadn't come over to continue the yard work, Dan would've driven himself nuts with the circle of anxiety. Right now they were in the backyard doing battle with more weeds than Dan had ever known in his life.

"I broke up with Ronnie."

"I figured. Eh... eh..." The first time Dan heard George emit those "eh... eh..." sounds, he thought the old warrior was going to his glory.

"It was a mess."

"Usually is. Eh... eh..."

"We have nothing in common. I didn't see it before."

"Eh... eh... It's high school, big guy. This is when Daniel is intro-duced to Daniel. Failed relationships help with that. Funny, right?"

"But you and Hortense met when you were in high school. And the Grandparents Roggebusch. They met in junior high."

"So much in life depends on luck. Worst thing you can do is hold up how life worked for someone else and expect it to apply to you."

"So depressing."

"Only problem you really have right now is you're a teenager. Eh...eh... That'll pass." George chucked the weeds into his sack, stood up, and wiped off his gloves. The gleaming sweat heightened and deepened his face's crevices so that they looked like fissures fit to spew steam. "Okay, big guy. Get started on Faith's here garden. I need to water the front of the house. Mind binding this up? Appreciate it, buddy."

Dan had just started tilling the vegetable garden when Frank emerged, followed by a panting Gorbie.

"Daniel, sir! I'm here to discuss the prospect of your living in Maryland. Or rather, I'm here to offer you my take on the Maryland situation since I haven't actually arrived at what I would call a decision."

Dan stopped tilling. For a few seconds the only sound in all of New Jersey was George's distant "Eh... eh..." Then Gorbie scratched his ear with teeth-baring earnestness before plopping down in the vegetable garden to mop his sack.

"Let us call it an interim decision. And the interim decision is, I'm still weighing the costs and benefits of your moving to Maryland to live with Woody."

"Let's get my dad up here." Frank's face, always studying, always piercing, froze. "It's a huge deal, right? Then we can discuss the costs and benefits in person."

The old man stroked his mustache and picked his nose ("Eh... eh..."). "That's an interesting suggestion."

"My real dad's presence would make your deliberation go more expeditiously." Never in his life could Dan remember uttering such an adult-level statement. And never would he figure out how he'd managed to do it just now.

7

LOUIS

FLASH FLUNKEE AND STRONG UNSAFETY

L ouis's favorite show was *Miami Vice*. Watching Crockett and Tubbs carry the torch for the drug wars offered the perfect escape from reality. If there was a better way to unwind after another brutal week of ninth grade, Louis didn't know of it.

As you'd expect from a fourteen-year-old jock with a girlfriend, though, Louis wasn't always home Friday nights. You take this particular May Friday as a for instance. While his kid brother Barry glued himself to one of the kitchen pedestals to watch *Miami Vice* on the little black-and-white, Louis was heading to the Gardens, Mount Holly's mostly black neighborhood, to hang out with Tanisha.

Not only was she not home, but no sooner did he reach the front door than her younger brother Devon, a twelve-year-old repeating fifth grade, and a pack of his friends stormed out and beat the shit out of him.

Since he began dating Tanisha, Louis had become the Barry to Devon's Jonathan. Tanisha swore she'd convince their mother to ship Devon off to the same military school in Connecticut to which their older brother had been exiled. Devon assured Louis that even if he did go to Connecticut, he knew enough people in the Gardens to complicate Louis's well-being indefinitely.

"Your stupid ass wasn't going out with her, we wouldn't have to do this all the time!"

"Your sister is special, Devon," Louis said as he stood up, wiping off the blades of grass. His right elbow and both knees throbbed. Bells tolled in his skull. "I can only follow my heart."

"Your heart's heading that way, so you better follow it the fuck out of here."

During the walk home, Louis stopped by the Mount Holly Pharmacy. A kid his age with a mullet waited in line behind him and stood a little too close. When it was Louis's turn at the register, the kid all but growled down his neck. Louis knew who he was. Well, he didn't know who specifically, but he knew in general it was one of those heavy metal-loving evil-N-word-spouting punks who sometimes jumped him on the way home from school.

Louis couldn't worry about him right now. He paid for his two tins of Copenhagen tobacco and hurried out. Normally, the idea of doing homework on a Friday night was anathema, and now that failing ninth grade was a fait accompli, really, what was the point? But as someone who thrived at athletics—a freshman starting safety for the varsity squad—Louis grasped better than most the importance of momentum. If he could get some wind at his back going into the summer, maybe it would carry him through summer school and into his second attempt at being a frosh.

As he cut behind the church and down the alley, he racked his brain for anyone at school who'd accept payment to protect him against Devon and the boys. It would be a win-win, as it was for Louis whenever Barry paid him, like he did at dinner the following night.

Heading into the kitchen with Alexander and John, Louis made a beeline for the table when he saw Barry already sitting there, swinging his chubby legs. With only the two of them seated while everyone else dilly-dallied over what they wanted to drink, Barry slipped him the Honest Abe.

"Lou-*is*?" Frank said several minutes later when they were all seated.

"Bad Thing first 'cause that's the easiest." He chuckled. "I'm repeating ninth grade. Have I used that one before? It really sucks."

"Which summer classes are you taking?" Faith asked, her hand clutching the large spoon she used to shovel peas down her gullet.

"Algebra and English."

"Yes, I attended the most recent summit between the teachers and the parents of their students," Frank said while making short work of the meatloaf. "I met with all of Louis's instructors, including those of algebra and survey of American and English literature. It appears his performance of late, and for the whole year, in fact, for the most part, on tests, quizzes, as well as basic homework tasks and assignments, has borne out to such an insufficient level that a repetition of his freshman year is generally agreed upon to be inevitable and in the best interests of all."

Louis chuckled again. Only in the past year or so, since his voice started changing, could he hear Woody's chuckles in his own to an uncanny degree.

"What does that feel like?" Stephen said. "Knowing there is no hope." Just as his father would've done, Stephen offered an open hand at the words "no hope."

"My New Thing is that Tanisha and I are seeing a play next week. I've never seen a play before."

"Which one?"

"It's in Philly. I forget what it's called."

"Sounds boring as shit," Jonathan said.

"You've seen plays before," Dan said. "Mom took us."

"Your mother and I went to the Kennedy Center, oh, once or twice a year, I would guess," Frank said. "Usually my parents would accompany us. We ever take you guys?"

"Maybe you took Jerry's Kid over there," Jonathan said.

"Barry, if you fall asleep at the theater, do you wet your seat?" Alexander asked with nary a hint of facetiousness. His mother smirked.

"Bawrence Barney!" Stephen said with both palms proffered.

"And my Good Thing is that my dad's coming up. Thanks a lot for doing that, Frank, you know?"

"Well, and it makes perfect sense." Frank folded his hands in front of him. "This would mark a significant life change for Daniel, so significant that I had to take a few days to consider the implications fully. It was an interesting argument Daniel put forth, well thought out..."

Louis stopped listening, as he was wont to do whenever someone, usually Frank or Faith, sang his big brother's praises.

After dinner, while Dan did the dishes, Faith played piano, Frank lounged in his recliner, John and Stephen played the Commodore, and Alexander went out to practice his bass in his friend's garage, Jonathan beat the shit out of Barry in the first-floor hallway. Louis sat on the hallway couch petting Gorbie until Jonathan started throwing a few genuine punches to make Barry cry.

The whole thing was such a joke. Jonathan made no effort to hold back his laughter while Louis did a Hulk Hogan to his Rowdy Roddy Piper. He put in a few good licks he knew Jonathan could handle, manhandled him with a few of his favorite WWF moves, while Barry sat on the couch next to a crotch-licking pooch.

Barry used to love the spectacle of his beating up Jonathan, but now it was hard to tell if he was into it at all. If he was onto the ruse, why didn't he say anything? Why did he keep giving up his allowance?

"Because if he doesn't, you'll beat his ass," Tanisha said later that night.

"Nah-ah."

"But he thinks you will because sometimes you do anyway. And Jonathan does even more. Just pretend you're Barry for a second. You and Jonathan are much bigger. Just one of you is enough to scare that boy, but two?"

"Do I scare you?"

"Boy, I'll jack you up."

Louis chuckled. "You sound so different from Frank, but you both say things in a convincing way. I suck at forming words."

"How many times have I told you that you need to start reading?"

"They're really impressed we're seeing a play." He chuckled. "'Cause they think I'm only into sports. But you told me I'm more... What was that word?"

"Complex."

He looked around for his Copenhagen. "That's a scary word."

Tanisha lowered her voice. "The Lumberton crew's going to be looking for you tomorrow. Maybe stay for ninth? You need the extra help anyway."

"Fuck them."

"You want to repeat ninth grade in a wheelchair?"

Louis found the hockey puck tin under his bed and flipped it open.

"Stay for ninth in Mr. Connolly's class, they'll never think to check there. You should really be at baseball practice. Oh wait, you need a C average to play sports. Guess I'm trippin'."

Louis grabbed the plastic Baltimore Orioles cup that still had a little soda mixed with melted ice and used it as a spittoon, exaggerating his spit noises to get on her nerves.

He had no intention of staying for ninth period or otherwise devising a plan to evade roaming gangs. Soon as the bell tolled the end of eighth period at two twenty-nine, Louis bolted out of earth science, threw his bag over his shoulder with impunity, and headed for the exit. He didn't bother with his locker, having already stopped by after seventh to collect the books for the homework he probably wouldn't do. Tanisha would be loitering around there, and he was in no mood to be lectured.

Louis was heading down Ridgeway Street and had passed Franco Harris's mom's house, with the cemetery just ahead on the right, scene of the famous Barry trick-or-treating-glowing-eyes-in-the-bush incident a year and a half ago that Frank never tired of talking about. When he was still a good twenty yards or so from the cemetery, RV's resident gang o' mullets emerged out of nowhere and headed straight for him and bumped shoulders walking past him. Then they turned around.

They had just made the turn into the cemetery when Louis stopped and made to turn around to get this show started. One of them pressed a hand on his back to keep him walking. He went deeper into this place than he ever thought he'd go, at least while still alive. The drive curved gently until Ridgeway was out of view. That's when it started.

As you might have gleaned by now, Louis was one tough mother-fucker. Any fourteen-year-old who can hold his own as a strong safety against seniors much bigger than him is someone to be reckoned with. Any white kid in Mount Holly who had no qualms about walking through the Gardens at night and even dating one of their own obviously possessed a decent measure of self-confidence. No one else at 48 Broad could've pulled it off. How did he? While getting pummeled by the mullets and scoring more than a few licks of his own that exploded one of their noses with blood, Louis pondered this. He and Daniel were alike in some ways, but in even more ways they were nothing alike. Perhaps nothing illustrated this more than how they integrated themselves socially at RV. Daniel had a million and one friends. Everyone loved him, classmates and teachers and janitors alike. Louis knew better than anyone that Daniel wasn't sweating his breakup from Veronica because he could have scored another girlfriend in five minutes flat if he so chose.

Louis stood in stark contrast. His friends, if that was the right term, were limited to those he played sports with, football in the fall and track during winter and baseball in the spring, C average notwithstanding. His teachers loathed him as much as they loved Daniel. Like Daniel, Louis had inherited enough of Woody's charisma to make it relatively easy to land a girlfriend. Only, until Tanisha, Louis's girlfriends never lasted. Indeed, Tanisha was the first Louis had been with long enough for the term "girlfriend" to be legitimate. As the fists continued to fly, Louis wondered about this too. Why did she stick with him? Was she using him as an instrument of rebellion against the establishment, such as it was, of the Gardens? He didn't think so. She was way too mature for that. Or was he another of her award-winning science projects?

At this point, Louis was prostrate on the grass next to the grave of a couple who had lived a long time until passing away within a month of each other in the eighteen hundreds. A question Tanisha had posed point-blank rang in his bruised skull: Why was it so hard to believe she liked him? Overanalyze something and you see problems that don't exist. Another maxim from the World According to Tanisha Bradford.

When Louis heard shouting, he figured it came from him in response to the mud-caked boot that had just come down on his head. But no, he could tell it wasn't him because it was too high-pitched. Louis sounded more like Rocky when he shouted, and that was very much by design. This person was using the word "punk" like it was going out of style. That could only be one mulleted kid, and this particular mullet was on Louis's side.

Jonathan and a few of those same friends he'd recently gone to the Pine Barrens with had pulled up in a pickup and managed to land several solid licks before the Lumberton crew high-tailed it back to their eponymous home base.

"Dude, what the fuck are you doing?" Jonathan asked.

Jonathan, Louis, and two others, a guy and a girl playing hand-sies, were sitting in the flatbed as the truck roared and spat its way down Jacksonville Road toward the Springfield Golf Center. "Everyone at school knew they'd be waiting for you."

Louis's head was miraculously pain-free at the moment, but that could've been because every single pain receptor in his body was already homed in on his lower lip, which felt fat and deformed as Barry. The mere act of speaking shot liquid fire through his cheeks. He fished in his backpack for the tin of Copenhagen and came across a Health quiz from three months ago that he failed and was supposed to have had Frank or Faith sign (Health class for RV freshmen covered sex ed), as well as a copy of *Of Mice and Men* he borrowed from a cute Puerto Rican he some-times fantasized about when masturbating. Eventually he exca-vated the hockey puck tin from beneath his floor-crushing earth sciences text. While plugging a wad in his cheek, that kid making out with his girl asked Louis if he could indulge. His girl slapped his hand with a:

"I will kick your fucking ass!"

"Fuck!" Louis froze as the agony of chewing shot a bolt of lightning through his jaw. While he stayed completely still, the tobacco juice didn't. It had just trickled down his throat when he jumped up and spewed the wad and as much juice as he could cough up. Jonathan and his friends laughed their asses off.

"Why's your dad coming up?" Jonathan asked when they were at the driving range.

While Jonathan whacked one ball after another to the two-hundred-yard marker and beyond, Louis lay flat on his back on the grass a few feet behind. He found this position elicited the least protest from his body. "I think Dan's moving."

"He's not going to Temple?"

"He wants to reconnect with his roots or some shit."

"Sometimes I wish I had a secret other dad like you and Dan. I mean, if I were you? And I had this secret other dad who was coming up? I'd be like, 'So long, fake dad and bitch stepmom!'" Jonathan blasted the next ball clear over the two-hundred-yard marker.

Louis had too many pangs playing pinball inside him to understand what exactly Jonathan was talking about, so he just chuckled.

"If I decided not to go to Temple, Dad would fucking kick my ass. You know he hit me the other day?"

"At least he didn't throw a can of peas at your head."

"Know what the old douche said when I told him about that?"

"Take it like a man?"

"He got mad at me like it was my fault."

"You don't even know my dad."

"Tell me this. Who's fucking dumb enough to lose all that money? But wait! Someone stabs my basketball to death, and it's my fault. Stephen says it was me, so it must be me."

Louis tried to keep a leash on his chuckling to spare himself the facial fire.

"If I wet the bed like Barry? Dad would call the cops and send me to jail. But Quasi-fucking-modo? 'Leave him alone. He's just a baby. He can't help it.' Dude, seriously, when your dad comes up? Talk to him. Maybe he'll let me live with him. My dad took care of you and Dan. And Peggy. How about a little payback?" He sent the next ball soaring to the left and very nearly hit a cart. "Fuck you, Monty!"

"My dad doesn't know how to pay bills."

"But he's on the news. Homeboy's got to be raking it in. Hooooo...!" He sent the final ball clear over the cart. It landed just short of the woods. "Let's take off, eh?" Jonathan said in his best *Strange Brew* accent.

While Louis regained his feet more gingerly than he could ever remember having to do, he thought of the Swiss Army knife Alex had gotten for his birthday. "Frank told me this saying once," he said when he and Jonathan were zooming along the links in a golf cart. Louis used one hand to grip the edge of his seat tighter than he'd gripped anything in his life. Jonathan went out of his way not to drive along the fairways. "The grass is always greener on the other side of the fence."

"Yeah, buddy!"

"What the FUCK?" Louis cried out at the agony as the cart dove into a sand trap. The spray didn't have time to land before Jonathan peeled up the slope, soared across the fairway, and barreled into the next rough patch.

"I just wish it was that easy when it's you and the iron."

"It means everything looks awesome for someone else while everything sucks for you. But if you think about it, things aren't awesome for that person. It could be worse and you don't even know it."

"Pardon me, are you a golfer?" Jonathan asked in a mock official tone. "Why, yes, I'm a golfer." Switching back to his regular voice: "Dude, if I don't go PGA, I could be a groundskeeper. I would get to make sure the grass is always greener than a motherfucker. Green grass, bitches!" He floored it into another trap and roared up the slope with air to spare and zoomed across another couple of holes' worth of rough. "Whatever I do, I'll have to work my ass off. Not like you and Dan. Fuckers get away with everything."

Louis chuckled, then grunted in pain. "Dude, that's the green grass."

"Fuck you. You owe me."

"I don't owe you shit. You're the one who owes me."

"Who had to mop the kitchen floor after we threw charcoal? All you had to do was sit by the fake fireplace in the music room."

"You ever think you might get off easy because you're Frank's son? I'm no one's son in that fucking house. It's like an orphanage. Sometimes I wish I was a bed wetter."

"That whole thing with Barry is getting obvious. Even he's going to figure it out."

"You still owe me."

"I just saved your ass. We set it up so I could pay what I owed you, you'd fuck with Barry to get him to pay you to protect him from me, and I was the one making him do that, that money counted toward the debt. Don't fuck with me, man. My dad already exploits me for free labor."

Louis held a hand to his cheek to stymie the fire as he chuckled. "I'm the one who bailed your stupid ass out of jail with money I borrowed from Tanisha. She had to get it from her grandparents. I was in debt to her so she could pay them back."

"Whatever, man."

"You better pray we don't play putt-putt."

"Want to go, motherfucker?" Jonathan floored it and swung a hard right back toward the clubhouse. His boss read him the riot act when he parked at a wildly different angle from the rest of the fleet. Jonathan ignored him as he and Louis went inside to pick up a couple of irons and scorecards.

The adoptive brothers couldn't get through the first hole before Louis exploded and slammed his iron on the ground after shooting six over par. "MOTHER! FUCKER!"

He may have quieted down during the next couple of holes, but his apoplexy never ebbed entirely. Jonathan, undisputed golf master of 48 Broad and RV, scored worse than his personal average but still plenty well enough to cream Louis, who couldn't par even one hole. Jonathan missed no opportunity to rub his beat-up face in it. On the ninth and final hole, what should have been an easy putt for two over par turned into the punch line of a bad joke. Louis swung his iron into the tree so hard that the metal shaft wrapped around it. He dropped the ruined club and stepped back as the two brothers gaped at it. They exploded in hysterics.

When Louis and Tanisha were parked on RV's front lawn during lunch the next day, she asked him if he was excited about this weekend.

"I was talking about the Os and you bring up my dad?"

"I can see you're thinking about him."

He scanned the sloped expanse of the lawn. Not as many people were staring at them as when they had first started dating, but now Louis was the object of mild curiosity for having gotten beat to shit in the cemetery. He always made sure they sat toward the Jacksonville Road side, closer to the gym and football field where his fellow jocks tended to gravitate. He nodded at the offensive line, who also played baseball together. A few Lumberton mullets were in the vicinity, smoking against the wall. About the same number of Devon's friends loitered by the curb and ignored the vice principal's recurring calls to stay on the grass.

Tanisha slapped his arm. "The storm has passed. Why bring it back?"

"Ain't shit has passed."

"Hey."

"I just want to eat my chili dog in peace."

"All I'm saying is your dad's coming up. It's a cool thing for you. That's all I'm saying."

He nodded as he gobbled up half the dog in a single go.

"What do you plan to do when he gets here?"

Louis chuckled at the two chubby fourth graders who'd darted across Jacksonville, heading straight for them. "What the fuck, Barry?"

"This is Patricia. She's in fourth grade also."

"I can introduce myself!" Patricia's Air Jordans were newer than Louis's.

"I told her she didn't need to come with me, but she kept saying she wanted to come with me so she can protect me."

"How cute," Tanisha said. "Nice to meet you, Patricia."

"Rad sneakers."

"That isn't what I said, idiot," said Patricia. "I wanted to come with you in case you got run over by a car or kidnapped by a stranger and then no one would know what happened to you."

"Not if you get run over or kidnapped too!"

"Barry, why are you here?"

"Barry has the dumbest idea in the world. Tell them, Barry."

"You know how I give you money to beat up Jonathan? I can give you lots more and then you can give it to those people who beat you up so they don't beat you up anymore."

"This a joke?"

"Like a couple hundred maybe."

"But you don't have that much," Patricia said.

"Yes, I do!"

"You have a job?" Tanisha asked.

"Allowance." Barry jutted his hand at them with the five little sausages splayed. "Five dollars every week."

Tanisha glanced at Louis.

Louis offered his girlfriend a shit-eating grin. "Isn't he just the awesomest baby brother ever? Come 'ere!" He grabbed a fold in Barry's *Empire Strikes Back* tee and pulled him to the grass and play-wrestled. Barry's protestations turned to giggles while Patricia's laugh was the uproarious, ridiculing kind.

Tanisha's laugh was more of the bemused variety.

"You messing with me, Bawrence Barney? This some sort of prank on your big brother? Huh? Huh?"

Barry could barely get out the "No!" amidst the giggling and kicking.

Only now did Louis notice the stares. The entire offensive line and many others were watching. The mullets were shaking their mullets. Louis lifted his brother back on his feet. "Probably time to go back to Folwell before someone tells on you."

"But I want to give you money so you can give it to the gangs so they don't beat you up and stuff."

"Get out of here."

For the rest of the day, Louis could think of nothing else except the idea of ending the skirmishes once and for all with a single lump payment. When Tanisha came over that night, they made out in Faith's wardrobe closet, their preferred venue for nooky. Normally, Louis lived for this, but right now he couldn't focus.

She abruptly pulled away. "Care to explain yourself?"

"He wasn't joking. He really has two hundred dollars. Probably more." When he told her where Barry most likely got it, he proposed giving all of it to Devon. By helping Devon fix those longstanding issues he always complained about, like his cousin's car and the broken dishwasher, and leaving him enriched besides, Louis would gain a formidable ally.

"You crazy? That money needs to go back to your father."

"He's not my father."

"The man's been raising you like his own for over ten years."

"Woody says he got fucked over and that his kids were kidnapped." Louis chuckled.

"But he let it happen. No one put a gun to his head."

"Yeah, yeah, yeah. My real dad's a fucking idiot, Frank let Barry take all that money, you're the genius of the family, and I'm the asshole."

"You want me to leave?"

"I'm the asshole."

"Something very wrong happened in this house, and you are in a position to set it right."

"But then Frank will know it was one of his kids."

"So?"

"He thinks Donald did it."

"So hold up. You're perfectly fine with an innocent black kid being blamed?"

"AAAAAAAAAHHHHHHHH!"

The scream curdled Louis's blood as he jumped up.

"AAAAAAAAAHHHHHHHH!"

"A little girl's in the house!"

"That's no girl. It's Barry!"

As Louis darted up to the third floor, he remembered coming up here late that Saturday night right after *SNL* and finding Dan holding a limp, sweaty Barry in his arms. The deathly ill child had wept with the pathetic wail of a dying animal. Dan and Frank dipped him into a cold bath every day during those two interminable weeks to keep his sky-high temperature in check. Why didn't Louis offer to help?

Luckily, it wasn't a deathly illness that was making Barry shriek like a bat on this night. It was, in fact, a bat that was making him do it. No sooner did Louis storm into Barry's room than the black, firm wings slapped him across the face. It zipped away and slapped one wall, followed by another, before shooting back to the center of the room where it hovered, the only sound its frantic wings. Was Louis imagining it, or was that supposedly blind creature giving him the once-over with those beady little eyes?

While his kid brother broke into a fresh round of damsel-esque screeches, Louis bolted across to Jonathan's room for anything he could use against the intruder. Inside the little pot farm closet below the Mötley Crüe bumper sticker, he found an old wooden tennis racket, one of the rackets the Roggebusch kids had used their first summer at 48 Broad when Faith enrolled them all in tennis lessons at the Westwood pool.

Too paralyzed with fear to make a run for it, Barry had resorted to lying flat on his stomach while keeping up a steady stream of screams. Louis, armed with the racket and clad only in his under-wear, felt heroic and ridiculous. The bat's radar was no doubt baffled by him as well. He assumed a pose not unlike that of a tennis player awaiting the serve, becoming as still as the bat was kinetic. Your move.

Tanisha ran partway up the stairs and called out to see if everything was okay. With eyes locked on the night bird, Louis reached behind him and opened the door and whispered for her, for Christ's sake, to stay the hell back.

The bat shot to the far wall, slapped along it several times until it reached a window pane, then shot back to the middle of the room. Louis leaped and brought the racket down. It collided squarely with the little fanged bastard. The bat, in turn, collided with that same window and couldn't recover before Louis was on top of it, swinging and hacking like McEnroe gone berserk.

Tanisha burst through the door, startling the bat into ear-cracking screeches. Louis threw open the window while continuing to swing. Most of the time he missed, but the bat was too confined to get around him. He pretended he was playing Whac-A-Mole at Great Adventure. In this case, the open window was the one big hole Louis had to swat the cuddly mole through in order to win the dual prize of its absence and Barry's silence. Well, at least its absence. Perhaps out of desperation, the bat fluttered and flapped against his chest. If it was thinking Louis would jerk back and let it by, it was sorely mistaken. "Fuck you!" He reached back as far as his racket hand would go before letting loose with a powerful, if awkwardly angled, swing. Awkward be damned, the racket connected and sent the creature smack into the Garden State night. Infuriated by the juice it took to get rid of that thing, Louis bashed the sill repeatedly before hurling the racket out the window. He stuck his head out and cursed the world it flew through.

Only when he slammed the window shut did he notice the film of sweat coating his entire body. His crotch, drenched and steaming hot beneath his tighty-whities, itched like a mother. "Avert your eyes, class," he said before doing the deed.

"You better wash your hands before you touch a single thing in this house."

Louis pretended he was heading for the door when he stopped and brushed his palm across her face. "So cute."

"No you didn't!"

He reached down and ruffled Barry's hair. "What a swell kid!"

Louis ran the tap hot as he lathered his hands beneath it. Shutting off the water revealed the sound of tinkling from the other side of the room. He leaned back to find Barry sitting on the can.

"It's so I don't wet the bed."

Louis ran the brush through his hair to freshen the feathering. He turned back just in time to catch his little brother flicking him off. "What's your problem?"

"Nothing."

"Why do you piss sitting down? Only girls do that."

"I don't know."

"That's fucked up."

"Jonathan beat me up and said from now on I should pee sitting so I don't get any on the sides."

When Louis came back down from the hysterics, he said, with intermittent chuckling, "Everyone gets a little on the side. Even if you manage to piss squarely into the toilet, little drops splash on the rim. You can't keep taking shit from Jonathan, man. At some point..." But it was easier just to chuckle. A red-faced Barry pulled up his undersized britches around his chubby midsection and headed for the door. "Hey, Barry." Louis checked the hallway before closing the door and kneeling. "Hey. You still willing to give me that money?"

Barry's right eye widened.

"I know I can be mean sometimes. But that's just because I have to be. You know that, right?" The kid just kept half glaring. "It's like at RV. They don't respect you if you're nice."

"What's respect?"

"Like, on *Cheers*? I bet you respect Norm. Right? Whenever he says something, you listen. That's respect."

"But Norm's nice. Why do they respect him if he's nice and not an asshole?"

"You know he's not real, right? His name isn't really Norm. He's an actor."

"I'm not a retard, asshole."

Louis offered a weak chuckle. Where was Tanisha?

"Alex is nice, and he has lots of friends. And Daddy respects him. That's why they talk all the time. And Alex respects Daddy and Daddy's nice to him."

"You're lucky Frank's your real dad."

"Why are you mean?"

Louis imagined Alexander's Swiss Army knife, the knife he needed to carry out his plan, floating into the room and snipping the tension with that tiny pair of foldout scissors. "I'm not like Faith, am I?"

"I hate her guts!"

When they came back down from laughing, Louis said, "You still have the money?"

"Are you going to tell Daddy?"

"You met Tanisha's brother? Real douchebag."

"What's a douchebag?"

"How about two hundred?"

"What if it doesn't work?"

"Barry, if it doesn't work, I'll go to Frank and tell him I was the one who stole the money. All right? Promise." And he meant it.

Following his little brother down the hall, Louis stopped at the suddenly startling realization that his father, his real father, would be here in less than forty-eight hours. Woody could be standing right here. Talk about two worlds colliding. Louis's chest felt light. He wanted to chuckle. Would that have been the right response? What would Woody say to both Dan and Louis moving in with him?

By the time he caught up with Barry, the little porker was sticking half his body into the square on the lower right of his toy shelves. The clock radio was humming with Simply Red's "Holding Back the Years." Han, Luke, Darth, Boba, a couple of stormtroopers, and some hideous bounty hunters spilled out onto the carpet to make way for the AT-AT. Barry unfolded those huge mechanical legs that had nearly squashed Luke and stood the walker on the shag carpet. He scooted back to consider it from a distance, a connoisseur of Imperial weaponry. "It's in there," he finally said.

Louis was about to ask what he was talking about when he spun back to the AT-AT. He got down on his haunches in front of the toy. The thing looked like some kind of creature that stalked the land with a cold, steely, mechanical indifference. The midsection was where the stormtroopers would go. Of course, that's not what was in there right now. Louis slid open the side door very delicately. When it jammed, he shook it with a "Fuck you!"

Barry giggled as he reached into the walker and undid a tiny plastic latch.

When Stephen started practicing his trumpet in the music room, Louis suggested to Tanisha that they hit up the 7-Eleven. After they made the turn onto Garden Street, well out of sight of the house, he spilled it.

She froze. "Tell me you're joking."

He pulled out the wad and really wanted to smile.

"Go back right now and give that money to Frank."

"Listen to me."

"Louis, this is crazy."

"Let's get our Slurpees, and if you still think my idea's bullshit, I'll give the money to Barry."

"To Frank."

When they resumed walking, Tanisha went at a considerably faster pace. Louis couldn't help chuckling as he sometimes had to break into a jog to keep up.

No sooner did they arrive at the store than Tanisha gave his arm a sharp yank. She led him to the grassy area beside the narrow, finger-shaped lake that curved around out of sight. "I have no interest in making a scene."

"What-the-fuck-ever."

"Every time you mumble, I hear exactly what you say, you know that, right?" When she laughed, it was a new kind of laugh he'd never heard before.

Louis stared at the water. It looked black in the night. One time, when he'd been here during the day, he spotted tadpoles frolicking. Were they frolicking right now?

"When I was in fourth grade, I had Ms. Bradley. She had this little library in the back of class. Whole lot of books. One of the books was *Charlie and the Chocolate Factory*. Guess what? I stole it."

"Get the fuck out of here."

"Last day of class. My last day at Folwell forever. So there I am walking back home and I'm carrying *Charlie*, skimming through it, all giddy and shit. And then Sharon sees me. She's like, 'That from Ms. Bradley's class?' I told her I was borrowing it. And then the next day Sharon and her mom are at the Acme and guess who they run into?"

"No way."

"So then Ms. Bradley comes to my house. She's all nice and everything. But I was humiliated. I never saw Mom get so mad. I cried my eyes out. She grounded me for two weeks."

"I throw charcoal at cars."

She looked at him.

"In the summer. In the winter we throw snowballs. We always do it from Barry's room. The last time, Barry nailed this car right on the roof. Guy gets out all pissed and shit, he tells Frank what happened, and Frank just assumes it was me and Double. We had to sit in front of the fake fireplace while he and Faith watched TV."

"What happened to Barry?"

"Fucker got off clean." Tanisha cracked up. Louis couldn't help chuckling himself. "How's Grams?"

"You're not giving the money back, are you?"

"I'm serious."

"She's got emphysema. How do you think she is?"

"Devon likes her, right?"

"She practically raised him."

"So I guess if she dies, he'll be pretty bummed, huh?"

Tanisha looked at him.

"Check this out." He laid out his plans for the money.

They took in the lake for a while. Louis had no problem waiting her out. This was Tanisha, after all. She couldn't stay quiet forever. "Why would you do that?"

"I want to hear what Devon thinks. He says go fuck myself, I'll give the money to Frank."

Tanisha considered the lake for another minute before she took his arm. "Come on, fool."

When he said Cherry Coke Slurpee, Louis meant fill the cup half with Coke, half with the cherry flavor. As he did the deed now, though, he decided on a whim to layer on some orange Creamsicle. Tanisha stuck with cherry. On the way to the counter, they scooped up Charleston Chews for her while Louis opted for a Babe Ruth, a Zero, a packet of Red Man bubble gum, and a tin of Copenhagen.

They took their time walking to the Gardens.

"Want me to do the talking?" she asked.

"Maybe you're right. This is all bullshit."

West of High Street, Garden Street became Rancocas Road. Just past the pharmacy and the Mount Holly State Bank were the court-house and jail. Louis was reminded again of Double's call. Tanisha laughed as if reading his mind. "You hadn't bailed him out, he'd've gotten out soon enough. He's a juvenile." She looked at him and tugged his arm. "It's going to be fine."

"My third grade teacher read us *Charlie and the Chocolate Factory*. I remember the gum and thinking how rad that would be."

"I read somewhere they might be able to make gum like that for real."

"No way."

"That would totally be my new favorite candy."

"But how many kinds would there be?"

"How many different things can you have for dinner?"

"Frank likes to cook London broil. That's one course."

"Then baked potato. And asparagus."

"Faith would get the gum where it's salad, then peas, then beets."

When they reached Tanisha's house, they went around the back. The screen door was closed, but the door itself was ajar. Devon was talking on the kitchen phone, taking advantage of the cord's length by ambling down the hallway before wandering back and rummaging through the fridge. Louis could just make out Bill Cosby's voice. Right now the entire family at 48 Broad would be crammed into the living room. A homesick pang hit Louis simultaneously with a jonesing for Copenhagen.

Thirty-six hours from now, his father would be on his way.

Tanisha hopped up the steps and threw open the screen door. "Get your bee-hind outside."

"I'm on the phone!"

"You go to the Acme like I asked you?"

"What the fuck?"

"You fools shush so I can watch my shows," came a brittle voice.

"Just want to talk, yo," Louis said.

Devon turned away and mumbled something profane.

"Two choices, knucklehead. Be an adult or be a child."

"How about I call Darren and Bernard? Sure they'd love a piece of this white-ass honkey."

"Bernard's a pussy." Louis chuckled.

"Quickest way to get rid of him is to let him say what he needs to say."

Devon mumbled as he looked around at everything but them.

"I didn't know you guys watched *Cosby*. You watch all the other ones too?"

Devon looked ready to pounce. "The fuck you think? Thursday night's the best night on TV, everyone knows that." He polished off his soda and waved the bottle at Louis. "This some bullshit, I'm going to break this on that thick-ass skull of yours, you understand?"

"So here's the thing. You know my dad Frank, right? Someone stole his money."

"Yeah I know."

"You know?"

"Everyone knows. Five hundred dollars or some shit."

Louis chuckled. "My dad's coming up this weekend. My real dad. So this may be the last time you have to deal with me. But first I have a lot of that money. And I'd like to offer it to you. On one condition." When he finished the pitch, Devon stared at him for one very pregnant minute. Louis could just make out *The Cosby Show*'s closing credits. One or two of his brothers would now be scrambling to the kitchen to refresh their ice cream while Frank did the same to his scotch.

Devon turned to his sister. "He lost his mind?"

"Money's got to go somewhere," Tanisha said.

"I don't want no fucking charity."

"If your grams doesn't get the care she needs, she could die. This shit is real."

Devon studied the doorjamb.

"*Family Ties* is filmed in front of a live studio audience," Meredith Baxter-Birney announced.

"Emphysema can lead to cancer, Devon," Tanisha said. "Poor woman can't walk to the bathroom without stopping to catch her breath."

The audience was rolling on their asses at something Michael J. Fox had just said.

Still peering at the doorjamb, Devon said, "Your brother took that money? That kid with the whole..." He gestured to his face.

Louis chuckled. "I know, right? No one would believe it even if he admitted it." He pulled out the wad and dropped it at Devon's feet. "I'm being philosophical. Know what that means? Me neither. Frank always says he's being philosophical whenever he reacts to something in a way that's totally opposite the way most people react. Like this one time when me and Double were so fucking high playing catch in the first-floor hallway with this big-ass grapefruit and broke one of the fancy windows in the front door." He chuckled. "Frank wasn't mad. He was philosophical. But he did make us pay for it with our allowance."

Devon picked up the money and examined it the way you would an ancient artifact.

"This is my first time trying to be philosophical," Louis said. "If it's all the same to you, I'd like to fail ninth grade in peace."

Devon mumbled something and went inside just as Michael J. Fox said something hilarious.

When he got home, feeling higher than if he'd indulged in Jonathan's herbage, Louis made his move for the Swiss Army knife.

With Alex and John watching *Night Court* in the living room with the rest of the family, Louis poked his head in their bedroom just above. It didn't take long to spot the knife on the desk. As he stepped carefully across the room, he became conscious of the two Broad Street windows. Was anyone walking by? Hogg? Squirrel Man? Why take chances, right? He flicked off the light. When you're treading thin carpet on an old, uneven wooden floor, creaking was inevitable. When it did creak, it sounded deafening. Louis froze. Looking at the windows, he wondered if his father would pull up on Broad or over on Buttonwood? Had anyone explained to him that the Buttonwood door was the one most people used?

Knife in hand, Louis was slipping out of the bedroom when:

"Lou-*is!*"

His heart stopped.

"Tanisha's on the phone!"

He snatched up the hallway phone and took refuge in Faith's wardrobe closet.

"I thought of something right after you left. Don't think I'm crazy now, okay?"

His heart was beating too fast for him to speak. Had anyone seen him? Or heard him?

"What if we took your dad to the play?"

Faith laughed at the TV below. He swallowed. "I don't think he likes plays."

"It's about father-son time. He'll go if you invite him."

Louis barely caught a wink that night. On Friday the weather was a postcard. During lunch on the lawn, stuffed with pizza and green beans, Louis conked out on Tanisha's shoulder while she jibber-jabbered with her girlfriends.

Good Thing Bad Thing New Thing was a no-brainer that night: His real father was coming up this weekend, he hadn't been sleeping well because of it, and he learned what emphysema was.

In his room that night, Louis popped in his brand-new cassette of Run-DMC's *Raising Hell* and turned off the light. Sometimes he liked to stare at that tree in front of the house. Sipping orange soda out of his Washington Bullets cup, he wondered how old it was. Would his father really be pulling up on the other side of that ancient tree in his almost equally ancient National Lampoon's *Vacation* station wagon? One of the branches on that tree bent upward slightly. Louis pretended it was the beginning of a smile.

He jerked awake in the gray light of early morning. No station wagon. He hopped over to the Buttonwood window but only saw the Dodge Caravan. Where was Faith's Rabbit?

Downstairs he found Barry in the living room watching *Goonies*. "Where is everyone?"

Barry looked at him with a mouthful of chocolate donut and shrugged.

Louis peered at the VCR clock: a few minutes shy of nine. He hurried back up to throw on an Orioles shirt, jeans, and Air Jordans. Down in the kitchen he dumped out the warm orange soda and used the Bullets cup as a spittoon while he took Gorbie for a walk. He had never plugged chew first thing in the morning, and now he could taste why. It came across like lukewarm spinach juice mingled with battery acid. Yet he continued chewing and spitting to keep himself occupied.

The Rabbit was there when he got back. He spit the chew into the cup and rinsed it out under the spigot by the flower bed. It blended with the mulch so perfectly not even George Taylor would be able to spot it.

"I got some wine and beer and snacky stuff," Faith said as Louis walked into the kitchen. She was wearing those abominable lime-green sweats that always made him cringe. Did other people feel that way as they passed her at the Acme? And the way her eyes looked so tiny and beady behind the Coke-bottle glasses reminded him of the bat.

Frank marched down the back stairs. "Morning, team! Faith, I see you've already tended to the hors d'oeuvres. Hello, Gorbachev!"

Louis fetched the box of Cap'n Crunch from the cabinet above R2. "Thanks a lot for doing that, Faith."

"It's not for you."

"I do not mean to minimize Daniel's anxiety or any consequences thereof," Frank said. "Such as, perhaps, insomnia."

"He says he hasn't had a full night's sleep in a week."

"But if I were a betting man, which of course I am, if only within the limits of common sense and low risk, I would wager that Woody will, in the end, be amenable to taking on Daniel as a dependent."

"That it?" Louis said as he parked himself at the island and crunched his cereal with his mouth open. He knew chewing with your mouth open was wrong, as did Woody, and yet they both did it because it seemed impossible not to. He was developing more in common with his real father the older he got. Moving in with him made perfect sense.

"The decision to bring a dependent under your roof is a big deal," Frank said. "Consider: You now have another mouth to feed, which means more groceries to buy, more medical bills if they get sick, more clothes. All those things. It also affects taxes. I ever give you my tax talk?"

Louis continued crunching with his mouth open.

"When you file taxes, first thing you do is declare your status. Are you single? Married? Cohabitating but not married? Number of dependents? Any changes from last year?"

Faith finished stuffing snacks in the fridge and stepped over to the island to glare at Louis with those batty beads.

"So let's see. How many children does Woody have with his current wife? Two, right? Two boys? And now Daniel will make three. Daniel could conceivably get a part-time job so he has some spending money, as many college students are wont to do. I made money playing jazz, for example."

"Yeah, you raked it in." Louis chuckled.

"But my parents still claimed me as a dependent. Even if Daniel were to move out and get a roommate or live in a dormitory, he will still be claimed as a dependent so long as he isn't earning enough to support himself or is otherwise incapable of supporting himself."

"God DAMN it, I can't take it anymore." Faith stomped out of the kitchen. As she passed the poolroom: "Turn that FUCKING thing off before I blow it up. Go upstairs, brush your teeth, take a shower, and put on CLEAN clothes. That means socks you didn't wear yesterday and underwear you haven't PISSED in."

"So it's a big deal is my point," Frank was saying.

Someone was hurrying downstairs as Louis slurped down the milk and soggy Cap'n Crunch bits. "Shake it off, Bawrence Barney!" Dan said while a whimpering Barry thumped up past him.

"Ah, here he is," Frank said. "Man of the hour."

Dan swooped into the kitchen wearing a sky-blue button-down shirt and tie with khaki pants. "Bedroom's clean, bed's made, and the bathroom is at least presentable."

Faith guffawed like Jabba the Hut as she thumped back into the kitchen.

"Costs and benefits," Frank said. "Bawrence the pigsty? Or a bathroom that perhaps shows evidence of swine habitation but is otherwise still a bathroom frequented by life-forms that are NOT poisonous to the environment?"

Louis wasn't sure why, but Dan's getup, especially that tie, pissed him off. He decided to make himself scarce before he did something rash like smash the cereal bowl over his brother's head.

He hopped up the stairs while they laughed their asses off in the kitchen. More laughter came from Alex and John's room. John was struggling to say something through the hysterics. Alex stepped out and said with perfect deadpan: "You seen my Swiss Army knife?"

"Fuck your Swiss Army knife," Louis said as he skulked past.

This cracked John up even more. Alex stayed rooted in the hall as if Louis had slapped him.

Stephen was throwing on his sleeveless Tampa Bay Buccaneers shirt and jogging shorts when Louis punched the door on his way in. He flipped *Raising Hell* over to side two and pressed play before plopping himself on the bed. Only now was the May sun breaking through the clouds.

Stephen stopped at the door. "I support Daniel's decision not to take advantage of the free tuition at Temple. Know why? Because that's a HANDOUT!" He stabbed the air with his index. "And HAND-OUTS are for Communists and pussies too lazy to get a job."

"If I told Tanisha I shared a room with a racist, she'd probably break up with me. So the fact that I almost never acknowledge you and think you're fucking crazy? You should take that as a compliment."

"A compliment that you don't acknowledge me? Or that you think I'm crazy?"

Louis swung the volume knob up to ten. When Stephen droned on about how Reagan should get rid of taxes because that was the only way to help "those people" help themselves, Louis grabbed the Capitals cup with the two-day-old spittle and flung it at him. A good bit of juice found the Bucs tee.

They both knew Stephen wouldn't try anything. It would've been like the Missing Link trying to outmove Superfly Snuka, only more ludicrous, and the contact wouldn't be faux. A grin plastered on his mug, Stephen walked calmly to his side of the room while removing the tee and replacing it with another Bucs tee.

Stephen's whole comportment, his love of debate, his conservatism, the roller-coaster weight struggles, the way he murdered the air with his finger... The parallels between him and Frank were as uncanny as they were innumerable. Could Louis say the same about himself and Woody?

He carried his boom box up to the third floor and banged on Jonathan's door. Quiet Riot came from the other side. Jonathan opened the door a crack. "Turn that black shit down."

"Open up, dick."

"I'm doing my fucking homework before your dad gets here. Punk." Barry walked by on his way to his room, fresh from the shower and clutching a towel around his waist with both hands. "You clean now, you little shit?" Barry stomped into his room and slammed the door. "Stop talking to yourself and blaming it on a fucking ghost!"

"Got any pot, yo?"

Jonathan gave him a look as if waiting for the "just kidding," then burst out laughing.

"Just a little, man. Don't be an asshole."

"Turn that black shit off first."

Louis stormed through the door and flicked off Jonathan's stereo before stopping his tape and switching to Philly sports radio. He dropped to the floor with his back against the door. Jonathan, meantime, stooped inside the hobbit door to the magic that lived deep inside. When he reemerged, he sat on the bed and rolled a J for each of them with great care.

Louis had only taken a couple of hits before the small door seemed ridiculous. "Seriously, man." He chuckled. "What's that door for?"

Jonathan burst out laughing and stuck out his tongue à la Gene Simmons. Louis chuckled seemingly forever. "George Taylor would know."

"George Taylor..."

"That crotchety old fuck hates my guts."

"He loves Dan." Louis took a deep hit.

"You okay, dude?"

"Did you fucking see him in the kitchen? Those fucking clothes. And they buy his bullshit. And now he's going to bullshit our dad. Our real dad."

"He's the oldest, man," Jonathan said after exhaling. "They get away with everything. It's like Stephen. That douche could fail all his classes, it wouldn't fucking matter. Dad would still worship the ground he walks on."

They nodded and mumbled and inhaled and sank into a lugubrious reverie for an indeterminate span.

"LOUIS!"

"No fucking way." Jonathan hissed.

Louis jumped up and opened the door with his brightest shit-eating grin. His eyes felt leaden. "What's up, Faith?" Jonathan pressed his middle finger against the wall.

That deathly pale face glared at him through the balustrade with eyes black as an eight ball. "George Taylor needs help."

"Isn't that Dan's thing?"

"Go out back and ask him how you can help. Now."

Jonathan stuck his tongue out and bopped his bird against the wall.

Faith gave Louis a look before thumping down the stairs. "And my advice to both of you? Open the windows so the whole fucking place doesn't stink."

"Hey, big guy!" George Taylor was sprinkling seedlings along the barren patch of dirt on the Hogg side of the house. "Pinch-hitting for Daniel, eh?"

"I suck at gardening." Louis offered a weak chuckle, so high he couldn't be sure he was really out here.

George Taylor's grotesque belly laugh only made reality more ambiguous. "Daniel reminds me of my father-in-law, the late Don Saft. Very polite. Not sure all of it was genuine. All due respect to both of them, but I'd say you're better built for this line of work."

"Jesus fuck, is it hot out here, or is it just me?"

George leaned back with a hand on his hip and laughed his gray ass off. They continued spreading the seeds as Hogg lumbered by. The hunched old man seemed naked without his old naked pooch. He even walked with one hand outward and clenched as if holding a leash. When they finished laying the seeds up to where the patch of dirt met the sidewalk on Broad, George led them to the Buttonwood porch where the hose lay curled up. "Alrighty then, big guy. Time to give those babies a shower." Louis made to help carry the huge coil, but George hauled it up over his shoulder as if it were light as a paper towel roll. When he started walking with those massive strides, Louis thought of the Imperial Walker where Barry had hid the money.

"Hey, George, no matter how hot it gets, you always wear that heavy shirt, pants, boots..." Louis chuckled. "You trying to burn off weight? Like how jockeys put on all those layers and shit?"

"I haven't given two shits about my weight since we took it to the Huns. And that's the truth."

"Cool, boss man. I'll take it from here."

"I'm sure you can handle it, but you know what you forgot?"

"The pot in the hobbit hole?"

George marched over to the spigot with the purpose of a soldier. It took a few seconds for the water to wind its way to Louis, and when it did, it spurted out in a pathetic little stream that dropped straight to the dirt. "Now here…" From his mud-stained khaki pocket, George pulled out one of those little plastic hose pistols and screwed it on. "All's you gotta do is squeeze. These babies need love, but they don't need to be smothered. So careful with that trigger lock there. And if you don't mind, once you're done with these babies, go ahead and give some affection to the front of the house. Okay?" He handed over the pistol and gave several pats on the shoulder that ended with the warmest grip Louis could ever remember feeling.

When he reached the front of the house, Louis felt like he needed to lock the trigger to contend with the much thicker bed of grass up here, not to speak of the freshly planted flower bed with all those maddening colors and those bushes that blended together so you couldn't tell where one ended and another began. The heat was unrelenting. The sweat bathed his forehead and matted his pits and made his crotch itch like there was no tomorrow.

This pistol had pretty decent range. Louis backtracked to the side of the house where there was plenty of shade. He could stand right here and still water most of the front.

"Hey, buddy! You with me?" A deafening guffaw.

Louis's eyes snapped open to meet the sun's mocking smile. He instinctively rolled over only to squash the side of his face into warm goo. When he shot up and wiped off the mud, he thought he was going to puke. He might have if George Taylor's guffaw hadn't distracted him.

"You're okay, big guy. Here…"

Jesus Christ, the old warrior was strong. Louis was reminded of the end of *The Terminator*, when we get to see what Arnold really looks like. With one hand clutching Louis's cold, wet pit and the other gripping his sweaty arm, George lifted him right up like an empty cardboard box. Louis was so caught off guard by the brute strength that his feet nearly gave way.

"Well, bad news is you drowned all the babies."

Louis spun around and nearly barfed at the sight of the small lake.

"Buddy ol' pal, guess what? Those seedlings? There's more of them. Lots more."

"You probably want Dan to help this time."

"Nah! He's busy trying to win over his old man."

This time he couldn't keep it in. When Louis turned and beheld the green-and-brown station wagon, out spewed Cap'n Crunch. Someone laughed. It wasn't George. It sounded like someone in the house, upstairs.

Louis hauled ass around to the Buttonwood porch and leaped up the steps in two strides. He froze the moment he stepped inside. The screen door hissed behind him.

Someone, a woman, was speaking in the living room. Why was she speaking in such a hushed tone? And then someone answered her.

"Got it."

Woody!

Louis had no idea how long he stood there listening to the barely perceptible voices of his real father and fake mother. He took a step in that direction when suddenly Frank's voice boomed into the hall. "I admire and respect the way Daniel approached the topic. Maybe it's my background. I'm sure my mother has something to do with it. Presentation and decorum, shall we say, rank highly in my view of the world and how it should work."

"Absolutely, absolutely." Woody chuckled.

Louis chuckled too, but quietly.

Oh fuck it. Who cared if he was interrupting? The least he could do was poke his head in and say hey. Well, maybe not poke his head in. To keep a respectful distance, he stopped at a point in the hall equidistant from the living room, music room, and stairs. No one in any of those places could feel their personal space was being encroached upon.

Gorbie was resting his head on Faith's lap. The excitement of a new visitor had worn off apparently, but he still took the occasional sniff in Woody's direction without lifting his head. Dan sat still as stone on the couch, lips sealed and eyes wide.

Except for during newscasts, Louis had never seen his dad's hair combed so neatly. At home it was always messed up because he slept so much. The blond was still in the process of giving way to the gray, a bit more than half in favor of the latter at this point. And while he always wore those big square specs, for some reason they were making him look especially dignified as he nodded at something Faith was saying. Or maybe it was the black golf shirt Louis had never seen him wear before. If Louis were standing closer, no doubt he'd catch a whiff of Old Spice.

"I have another question," Frank said.

"Hi, Daddy!"

No one looked in Louis's direction. Not even Gorbie.

Louis was about to say hi again when Woody launched into an enthusiastic answer to whatever Frank had just asked. A couple more steps. Now Frank was saying something which Woody cut off with more head-nodding enthusiasm and now a smile. The two bantered and gesticulated like the pair of drinking buddies they used to be.

Louis now stood at the border of the room.

"Dad?"

It seemed his father grew more immersed in the conversation, and more smiley, each time Louis called to him. Look at how he sat on the edge of the couch like he did during Redskins games.

Louis was walking up the stairs when he heard Faith say, "Wouldn't it make more sense to come down at least a week before the semester starts?" He parked himself at the top of the stairs. He couldn't hear anyone on the second or third floors. Who had laughed?

"Sherry and I will need some time to rearrange the house, get it ready for Danny."

"Am I living in a dorm, Dad? Should I?"

"It's a good half hour to College Park. Usually more. Think you can get a roommate? I'm not sure how it all works."

"Would you and perhaps your wife consider sharing the cost if Daniel decides to live on or adjacent to campus?"

"Whatever Danny wants."

This had to be the most repulsive conversation Louis had ever had the terrible luck of eavesdropping on. That slapping sound that could only be Woody patting Dan on the back wasn't helping matters.

"But if I wanted to live at home, could I use your car? Or Sherry's?"

"My hours are long, Danny, you know that. Same with Sherry. Not sure if Danny told you, but my wife works at the State Department. Been there since Nixon. First boss was Kissinger."

Faith made a performance out of clearing her throat. She was probably glaring meaningfully at Frank. Louis wanted to chuckle, but his innards still felt gelatinous.

"But if Daniel opts to commute, would you and your wife consider sharing in the investment of a vehicle for him to use?"

"A car is a very expensive investment, Franklin."

"Well, actually," Frank said. "If you do the math, the per-semester cost of dormitory accommodations could be equal to or even greater than the cost of a vehicle that is pre-owned but still in good enough shape to handle Gaithersburg to College Park."

Louis heard his father sigh the way he did when the Redskins gave up a lead.

"Daniel. Do you have a preference between commuting versus the dormitory?"

"I'm going to get a job," Dan said. "I just want everyone to know that. I could help pay for the dorm. I might also join a fraternity."

"I pledged at GW," Frank said. "Many of my friends today are the friends I made there."

"I need to come down a week early, Dad," Dan said. "At least a week. So I can move into the dorm and find my way around campus and stuff."

"Whatever you want, Danny. Your call."

"Team. I believe we have done it. Woody?" Louis heard them all get up followed by the sound of two hearty male palms colliding.

"Thank you for coming up here and considering and agreeing to Daniel's proposal."

"Daniel, the way you handled this was very mature and very proper," Faith said. "Bravo, as they say at the opera."

"Danny will be the first from my family to have a college education. In the news business, we call that a trailblazer. I have to run. The news is a demanding mistress, ladies and gentlemen." Woody bumped the two sets of double doors as he hurried through them.

After listening to the station wagon rumble away, Louis ran upstairs and knocked on Barry's door. "Hey, Bawrence Barney, let's go to the library lot and play catch."

When they got there and Louis started mapping out the first play on Barry's palm, the little guy said, "Why are we here?"

"Just run that route."

"You're going to yell at me and everything."

"Ready, break!" The kid surprised him and, by the look on his face, himself by how fast he hauled that chubby little ass downfield, tracing the route flawlessly and making the catch in stride. "Fuck yeah! Let's go again." This time Louis traced a down and out. Still panting from the first play, Barry wasn't able to match his previous speed, but in the end he ran the route and made the catch. "All right, this shit's too easy."

Barry giggled as he jogged back with the ball outstretched. He stuffed it into Louis's gut and kept running. "I handed it off to you! Run!"

"Holy shit!" Louis booked it down the entire length of the lot, weaving in and out between imaginary defensive backs. He spiked it before bouncing off the tall wooden fence. "All right, let's make this a challenge, bitch! Get over here!" Barry's smile dimmed a bit, his step tainted with trepidation. "Everything is on the line. We're down by three. No, fuck it, four. That means a field goal won't cut it. We have to score a touchdown. Five seconds on the clock. You ready for this?"

"But what should I do?"

"Down! Set! Hut-hut! Hut! HIKE!" Barry's pace was still tepid. "Faster! Go long! GO LONG!" Louis backpedaled and danced around as if dodging pass rushers like Too Tall Jones and LT and Mike Singletary. Thunder rumbled just as the pigskin left his fingers and soared clear across the field in the tightest, most graceful spiral he had ever thrown in his life. He knew Barry had a better chance of keeping his bed dry than catching this highlight reel clip, but he couldn't help beaming at those pudgy paws jutting out at different angles like a slug's roaming antennae. The ball landed right in front of him and made him trip and soar.

"You okay, man?" Louis let out a hearty chuckle to let his brother know everything would be okay. The sky flashed. They took in the mother ships settling in over South Jersey. "Who do you talk to in your room? It sounded like you were arguing or something."

Barry peered up anxiously at the groaning sky. Raindrops fat as his fist started falling with a vengeance.

"Come on, Bawrence Barney!" Louis sprinted the two blocks down Buttonwood and scaled the steps in two jumps. Soon as he stepped inside, he saw Dan doing something he never did: playing the Commodore 64 with Stephen.

"Lou-is!" Frank thumped into the hall from the kitchen. "I was just speaking with Tanisha. She asked if you and she were still planning on attending the theater with Woody. I informed her of Woody's departure."

"Hey, Louis!" Dan called. "I'm a Terp!"

Louis hurried into the bathroom and slammed the door. Finally he could breathe. When they moved here, they had had keys to some of these old doors. They looked just like those old-fashioned keys you see in period movies. What happened to them? The only window in here was the stained glass facing Buttonwood. The red was especially deep and rich against the charcoal sky. A lopsided blob wobbled by. "Aw shit."

"Where the FUCK did you go?" Faith roared at Barry from the kitchen.

Instead of a vanity or mirror cabinet, this bathroom's storage was in a small closet, the ceiling of which was the underside of the stairs. It wasn't as small as the hobbit hole in Jonathan's room, but Barry was the only one who could walk in without stooping or ducking. Who knew how many times Louis had dipped in here for one reason or another, usually for first aid? He felt a perverse pride at physically wounding himself more than anyone else in the house. Never had the inside of this closet looked as ridiculous as it did right now.

"Baw-*rence*. You seem to have been caught in a deluge. If you require linens, you might find some in the second-floor wardrobe closet or perhaps the closet in the third-floor hallway."

"Even the dog knows to take shelter when it rains," Faith said. "Wise up. Do what the dog does."

Frank thumped upstairs. "Looks like I will not be jogging today. Oddly, my heart isn't breaking."

Louis figured the only way to make the closet look less absurd was to rearrange its contents. He executed a sweeping slow-motion chop right out of *Kung Fu*, knocking everything off the shelves. After rubbing his hands through everything, he grabbed the bottle of alcohol and delicately dressed the salad.

As he closed the closet door, he spotted the new bottle of hand soap on the sink rim. He unscrewed the dispenser and poured the goo on the floor around the sink and along the radiator and toilet seat. He then dropped the dispenser itself into the toilet.

"My Bad Thing is that it's only May," Dan said at dinner.

"Most people would use that for Good Thing," Alexander said in his usual deadpan way that for some reason was making Louis roll on his ass. "May's a great month. Warm. School's almost, you know, out. Because it's May."

"But I'm not moving until August," Dan said. "Oh yeah, that's my Good Thing: Maryland bound, baby!"

"I would call that a Good Thing as well," Frank said. "Let's say Very Good Thing."

"Aren't you two kids forgetting something?" Stephen said to his father and stepmother. "It's taco night."

Honoring a tradition that began by accident soon after the brood arrived at 48 Broad, Frank asked Faith to pass him the bowl of taco shells. Instead, Faith picked up a shell and chucked it at him. Not heeding its brittleness, Frank didn't catch the shell so much as crush it between his palms. Everyone laughed, although not as uproariously as they did that first time. Except for Louis.

"And my New Thing is a twofer: I'll be living in a dorm and pledging a fraternity."

"So you'll be scoring lots of chicks," Jonathan said. "Pretty rad, man."

Barry turned to his father from underneath the Orioles cap. "Daddy, what's a pledge?"

"Take advantage of this, Daniel," Faith said. "And think long term. It's not about partying. This is where you start to develop a professional network."

"Daddy, what's a network?"

"You are excellent at befriending people. You have a charisma and charm that can't be taught. Alexander? John? You're my flesh and blood, I love you both, but I'm sorry. You'll never be Daniel."

Louis considered his salad, smothered with blue ranch. Had anyone discovered what he did in the bathroom?

"I have a Good Thing that could also qualify as a Very Good Thing," Stephen said. "But I'll save it for last. My Bad Thing is that Daniel will not be living at 48 Broad next year. You are now, all of you..." He waved his hand side to side to make sure his outstretched fingers found everyone. "...completely shocked. You no doubt thought I'd be happy to have one less brother in the house. But Daniel? Whatever our differences? You're the only one here who *gets* it." He stabbed the air with both hands in Daniel's direction. "Now my New Thing. This is where it gets interesting. My New Thing is that I've taken to cleaning up my room. Or I should say, my half of the room. I don't have my own room like Daniel because I lack his charm that can't be taught. Karen going AWOL has taught me not to be quite such a slob. Unfortunately..." Now he stabbed the air at Louis. "Louis's busy social schedule hasn't permitted him the time to learn that same lesson. So the room as a whole is half neat. This makes the New Thing a Neat Thing. Now my Good Thing. Yes! My Good Thing is not only a Very Good

Thing, it's a Very Musical Good Thing. Thanks to the cutting-edge technology of my musical setup on my neat side of the room, which includes a drum machine and synthesizer, I have written and recorded five original compositions. This is enough for what they call an EP. By the time I start Temple in the fall, I will have recorded enough for a full-length album." Stephen beamed at all the blank faces.

"Daddy, what's EP?"

Frank looked around at everyone before circling back to his first-born. "Congratulations, Stephen. Would projects like this, worthy though they may be, perhaps interfere with any attempt you may make or have thought of making apropos of seeking part-time employment over the summer, which may continue when you begin your studies in the fall?"

Now it was Stephen's turn to look around at everyone before circling back to his father. "I hadn't thought of getting a job at the moment. Or later. Or ever. In fact, I believe the last time you and I spoke, we agreed to take the wait-and-see approach. Since I will be a full-time student playing in the marching band, it might not be the most, shall we say, economically feasible, temporally speaking."

"That is an interesting recollection of our conversation on that matter," Frank said with his hands on the table. "I might be remembering it a bit differently, but in any case, good! I'm pleased your musical interests and passions are showing signs of fruition."

"My band was going to have a full-length by the end of the summer," Alexander said to his half-eaten taco. "But now that won't happen because someone, you know, saw fit to steal Frank's money."

When he ran up to his room, Louis flicked off the light and sprawled across his bed with the boom box on his belly. He blasted the Fat Boys and waited for someone to pound on the door in protest. No one ever did. When the album was over, he dragged himself out of bed and stepped carefully to the door and only had to open it a crack to let in the explosion of laughter. They were playing Oh Hell! He smacked his toe on the way back to his bed and caught the "FUCK!" in his mouth. Should he call Tanisha? They'd probably end up talking for hours. No, the only company he wanted right now was his rap music.

Next thing he knew, Louis was jerking awake to the sound of neighing horses from across the room. He was about to tell Stephen to turn it down, but when he heard Grace Jones talking to Arnold, he could tell *Conan the Destroyer* was already set to their agreed-upon volume.

Louis set the box on the floor as he sat up. Stephen had conked out in a slouch position with a half-eaten bowl of popcorn perched precariously on the side of the bed. His musical setup, which more or less formed the boundary between their halves of the room, included an electronic piano and a mic in addition to Stephen's prized synthesizer and drum machine. Louis could trace the silhouettes of the various cords against the light of the TV. The setup wasn't so complex. Stephen took a page from his father in how he loved making his shit sound like only a genius could pull it off, but Louis knew better. And now was the time to prove it.

Gorbie and his spotless balls were dead to the world when Louis stepped out on the back porch. Something about being outside in the wee hours felt absolutely thrilling, all the more so because he was wearing only his pajama pants and untied Jordans with the splayed tongues. It was pushing June, and the balmy air behaved accordingly. Just for the hell of it, and because it might lead him to the tools he was looking for, he decided to make a full circuit of the house. The space by the curb on Broad where his father had parked the station wagon seemed like the one spot not catching any moonlight.

When he came full circle to the backyard, he headed over to the garage and hauled open the door. Sure enough, neatly arranged in that old metal Oscar the Grouch garbage can, stood George Taylor's arsenal. Gorbie sniffed the shears as Louis stepped onto the back porch. "The fence is open, Gorbie. Go on. Go. While you've got the chance."

One of the laundry room fridges had two leftover Sal's pizza slices from several nights ago. No one would miss them. Louis gave one slice to Gorbie and threw the other across the lawn. Gorbie made short work of the first before blasting off for the second like a furry white rocket.

Watching that ravenous pooch excited hunger pangs in Louis's gut. When he cracked open the freezer chest, he reveled in the arctic blast giving his bare chest a big polar bear hug. There before him stood not one but two giant plastic bins of ice cream, strawberry and chocolate, a pillar of pink and one of brown, towering over the frozen meat and veggies. Louis hauled out both bins by their stiff metal wire handles and dropped them on the kitchen island. Dan had no doubt cleaned up after dinner, judging by the sheen of the surfaces. It usually took a good fifteen or so minutes for the ice cream to thaw enough for easy scooping.

Back up in his room, Conan was going toe-to-toe with Wilt the Stilt. Louis sat cross-legged on the floor behind the equipment and used the shears to clip the cords, the noise masked by all that clapping steel and macho grunting. It wasn't as easy as cutting hedges, but Louis managed, and with a smile to boot. Basil Poledouris's rousing score egged him on. Only when he was sitting back with a lazy chuckle and taking in the electronic carnage did he decide it was only proper he balance this out.

The boom box was out of the question, but the bed? If you measured value by square footage, his bed won hands down. But what could the shears do to it? The way the sheets and blankets jumbled and bunched and clumped reminded Louis of mashed potatoes. A smile snuck into the corner of his mouth.

With the sheets crammed under one arm, Louis grabbed the boom box and shears and took everything down to the poolroom. After nudging the couch toward the TV and rearranging the desk chairs to free up space, he pressed play on Doug E. Fresh and went to work.

"You IDIOT!" Frank swallowed and took a breath and slaughtered the air with a finger. "Lou-*is*! Let me introduce you to the concept of chemistry. When you take something that solidifies upon freezing, such as water, or most any liquid, when you unfreeze it, it performs an action called MELTING! It reverts back to its liquid FORM! This equally applies when you remove two significantly large objects that are frozen from the location that keeps them frozen, setting aside the odd fact that you felt compelled to take BOTH bins out when, based on my forty-six years of anecdotal data gathered from simply living on this planet, a single serving of ice cream does not require two bins. Apparently, you are unfamiliar with this concept. Now. This could be that being up at a late hour made you forgetful of certain principles, such as common fucking sense. Of course, perhaps I shouldn't be too surprised given that you're failing your first year of high school. Just so you're not surprised, but as you progress from ninth grade to tenth grade and so on, it gets harder. Unless you acquire at least a partial intellect, this next stage of your scholastic career will be a very brief one. Or a very long one, depending on how you look at it. Now. I would ask you to explain yourself, but based on your utter lack of common fucking sense, I'm guessing you wouldn't be able to form a coherent answer. But just in case miracles DO happen, then I will pose the question: Do you have a compelling reason behind the fucking travesty in the kitchen?"

Parked on the cold marble in front of the faux fireplace in the music room afforded Louis a straight-on view of Frank's red knee. Apparently he and John had convened in the kitchen for their usual coffee klatch and didn't notice the pink and brown pools before it was too late. "I... I, uhhhh..."

Frank closed his eyes, took another breath, and stabbed the air again. "Then there's the business with Stephen's musical equipment. Understandably, he's pretty upset. After all, you have completely ruined any chance or opportunity he will have to play or record his music. And per last night's Good Thing Bad Thing New Thing which, as you'll recall, he delivered with sufficient passion and fervor to make him wave his arms all about, he had been looking forward to having a set number of songs recorded by the time he entered Temple's music program this fall. Now, of course, that won't happen. He's upset with you. And he's upset with me. Before he stormed out this morning, he said something that indicated I was somehow in league with your machinations to sabotage his musical ambitions. Of course that's all bullshit, and once he can stand the sight of you enough not to PUNCH you, you can explain with as much eloquence you can muster, even if it isn't very much, which I suspect it won't be, that you, like Lee Harvey Oswald, acted alone. Now. Given that you performed this act within hours of Stephen's Good Thing Bad Thing New Thing, one could surmise that you, for devious reasons of your own, do not wish Stephen to realize his musical ambitions. Would this be an accurate supposition?"

The grogginess weighed a ton. "Uhhhhh..."

"So you fucked up THOUSANDS of dollars' worth of electronic equipment for reasons that escape you? Louis, that doesn't make any sense. Of course, having a reason won't undo the damage, but having a reason would at least mean you're not out of your fucking mind. Speaking of which, at some point we should discuss your sheets."

The back porch screen door slammed shut. Footsteps punished the laundry room floor, the kitchen floor, and the hallway with the most unforgiving thunder Louis had ever heard or felt from any pair of feet.

"FOUND HIM!" Faith's deathly pale visage appeared. She cradled a shivering, wide-eyed, terror-struck Gorbie.

"Fuck this." Louis jumped to his feet and made for the doorway, willing himself to shut that glare out of his peripheral vision.

"Your father is talking to you!"

When she clutched his shoulder as he slid past, Louis grabbed her wrist with one hand and used the other to shove her to the ground. On his way out the front double doors, he muttered, "He's not my father."

He stopped in his tracks. Where was he going? He spun around and saw sidewalk corners all around him. Louis was standing smack in the intersection of Broad Street and Mount Holly Avenue. Not a single car could be seen or heard. He continued looking around until the dizziness overwhelmed him. Sprawled on his back, Louis placed his palms flat on the asphalt and opened and closed his eyes in a slow, deliberate fashion. One of the clouds looked like a station wagon.

A station wagon peeled around the corner from Jacksonville Road. It was green and brown.

"No fucking way." He sat up just as the driver honked. It was an old woman with a white perm. He jumped out of the way with a mixture of blood-pumping adrenaline at coming this close to getting run over and relief that it wasn't his father.

The old woman blared her horn and screeched at him through the window.

Louis took off up Mount Holly Avenue to the intersection with Ridgeway Street and the entrance to the cemetery. The side of his head throbbed where one of the mullets had kicked him. The church on High tolled eight.

He headed up to the Mount. The utter silence would've gotten to him on any other day, but today it was just the balm he needed. Louis headed to the top and lay on his back and studied the foliage against the changing light. How realistic would it be to live up here? What essentials would he need?

At some point he decided to head to Tanisha's. He was making the turn at the Mount Holly Pharmacy when he remembered that she'd be at church. They usually didn't get home until midday. He killed time detouring to the 7-Eleven in a very roundabout way that involved passing RV and Folwell. Louis could try hiding everything from her, but that would've been futile with her sixth sense. As soon as she answered the door, he spilled everything. He concluded by saying, "I'm not in the mood for a play."

He spent the day at her place. She took advantage by having him help rearrange the furniture to make the space more easily navigable for her grandmother. Devon came in and out, and while he didn't shower Louis with pleasant greetings, the fact that he wasn't threatening bodily harm was a vast improvement on their relationship.

Tanisha took more advantage of Louis by having him help prepare the kitchen for dinner.

"Mind if I spend the night?"

"You going to call your folks?"

After dinner, Tanisha called Frank to let him know Louis was safe.

"He sound pissed?"

"He said he feels bad."

Louis chuckled. "You don't have to lie."

"You're going to have to go back there at some point. Watch, it won't be as bad as you think."

The sofa folded out into a bed. Last night's lack of sleep caught up with a vengeance. Louis slept straight through Devon leaving for school.

All day Monday Louis spun in his mind the first thing he'd say to Frank when he got home. He was in sixth-period earth science watching an episode of Carl Sagan's *Cosmos* when he decided that whatever he said, he should start out by telling Frank he was being philosophical.

He was on his way to seventh-period algebra when: "Hey, douchebag!"

Louis turned to find four mullets facing him in the center of the hall while students flowed by on either side.

Five or six additional mullets emerged from behind them. The passersby finally started to notice.

"What's it like to fuck a black chick, Roggebusch?"

"What's it like to fuck your sister?" Louis shot back.

"That's right. Keep digging that grave, Roggebusch."

At this point the passersby had gelled into two masses of spectators, one behind Louis, the other on the far side of the mullets.

"What the hell's going on here?"

Louis chuckled at the steaming, red-faced visage of Laz. "Hey, coach."

Laz made to step into the pending melee when three of the mullets blocked his path. "Out of my way, jackasses."

"Fuck off, old man."

"Touch Roggebusch and you're dead, faggots," Devon said from somewhere behind Louis.

"This don't concern you, homes," one of the mullets said.

"Homes? Bitch just said homes." Devon and his friends laughed.

One of the mullets launched and somehow got around Laz to

land a sock to Louis's jaw. Flat on his back, Louis caught a glimpse of Devon & Co. rush into fisticuffs. One of the mullets got down to deliver more licks while Louis returned the favor.

One of Devon's people pushed a redheaded mullet into Louis's mullet.

Now!

Louis whipped out the Swiss Army knife and flipped open the large blade in a single fluid motion that would've made Lone Wolf McQuade proud. The mullet's reaction time split the second in two. He dodged the thrust. The blade landed in the gut of the person behind him.

It was Jonathan.

"Fuck," the stepbrothers said in unison.

8

FAITH

NOOK 'N' BOOK AND ORGAN ICK

"You've got to wonder, Faith. Is the kid fucked up?"

Faith and Frank were lying side by side in bed after having had their longest bout of sex in months: thirteen minutes. Thirteen and change if you counted Frank's extra mini-tap-tap. You might think Faith weird to keep such precise measurement, but that just means you don't know Faith. She could've gone longer, but often she was too exhausted from trying to exorcise that maddening sense of entitlement from Frank's kids, biological and adopted alike. As for tonight's stamina, she and Frank could share the credit, as their motivation, shall we say, stemmed from a common source: the fact that one of the aforementioned adopted kids had stabbed one of the aforementioned biological kids. Using a knife belonging to one of Faith's kids.

In a perverse way, Faith was glad Louis had stabbed Jonathan. The whole ballyhoo was just the distraction she needed from this morning's biopsy. And besides, Jonathan would be fine. The blade caught him in the meat of his flank. Bloody, sure, but nothing permanent, at least not physically. Meantime, Faith was wondering if she should call her sister tomorrow or wait until the results came back. They'd long suspected something like this might happen. But nothing had happened yet, not officially. Why stir things up? She'd never shared with Frank this tidbit about her mother's side of the family. If the results came back the way she figured they would, how would that conversation go?

"I never thought I'd have anything to thank my shithead father for," she was saying. "But maybe, in his own special way, he honed my asshole radar. The second I laid eyes on Woody, I saw another version of Dad. A selfish coward with a natural-born charisma that hoodwinks ninety-nine percent of the people he meets. I can't believe you two used to be friends."

Frank slurped his scotch. "Well, to be fair, I hadn't started sleeping with Joanne at that point. I was what? Hardly thirty. I certainly didn't have any radar for assholes. Some people may have thought I was an asshole. Certainly Stephen and Jonathan's mother would say so, but when it comes to Count Dracula's opinion, I have to admit it doesn't keep me up at night."

"Of course Louis is fucked up. He's fucked up for life. But is it any wonder why?"

"I suppose you could be right."

"You were blessed, Frank. I've said it before, but you don't God damned get it. You grew up with parents who, from what I can tell, never introduced you to the word 'no.' You were this prince who could do whatever the hell he wanted. I'm not sure your childhood and mine could've been more different. Trying to explain to you what it's like to have a father who punches you out at the dinner table would be like talking to you in Swahili."

"I don't think Woody punches his children."

"But coming all this way and not even acknowledging one son while showering praise and affection on the other? That's the psychological version of being punched out."

"Well." Frank picked his nose. "Hmm. Let's give him some time. Having him and John switch rooms should be a step in the right direction."

"I'd prefer him sharing with someone on the third floor to get him farther from Stephen. Jonathan's room is too small. Daniel shouldn't have to share a room. And no one in their right mind would cohabitate with Bawrence. Waking up to the smell of piss every day..."

Frank finished off the scotch. "I just hope Jonathan doesn't tell his mother about being stabbed. Of course, he probably already has. Night-night, love."

Faith read a mile a minute. It took her all of a week to polish off Ursula K. Le Guin's Earthsea trilogy. She hadn't read it in years and appreciated it much more this time. In that same spirit, she felt it was time to revisit Tolkien. Tonight she made it through the first hundred pages of *The Hobbit* before her eyes felt heavier than the Sackville-Bagginses.

Her eyes snapped open at three in the morning. It wasn't biopsy stress that flicked her brain back on. It was Jonathan. This Saturday, the last day of May, was his birthday. Frank hadn't said anything about it. She was sure he'd forgotten. That meant everyone else had too.

She slipped out of bed and shuffled into the nook overlooking the backyard. You won't be surprised to learn this was hands down her favorite spot in the house. It was the only spot where she felt separate from the house. It was a tiny space, to be sure, a few feet by even fewer feet, leaving just enough room for the old cushioned armchair and matching stool Frank had brought with him from Kensington. Apparently, this had been his main TV-watching chair in those days. At first it felt awkward sitting in a chair her husband occupied daily during the ten years he was married to Bawrence's mother. They could have had sex in this chair. That chubby half-faced bed wetter could've been conceived right here on this very piece of patterned kitsch.

No matter. The chair wasn't dwelling on it. Why should she?

On the wall she'd taped up old photos showing various combinations of herself, her sister, and their mother. You wouldn't think Faith would want any vestige of her father in her sanctum sanctorum, but to her it made perfect sense to slap up at least one photo, and a large one to boot, featuring the shit-eating grin that fooled the world. That photo reminded her that she was a survivor.

Her father's photo especially made sense when she did stuff like this. "Think I'm selfish, Daddy? Then why am I thinking about Jonathan? His birthday's coming up. You were never into birthdays."

Faith could go weeks, months even, without doing this. Indeed, for most of last year Faith's father had left her head alone, but 1986 had seen her guilty conscience kick her ass up and down the block. Just a couple of weeks ago she'd had a nasty episode in Bawrence's room.

"But what should I get him?"

She stood up and surveyed the backyard. The most obvious ideas were the athletic kind. A new hoop to replace that sad one on the garage? A jersey maybe? Golf clubs were out of the question. A lot would have to be out of the question courtesy of whoever stole the five hundred fifty-eight dollars out of Frank's sock drawer. Of that amount, two hundred ninety-one had belonged to her. She'd been gearing up to get presents for Jonathan as well as John, whose birthday was in mid-June. And don't even get her started on Alexander's band camp.

At some point her eyes wandered up to the full moon just past its zenith. Orion's Belt sat a few degrees away, like salt that had been mis-sprinkled. That's when it hit her. Of course she knew what to get Jonathan. He didn't think anyone knew about this passion of his, but Faith made it a point to know everything that went on under this roof.

On her way home from Princeton the next day, she stopped by the Burlington Center. The hobby store featured several different kinds of telescopes on sale, all lined up in a row from smallest to largest. Faith had no idea where to begin.

"What do you want to see?"

"Pardon?"

The Ichabod Crane look-alike smiled through the specs perched on his nose and nodded at the telescopes. "Certain constellations? Galaxies? Me, I've got Big Red over there. You can get the Large and Small Magellanic Clouds with that baby. The North America Nebula. Pretty rad."

"I met Carl Sagan, you know."

"Get out!"

"On two different occasions he visited the University of Colorado in Boulder while I was a student there."

"My hero!"

"He gets on my nerves."

"He's so rad to talk to, you know?"

"It's my stepson's birthday on Saturday. Kid's down in the dumps because he got stabbed at school by his brother."

"Unreal!"

"And since I'm the only one who remembers his birthday, the onus, if you will, is on me to rally his spirits."

"Freaking awesome."

"He doesn't know I know he likes astronomy. He doesn't want anyone to know because apparently it's not cool. So a gift like this will either thrill him or piss him off. After weighing the risks for weeks, I've opted for potential short-term scorn for longer-term gratitude. How much is that one?"

"The black beauty? Check it out." He led her down to the largest of the selection, a gleaming black cannon with a dangling yellow triple-digit price tag. "It's really rad that you and your son have this hobby together. Know what? Here's a secret reason I look at the stars. I almost never tell anyone this. But it's a weeknight, it's quiet. Plus you seem like a nice, smart lady. I do it to get a rad perspective on things. Know what I mean? Those times you're feeling like everything's a bummer? You can escape through this. You can get away from this depressing planet. I totally sound insane to you right now."

"In fact, I can relate to that sentiment."

"Your kid's going to love this."

"Of course, the lofty price increases the risk. I must acknowledge the possibility that he'll be too embarrassed to accept this. He'll refuse to admit it's something that can help him graduate his passion to the next level."

"I so love how you say that."

When she got home, Frank had just finished whipping up

Cornish game hens with rosemary potatoes and peas. Faith sat down at the table with a grin and a swell of pride. Yes, she knew it was a stupid grin. And yes, of course she knew the kids made fun of her and Frank when they weren't around. John would sit at one end of the table, Daniel at the other, and they'd role-play the grinning much to the ass-rolling hilarity of the rest of the brood. But who gave a shit, right? She thought about her biopsy. Her grin dimmed a bit. "My Good Thing is that Jonathan got through the stabbing in one piece."

"Coming from the woman who did a Nolan Ryan fastball with a can of peas to my head, I'd've thought you'd be celebrating."

"Not seeing eye to eye with someone doesn't mean you wish them ill, Jonathan."

"Said the woman who threw a can of peas at Jonathan's head."

"Ow! It fucking hurts to laugh, man."

"My New Thing is that now I can say I live under the same roof as someone who stabbed their brother," Faith said.

Louis kept his eyes pointed at his plate while he mumbled and squashed one of the little potatoes between his fingers. He dropped the mush and moved on to the next victim.

"If you're interested in having a constructive conversation, you'll have to articulate."

Louis continued mumbling and squashing.

"If you can't form words, perhaps you shouldn't open your mouth at all."

"Jonathan's not my fucking brother."

"Watch your mouth."

"I've said sorry a million times. What more do you want?"

Stephen sliced the air with gesticulations in a picture-perfect imitation of his father. "I was pissed about my musical dreams being blown up. But now? After you knifed Jonathan? I'm just glad it was my dreams you blew to a million pieces and not, you know, me." He giggled in that maniacal way that Faith could only assume he inherited from his mother. Lord knows Frank never wore his square specs crooked or pulled off such an uncanny impersonation of the Joker.

"None of these people are my brothers. I'm living in a house with a family that's not my fucking family."

"Well," Frank said. He looked around at everyone.

"Dan's about to leave," Louis said. "Why am I still here? Whatever."

"But what about this gem?" Stephen splayed five fingers in Barry's direction. "Bawrence Barney, did you know you were born out of an illicit affair? The half of you related to Louis will be the only thing he's related to in the house after Dan leaves. Look at the bright side. At least he won't stab you. Or if he does, it won't be on purpose."

"Those are called bragging rights, Bawrence," Frank said.

Stephen cracked up.

Faith furtively watched Louis stuffing some of the mashed rosemary potato in his mouth. She knew the kid was at an emotional nadir, but everything was still relative. From where she sat, she'd've given one of her breasts to switch places with him right now.

"And your Bad Thing, love?"

"Didn't I say it already?"

"Don't believe so. Although after the present conversation, you might have some ideas."

I have a lump in my breast that in all likelihood is cancer. Statistics say I have less than five years to live. "Today I learned that the robot I've been busting my ass on for the past six months will have to be shelved so I can pitch in on another project that's behind schedule."

"Oh too bad."

"I'm pissed off."

"Is that the robot that's, like, an arm?" John asked with a mouthful of blue-ranched salad.

With Frank parked in the recliner with his scotch, Daniel handling the dishes, Louis hanging out at Tanisha's, Alexander practicing bass in the music room, and the balance of the brood playing the Commodore, Faith fled to the master bedroom with a tall cup of water. She tried to distract herself by mulling what to get John for his birthday that would top Jonathan's telescope. It was in vain, though, as her thoughts, like a tributary that wouldn't be denied, streamed into the main river of anxiety: the biopsy.

If the worst came to be, she'd have to turn her thoughts to more practical questions, from what to get John for his birthday to what to get him and Alexander for their next umpteen birthdays, what to leave them. Did she have life insurance through Princeton? How could she not know that? Should she leave anything for Sarah and Eddie? Faith had no illusions that Eddie, even though he was the oldest, would outlive his sisters. Cancer only hit the Drummond women.

Maybe that's why these women were such tough bastards. Faith laughed at the memory of when she and Frank had flown out to San Francisco when they were still engaged. Their first stop was Aunt Suz. All three daughters were there, two of them with their husbands. At the end of the night, Aunt Suz, beaming, announced to Frank that he passed the test.

"Test?"

"My girls and I have been gauging your character to see if you belong in our family. Faith knows we cherish things like integrity, traits that add up to a well-rounded individual with a healthy, robust intellect. She knows this well because, as my sister could explain, Faith has struggled to fit this mold. Congratulations. I look forward to the wedding."

Frank's eye took on the gleam that Faith had since come to under-stand was his own sort of thinking nook, a portable real-time nook for nipping conundrums in the bud. "That's very interesting. As it turns out, I have been conducting a similar test. Faith wasn't cognizant of it, nor was I planning to bring it up until we left. Would you like to know the results thus far? After having sized you up and your well-accomplished children, well, as it turns out, the results of my scrutiny are not yet in."

That was when Faith knew she was marrying the right man.

Laughing at the memory was just the balm she needed. It freed up some mental bandwidth to ponder how to patch things up with Alexander. How could she make up for his missing band camp? Last summer all the kids took tennis lessons at Westwood. Alexander seemed to enjoy it the most. If she enrolled him this summer, would it distract him from his indignation? Or only remind him he wasn't doing what he really wanted to do? She couldn't help the broad smile. How wonderful it was to focus on the quotidian tribulations of being a parent.

Frank stumbled into the room a little after nine and, by the sound of his voice, was swimming four or five scotches deep. "Hello, love!" Gorbie darted in and jumped up on her lap. Frank stuck his hands down the back of his sweatpants. "Question for you. I have been thinking, as I sometimes do. Now that it's been nearly a month since the five hundred dollars were stolen, perhaps it's time for Karen to return to her normal Wednesday schedule. What do you think?"

Faith's Gorbie-petting hand tensed for a second. "How's her mother faring?"

"A very good question."

"If she's amenable, then it's perfectly one hundred percent acceptable by me."

"I haven't really studied our books very carefully, at least not in the past, oh, three or four days or so."

"Has it been that long?"

"But when I did, I remember thinking, 'You know, when we get to June, between the end-of-month checks from Temple, Princeton, and my consulting for the Department of Energy, we should have enough to bounce back.'"

"I feel like we're talking to two different points. Everything you're saying seems predicated on Karen's service having been suspended due to the stolen money."

Frank bobbed his head in that fluid way he could only pull off after having ingested enough, well, fluid.

"But it was my understanding she stopped coming because her mother fell ill."

He continued bobbing his head. "In a sense."

"What does Karen say?"

"What do *you* say?"

"I defer to Karen's judgment on the status of the condition her mother is supposed to have."

"*Supposed* to have? Theory versus reality? Because we can talk about that until the fat lady sings."

"Frank..." She closed her suddenly very heavy eyes.

"You and Karen haven't always seen eye to eye. Now that she's been gone a few weeks, it's possible you've come to enjoy not having her around."

The hand froze on Gorbie's head. "I'm baffled."

"Allow me to unbaffle you."

"*You* want Karen to return. Without having first asked Karen if returning is an option. From her point of view."

"I shall phone Karen first thing tomorrow."

"The house all to yourself. So you can phone Karen."

"Or maybe I won't phone Karen."

Faith took in the grease-stained golf shirt stretched over that expanding gut, the same filthy garment he'd worn last night, and his bare feet, and smiled as she resumed petting the pooch. Gorbie licked her hand.

"Fine. I won't phone Karen. I hope this meets with your satisfaction."

"You have failed to explain the relevance of the theft of the five hundred fifty-eight dollars to Karen's supposedly ill mother."

"Who said it has anything to do with it?"

"When you stumbled in, nearly falling over, I might add, you prefaced this discussion by establishing the approximate length of time since the theft and that our funds would sufficiently be replenished after the next pay cycle to compensate for the theft, which therefore meant taking Karen back on would be tenable. Correct? That clearly implies she stopped coming due to pecuniary reasons and not, as she has said, to nurse her mother."

Frank stopped rocking on his feet and squinted at the windows. When he resumed rocking, he pulled one hand from his sweats and stabbed the air. "Karen performs a service that costs money." He looked at her. "Agreed?"

Faith returned his look but said nothing. The hand continued petting.

"One hundred dollars a week to clean the house. That includes vacuuming and mopping."

"Vacuuming and mopping what?"

"Say again?"

"For what services specifically are we paying her a hundred dollars a week?"

"*We* don't pay her anything. I pay her."

"Why do *we* pay her a hundred dollars a week?"

"Karen is paid."

"For?"

"Services rendered."

"Is she a prostitute?"

"Karen is a professional."

Faith had to lean forward as the laughter defeated her. Gorbie jumped down, waited for her to recover, and jumped back up. This time he sat only on his hindquarters to be sure his head was high enough to lick her face. "Gorbashay, what are your thoughts?"

"You are consulting with our dumb dog?"

"Do you miss Shadow? Hmm? I'm sure he misses you."

"Karen mops the kitchen floor, the laundry room floor, all hard surfaces."

"So she mops the second-floor hallway?"

"The surfaces she deems to require mopping, drawing upon her years of professional insight and experience. She vacuums all carpeted surfaces. Does this description meet with your approval?"

"What happens after the hard surfaces are polished and the carpets are refreshed?"

"I issue her a check from *my* bank account."

"Have you ever had to clean up after yourself in your life? I know you didn't when you were growing up in that big pillared house in Washington. You had staff."

"I do the dishes. Whenever Daniel doesn't do them."

"The bathrooms would be fucking swamps if not for Karen. She earns her money from that alone, far as I'm concerned. And she dusts. Have you ever dusted a single fucking surface in your life? Karen also comes armed with all those cleaning fluids. Have you ever wondered what she does with them? Why does she need a glass cleaner, for example?"

"As, per you, I lack the requisite experience to possess such knowledge..."

"Frank, all I want to know is the connection between the stolen five hundred fifty-eight dollars and Karen's having to take time off to care for her mother."

"I won't call her. Done." He stomped out.

Whenever Faith scored a win, it was Pyrrhic at best. Her state of calm, once realized, would always be antique brittle. As her husband's footsteps receded down the back stairs to the kitchen, where yet another glass of the hard stuff was no doubt calling his name, her equilibrium was left in tatters.

To regain her focus, she clocked long hours at Princeton the next day. Frank was working from home, leaving him oodles of time to phone Karen before the kids started trickling in around three. Having to change projects midstream, even though she'd used it as a Bad Thing at dinner, provided just the distraction she needed. Only three times throughout the day did she devote any mental energy to stressing over Karen coming back, with two of the three happening during lunch when it was easy to camouflage with the rapid chewing she was known for.

She meant to get home in time for supper, but turnpike traffic, coupled with the humongous telescope in the back weighing down the Rabbit, conspired to slow her down. It was twenty-one minutes past seven when she walked in the door to the smells of spaghetti and steaming french bread and the sounds of far too many male voices.

"Hi, Mom."

"Hey, Mommy."

"I had faith in Faith's making it back on time," Daniel said.

"Very original," Stephen said.

"Where's Louis?" Faith asked.

Frank cleared his throat and turned in his chair. "Hello, lovey. You never called. Although I assumed, based on what you said last night, that things were kind of hectic."

"He upstairs?"

"Louis is dining at Tanisha's residence. Here…"

"Don't get up. My workday is not over."

"It almost appears as if you're about to head back out."

"Boys." She faced the room. "We'll be adding chores for each of you on the chalkboard to make up for Karen's absence."

"She ever coming back, Pop?"

"The house is turning into a pigsty, and while that might be okay for you, it's not so nice to come home to at the end of the day."

"Lovey. Here. Have a seat. Your Bad Thing for this evening will be a dirty house."

Faith would've given a breast to slap that grin right off his face. She plopped some spaghetti in a bowl, tore off a hunk of bread, and filled a thermos with water to take upstairs to her nook. She wasn't lying when she said she needed to get more work done. What she left out was why.

Faith knew Karen lived in Lumberton but not much else. She'd never memorized her phone number because she never needed to call her. Her coming on Wednesdays had been progressing like clockwork for three years.

Sometime after dinner, she set her papers and Gorbie on the carpet and crept into the hallway to gauge everyone's location. Between the living, music, and poolrooms, it sounded like the brood was all downstairs. The kitchen black-and-white blared up the back stairs, too loud for whomever was watching it to hear her. If anyone was upstairs, it would only be Barry, and Faith was 99.9 percent confident he wouldn't be coming down the rest of the night. If he ever emerged from his room, it would be for the bathroom, and once he crashed, not even for that.

When she flicked on the light in Frank's office, her heart sank at the sty of papers while Baltimore yapped from his three-story birdcage across the room. Frank had bought six or seven desks of a similar style to what the kids used in the poolroom during homework hour. Two or three were arranged in the middle of the room with the Radio Shack TRS-80 and dot matrix printer, in addition to software books, legal pads, loose sheets of paper, a roll of paper towels, used paper towels, several coffee mugs containing various measures of cold coffee, and the small plates he used for the peanut butter bread quarter slices he enjoyed after jogging. The three or four tables arranged along the left side were more of a storage dump for various office supplies and even more dishes. Sections of carpet were a winter wonderland of paper hole dots.

Protruding from the wall over to the far right was a rusted white porcelain sink. She'd always meant to ask George Taylor about that. Had his in-laws used that when it became harder to get about the house? It looked positively ancient, of the same style as that rusted porcelain tub that had awaited the Roggebusch clan in the third-floor bathroom.

To her immediate right, against the wall opposite Baltimore, stood a pair of metal bookcases crammed with stacks on such topics as calculus, statistics, economic models, and programming languages. Some books were stacked standing up while others were laid atop each other in sloppy pillars. The bottom shelves featured a bunch of those boxes you bought flat and then formed into a box by folding it in at the indicated corners. The ones nearer to her were choking on bloated yellow envelopes. Faith lifted the partially displaced lid on one and spotted the word "Taxes!" scrawled in black marker on the top envelope.

When she lifted the lid off one of the boxes in the next book-case, she was greeted by a letter written in blue ink. It was Frank's handwriting. Faith slipped it out delicately, holding it by the edges. It was dated a few weeks ago, before Barry found out from his mother that he would have to wait one more year before living with her.

JOANNE: [Frank still addressed Barry's mom by her old name even

though it had been a year and a half since she relocated to North
Carolina and changed it to Joan.]

*This letter is written confirmation of our agreement that Bawrence will
relocate to your residence in August of this year. Excepting visits up here
during Christmas and a certain portion of the summer, a portion to be
determined jointly by you and me at the appropriate time, Bawrence will
reside at your address from August of this year until August two years
hence.*

*Built into this agreement is the assumption that Bawrence will attend
grades five and six during his North Carolina tenure. You and I agreed he
would do so in your local public school system, as public schools will incur
neither you nor I any cost.*

*You and I also agreed that your income at the University of North
Carolina, paired with your income from the part-time night and weekend
job you mentioned (was it medical receptionist?), was sufficient for you to
support Bawrence without any external assistance, such as monthly
payments from me. In contrast to my divorce from Stephen and Jonathan's
mother, our separation was free of legal intrusion, interruption, or compli-
cation. You and I were, and will hopefully remain, of a reasonable level of
equilibrium without any external arbitration or moderation.*

*I freely admit you are better equipped than I to gauge Bawrence's well-
being. To this day I feel guilty for not having caught his near-fatal illness,
and given the logical way you explained how to discern an illness in a child,
I sometimes wonder how that kind of intuition eluded me. Perhaps this is
yet one more reason why I doubt the wisdom of the decision that has placed
me in these present circumstances (I am sure you will never show anyone,
anywhere, at any time, this letter).*

*I trust Bawrence will enjoy his two years with you and look forward to
his return in August of 1988.*

FAITH SLIPPED the letter back into the box and pushed the lid shut
with the nonchalance of someone who'd come upon an old shopping
list in one of the carts at Super Fresh.

She stood back up to survey the room. If she were Karen's contact information belonging to a man who had no Rolodex, where would she be? Given how said man spent the majority of his time in this room parked in that squeaky swivel chair, she had to figure he kept important contact info within easy reach of that spot.

Closing the door to keep Baltimore's yapping from spilling out, Faith tiptoed over to the central desks and flipped through papers and notepads. In the hallway she heard Gorbie's paws click-clack up to the door. He scratched and squeaked in complaint. This was beyond hopeless. Frank's desks were such a collective heap that she doubted even he could've found it.

Faith was standing there, hands on hips, trying in vain to block out the fluttering and chirping finch, when her eyes caught a Post-It protruding from the side of the computer screen, one among a forest of yellow with black scribble. This one had on it a vaguely legible "Karen" with a phone number beneath it. She grabbed one of the black felt-tip pens scattered near the printer and copied the number on a fresh Post-It. As if sensing her excitement, Baltimore fluttered more wildly around the cage while Gorbie scratched and squeaked in earnest.

Boss Hogg was watching her from across the way, one of his kitties perched on his rough ham of a shoulder, bathing a forepaw. She peeled off the Post-It and squirmed her way through the jungle and out the door to an ecstatic Gorbie.

Amazing how warm milk could calm a restless mind. This was perhaps the only lesson her father had taught her that made any sense. Afraid she'd be up all night playing and replaying all the possible scenarios of confronting Karen, including one that saw her walking in on her and Frank fucking on the kitchen table while Karen's mother died slowly in the next room watching *The Price Is Right*, Faith crept down the back stairs. She was desperate enough for her father's remedy that she was willing to tolerate social interaction. Fortunately, the black-and-white was playing to an empty kitchen. She smacked the knob into the off position before nuking herself a glass of skim milk. When she awoke the next morning to Frank's getting suited up for Temple, her tranquility made her forget, if only for a moment, that she had an important mission today.

Faith couldn't help smiling as she watched her husband tie his tie in the body mirror, his entire left half doused with the sunlight pouring in through the nook. On the one hand, he and his big tummy and the way his tie sat on it were absolutely adorable. On the other, she could read in his countenance how much his sense of entitlement made him resent the whole idea of getting dressed for work. That pissed her off.

"Have a good day, love."

Most Tuesdays and Thursdays, she would only wait for Frank to leave before pulling out her vibrator. On this morning, though, she needed the whole house empty. She lay on her back and watched the sunlight float across the nook doorway while listening to Frank and John down in the kitchen exchange a few philosophical words over coffee. It took a good hour or so for everyone, one by one, on their own time and with their own attitudes and footfall patterns and throat-clearing noises, to make their way out the door.

After phoning her boss to tell him she was under the weather, Faith headed into the bathroom for a long, scalding-hot shower. Today she'd wear her most comfortable blue jeans and the emerald blouse she hadn't worn since that house party Frank hosted for his grad students. She brewed a hot mug of tea downstairs and came back up to take the phone into the nook. The sun speckled the grass and bathed her vegetable garden. What with the sparkling dew and sparkling chirps and the absence of antisparkling car noises, Faith would've gone outside to do her thinking if she didn't need to make this call.

"This is Karen, can I help you?" Karen spoke fast, and her breath sounded heavy.

"Hi. Or good morning, I should say."

"Morning."

"You know who this is?"

"Voice sounds familiar."

"It's Faith. Faith Roggebusch."

"Oh hey!"

"How are you?"

"Caught me in the middle of a workout. Wow!"

"Are you being literal?"

"Sorry?"

"Are you using the word workout in the literal sense? Like you're exercising? Or figuratively? To indicate you've been having a busy morning?"

"You know the Jane Fonda video?"

"I have it myself."

"Yeah, yeah, yeah! I do it five times a week. She is one rad chick."

"Bit too liberal though."

"Huh?"

"But yes, Ms. Fonda's energy and enthusiasm are contagious. I only wish I could get to it five days a week myself."

"Yeah, yeah, yeah."

"Would you happen to have thirty minutes to spare for a chat? Preferably in person? I could come over to your place."

"Shadow, get down from there. Shadow!" She laughed. "Stupid mutt. How's Gorbie?"

"Shadow is the only dog he gets along with. How's your mother doing?"

"What's that?"

"Your mother." In the background Faith could hear Jane cheer-leading her viewers through those dreadful leg-flexing maneuvers that always lit her quads on fire.

"Oh man. You have no idea. Or maybe you do. Are your parents, um...?"

"My father's never been sick a day in his life and will probably outlive us all. Mother died of breast cancer after spending most of her adult life bent over with arthritis." Were Mother standing here right now, leering while Faith chatted with this younger, attractive woman, she'd probably taunt her by asking if she wished she had breasts like Karen's.

"Holy shit, Faith."

"It was genetic. She lived her whole life in physical agony."

"Fuckin' A."

"That's why I was worried about your mother."

"Yeah, yeah, yeah. Mom's... I mean, it's hard to explain. She was in bed a lot at first. It wasn't pneumonia really. I mean, it kind of was."

"Did you have to put your other clients on hiatus as well, so to speak?"

"It's been crazy. And I've got bills. Mom's got doctor bills. Totally. And I'm going to school. I mean, it's like, holy shit, what am I going to do?"

"But things are okay now?"

"Huh?"

"Or at least improved?"

"Eh."

"Maybe we could have lunch."

"Yeah, yeah, yeah. Totally. I mean, I'm not the biggest lunch eater. I try to keep my meals small. But then I snack a lot because I have no willpower."

"Would noon work?"

"Normally it would, but one would be better if you can do that." She gave Faith her address in Lumberton.

When Faith took Gorbie on an extra long walk to kill the rest of the morning, additional scenarios for the meeting spun around her skull with a much-improved note of positivity compared to last night's stormy speculations. One of them, the one Faith wasn't ashamed to admit was optimistic to a fault, saw her and Karen becoming fast friends and shopping buddies. When she and the pooch got back, she snapped out of it, accepted that her personality was diametrically opposed to Karen's, and only prayed she could survive the meeting sans conflagration.

Lumberton, like Mount Holly, had no shortage of three-story Victorians, many of which had been converted into apartment buildings. Some of them even saw their screened-in back and/or front porches turned into studios, with the building's side entrance repurposed as the main entrance. Karen lived on the third, steep-gabled floor of a Queen Anne that was originally sky blue, yellow, and red but was now a faded melding of the three.

"Hiya! Come on into my humble abode over here!"

Faith was reminded of the studio she lived in during her undergraduate years at Boulder, a tight space that had evolved in her mind from cramped to intimate. And just like Karen, she had a Murphy bed. The fridge wasn't much bigger than Baltimore's birdcage. Parked on top of the chipped and scratched wooden dresser, the kind that only seemed to exist at garage sales, was a black-and-white TV, just a bit smaller than the one in the kitchen back home. It was currently showing a soap opera with the sound turned down. The empty Jane Fonda sleeve lay atop the little VCR. The only sound came from an elderly guy weed whacking across the street.

"Want some water? I'm sorry, I know. Grocery shopping, I've been putting it off."

"Where's Shadow?"

"That stupid mutt?"

Faith had always prided herself on superb peripheral vision. She never once had to look directly at Karen to appreciate her figure, nicely defined by the light purple blouse and jeans. "I thought I heard a doggie door on the phone."

"Yeah, yeah, yeah. We have a community kitchen with a doggie door in the back. Shadow's not the only stupid mutt in town. Hey, you look like a Perrier kind of gal. What do you say?"

Faith adored Perrier and made Frank get six-packs of it during his and Barry's weekly two-cart Super Fresh run. "I am not opposed to Perrier."

Karen dug two out of the baby fridge. "I love how you guys have three refrigerators. I have all three memorized, like what's in each one. There's no better way to get to know people than to look in their fridge. You guys always have Perrier in that one fridge in the laundry room that has the veggies and stuff. That's your fridge, right?"

Faith couldn't help cracking the slightest of smiles as she took a quick pull from the green bottle. "Interesting observation. Linking personality to refrigerator contents." She took another pull and wondered why she hadn't thought of that. "Perrier has healthy qualities in addition to the healthy aspects of drinking water."

"Cheers, girlfriend!"

"They say sixty-four ounces is the ideal water intake per person per day, which amounts to eight eight-ounce glasses. Of course, no one really measures how much their glass holds. Mine is definitely bigger than eight ounces, so I could probably get away with five or six servings of water and still achieve the sixty-four-ounce ideal."

"If eight is such an important number, you'd think they'd sell Perrier in bottles that only hold eight pounds."

"Ounces."

"And then sell eight of those at a time. So you could get an eight-pack of eight things per bottle, and there, just get one of those every day and drink all of it. You like music?"

When the organ started filling the room, Faith's mouth fell open before she caught it. Willing herself to be restrained took more strain than ever and triggered a tickle in her chest that made her titter. "Sounds like Bach."

"It's so calming. So rad. It's great when I'm doing homework or reading something for class. I like all kinds of music. Madonna. Cyndi Lauper. I know, I know. Guilty. Depends on my mood, I guess."

"You know, on Sundays I play the organ at the Episcopal Church in Medford."

"Here, sit down. Sorry for the mess. You are so smart!"

Faith sat on the round footstool after Karen cleared the clothes off it. Karen rolled her desk chair around to face her and sat perched on the edge of it. Faith leaned back just a bit and crossed her legs. "You might find this amusing, Karen, but in fact, in a certain sense, I derive more enjoyment from playing the organ one day a week than working in robotics five days a week."

"That is so radical you work with robots."

"What I mean to say is that this art form, which is centuries old, gives me more pleasure than the most sophisticated technology of today. Think about that because there's a lesson there."

"Yeah, yeah, yeah. Totally!"

"I've noticed that when you come over, you often wear a Walkman. I assume house cleaning requires a different soundtrack than the ecclesiastical kind?"

Karen giggled and blushed. "'Material Girl!' and 'Girls Just Want to Have Fun!'"

"No one is as familiar with our house as you are. That is, among those who don't already live there. It's important to keep the house clean when so many animals live in it."

"But you only have two pets, Gorbie and Baltimore."

Faith grinned. "On that point, and since your skill set is an ideal fit, I was wondering if you'd entertain the idea of resuming your weekly schedule. Of course, it doesn't have to be Wednesdays. Whatever works for you." And then came the words that ambushed Faith as much as Karen: "And we'll give you a raise." Karen took a long pull from her Perrier, providing a full-on view of her well-toned shoulders and neck. "But I want to confirm that your mother's health is such that you are comfortable coming back."

"Mom keeps saying getting old is never fun. I'm like, 'Yeah, thanks, Mom.'"

"Could you return, say, next week?"

"You guys have one awesome house. One time me and my girlfriends drove by just so they could see it. I was like, 'I get to work in that place every week!' They went nuts."

Faith grinned.

"Yeah, you know, it's an interesting prospect."

"Between you and me, the house has turned into a shit heap since you left. Frank's office alone would take up a whole day."

"And so. Like. What kind of a raise would it be? I don't want to sound greedy or anything."

"Raises are traditionally percentage based and involve multiple variables that fall more squarely in the court of an economist and statistician like Frank than someone in applied mathematics like myself. However, I hesitate to bring it up with Frank if you feel like your mother is still dependent."

"Yeah, yeah, yeah. I mean, she's fine right now. I could totally work. Gosh. Sometimes it's just... With Mom's medical bills, school, Shadow, the rent for this dump..."

"Add in a bunch of kids, most of whom aren't yours. And a mortgage." And the very real possibility that you'll be dead in a year.

"What stinks is that if I do come back to work for you guys, and Mom gets sick again, then I have to stop coming and devote all my time to playing nurse."

"I'll consult with my husband about the percentage of the raise. If our conclusion meets with your satisfaction, you can tell us which day of the week would be ideal."

"Sounds like a plan, Stan!"

"There a bathroom up here?"

Faith didn't know what possessed her to rummage through the little wastebasket next to the toilet while she was doing her business. She didn't have to rummage through more than a layer or two of cardboard toilet paper rolls and cotton swabs and scrunched tissues and soap wrappers before arriving at something she had to stare at hard before she trusted her eyes.

KAREN:

It has been two weeks since you last cleaned my house. Given the timing of your mother's illness, combined with your, let us say, abrupt behavior and tone, and given my own understanding about money and its uncanny ability to alter so completely a person's behavior (my first wife being a superlative example), I have come to the conclusion that my inability to lend you the five hundred dollars has contributed, somehow, to your absence. I know I said I'd lend you these funds, I know you said you needed these funds with an acute urgency, but, just to minimize the chance or opportunity for misunderstanding, assuming my previous phone calls have failed to minimize such a misunderstanding, please know that I will still provide you the funds should they become available to me to provide.

THE HOME PREGNANCY kit beneath it had a plus sign.

No one likes to barf, but that accursed purple prose filled her with something that would not, could not, stay down.

"Babe, you okay?"

After flushing and squeezing back into her jeans, she extended fifteen seconds of good hard thought toward wondering if she should put the letter back in the can and cover up her rummaging. Her father's voice asked why she'd give two bits about this hussy knowing what she'd done.

"Hey! You all right? Was it the Perrier?"

Faith hurried past those inscrutable green eyes, too green for their own good. "I'm sorry." The tiny hallway seemed endless. As did the stairs. And the sidewalk.

"Hello, lovey," Frank said when he found Faith in the nook. The sound of Louis grilling Barry for sucking at Wiffle ball bounced up from the backyard. "Home early."

"I clocked eighty-six hours last week. Eighty-one and a half the week before. I just needed some time to rest. Relax my brain." She offered a weak smile.

"Sounds perfectly logical."

"Do you want Karen to come back? And please, Frank, no bullshit."

Frank bobbed and swayed and swiped a finger across his mustache. "If it's all the same to you, I would prefer we take that discussion outside the house."

While Frank got changed into shorts and a Redskins tee, Faith headed downstairs to find Gorbie. The Lhasa apso was curled up under the couch in the poolroom. Faith was the only person on earth who could coax Gorbie out from under that couch simply by calling his name. She and the leashed-up, ear-scratching pooch were waiting outside when Frank came down.

When they were on their way, Frank stalled with moans about how some of his students were having a hard time with his quizzes even though he all but gave them the answers ahead of time. The only faculty they need possess, he said, was that of literacy. When they reached the top of Buttonwood and rounded the bend at the foot of the Mount, he said, "I'm afraid I haven't been, let us say, one hundred percent straightforward about why Karen discontinued her services. Her mother, so far as I understand it, is in a bad way. What manner of bad way? I haven't asked. Not sure it's my place to. But as science tells us, the older we get, the more opportunities there are for things to go wrong with our bodies. To complicate matters, their health insurance is insufficient to shield them from the expenditures of the care her mother requires. Given your experience with your mother's debilitation, you may understand Karen's predicament better than myself."

"I don't really know what's going on at all."

At the bottom of Hillside Road they let Gorbie dawdle and sniff among the bushes until he lifted a leg and did his business. They swung a right onto High Street and continued up toward the Fair-grounds and the Acme. Kids from Holbein were heading home. Several played leapfrog with a fire hydrant across the street. The more Faith thought about it, the more she was convinced today was the most beautiful day of the year thus far.

When they reached the Fairgrounds, Gorbie wanted to cross the street while Faith and Frank were angling to the right down Ridgley. "This way, Gorbashay. More greenage down here." Faith waited for the next traffic lull before she asked, "Are you going to admit you screwed up?"

With a delayed nod: "I screwed up."

"You should not have wanted to lend Karen five hundred and fifty-eight of *our* dollars."

"I believe you mean *my* dollars."

"Frank..."

"I am not sure what the source of that assertion is. *Our* dollars. Nor am I entirely sure of the exact amount nor how you could think it was five hundred fifty-eight."

"Let us set aside the ownership of the money. Do you, as a purportedly intelligent, PhD-educated economist, feel in any way ashamed that a woman half your age nearly duped you?"

"I don't know about duped."

"We have no proof her mother is sick. I've never even met her mother."

"When would you have expected to meet Karen's mother?"

Gorbie stopped to lick his nuts. "Where is the data, empirical or anecdotal or otherwise, that her mother is sick? I could just as well tell my colleagues at Princeton that my father is on his deathbed and do they have a few hundred bucks to spare?"

"What would Karen's motivation be for such a scheme?"

"For three years she's been cleaning up after a horde of males who think of no one but themselves, who think that this God damned planet owes them something. Once Karen resolved upon her scheme, she didn't think twice. Gorbie..."

"Allow me to say that, although I did perhaps make a mistake in wanting to lend Karen *my* money, it should be remembered no money was actually lent *to* her. Further, beyond any miscalculations I may or may not have made relating to Karen's nature, in the bitter end the miscalculations remain strictly of a fiduciary kind. And theoretical, given no money actually changed hands. Have I engaged in some innocuous flirtation? Sure. But have you not done the same with the gentleman you work with at Princeton?"

Stubborn twigs poked Gorbie in the face while he tried to sniff deeper into the blooming shrubs. "Oscar's harmless."

"I believe it would be best if we did not bring Karen back," Frank said. "I am confident you and I will resolve our differences concerning her and move on with our affairs appropriately."

"Affairs? Gorbie!" All things considered, Faith allowed for a sixty-forty chance that he was telling the truth and that no additional truth remained to be found here, at least concerning Karen. She also allowed for a fifty-fifty chance, amazingly, that she'd never told him she was storing cash in his sock drawer.

Ridgley eventually merged with Front Street. They continued a bit farther before taking a right onto Walton followed by another right onto Jacksonville Road. At this point they were approaching RV and Folwell from the opposite direction of how their kids came here. A beat-up, sputtering hatchback honked at them before swinging a

U-turn, nearly T-boning a passing station wagon, and pulling up partway onto the curb.

"Team!" The hulking middle-aged man with the flattop jumped out. "Dan and Louis's folks, right? The Roggebusches?"

Husband, wife, and pooch all froze in unison.

"Laz. I have a couple of your kids for history. And Jonathan's a regular in my ninth period. I think we met at a football game. I'm the coach." He didn't shake their hands so much as turn them to powder. Gorbie jerked back a couple of steps and gave a couple of impulsive licks of nothing in particular around his mouth.

"I'm Faith. This is my..."

"I know you, Dr. Jones! You're at Penn, right? We met!"

"Temple actually."

"Rutgers here. Before that, I was a teamster. And before that, a scab. Scary, my friends, very scary. I don't recommend it."

"You mentioned Jonathan's in your ninth period," Faith said. "Ninth-period history?"

"That punk wishes. Naw, ninth's for study hall. It's also for detention. He-he!"

Faith looked at her husband, who didn't seem to register that.

"I have to compliment you on Dan. Great kid, great kid." He smiled the smile of a James Bond henchman.

"I agree," Frank said.

"Getting a part-time job just because he wanted to learn responsibility, earn his keep. Know how rare that is? And he's one of the few who stays for ninth not because he has to but because he wants to put in the extra effort."

Faith glanced at Frank again. Still nothing.

"He's not really ours," she said. Her blood was simmering, and while she wasn't entirely sure why, she was eighty-five percent certain it had something to do with this behemoth. "And I've been tutoring him. Algebra, geometry, trig, common fucking sense. Filling in the gaps where his real parents can't or won't. His mother lives in North Carolina. His father's in Maryland."

"I said God damn, jump down a trucker's throat, why don't you?"

"Same goes for Louis."

"I can't keep up." Laz guffawed. "I'm just messing with yas. Yeah, I know, I know. Woods Roggebusch, Roggebusch Woods. And then there's Jonathan. I know he's yours, Dr. Jones, but I had to guess? I'd've said that punk comes from friggin' Mars."

Faith tried a fake grin. It hurt like hell.

"That boy could have a bright future in golf if he didn't get in his own way all the friggin' time."

"Next year you can look forward to one of mine. Alexander Peterson."

"Peterson? Shit!"

"He's showing true promise as a musician. This summer could've been his summer to shine. But what they don't tell you in the parent manual is that shine costs a fuckload. And what do you do if one of your kids steals your money? But they're not really yours? Stepkid. Years of practice, and Alexander's promise will remain just that, a fucking promise."

"Faith..."

"Fuck calm."

"I think Jonathan mentioned that. Something like five hundred bucks, right?"

"I find it rather interesting that my boy would talk to you about internal domestic matters that don't concern you," Frank said. "Not you personally. What I mean is, that he would tell anyone outside the house."

"Just a sense I have, but I don't think he's got many people to talk to there. Why else would he get diarrhea of the mouth in detention?"

"I'm glad you've become a surrogate parent to the children who reside at our house. Especially fuckups like Jonathan, he needs all the help he can get."

"That is very interesting that Jonathan would relate pecuniary matters to anyone at all who isn't me, as I am and have always been the sole source of his income."

"Patently false," Faith said.

"Has Jonathan, at any point during these domestic ruminations, ever ruminated on who could be responsible for the theft of the five hundred dollars?"

"Five hundred fifty-eight."

"He says everyone thinks it's him and how that's not fair because he's never taken any money from anyone in that house that he hasn't paid back. He's a funny one. We all know he's a dealer, right? Let's not bullshit each other."

"That's an interesting insight," Frank said. "And perhaps it demonstrates that, while I have sometimes suspected his being deaf to everything I say in his general direction, perhaps my words have sunk in to some extent."

"He thinks it was the little fat kid. What's his name? Harry?"

"Barry," Faith corrected.

"Apparently, no one's thought to ask him about it. Ms. Kruger, English teacher here? She'd call that ironic. I gotta run. Be good!" Laz's girth shook the weary hatchback as he hopped back into it. Both man and car coughed as they took off down Jacksonville Road.

Husband and wife didn't say anything the rest of the way home.

When she got home from work the next day, Faith took shelter in her nook for a good cry. Oscar had let her go home early to make up for all the grinding she'd been doing these past few weeks. It was a small gesture that touched her more deeply than she expected. While the tears gushed hot and heavy, she realized it was the first time anyone had done her a favor for as long as she could remember.

The kids were playing Wiffle ball out back. As they'd long since lost the plastic ball that had come with the skinny yellow bat, they were using the blue rubber ball Jonathan and his friends used when they played hockey in the church parking lot on the other end of the alley. Using the side of the garage as the backstop meant they were hitting the ball in this direction. Faith knew she should've been concerned. Lord knows it wouldn't occur to Frank to care.

Frank's office chair squeaked. Had he heard her come up the back stairs?

Gorbie zipped into the nook and leaped up on her lap. The forward momentum thrust his head into the besieged breast. The lump was most likely too small to be felt with a bop from the furry little head, in which case it must have been her knowledge of its being there that made her think she felt it.

Faith put a palm to her mouth to suppress her laughter at an image that materialized out of nowhere: Frank, middle-aged widower, waiting by the altar as his beaming, cleaning, rubber-gloved bride traipsed down the aisle, a spotless aisle that she had just scrubbed, with an obscenely long train. And then they came home, to this house, in the Dodge Caravan. And he carried her up to this very room. Via the back stairs naturally. And they had sex to the sound-track of Bach.

Did Karen play an instrument?

Her muffled laughter turned into a fresh round of hot tears. She rocked back and forth, not sure if she was still laughing or if this was something else entirely. Gorbie, reveling in the motion, sprawled on his back across her lap and conked out.

The blue ball shot through one of the mini panes framing the pane proper. Like a bullet, it ricocheted between wall and windows several times before spending its velocity, knocking two of the photos to the floor. It caught Faith's head once. Gorbie was gone in a flash.

"That was rad!"

"Outta here home run Michael Jack Schmidt!"

Frank's chair squeaked.

Faith picked up the ball and gave it a squeeze. The rubber was more pliant than she expected. You couldn't help but be impressed, both at how it was hit hard enough to break any window and how it had obliterated that little square of glass so cleanly.

"All is well?" Frank called from the bedroom doorway.

She stood up and beamed at the kids while tossing the ball up and down.

"Sorry, Faith!" Jonathan raised the bat. "Totally my bad!"

"That was one rad hit, Jonathan," she said.

"He sucks!" Louis barked. "Barry, you suck. Next time, catch that shit."

"You're a pain in my ass!"

"Hang on a second, guys. These windows don't open. Hang on." Faith hurried into the bedroom and willed her husband out of her peripheral vision. Of the three windows in here, only one faced the backyard. With a grunt and a strain, she finally plied it open. Throwing the ball felt terribly awkward. She guessed it looked doubly so from down there. Instead of throwing it in their direction, she had somehow managed to throw the equivalent of a golf slice, sending the ball into Hogg's backyard. The kids cheered and clapped with naked sarcasm that made her crack up.

"What happened?" Frank asked after she closed the window.

"Double can hit like the vicious motherfucker he is."

"All is well?"

"Didn't you say you were going out tomorrow?"

Frank stuck his head into the nook. "There's glass on the floor."

"I believe we agreed the nook was the one part of the house I could have to myself."

He turned and stomped out with a brush of his thumb through his salt-and-pepper hair. "I have come to check on the well-being of my wife, which apparently makes me an asshole. Baltimore, do you think I'm an asshole?"

Saturday could not have worked out better had Faith been a master planner. She was right about Frank's going out. Barry and John had convinced him to chauffeur them to the Cherry Hill Mall. Stephen had nothing else to do so decided to tag along. Meantime, Alexander was jamming at a friend's garage, Louis was hanging out at Tanisha's, Daniel was doing yard work with George Taylor on the Boss Hogg side of the house, and Jonathan was heading off to the Pine Barrens with his new girlfriend and a bunch of pals.

Daniel's being Hogg-ward was the only part of the above that was by Faith's design. She had called George Taylor to concoct the scheme the night she bought that behemoth of a stargazer. She figured they could carry it up together. No sooner did she pop open her Rabbit's hatchback, though, than George clutched the box with hands the size of Kong's and hauled it up to the third floor on a granite shoulder.

He parked himself on the floor by the Broad Street window and flipped through the manual. Every once in a while Faith made out a word or two as he processed the instructions. Finally he put it down and pulled out a Swiss Army knife to open the box. "Never pegged Jonathan as a space man."

"I have no idea what he'll think of me after this. It could quite literally go either way."

George beamed as he spread the parts across the floor. "I remember when the Commies launched Sputnik. I was in the study putting together a bookcase when Hortense runs in all shook up, like she seen that giant vegetable monster James Arness played just before *Gunsmoke*. It was all over the papers. I felt sick to my stomach. First time I realized we might actually lose. Whatever losing means when you're not actually pulling a trigger."

"George, have I ever told you that Admiral Nimitz was my neighbor growing up?"

"Get outta town."

"We moved to Berkeley when I was in grammar school. The neighborhood was on a hill with a beautiful view of the bay. Being a stupid kid, I took it all for granted."

"Ain't that always how it goes?"

"Walking home from school, sometimes I'd see this old guy working on his lawn, tending his flowers, watering, weeding."

"That was Nimitz?"

"'Call me Chester,' he said. Most of the time we didn't say more than, you know, 'Hello, how are you?' But once in a while I'd stop and we'd chat. Sometimes I'd vent about the asshole kids who made fun of my glasses or my chest."

"Ain't that a thing? Humble advice from one of only six men ever to be a five-star admiral. Commanded the largest navy the world had ever seen."

"Chester always counseled patience. He also said if things got really out of hand, then I should invite all the assholes together to talk it out." She grinned. "That was the first time I heard the word parlay."

Having already made decent progress on the telescope, George sat back against the wall and spread out his legs. "Ewwee. That's just something."

The house was completely silent. Faith strained to remember what Chester's smile looked like. She remembered how it made her feel: warm, reassured, secure. There are no wrong answers, and we're all in over our heads.

When George resumed the work, he said, "Memories are like ghosts. Like little missy across the way."

Faith stopped wandering through her Berkeley neighborhood. "Pardon?"

"You hear her?" He squinted. "Not sure who that one is. Who's the Russian fellow?"

"You've lost me."

"You know violin, right? That Russian fellow. Right on the tip of my tongue."

"Tchaikovsky?"

"That would've driven me bonkers all day and through the night."

"George, what...?"

"My best pal Barry probably never told you about that there little missy over yonder. Been playing the violin almost nonstop since the day she died. Probably figured you'd think he was the one going bonkers. But believe you me, it's true as two plus two is four."

Faith peered over her shoulder at Barry's room. "You cover an impressive breadth of topics, George."

"I'd've never known if Hortense hadn't gotten to know her. She was pals with that girl when she was growing up here. That was her room. Hortense told the ghost everything, including stuff about me when we started dating. He-he. The nerve."

Faith couldn't help but wonder if the old warrior was pranking her on behalf of Barry.

"Want to meet a real skeptic? Look no further than yours truly. I didn't believe my wife for the longest time."

"But you can't see her."

"Hortense stopped talking about it eventually. I forgot about it. But then one night, after supper with Don and Frances, I came up here to fix that door down the way. At one point I go into the john to do the deed. Whenever Frances made her famous quiche, I'd pay a toll if you know what I mean. So there I am, me and my thoughts..." He looked up at her with awe mixed with dread, the likes of which Faith had never seen in a man his age. It tickled her spine. "...and I hear it. To say my blood went colder than the poles doesn't do it justice. You kidding me? I went head to head with the Huns. Battle of the Bulge. Yet there I was, paralyzed." He finished assembling a particular section. "I reckon I couldn't face my wife again if I let myself get scared silly of a little girl. So I walk in. And the room's empty. Violin still sounded far away. Not quite as far but a ways off. And that's when the craziest thing happened: I shed a tear. Music's never made me cry before or since." He stood the tripod upright so he could attach the instrument. "Every time we visited Don and Frances, I tried to make up some excuse to come up here. Bit by bit, each time, it was louder than before."

"And Hortense? What did she say?"

"Never told her." He smiled at the look on her face. "She'd had Bunny to herself for so long. Reckon I wanted the same." He secured the eyepiece and double-checked its tightness.

"One thing is not computing: Why can you hear her? And I can't? Sorry, it's the mathematician in me. I'm being überlogical."

"Eh. We should all be more logical."

"Could you tell Frank that?"

He grunted a laugh. "Don't fret that we're talking about you, Bunny. I just don't want Barry's stepma thinking he's losing it." He double-checked the base before positioning it in front of the window and peering through the eyepiece.

Faith swallowed hard at how massive that thing looked in the little niche. Jonathan had to love that. Maybe she could will that response in him. So much for logic.

"Hello there, little lady." George was standing out in the hall, staring into Barry's room. "It's not the Russian now, but boy, is it pretty. It's like the music knows how pretty it is, and it's taking its time so folks can enjoy it."

They headed out to the backyard where Daniel was whacking weeds along the Buttonwood side of the fence. Faith whispered thank you to George before heading down the alley and across High Street to the Mount Holly Pharmacy. She snagged the first birthday card that wasn't drowning in sap. Soon as she got in line, her eyes landed on the rows of Garbage Pail Kids, a seemingly infinite number of toddlers with mushroom clouds booming out of their swollen noggins.

"My stepson loves those," she said to the mustachioed pharmacist while he rang up the card.

"All the kiddies do. Some even try to take them without paying." He shot her a look over the rims of his specs.

Her eyes wandered to the cigarettes lining the back shelf. She spotted the brand Jonathan smoked and asked for a pack. By including this with the card, it could be a sort of consolation prize if the telescope struck the wrong nerve.

"He the one celebrating the special day?"

Her eyes fell back down to the mushroom clouds. Oh why not? She plucked a pack and dropped it next to the cigarettes.

"Just one?" He smiled at Faith's bemused look. "My experience, kids prefer several because the cards repeat themselves."

"I shouldn't even be getting him this."

Within minutes of jotting a message on the card and stuffing it and the cigarettes into the fuchsia envelope and taping it to the side of the telescope, everyone started trickling in from their Saturdays. Jonathan was the last, showing up in a blissful cloud of pine, pot, and sex.

Frank ordered a couple of pizzas from Sal's and left them on the kitchen island for anyone to graze as they passed through. Faith prepared herself a giant bowl of steamed peas and parked herself in her blue leather high-back chair to watch a PBS nature show with Frank, who was half watching while half reading a Civil War book and chasing pizza with slurps of scotch. Barry sat in the cushioned rocking chair with three huge floppy triangles dangling off the sides of his plate and a Washington Bullets cup filled near to overflowing with that green sugary soda that did him no favors.

"You tell Jonathan happy birthday?"

"MMMM!" Frank exclaimed with his mouth full. After swallowing and coughing: "God damn it. I was so focused on..." He jabbed a finger in Barry's direction. "...obeying his every whim. He home?"

"7-Eleven. With Louis." If tonight was going to be par for the Saturday course, Frank would conk out in his recliner and eventually come up around midnight or one. That should allow plenty of time for Jonathan to discover the surprise and, if it came to it, confront Faith. "Anything else on?" She tittered. "Not sure this is holding Bawrence's attention."

"Hmm?"

"Bawrence, is there something else you'd rather watch?"

With a mouthful of cheese and pepperoni: "I don't know."

Frank belched. "Baw-*rence*! Getting enough to eat?"

"I don't know."

"Would you say we had a successful day at the mall?"

"I don't know."

"You have two more Transformers, so that can't be bad. And now you get to end the day by not starving to death and dying. Hey!"

The secret operation on the third floor must've taxed Faith more than she realized. She didn't eat the peas so much as shovel them. Still hungry, she figured she could crimp two Soft Batch cookies from R2 without Barry being the wiser. After wolfing those down, she grabbed a can of tomato juice, a Perrier, and one more cookie to take up to the nook. Soon as she plopped down in the chair, she didn't sigh so much as spew a gust of air that had been trapped all day. Her eyes felt heavier than that telescope. She considered her father. "Fuck you."

Faith might have overslept the Sunday morning service if John's laughter hadn't rung up the back stairs. She woke up in bed without remembering how she made it there. As she stretched and reveled in a full night's sleep, she thought of Jonathan and shot up with a jolt.

By the time she was bathed and dressed, John had left for Tara's. Frank was perusing the *Philadelphia Inquirer* in the living room. He chomped and smacked his butter-soaked bagel cut into quarters topped with cut strips of bacon. Without looking up: "Morning, love."

"Jonathan up yet?"

While still chomping and smacking: "Dunno."

"You see him last night?"

He smacked his lips. "Last night?"

"When did he come home?"

He looked up at nothing in particular as he thought about it. Then he started chomping and crunching and smacking the next buttered bacon bagel quarter. "Let's see. After you went up, Bawrence asked if we could watch that movie he's seen fifty billion times. Um..."

"*Goonies.*"

"I fell asleep."

"So you didn't see him?"

"Bawrence?"

She bit down on her tongue and focused on breathing. "It was his birthday. Maybe they went to a party."

Frank stuffed the next quarter bagel into his mouth and shrugged.

If Faith didn't leave for church now, she might say something she'd have to own up to later with the pastor.

Feet thumped down the stairs behind her. "Yo, Pop!" Jonathan clung to the banister with one hand so he could hang over the last two steps. "Going to Springfield to hit some balls."

"Good morning, Jonathan," Faith said far more formerly than she'd intended.

Jonathan rushed out the door and thumped down the steps.

Frank wiped his mouth and mustache. "You know, he keeps this up? He could qualify for the PGA."

Nothing then? Not a thank-you? Even a fuck-you would've sufficed. By the time Faith arrived at the church in Medford, her indignation was nothing short of righteous and holy.

In a mood like this, she would've very much preferred to belt out Bach's "Toccata and Fugue in D Minor." It was a gorgeous piece, but

at some point it had taken on a Halloween haunted house connota-
tion. She nearly did start playing it, but the sight of those adorable
toddlers in the front pew shifted her fingers to the chords of "Prelude
and Fugue in E-flat," followed by *"Liebster, Jesu, wir sind hier"* as one
last touch to help people get settled and in the mood to be preached
to.

Until today, the music never failed to calm her. It didn't matter
what she played. By the time the service came to a close, her nerves
would be slack, a dangly jumble lined with balm. Not today. Today
marked the first time ever that her nerves were impervious to the
music. She knew she was banging the chords with too much punch
but didn't give a shit. Jonathan's was one snub too many. What with
Karen pregnant, possibly by Frank, Alexander's being pissed at her
for not letting him go to band camp, Louis going off the deep end,
and her younger son having coffee every morning with his stepfather
and in general preferring his company over that of his own mother,
Jonathan's blowing her off didn't just take the cake, it burned down
the God damned bakery.

During the drive home, Faith mulled next steps. The nook
wouldn't cut it. By the time she pulled her Rabbit up to the curb, she
was still drawing a hot-blooded, steaming blank. No sooner did she
step into the house than she came upon a scene in the living room
that amounted to a gift.

Barry was splotched in the cushioned rocking chair, but instead
of facing the television, which wasn't on anyway, he was facing his
father in the recliner. Jonathan was sitting with Gorbie in Faith's
high-back chair. Stephen sat in the chair over by the bookcase while
Alexander, John, Daniel, and Louis hovered on their feet near the
hallway.

Faith half dropped, half threw down her purse on the stairs
before bumping into the kids on her way into the room.

"Hey, Mom," John said.

"Come on, Barry, the sooner you fess up, the sooner you'll feel
better and we can all move on."

Faith stood in the center of the room. Barry was a wreck. The tears had turned his chubby, half-dead face into a glazed ham. The last time he looked like that, his mother had just broken the news that he'd have to wait another year before living with her.

"Bawrence Barney!" Stephen said with his signature mock indignation.

"Baw-*rence*. How much money did you, quote, see?"

Considering her husband, a few bagel crumbs still on his butter-stained golf shirt, Faith spat, "Have you not moved from that fucking chair since I left?"

Frank folded his hands on his belly and cleared his throat. "It appears Bawrence has information concerning my missing five hundred dollars."

Stephen held up his fingers to indicate quotation marks. "He's 'seen' it. Or wait. I'm sorry, Barry, you only 'saw' some of it."

"He stole it, man. Just so he could collect those ugly fucking cards."

"Maybe he didn't steal it though," Louis said through his trade-mark chuckle. "Why does everyone have to be so down on the kid?"

"'Cause he's a thief!" Stephen said with an open-palmed slice through the air.

Barry spluttered something about having come upon a hundred dollars in the empty metal wine cooler that sat on its stand in the corner of the second-floor hall for reasons no one could remember. The sight and sound of him boiled Faith's blood for a completely different reason than would've otherwise been the case as recently as yesterday.

"And on the stairs too," Barry was saying thickly with mucus nesting in his throat and on his upper lip.

"The stairs," Alexander said with nary a trace of emotion.

"Ah yes," Stephen said. "The one place no one else would think to check."

"But which stairs, Bawrence Barney?" John asked.

"The back ones." Barry sniffed and ground his fists into his eyes.

"Guess that means you're blind, Pop!" Jonathan giggled in that high-pitched way that stuck in Faith's craw even in her better moods.

"Baw-*rence*." Frank thumbed his scalp before refolding his hands on his belly. "This discussion of my missing five hundred dollars might proceed more smoothly and with less interruption if you could provide an itemized list of the various locations where you came upon portions of said sum. Then you and I can explore the house, floor by floor, perhaps with assistance from others, to see how many of these portions are still locatable in the hopes of piecing back together the original sum. Does this sound like a satisfactory plan to you?"

"Bawrence Barney Roggebusch," Stephen said. "When you cry, do tears only come out of the living side? The Jerry's Kid side of your face looks dry."

Jonathan leaned forward. "No way!"

"That's a scientific marvel if you think about it," Alexander said.

Several of the kids laughed. Frank smiled.

"I TOOK THE FUCKING MONEY!"

Faith didn't know the words had exploded out of her very breast until all eight pairs of eyes were pointing at her.

"Mom?"

"I took it, Frank. All of it. *Our* money. All five hundred fifty-eight fucking dollars. Since some of it was mine, more than fifty percent, in fact, I don't consider it a theft."

Stephen looked like he wanted to say something but couldn't find the words. Frank went through the motion of looking around at all the books. When his eyes returned to her: "May I ask why you didn't see fit to inform me of this before?"

"It was for medical bills. I have a lump in my breast. Probably cancer. As you like to say, doctors cost money."

"Cancer?"

"Were you ever going to tell me about the letter you wrote to Karen? Or the letter you wrote to Barry's mother? Does his mother still think you didn't meet me until after you moved up here? I don't know her, but something tells me she's not that obtuse. And it makes *me* look bad. You ever stop to consider that? Like I'm in on the deception? Why can't you just be honest? Otherwise, you set a shitty example for the kids. Right, Jonathan? Does Carl Sagan know you're a fan? John, no one will get mad at you for still being friends with Donald. As we can see, he is clearly not at fault for all the shit going on in this fucking house. Louis, there's no shame bribing your enemies to be your friends, especially when you have so many of the former. Stephen, you fool absolutely no one skipping school on the days your father teaches so you can eat popcorn and watch *Conan* for the umpteenth fucking time. Honestly, the only person I can't chastise for keeping secrets is Bawrence. He's tried to tell people about that ghost, but everyone just makes fun of him. For what it's worth, Bawrence? I believe you."

The room was dead quiet for an eternity, interrupted only once when a pickup roared by and shook the asphalt with Quiet Riot.

"Mom?" Alexander said. "Are you going to die?"

Stephen considered his stepmother while rubbing a palm up and down his chin.

"But you still might not have anything, right, Mom?" John said.

"I will assume everything is fine apropos of the ultimate purpose of the medical bills," Frank said. "As for the money, at some point when we have the time, it might be worth a more thorough accounting of how you calculated the percentage of the amount that belonged to you versus me."

"I have records of everything going back to when I opened an account at Mount Holly State Bank right after we moved here."

Frank displayed a palm. "We can discuss it."

"We'll also look at receipts."

"Mom?"

"You're pretty fucking proud of yourself, eh, Jerry's Kid? Your proud fat ass."

"Jesus Christ, Frank. I know your philosophy of parenting is, in essence, not to parent at all, but could you *possibly* be bothered to raise even a pinkie in objection when one of your kids speaks to people in such egregiously profane language?"

Frank thumb-scratched his scalp. "Jonathan. When addressing someone, whether it's Bawrence, another relative, or a stranger on the street, it is customary to do so in a manner that is nonprovoking and thoughtful. Others might say polite. One way to demonstrate that is to refrain from any profane verbiage, whether it be verbiage aimed directly at your addressee, or that which is sometimes used to spice up the language in general."

"I know people who swear all the time. They're considered polite."

"Ah!" Stephen jabbed his finger. "I believe Jonathan is referring to politeness as a subjective concept."

Only when Faith arrived at her nook did she notice her panting. As she closed her eyes and willed herself into calm, the kids darted out back to play Wiffle ball. She tried to tune them out at first, but it was hopeless. At some point, standing there and watching the game, she realized she was their only spectator and a secret one at that.

First thing next morning, while Frank and John were having coffee down in the kitchen, Faith rung Oscar to say she'd be late because Alexander had come down with a nasty bug. She knew how risky it was to lie so soon after the previous one, but after calculating the risks innumerable times during the sleepless night, she'd resolved that it had to be done.

No sooner did she reach the bottom of the stairs than Barry barreled down behind her and pounded down the hallway and out the door, trailing a wind gust that wafted a slumbering Gorbie. "Have a good day at school, Bawrence," Faith said for the first time ever. She poked her head into the living room and pointed her eyes at the window just behind the recliner so she could affect the appearance of looking at her bagel-chomping husband without actually doing so. "I'm not back by seven, have dinner without me."

"Smoochie."

She grinned. Now she had no doubt that what she was about to do was the right thing.

"Is that a thousand, it says?" The elderly teller's fragile voice reminded Faith of the wooden creaks of her wardrobe closet. With great strain, the teller budged her huge round specs up the bridge of her brittle nose so she could see the check up close with her veiny eyes.

"Mm-hmm."

"I remember when a loaf o' bread cost a nickel. This here's a lot of nickels. Hey, Sherry? Sherry! One moment, ma'am. I need approval."

Faith's frustration simmered down a bit at the sight of these two arthritic creatures whispering and nodding at her check as if it were the monolith from *2001*. When the teller returned, Sherry accompanied her, check in hand. She leaned forward until her sloppy, clumpy, flame-dyed perm nearly blinded Faith. "Might I ask you what you plan to do with the money?"

Faith couldn't find the words.

"It's a lot of money, ma'am."

"Not safe for a young woman to walk around with this much money."

Faith couldn't help but be softened by the "young" comment. "I won't have it for very long. If that reassures you."

"I've been working here thirty-eight years," Sherry said.

"Thirty-nine come October."

"When someone does this, it means they're in trouble. Sweetie, you and I both know this isn't entirely on the level. It's written all over your face." Sherry handed the check to the teller. "Look up Ms. Roggebusch's account please."

"I know these people," the teller said as her garish fake nails clackety-clacked the keyboard. Her squinting scrunched her nose and pulled up her upper lip, baring her chompers in a way that reminded Faith of Gorbie's underbite. "Usually it's Mr. Roggebusch comes in." She clacked some more. "That much for a telescope?"

"Why do you look so familiar to me?" Sherry asked. "You from around here?"

"I grew up in the Bay Area."

"You don't say! My family's originally from Marin County."

"Mine's from Europe and the Pacific Islands. How's it coming with that check?"

"Went to Berkeley for two years. Business major."

Faith was about to spit venom at the teller for dawdling over the green font on the screen when Sherry's comment caught her short. "Did you know a Humphrey Drummond? Taught math?"

"He bald? Wisps of hair dangling all about? He was so nice. Soft-spoken. Seemed very gentle."

Faith opened her mouth to answer, then froze. She'd never seen her father teach. Ditto Frank. Did her husband wear a different persona in front of the students?

Sherry bound the bills with a thick rubber band and slid them delicately into a crisp yellow envelope. She handed the envelope with one hand and took Faith's hand in the other. "It's none of my business, but that doesn't mean I can't say good luck." She gave Faith a mock warning look. "Don't make me call your father."

Climbing the stairs to Karen's, Faith tackled two steps at a time to vent lingering frustration as well as to gauge the kind of shape she was in. How did Daniel make this look so natural? Her quads were positively on fire by the time she knocked on the door. "I'm so sorry to show up unannounced like this," she panted. Her heart stopped when Karen swung the door to within a sliver of the jam. But no, it was only to keep the dog inside.

"Shadow!" Karen opened the door just enough for Faith to see she was wearing aerobic tights. "Crazy mutt."

"Everything okay?"

"Yeah, yeah, yeah. Totally! Just burning off Mom's cake from last night. Shadow! Back!" When she opened the door a bit wider, Faith caught the heavenly aroma of fresh pancakes and syrup. "Trouble-maker needs to go for a walk."

They walked a couple of blocks before either of them spoke. "How's the house doing?"

Faith said nothing until they crossed the street. She pulled the plump envelope out of her purse. "Here..."

"Shadow!" Karen glanced at the envelope before giving her pooch a little tug to stay on the sidewalk. "It's not Frank's."

"I know. I also know you don't want it. Frank can forecast energy consumption into the twenty-first century, but he's too obtuse to figure out that nothing's wrong with your mother."

"Shadow, either lift your leg or let's go." As they waited to cross the next street: "I'd put that away, I was you, hon." They walked another block. "Look, okay? I didn't mean to cause all this trouble."

"I was ready to give up on ever getting a man by ninth grade. But I said Faith, give yourself another four years. High school, right? If it's going to happen at all... Next thing you know, this first-place mathlete is graduating, still a virgin. That's when I resigned myself to the cold hard facts. The data are the data, and you can't escape it."

"But you have Frank."

"I have two great kids. They're pretty rad. That's their favorite word." They were quiet for another block or so. "You know that in some countries, if a woman is raped, she's punished? Stoned to death?"

"Unreal."

"You need to be more culturally aware of the world you live in so you can get pissed off about it."

"Are we so much better? A married man hits on another woman, and when the shit hits the fan, she's the home wrecker."

"Someone tries to throw a rock at me, I'll kick their balls in." A pang shot through Faith's midsection when she thought about the can of peas. Given they'd most likely never see each other again, she mentioned it.

Karen bent over red in the face. "Oh my God! What I would have given to see that!"

"Still. The wrong thing to do. Cooler heads, am I right?"

"No offense, right? But when I get married? I don't want to be a stepmom. They're always the bad guy."

"I had reservations, believe me."

"But it's funny. Part of me really wants to have this baby."

"Believe it or not, I do understand the nesting instinct."

"That's such a great name for it." They crossed the street to a particularly scenic tree-lined block. "Know what's funny? I've cleaned your guys' house so much it's like I stopped seeing it after a while."

"Quite a feat."

"But when I think about it? After three years? I've learned a lot about kids. And they're rad and everything. But..."

"Except for when Bawrence told you to clean up his spilled popcorn because that's what you're paid to do."

"He gets that from Frank."

The kids were especially active that night. Pairs of feet stomped up and down the stairs like an evacuation drill that didn't know how to end. Faith chalked it up to being the first week of June. The end of another school year was finally, at long, interminable last, in sight.

"Faith?"

"Jonathan."

Not even in the shadows could his freckles hide. "Hey. So. Um. I saw the, uh..."

"I presume it lets you see farther than its predecessor."

"Processor?"

"The telescope you had previous to this one."

"Oh yeah. Yeah, this is much better than that piece of shit. Sorry."

"Oh please. Say 'fuck' until your freckles turn blue."

Nodding at the windows: "Sorry about that."

"What will you see now?"

He thought about that. "Ever see Jupiter's moons? Phases of Venus?"

"Isn't it nice when you find a topic you can teach your elders about? Ask your father about the phases of Venus. I doubt he'd have a fucking clue."

They stared at the glassless hole for a while. "You can come up."

"Pardon?"

"If you ever, you know..." He chuckled. "Maybe I can show you the California nebula. Since you grew up there and junk."

That's when she heard it. George was right. Even as the notes wafted down from Barry's room, the music sounded like it was coming from another world. She closed her eyes.

Tchaikovsky's Violin Concerto in D Major.

9

ALEXANDER

ACE OF BASS AND DEADPAN ALLEY

"Hey, Gorbie? Hey. Did you know that you have grass growing out of your shit?"

Alex wasn't trying to be funny. He sincerely wondered at this amazing fecal phenomenon before him. He'd been on his way to the bathroom for a turn in the steam room shower and Jacuzzi when he came upon the trio of knotted, crusted logs, each sprouting an uneven smattering of green blades. This wasn't your garden-variety grass either. George Taylor wouldn't have any idea what to do with this. Jonathan might.

"Gorbie?"

If Alex had to guess, the pooch was probably under the poolroom couch. He squatted down and picked at the blades until he managed to pick off one of the longer, wriggly ones. The rank shit was no match for one whiff of this homegrown product. A small smile cracked the corner of his façade. Yes, this was definitely Jonathan's handiwork.

Alex pulled out his Swiss Army knife and turned the phrase "cut the shit" into a literal act, albeit a delicate one. The shit's feel on the blade was not unlike that of fish sticks fresh from the oven. The first couple of cuts caused some crumbling. The last thing he needed was more of a cleanup job than he already had, so he proceeded with extra care until he'd cut all three logs into little coins.

This freed up most of the grass. He then used the blade as a sort of sweeper to separate the pot from the shit. While the stench had renewed its vigor upon his cutting into it, it was still losing ground to the liberated weed. Once he'd separated as much of it as he could, he fetched some toilet paper and scooped up the coins before wetting more toilet paper to mop up the little bits.

Before you jump to any conclusions: No, Alex was not a regular smoker of this stuff. He looked like he could've been, what with the long, feathered hair, the metal tees, that rocking electric bass. But hiding behind that façade was his mother's son, a genuine math and science geek. At first it was just the thrill of discovery that fueled his patient examination and separation of Gorbie's shit from his step-brother's harvest. But as he sat back on the carpet and considered the wiggly, brown-dusted blades from a distance, an idea flashed across that feathered hair with a blinding suddenness.

"No fucking way," Meredith said. She was playing a version of darts that required you to throw little plastic balls with Velcro patches at a Velcro bull's-eye.

"It could work. If you think about it."

"Pot? Brownies?"

"People love pot. And they love brownies. Why not both? At once? Others do it. Or so I've heard."

"You mean Jonathan-an-an-an?" Bruce was parked on the box of Meredith's old family photos. He stood his acoustic guitar on its big butt and rotated it absently while squinting at Alex through those long red feathered works of art that were his bangs. "And that's why the cops are always after him. Can't play bass behind bars, dude."

"Especially that one cop that's always riding his ass, what's his name?" Clayton, the other guitarist, sat cross-legged on the garage's cement floor with his electric-blue electric guitar. He strummed it absently even though it wasn't plugged in, so all you heard were the faint metallic notes.

"James Douglas, dude."

"He's so hot."

"James fucking Douglas." Clayton unbound his blond ponytail, shook it out, straightened the main with a comb, and bound it back up.

"I can't believe your brother is going out with his daughter. Lucky piece of shit."

"So messed up, dude."

"Ugh." Meredith groaned with an upturned lip, flicking both hands outward repeatedly as if wiping something away. "Katherine hates Tara with a passion, you guys. She's so stuck up and snobby. No offense, Alexander. I mean, you know, my sister says that, not me. And she can be full of shit, so take it seriously or not, I don't give a rat's ass, okay? Fuck you guys."

"If the cop doesn't get you, your stepdad will."

"Alexan-*dor!*" They all said in perfect mimicry of Frank Roggebusch.

"Jonathan runs his business from the third floor of our house. Not entirely, but mostly. A lot of it. And Frank still hasn't caught him."

Meredith grew tired of Velcro darts and sat on the overturned yellow plastic crate behind the drums. She didn't miss a beat putting on a mock jam in time with Bruce's mock rocking.

"I still think your stepdad's a spy."

"Yeah, but Roger Moore will always be the best James Bond, dude."

"Do you know what a PhD even is?" Alex asked.

Bruce guffawed. "My uncle's got a PhD. My aunt says it means philandering dick. Hawhawhee."

Alex scooped up his bass and plugged it in. "Meredith, you already bake rad brownies. Most rad ever."

She mimed throwing a drumstick at him. "Why do guys with long hair always have to be a pain in my ass?"

"Ms. Urso loved your cupcakes that one time."

"Ms. Urso weighs like a thousand pounds, okay?"

"Given the amount of shoplifting you do at the 7-Eleven, especially for Peppermint Patties. And M&Ms. Especially M&Ms. Especially when you need to include Peppermint Patties and M&Ms in your rad baked goods. I find it inconsistent that you would, you know, have a problem making money selling pot brownies."

"How much money?"

"Enough so I can go with you guys this summer. With plenty left over for your take."

"What about me and Clayton, dude?"

"Depends. Because if I get caught and Meredith gets caught, you both get caught too. But if you don't want to share the profits, well then. I guarantee you won't get in trouble."

"Hang on, douchebag," Meredith said. "Don't I get a say in this?"

"Even if you don't go to jail, it'll be on your record and junk," Bruce said. "Like, you'll be trying to get into college, and they'll be like, 'Holy shit, dude, you put pot into brownies and sold it to a whole bunch of unsuspecting people! Sorry, application denied even though all your grades were perfect and you rocked.'"

"Okay, I never thought I'd say this? But listen to Bruce."

"We're a band, dudes. We're the Glyphs. Let's act like it."

Meredith deviated from her rhythm and started banging hard, the sticks and her head. Her black hair swished all over. "Don't underestimate me, fuckers. You think I can't make the best pot brownies and rock the Casbah at the same time? I know when my folks aren't home. And I can always tell Katherine to fuck off."

"But, so, like, where do we sell them?"

"Now that's a great question," Alex said. "I was thinking the gym. At RV. Tomorrow."

"During auditions for the end-of-year dance? Dude!"

As always, they jammed until Meredith's sister Katherine whined to their parents about the noise. Even with his worn red bass slung over one shoulder, Alex felt like he was floating home. Cutting across the recreational fields behind Folwell, where a few kids played kickball in the growing murk, he pondered how to broach the topic of pot brownies with Frank.

A roar of cheers mixed with boos erupted from the pavement. One of the kids had booted the equivalent of a home run, clear over the basketball court and out into the field. One of the defenders, a chubby kid whose incredibly slow yet very earnest pace reminded Alex of Barry, bounded and bounced like a slow-motion equivalent of his prey. Alex scooped up the ball with his free arm.

"Good effort. Are you a fourth grader? You look like a fourth grader."

"Yeah, so?"

"Do you know Barry Roggebusch? He's in fourth grade too."

The kid spluttered out a laugh. "That freak?"

"I see."

"Doesn't he wet the bed?"

The other players were yelling at them to hurry up.

As soon as he stepped into the house, Alex was met by the caressing scent of lemon-seasoned chicken, the mundane sight of Jonathan pounding Barry into the very fibers of the hallway carpet, and the thunderous sound of his mother's classical piano playing in the music room down the hall. It was half past six. Frank would be in the living room sipping scotch and eating peanuts and cheese and reading the paper and watching the news and otherwise feeling, or at least looking, especially philosophical, what with his hair freshly combed and still a bit wet from the shower he'd taken after jogging, his clean-shaven cheeks redolent of Old Spice.

"Alexan-*dor*!"

"Frank." Gorbie was occupying his mother's blue leather high-back chair. Alex adjusted the pooch's position a bit so they could share. "How goes it, professor?"

"Dinner this evening will be Cornish game hens. Lightly seasoned with lemon pepper. Served with wild rice and steamed carrots. According to my father, our family hails from Scotland. Or at least Great Britain. One rumor says we're descended from Henry VIII. I've always wondered why Cornish hens seem so familiar to me."

"Did your parents make Cornish hens for you growing up?"

Frank folded his hands on his belly. "Perhaps. Once in a while. The staff would prepare it."

"Maybe that's why Cornish hens are familiar to you."

"Alexander, your sense of logic is not to be underestimated."

"But I do have a problem my logic can't tackle."

"Oh?"

"You could say it's a kickball problem."

"Kickball?"

"So here's my dilemma. Let's say I want to put on a kickball game. A professional game. That people will, you know, pay to see. But first you need all the, the… the ingredients. The players. The teams. The refs. The coaches. The ball itself. Or perhaps multiple balls. You know, in case one gets lost. Or kicked over the fence."

"Would the players and referees be part of a union?"

"Excellent question. Let us assume for the sake of argument that, you know, unions are not the problem. Because do you know what the problem really is, Frank? With my kickball game?"

Frank started looking around at all the books.

"Really is getting all the balls. And here's the other problem. The first game is tomorrow. And I only have one ball. So the real question is: How do I get all the other balls? The supplier who normally supplies the balls only supplied one because that's all I asked for. Do I risk breaking the contract? Should I find a legal way to do it? Even though that might mean delaying the first game? Or should I ask him for more? And tell him I'll pay him later? Or should I just find another supplier altogether? But if I do that, my original ball supplier might find out. And his feelings could be, you know, hurt."

Barry came soaring into view and landed on his head before performing a couple of lopsided rolls. Gorbie jumped with a start. Louis chuckled. "Okay, Bawrence Barney, if you don't want that to happen again, hand over the moolah."

"Barry, give him your allowance and I'll kick the shit out of you even harder tomorrow!" Alex could just make out John's laughter in the poolroom.

Remaining prostrate, which he'd learned was sometimes the best defense per his favorite holiday movie, *A Christmas Story*, Barry wrestled out a crumpled five from his too-tight corduroys and slapped it into Louis's hand.

"Fucking Quasimodo!"

Faith continued banging out Beethoven.

"Alexander. You are confronted with a common problem in the world of commerce."

"Rad."

"My father, you may recall, is a retired dentist."

"And he was a pretty rad dentist from what I've heard."

"Of course, given the enormous amounts of excruciating pain one suffers when going to the dentist, one can't help but wonder how the radness of dentists is gauged. Any event, part of the burden of being a dentist with your own practice is that you are faced with a greater degree of responsibility over many things related to the functioning of the enterprise, things that may be outside the more traditional purview of dentists, the traditional purview being the insertion of terrifyingly sharp objects into people's mouths. My father, for example, had to ensure, before inserting such objects into people's mouths, that his practice had the appropriate quantity of such objects to begin with." With a baton of the finger: "Now. Just to show you my father could never escape math, my chosen field, despite his best efforts, part of working with suppliers is knowing the demand side. Other words, who will this supply go to? Or, in this instance, serve?"

"The patients."

Another finger baton: "Bleeding victims. You need to know how many patients to expect during any given month, which helps you predict the number of patients you'll be getting next month, the month after that, the next year, next five years, so on."

"So this is how you know how much oil the government needs, right? For cars?"

"Not just for cars. Fossil fuel consumption over the next thirty years based on predicted weather patterns and past fossil fuel consumption. That's the simplest way to say it. I could go on, but the Cornish game hens will be done shortly. Suffice it to say that to perform the calculations by hand or with a calculator would take too long. So I used Basic to design a program that performs a large number of complex calculations at once."

"Rad. I know Basic. A little."

"Back to your ball supply problem. You have your first professional game tomorrow. You'll need more than one ball. What to do? My advice: stick with your current supplier. If the game is tomorrow, see him as soon as you can and arrange to get more balls. How many do you need?"

"Another excellent question."

"Let's say you need twenty. Well, you've already got one, right? Most likely your supplier won't have the additional nineteen on hand. Or if they do, they will most likely be reluctant to supply you with all nineteen for free and hope you'll recompense them at some future date."

"Even if I pinkie swear? I'm an honest man, Frank."

"Everyone wants to be paid for performing a service. That the service is being done for someone who is honest is definitely a plus. You need to work out some arrangement with your supplier for somewhere between one and nineteen additional balls. It's not uncommon for a compromise to be reached in such situations. Let's say you and the supplier agree on ten balls."

"Rad."

"Ten's better than one, right?"

"Should we make it formal and have a contract and all that?"

"As you may have noticed from the state of my office, Alexander, I am a strong believer in the paper trail. Everything I do for the government, and their compensation for what I do, is agreed upon ahead of time in writing."

"But here's the thing I'm hung up on, Frank. I'm still not sure how I can convince my supplier to meet me halfway."

"Collateral."

"Collateral. Let's see. Guarantee something of value, so if I don't pay the money…" What the hell did he have that Jonathan would have any interest in? Then, of course, there were the still-theoretical brownies. The auditions were less than twenty-four hours away. Unless he and Meredith skipped school, they realistically had only twelve or so hours to bake the batch. And where would she hide them?

Dinner never dragged like it did that night. Alex needed to get Jonathan alone. The collateral question nagged at him like nothing else. He had always prided himself on not needing much. If you were to go into the room he shared with John (and would soon be sharing with Louis), almost everything you'd see belonged to his kid brother, all the toys and trading cards and *Batman* comics and other evidence of their father's preferential treatment.

He was so distracted that he had no idea what to say for his Good Thing Bad Thing New Thing. Usually he was one of the better ones at this while Barry was almost always the worst. Tonight the roles were reversed, but as it turned out, it was for the best. While his little stepbrother banged them out—Good Thing was talking to Misty at recess, Bad Thing was getting yelled at by his teacher for misspelling too many words on a one-page "essay" on what he would do this summer, and New Thing was literally a new thing, a novelization of *The Last Starfighter* Faith had gotten him even though everyone knew he'd never read it—Alex solved it.

After dinner he headed up to the third floor and waited in the darkened hallway. He lost track of time when his head started spinning with all the different ways this scheme could explode in his face, starting now. He wasn't paying attention as Jonathan leapfrogged the stairs and flicked on the light. The freckled blond kingpin all but leaped out of his open-tongued tennis shoes at the sight of Alex's deadpan visage.

"What the fuck, man?"

"I need pot. Tonight."

Jonathan just looked at him.

"I am prepared to offer you a deal. Here is why I need it urgently." As Alex gave the backstory, a spindly, reptilian smile split his stepbrother's face. "And I'll give you my bass as collateral."

"You're my slave, bitch."

"You'll take care of it, right? Maybe put it in the hobbit hole next to your stash. It's my life."

More footsteps thumped up the stairs.

"What the fuck are you doing, Bawrence Barney?"

Even though half his face was dead, Barry still managed, thanks to three years of PT with his father, to form a countenance that conveyed stress. "My room."

"Go downstairs."

"But my room."

"Get your fat ass down those stairs before I kick it down."

"*You* get your ass down before I get Faith to throw a can of peas at your *dumb* head."

"Watch your mouth."

"You're a pain in my ass!"

"Bawrence, Jonathan and I are in the middle of an important discussion. Maybe go to the kitchen and enjoy another bowl of coffee ice cream."

"Move!" Barry squeezed past them and slammed his door and started mumbling.

They looked at the jagged "life is a beach" that Louis had carved in Barry's door when they moved here.

"Sell my pot to my customers and you're dead."

"Do your customers include the Holbein band? Plus, you know, I won't be doing it for very long."

Jonathan considered him for some time. Alex could all but feel his brain being poked and probed. Finally his stepbrother turned and headed for his room. Alex didn't move until Jonathan made the slightest jerk of his head.

What blew Alex away more than the mingling smells of socks and nicotine was the massive cannon-like instrument aimed out the Broad Street window.

"Fucking awesome, right?"

"That a telescope? Since when...?"

Jonathan opened the little door below his Mötley Crüe bumper sticker to reveal an Eden bathed in artificial sunlight, redolent of opportunity. "This isn't where I get the supply though. I have suppliers. My dad already explained that to you. What? You didn't think I'd know? You're so fucking predictable, man."

"Funny he doesn't know about this. Even though, you know, in a way, he taught you. About business. Irony."

"He thinks I don't listen."

"There enough there for, you know, brownies?"

"We're not touching that. It's not ready. I just wanted you to see where the magic is born. But over here..." In three long strides he stepped across to the closet adjacent to the telescope. "Catch!"

In Alex's hands landed a snake-shaped baggy of the dark green stuff that could make the world right again. It was a small snake though, like one of those copperheads the kids always talked about on the Mount.

"With pot brownies, you really don't need that much. Here..."

They sat on the floor. Jonathan unwrapped the baggie delicately like he was dealing with precious art. And then, very carefully, he reached in and pinched a minuscule amount. Indeed, Alex wasn't sure he had anything between his fingers until he separated them to let the flakes fall. "See that? That's one brownie."

As he walked to Meredith's that night, bass-less and pot-full, Alex slowed down when he reached the field behind Folwell. The utter emptiness and blackness only enhanced the feeling of not quite believing what he was doing. He didn't realize he was laughing until Meredith opened the door and spat: "What the hell's your problem?"

Giggling and thumping came from above. Alex stepped back and caught silhouettes flitting behind the blinds.

"My folks are at some bar association dinner, and now Katherine's got a bunch of her bratty friends over. Whatever." She turned and headed into the kitchen.

"What's a bar dinner?" Alex dug out the pot and set it gently on the island. Looking at the eggs and the mix, he felt the first rising of panic.

"That your stepbrother's pot? That's cool."

"My bass is gone."

"Fuck you!"

"Not *gone* gone. But it's gone." He explained the deal with Jonathan. An explosion of giggles and "Oh my God!" shook the second floor. "You sure they won't come down?"

"But why?"

"Collateral. I'll explain tomorrow when you ditch school to help me find a place to rent one."

"Jesus Christmas! Here, get started on this. I'll be right back."

Alex had no idea where to begin. The kitchen was kryptonite. Nothing good could come from him trying to boil water, let alone prepare an actual dish.

Meredith lumbered flat-footed back down the stairs the way she always did in her "less than thrilled" gait. She slapped down a wad of cash. "From my dad's drawer."

"And you just took it? Something similar happened in my house. This is not a good omen."

"Oh shut up. Let's just make this shit." When the brownies were in the oven, Meredith turned the small kitchen TV to MTV. She soon grew bored of that and started flipping channels until landing on a Phillies game on Prism.

"Oh my God!" A herd of footsteps stampeded down the stairs and punished the hallway as Katherine and her gal pals, clad in various shades of pink and white and glitter, poured into the kitchen. "Brownies!"

"Make yourself extinct, skid mark!"

"Can we have some?"

"It's for school, shit-for-brains."

"What about the bowl?"

Meredith's glare popped the thermometer.

"You never lick the bowl! You always say it makes you fat." Katherine's friends giggled.

"I don't mind." A pleasant scent had accompanied Katherine and her friends into the kitchen. Alex would never have been caught dead with a clique like this, but he had to hand it to them when it came to the aesthetics of presentation. He scooted the bowl toward them.

Meredith shot fire at him and turned up the game.

"So what's this all for anyways?" Katherine said when she came up for air.

"School," Alex said. "Band. Tomorrow."

She slackened her face to imitate him. "School. Band. Brownies. Rock." She giggled with her friends. "No offense, dude? But you're kind of creepy."

By the time she became a freshman, Alex would be a junior. God help them all.

Katherine must've been accustomed to her big sister's propensity for TV immersion, because it wasn't until the break between innings that she begged for a brownie to split with her friends.

"Get. The fuck. Out." Mike Schmidt had just smacked a double when Meredith pulled out the brownies. She slapped Alex's hand away. "Want to burn your finger off? Here." She took him by the arm and tugged him to the other side of the island where they continued watching the game. At some point she said, "Why do all lawyers like to argue?"

"They have to. It's, you know, their job. Look at your house."

"The fuck does my house have to do with anything?"

"It's a nice house."

"Look at that castle you live in, asshole."

"But this is newer. Everything's modern. And you don't have ghosts on the third floor."

"We don't have a third floor at all, show-off."

"And you don't have a crazy neighbor who looks like Boss Hogg. With a hundred cats."

"But do your folks argue as much as mine?"

"That's an excellent question."

"Dad just argues because my mom likes it. They can never have the same opinion."

After the next inning, they went back to the brownies. Alex hovered a palm over the thick brown bed and felt a deep warmth just this side of hot. "May I...?" When she didn't protest, he tapped a corner. Sure enough, his finger wasn't scalded but welcomed, all but embraced. "Want to split one?"

She crossed her arms. "God, fine. Kind of ruins the experience, doesn't it? They're meant to be consumed whole."

"I'm not opposed to eating one whole brownie each."

"Fuck off."

After he cut two small pieces, Meredith pulled him out back. "Just in case that ugly brat comes back down."

The pool stood out like a bright blue rectangular beacon. After they scarfed the brownie, everything in their worldview, plus everything outside of it, became perfect and perfectly hilarious. Alex wasn't sure how much time had passed, but the next thing he knew, Meredith was holding his hand to steady herself against a giggle fit. "Did you see Katherine? Her shit..."

"Shit? What shit?" He couldn't help feeling impressed with himself for maintaining his even tone.

Eventually she got out: "Shirt. Her shirt. So weird!"

"Very. Blue. So. Blue-esque." Just like that, the even tone crumbled. His hair blinded him. When he recovered, he found his hand still clutched in Meredith's.

"How much are we going to sell these for? We should charge a pretty penny given all the parts and labor."

"Parts and labor!" After losing control and getting it back: "No, you're right. And you know, we have more. I mean, I have more. Of the herbage. We could really make a lot of brownies. Maybe sell them for five or ten dollars each. Fuck it, fifteen. Fifteen dollars. Dollars-esque."

"You really like them?"

"Let there be no doubt. As my stepdad says. Actually, he doesn't say that. He never says that. But he should." The next thing he knew, Meredith was pulling away after kissing him.

"Are you mad at me?" Her eyes were so glassy and red Alex couldn't decide if they were creepy or pleading. "Asshole." She leaned in to kiss him again when her father called from the kitchen.

"Go through the back gate," she whispered. "They eat them, we'll be dead."

"For more reasons than one."

"Get lost!"

Only when he was on the other side of the pool did he remember. "Wait. Dude. Tomorrow."

"See? They're arguing!"

"But tomorrow."

She hurried inside.

When Alex got home, the first floor was empty. He walked into the living room and stood in front of a music video showing androgynous men with funny makeup and hair. Two Florida gators lashed out and would've surely reduced him to chuck had he not fled across the hall into the empty music room.

Staring at the amp in the corner, the absence of his bass reminded him of his predicament. It seemed unreal that by this time tomorrow, auditions would be over. Would he really be renting a bass? Had Meredith rescued the treasure from her parents? Even if he missed the auditions, he still had the rest of his life to consider. But without his bass, what would his life be? Was the pot making him ponder so deeply, or was he coming back down?

His head started to throb. Alex walked up the stairs the way Frank did, measured and assured and deliberate. Did this mean he was becoming more like his mentor? For the moment he'd believe that just to have something positive to bring into his room.

As it turned out, there was no need. Frank himself was there. The old philosopher was holding John's hand through the math homework that was known to reduce the kid to tears now and again. Just look at how patiently Frank explained concepts that Alex had picked up easily courtesy of his mom's genes. As for John, when was the last time he'd looked so tranquil and content?

Alex looked up through the balustrade. The hallway light was still on from when he and Jonathan were strategizing. Barry was still mumbling and thumping around.

"Alexan-*dor*!"

"Frank. Dude."

"You are free to join us if you wish and share in the mind expansion."

"I've expanded my mind enough for one night."

Alex slept one of the deepest sleeps he could remember. The only reason he woke up in time for school was Frank's "Good morning, Baltimore!" down the hall. He was positively famished and reveled in having the kitchen to himself while he scarfed two of those Entenmann's chocolate donuts in addition to a bowl of Peanut Butter Crunch, by far the largest school day breakfast he'd ever had. As he set out for Holbein, stopping by the poolroom to say bye to Gorbie under the Commodore couch, he was sated but not so full that his appetite wouldn't be back in time for lunch.

Alex was making his way up High Street to Levis Drive when thoughts of his bass encroached upon his blissful gluttony. With no bass and no clear plan for how to sell the brownies, did it make sense to audition? Especially since no one in the Glyphs went to RV?

Just as he was about to make the turn onto Levis, a hatchback screeched to a halt by the curb about a block farther up High. Someone was waving through the windshield's sky-reflecting glare. As he drew closer, he made out Meredith's scowl. Clayton and his dorky grin hopped out of the passenger side with his guitar.

"Dudes." Only now did he notice Bruce cracking up in the back.

"I can't believe you gave up your bass, you crazy bastard," Bruce said as he climbed out with his guitar.

"Whose car is this?"

"My bro's," Bruce said.

"He let you borrow it?"

"He has no idea."

"Good luck, dudes!" Clayton and Bruce headed down Levis toward the school.

Meredith scowled at him as he settled back into the cracked fake leather. The expired pine tree dangling from the rearview mirror did little to fend off the stench of sweat socks and nicotine. The steady flow of traffic meant they had to wait a few minutes before a gap opened up for a U-turn. Only when they were on their way did Alex notice this was stick, like his mom's Rabbit. She'd spent long Sundays in the Acme parking lot getting Dan and Stephen up to snuff, and they were years older than Meredith.

"My dad taught me when I was ten."

The Burlington Center was still closed when they got there. While they dawdled by the bank of glass doors, Alex made it a point to stand completely still, as immobile as the *Jungle Book* fountain inside, hoping in vain that it would help calm Meredith's fidgeting.

Soon enough, other shoppers started showing up, mostly retirees as well as young parents with tiny children. The occasional curious stare prompted Meredith to calm down and stay near Alex.

"Fuck, what are we going to play?"

"I was wondering the same thing."

"I really like the B-52s, but Clayton hates them. What an asshole."

"The brownies safe?"

"Oh my God, know what I realized after you left? We need more."

"Where are we going to sell them? It's illegal enough already. But if we sell them on school property, it's doubly illegal. We'll go to jail. But for twice as long. I think."

In the end they were able to rent a bass with the cash Meredith pilfered from her father's sock drawer. It was a sorry substitute that would provide a passable audition only if Alex could get to know it beforehand. That's why it was now his turn to fidget during the drive to Meredith's house. Soon as they got to her place, he headed into the garage to warm up the instrument, leaving the door to the kitchen open so he could soak up the aroma as she baked another batch. At one point he got paranoid about the pot and called out to her to remind her to use only a small pinch for each one.

"I'm not a retard!"

As he made friends with the bass, Alex pondered songs. He wasn't against the B-52s, but for an audition like this, the Cars would've been more up his alley. If they really had balls, they would've dipped into Quiet Riot or INXS or Joan Jett.

"Oh my God! You know how many brownies we have now? This is

crazy!" When she spotted Alex peering into the Tupperware containing last night's masterwork: "You touch, you die."

They split one. As he munched, Alex didn't realize he was staring at Meredith until she cussed him out.

"These are so fucking amazing," she said.

"Maybe we should play Hendrix. Or the Doors. Let's pick someone who didn't make it to thirty."

The next thing he knew, he was standing in the doorway of the bedroom Meredith shared with her sister. Had he ever been up here? It was blindingly obvious which half of the room belonged to whom. Meredith's side was plastered with posters of John Densmore, Phil Collins, and a black guy in a tux parked behind an impressive drum set.

"That's Cozy Cole! One of the best jazz drummers ever. And he was from Jersey. Here..." She pulled out a stack of vinyl from under her unmade bed (dark green sheets versus Katherine's white and pink) and flipped through them. You could tell the recording was from decades ago by all the crackle. Still, this Cozy Cole fellow had one helluva beat. Did Frank have this? This sounded exactly like something he'd play late at night when everyone had gone to bed and he'd had a few nips. "I so didn't mean to kiss you last night. Total fucking accident, oh my God. I know you hold it against me because you're such a jerk."

For the rest of his life, Alex would never know for sure who jumped on whom first. The next thing his brain could process was the two of them on her bed going at each other like emaciated hyenas to the soundtrack of nineteen thirties jazz.

He would also never be sure how long they lay there afterward. That old baby-blue blanket Meredith's grandmother had knitted a million years ago was tacked to the wall over the blinds, providing a cool dimness that removed any sense of time. He would definitely remember the poster of Gina Schock, drummer for the Go-Go's, on the ceiling. Was Meredith sleeping? For whatever reason, Alex would remember that, for a short while at least, it was just him and Ms. Schock.

"Time is it?" she asked.

"I don't think I've ever been this comfortable in my life."

She lifted her head to read the clock. "Asshole, it's almost two."

When they arrived at the RV gym at quarter to three, in the middle of ninth period, random clumps of kids were playing pickup basketball. Was that Dan ripping up the parquet at the far end of the court?

"Dude!"

Alex turned with a start to see Joe, a fellow rocker whose social circle occasionally overlapped with his because they both played in garage bands. Joe was a sophomore who seemed never to give any notice to the school's written rules on beards or the unwritten rules about using a rubber band to bind your unwashed hair. "Hey. Dude. How's it going?"

"Just putting in an appearance?" Joe's three bandmates were similarly bewhiskered and overweight.

"Appearance?"

"This is for an RV dance. Not some kiddie dance." His bandmates guffawed, their bellies bouncing as one.

"In your stinking dreams, Lyons," Clayton said.

"In your stinking dreams, Lyons," Joe said in an exaggerated mock kid's voice. The bellies jellied again. "No, Clayton, it's in your FUCKING dreams."

"What's your girlfriend got there, Peterson? Cupcakes and shit?"

"Hey, Meredith!" several girls called at once.

Alex figured his brain would've landed at this point, but apparently it wasn't ready to process all these faces. A headache was edging its way in just as the Pink Dreams made their ineffable entrance. Scuttlebutt on the street was that they were the only all-girl band in Burlington County. They were all RV students like Joe's band, the Smashers. When their original drummer graduated last year, they'd tried to get Meredith to replace her, but as Meredith told her fellow Glyphs during a jam session, she couldn't see herself joining a band called the Pink Dreams, not in her wildest nightmares.

Still, as she also liked to say, girls have to stick together, as evidenced by her "What's up, bitches?"

"Looks like the kiddies have come out to play," said Holly, their bassist, who made no secret of her eye for Alex. Sometimes though, it was a stink eye, which was why Alex took advantage of his long, feathered bangs to shut her out.

"Come on, people, take it outside! When practice starts, you come in. That's how it works." The Gomer Pyle voice of Mr. Masters, one of RV's gym teachers and football / basketball / baseball assistant coaches, draped itself like a drenched woolen blanket over the growing throng of musicians clustering near the bleachers.

"Chill out, yo," Holly said. She and Meredith whispered and sniggered.

"We're not in the school band, Gomer!"

"Name's not yo, it's Mr. Masters. Now make like a banana and split."

"Did he just say that?" Alex asked. "Seriously. I'm not sure."

Jonathan emerged from the pickup game, grabbed the Tupperware out of his stepbrother's hands, and ran outside. When Alex followed, the sun blinded him. Jonathan was nowhere to be seen. A few girls from the softball team were running laps while a few geeks pretended like they weren't watching from the bleachers. As he took everything in, Alex wished with each and every one of the zillions of hairs on his head that he was home right now, curled up in his bunk, with John somewhere far away so he could have the room to himself, perhaps with Gorbie there, but that was optional, and not a peep from Baltimore or a single decree from his mom. He'd even ask Frank to hold off on the philosophy.

"Alexan-dor!"

Jonathan and Louis were standing just outside the gate of the athletic grounds.

Bruce chuckled. "Dude, are they waiting to put the beatdown on us?"

"So much for the brownies," one of the Smashers said.

"Yo, Alex!" Louis shouted with that same drill sergeant voice he normally saved for Wiffle ball games. "Manure-for-brains! What are you standing there for? Get over here!"

"You're not going, are you?" Meredith said.

The other musicians gave her shit for being oh-so-concerned for her man.

Readjusting his bass so it sat securely on his shoulder, Alex stepped through the gate and, for a split second, felt that flash of anxiety he hadn't experienced since his mother whisked him and John away from Colorado forever. "Dudes." He tried to smile but failed miserably. His deadpan façade had become so common it was as if it had developed its own consciousness and would not be denied.

"Were you about to sell these in there?" Jonathan said.

"Give it here, bro." Louis chuckled and offered Alex a high five that went unreturned.

"You out of your fucking mind? Masters is in there."

"They any good?" Louis pried open one of the containers, shuffled them around until he spotted a particularly big one, pulled it out, and went to town. "Aw fuck yeah."

"Didn't you see the sign? No pussies allowed!" Laz plowed through the throngs like a hurricane. The salt-and-pepper flattop was in peak form today, a perfectly even bed of something unpleasant. The RV Red Devils golf shirt, redder than blood, looked ready to explode. He roared with laughter as the shadow of his six-four frame washed over their pale faces. "Can't hit for shit or catch for shit, so you're selling brownies? Give me one!" After affecting an amazingly convincing square-jawed sternness, he blew up with more hysterics. "I'm just messing with you faggots. How's the knife wound, gangster?"

"Don't you have a big game to blow, Laz?" Louis said.

Laz pretended to be crushed. "Oh shit, Rogge-*busch*. You got me. I'm done."

"The fuck out of here," Jonathan said with forced joviality.

Laz was about to spew more venom when he noticed Alex. "Someone call Kiss. We found the one who got away."

"Introduce yourself, shit-for-brains."

"Hey. Alexander. Their brother."

"You're shitting me."

"I'll be here next year."

"Looks like you're here now, Helter Skelter."

"*Step*brother," Jonathan said.

"I'm looking forward to high school."

"He's the one who baked the brownies."

Laz stomped through the gate and tongued his dentures. "Un-fucking-believable." When he came upon the nonplussed musicians, he barked, "Out of my way, God damn it!"

"Time for plan B," Louis said.

Jonathan handed the Tupperware to Louis. "Follow me." More bands had congregated outside the gym, a collective portrait of long hair, unkempt clothes, and pierced paleness that stood in stark contrast to the golden-tanned athleticism all around them. Only as they approached the group did Alex, for the first time ever, under-stand and appreciate the unique position Jonathan occupied in the social strata of high school. Most people only get one stratum if they're lucky. Jonathan somehow occupied at least two. On the one hand, this freckled six-footer was a jock, making a mark on both the basketball and golf teams. But he didn't dress like or otherwise associate with the jocks. No, with that unkempt mop of blond hair and metal tee, he easily blended into the musicians' clique. "Okay, kids, just remember it's an audition for a dance most people in the world don't give a shit about. Oh don't look so hurt, cupcake, you know it's true. Whoever wins will win, and the rest of you can show some decent sportsmanship and congratulate them. And then you should fucking congratulate each other on making an effort. I know there's more bands than this, but they chickened out. Fuck them. Shit, my stepbrother doesn't even go to this school, and even he's auditioning. That's balls. Now get this. After auditions, Alex is inviting everyone back to our house for a party. The rain's finally stopped, and we've got this big-ass puddle in our backyard. It's like a lake. Beer's free, but if you want one of these awesome brownies, you've got to pay. Twenty bucks per, that's how awesome these fuckers are."

Eight bands were competing to play the end-of-year dance. The Glyphs were going last. The four of them huddled in the upper corner of the bleachers and bickered over what to play. Alex was trying not to get involved. He wasn't sure where the confidence came from, but whatever they decided on, he knew they'd slam-dunk it. When he scooted away from the others to watch the auditions, his confidence only increased. The other bands weren't really trying. What a clever bastard, that Double. By telling them that this dance didn't mean shit and then inviting them over for pot brownies and beer, Jonathan had, in effect, compromised their focus.

"Hey. Dudes. I know what to play."

"'Hungry Like the Wolf.'"

"No, Bruce, not the song you suck at. Something we're already good at. My stepdad always says not to overthink the problem because the solution is sometimes right in front of you. Look at them. Everybody keeps messing up. All we have to do is pick a song we could play in our sleep. We do that, we'll win this gig. So I say The Cars. 'You're All I've Got Tonight.'"

"'Vacation.'"

"I've gotten a lot better at 'Hungry Like a Wolf,' dudes. Seriously."

"I hate 'Vacation.'"

"Said the one with a Gina Schock poster on her ceiling."

"Fuck off."

They continued the heated debate right up until: "Glyphs! You're up!"

As they made their way down the bleachers, Bruce turned to Alex. "How do you know she's got a Gina Schock poster on her ceiling, dude?"

They ended up playing "You're All I've Got Tonight," and yes, they nailed it on the first try. They didn't just go through the motions though. During one of his wistful, lubricated recollections of his jazz days, Frank had told Alex that no matter how many times you rehearsed in private, each public performance would provide the X factor. That wasn't always a good thing, as the other bands had just found out. But when the Glyphs dove in, the X factor became their best friend. Indeed, Alex forgot this was an audition. By the time the gym erupted in applause, those long, feathered bangs were matted to his sweaty face.

They wouldn't know the results until Monday, but that didn't stop him from floating home. Bruce and Clayton were still doubtful but only, he suspected, because they didn't want to admit he'd been right about the song. Meredith, meantime, seemed to withdraw into herself. As they approached the Queen Anne, Alex spotted the window with Jonathan's telescope and wondered what his target would be tonight.

Every band showed up for the backyard party. Jonathan and Louis held court behind two foldout card tables joined together. The open Tupperware burst forth with magic and dreams and visions of the future. While everyone eventually jumbled into a roughly coherent line, Alex braced himself for taunts and insults and shit giving. Instead, he got nods and small smiles.

John drew heavily from his prepubescent cuteness to endear himself to the Smashers. The way he was giggling and making Joe do the same indicated he was probably making fun of his big brother. Who cared? How could Alex get upset as he watched Louis and Jonathan collect all that cash?

Just as Jonathan had warned, a significant chunk of the backyard was out of bounds courtesy of a massive puddle. It covered the entire southwest quarter of the backyard, the space next to the garage that included home plate during Wiffle ball games. Throughout the shindig, one or two or three or more of the guests would wander over to it and point and smile and, occasionally, as in Bruce's case, gape. The higher they got, the more amazing that puddle became.

"Dude!" Clayton dropped an arm around Alex. "This... *rocks*! I never knew you were this cool. Right on. That tree green?"

Alex spotted John standing over by the puddle talking to Meredith and the Pink Dreams. "Clayton. Dude. You give John a brownie?"

"Brownie?" He frowned. "That a metaphor?"

Meredith and the other girls were rolling on their asses at something John had said. Curiosity finally got the best of Alex.

"What's up, blade runner?" said Holly as he walked up.

"You never told me about using your knife to cut cards," Meredith said. "You prick, I hate you."

"Hey. Any of you guys give him a brownie?" He examined his kid brother's eyes. They weren't glassy, but his face was redder than usual. "He's only eleven. For fuck's sake."

"I didn't give him anything."

"No way, man. I've got scalpels."

"Scruples, you dumb bitch." They cracked up.

"Hey. John. What sorts of bullshit have you been telling them? About me?"

"Alexan-*dor*! Cut the deck." John spat out a laugh. "I still can't believe you actually tried to physically cut it."

"You're full of shit."

Meredith slapped his arm. "He's just messing around."

"He got that Swiss Army knife for his birthday. Never goes anywhere without it."

"I've never seen it." Meredith gave Alex a look.

"I don't have it with me that much."

"See, girls. Alex doesn't get out all that much. Shocking, I know. What with his pale skin, the zits, the caveman hair. But yes, like our stepdad says, Alexan-*dor* is more at home with the Commodore than he is with a Wiffle ball bat."

"Same could be said about you, jackass."

"Alex."

He blocked out Meredith with his hair. "You play the Commodore more than me. You're always in there. You and Barry. Because he's the only one you can beat at anything."

"Hey, girls, you see that one guy selling brownies? He used Alex's knife to stab that other guy selling brownies. True story."

"I heard about that!"

"I was there!"

"What the fuck else are you keeping from me?" Meredith said.

"Heads up. Girlfriend's pissed. Cut the deck!"

"I didn't cut the fucking deck."

"My stepmom likes Atlantic City," one of the Pink Dreams said. "She likes to play 21 and chain-smoke."

"Let's go to Atlantic City and cut the deck."

"Shut up."

"Alexan-*dor*!"

"I'm asking nicely."

"Cut the deck!"

Alex gave John what was supposed to have been a shove in the shoulder but ended up more like a tap with his fingertips.

John cracked up. "*This* is a push!" He caught his big brother off guard with a two-palmed shove that threw Alex into the keyboardist from Garden Hate, a band made up of very tall seniors. The keyboardist had been halfway through savoring a brownie that Alex's collision pushed out of his hand and into the grass. Gorbie made a beeline for it but was stymied by Louis.

"God damn it!" the keyboardist raged with frothing indignation. "You owe me twenty bucks, you fucking juvenile!"

Alex would have to reckon with that debt some other time. Right now he had a kid brother to beat the shit out of. Once again without putting any serious thought into it and using his bangs to shut out everyone else, Alex charged John like a deranged bull. Just when he would've collided with him, John sidestepped like a natural-born matador. After years of assuming how much smarter he was than his little brother, Alex knew this one matador move would be the great equalizer. His unstoppable momentum carried him full bore into the center of the colossal puddle, splashing those who'd been admiring the water's discreet beauty. Apparently, one of them had been wearing a new pair of jeans and cursed Alex for besmirching them.

All conversation came to a stop. The guitarist / vocalist who'd been in the midst of offering Jonathan two tens froze (Jonathan discreetly accepted the money anyway). Even Gorbie lost interest in licking his nuts while he and everyone else waited to see what happened next.

It was Alex's move, and whatever Frank would counsel in this situation went out the window and into the filthy water. John raised his hands and tried to apologize. For some reason this pushed Alex straight over the proverbial cliff. He charged again, splashing water with impunity, and shoved his kid brother straight into the Pink Dreams. Not missing a beat while John regained his balance, Alex cupped handfuls of water and splashed him. Some got on Meredith, who yelled louder than he'd ever heard her.

While Jonathan and Louis and the upperclassmen cheered them on, Alex and John tore into each other with years of pent-up righteousness. That they were both getting filthy in stagnant rainwater didn't matter one dirty drop.

Neither threw any actual punches. No, as they pushed and pulled and scratched and shoved, occasionally clutching the other's shoulder to maintain balance, Alex thought of the fights between another pair of full-blooded brothers, Stephen and Jonathan. Neither one ever threw honest-to-God punches either (although if you asked Barry about Jonathan, you'd get a different story), but Stephen did offer a slap now and again. This inspired Alex to give John a healthy slap clear across his square head. The thick hair was quite the cushion, but apparently it didn't feel that way to John.

"What the fuck was *that*?" He backed up and stumbled and very nearly fell.

Alex felt a rush no pot brownie could match. He slapped his brother one more time across that noggin. For a split second, he thought John was throwing in the towel.

When he saw those eyes, though, he knew he'd gravely miscalculated. John clocked his brother with everything he had. Alex's glasses flew clear off and landed somewhere in the middle of the muck.

Literally blind with rage, and before he had any clear grasp of what was going on, Alex was gripping John by the folds of his Vikings tee several inches above the water. Awed by his own strength, he tested it further. Could he toss John onto the grass? Not even close. His baby brother landed with a splash in the deepest part of the wet.

Alex would've thought the world had frozen if not for the quiet sobs of his brother. He used his bangs to block out the shocked and disgusted looks all around him.

Suddenly, like a furry white bullet, Gorbie whizzed into the water and hopped around like the Easter bunny at a rave. He stopped in front of John and sniffed with some urgency. Apparently, he was expecting an assist, but John didn't appear to know the little pooch was even there. After sniffing some more, Gorbie dipped his head into the water, came away with Alex's specs, and brought them over to the blind bassist.

Alex put them back on just in time for Meredith to fill the space between his bangs. He nearly puked. His heavy footfalls splashed several people as he fled the backyard and turned tail down the alley. He hadn't the slightest idea where he was going. Only when he reached High Street did he decide to duck into the Mount Holly Pharmacy.

Barry was standing in line. Alex was struck by how normal the nine-year-old looked as he waited patiently, the only child in a line full of adults on their way home from work, nothing in his hand since what he wanted was at the register. Barry pawed the GPKs with his pudgy hands and dropped several packs in front of the man with the specs perched on his nose. Look at how he gave him the money and accepted the change. The man wasn't making fun of his face, wasn't making fun of his bed-wetting, his unkempt hair, his too-tight pants. No, it was just your garden-variety Garbage Pail transaction.

"Hey, Barry. Hey. How's it going?"

Barry shot a one-eyed glare at him on his way out the door. The bell seemed to jingle as angrily as he looked.

Alex froze when he noticed the stares of everyone else. Only now did he register his wet jeans and mud-caked sneakers. He hurried out and caught up with Barry.

"Leave me alone."

"Hey, Barry. So. It's a shorter walk if you, you know, take the alley."

"Stop being a pain in my ass."

Barry crossed over Broad before making the right toward their house. This meant that when they reached Buttonwood, they'd have to cross back over. Alex was about to inquire about this peculiar way of walking home when Barry slowed down. He followed his gaze to one of the houses on this side of the street, probably the most unique house on all of Broad. All the kids pointed it out and gossiped about it at some point. Its stone masonry, that cylindrical turret... How could you not be reminded of a castle?

Barry considered it with the half smile he usually reserved for Garbage Pail Kids and Zero bars.

"Rad, huh?"

"I wonder who lives there."

"You know something, Barry? That's an excellent question. Let's find out." Alex walked up the small hill to the front door. Only as he got closer did he appreciate just how massive this structure was. What it lacked in 48 Broad's height it more than compensated for in girth. It was hard to tell how far back the house stretched with all the vegetation. He wondered if they had someone like George Taylor to maintain all this and to make sure that Cupid fountain near the porch always had water.

"What are you doing, stupid?" Barry protested. "You could get shot!"

Alex waited for him to hobble up the hill, the plastic bag of GPKs slapping his thick thigh. "Okay, Barry. Ready?" He couldn't help chuckling at how similar the doorbell sounded to 48 Broad's. No one answered. He tried knocking. Still nothing. Barry kept looking over his shoulder.

When they got home, Barry made a beeline for the living room to watch as much of *Goonies* as possible before Frank and Faith got home. The music room door was closed as Stephen used his father's keyboard and drum kit to put on a one-man concert.

Alex crept up the stairs while trying to gauge where the voices were coming from. By the time he reached the second-floor hallway, he figured out that John was up in the third-floor bathroom soaking in the Jacuzzi, the four pairs of jets sounding like a prop plane engine from down here. While Alex changed into clean clothes, he heard other voices above. Louis and Jonathan were cracking each other up.

"I'm getting in the steam room now, John-n-n-n!" Louis said. "No looking at my ass!"

Alex took his dirty clothes to the laundry room via the back stairs. Dan was watching a repeat of *Diff'rent Strokes* on the little black-and-white. He glanced at the bundle in Alex's arms before turning back to the screen and taking a pull from his cream soda.

Algebra turned out to be just the distraction Alex needed. There was nothing quite like the order and predictability of numbers to help set the world back on its feet. For the first time ever, he felt genuine pity that John had missed out on their parents' math gene. Perhaps as part of his reparation, he could assume the tutoring responsibilities from Frank.

One look at his kid brother's face as he walked speedily into their bedroom clad in his Daffy Duck tee and tennis shorts, only to balk at who was already there, made Alex think maybe now wasn't the right time to ask about math tutoring.

John's combed wet hair smelled strongly of Pert. "You know I should kill you, right? Right?" The quietness of his brother's voice rattled Alex more than it should have. "I'm telling Mom. You know that, right?"

"I did not know that before. But I do now. Because you told me." Alex wanted desperately to sound like Frank, to summon just the right words to give the whole brouhaha the philosophical perspective it needed to be defused.

Below them they could hear Mikey and Chunk and Mouth and Data all messing around in the attic, where they found that map that would send them on their booby-trapped quest for the riches needed to stave off foreclosure. Two things occurred to Alex at that moment: It was amazing all those kids could engage in two hours' worth of shenanigans and get away with it; and Alex would literally give up an eye—just like One-Eyed Willie—if it meant he could vanish from here and join Barry down in the living room.

"I understand, John. You do what you feel is right. Within reason." He was sure Frank would've added "within reason." Christ, but his current rattled state was keeping him from being sure about anything. Frank used the word "reason" all the time. Wasn't it usually preceded by "within" or "within the boundaries of?" Maybe the latter, so he added that as well.

"Fuck you." John walked out and joined Barry downstairs.

Alex remained frozen to the spot for a good long while.

As Frank and Faith got home and people shifted rooms and ran up and down the stairs, Alex kept his nose buried in his homework. His focus held fast, all the way until John paused G.I. Joe and thumped down the hall to the living room. Frank's voice rang out as clearly as if he were right here in this room.

"Hello, John-n-n-n!"

John spoke very quietly. Eventually Faith spat, "What?"

Alex picked up the phone to call Meredith. A girl was giggling.

"The fuck's there?" Jonathan said, both on the phone and directly above.

Normally Alex would've hung up without betraying his identity, but for whatever unfathomable reason, he decided on the opposite. "Oh. Sorry. Sorry, Jonathan. It's me. Alex. Your brother. Stepbrother, actually."

"Hang up the phone, faggot."

Alex tried to get more homework done while he waited for Jonathan to finish talking to his flavor of the month. But who was he kidding? All he could do was stare at the pages without seeing them, clenching his teeth until he heard the grunted goodbye.

"Katherine. Hey. It's Alex. Meredith there?"

"Like, I'm kind of on the phone right now."

"Well, okay. It's kind of urgent. But hey. We won't talk long. And then I'll tell her to, you know, return the phone to you."

"This is *my* phone!"

"I mean, you know, the line. The availability to use your phone."

"Freakazoid! Mer!"

Soon as Meredith picked up, she spat: "Hang up the phone,

dipshit! Hang up, hang up, hang up..."

The phone clicked.

"Meredith. Hey."

She sighed.

"Ready for the corniest line in the world? I needed to hear your voice. I've never said that to anyone. You still there? Because, you know, if you hung up, I'd be really bummed. But I would also understand."

"What are you saying, retard?"

"Oh. Hey. I thought, you know, you hung up."

"How could you be so harebrained? Oh my God. He's just a little kid. I hate you."

"Usually, you know, I don't agree. When you say that. Use the word hate, that is. But for once? This would be an accurate usage of that word."

"You're just like those jerks in gym class who make fun of me when I can't do any pull-ups. Assholes!"

"Will you visit me? If I go to jail? Hey, I ever tell about that one time Jonathan went to jail? And then Louis bailed him out? Too funny. I wonder if that will happen to me. But who will bail me out?"

"Can I go now?"

"I think we'll win."

She didn't say anything for a while. Then: "Why'd you do it, Alex?"

"Meredith? That is an excellent question. I'm sorry. I'm very sorry."

"Tell John you're sorry."

"Have you ever done something shitty and then wondered why you did it?"

She adjusted the phone. "I don't think we'll win. We don't go to RV. Why did we even try? The whole thing's a goddam bust. I have to go."

"Are you sorry we humped?"

"What did you just say?"

"You never, you know. Said anything after."

She was quiet for a moment, then hung up.

The dinner bell rang.

On the menu was fondue. If you'd asked Alex about his final meal, which was what tonight felt like, a meal that involved sharp instruments and boiling hunks of meat would've been his very last choice. Worse yet, John was sitting directly opposite. They always sat across from each other, but it never mattered until now. Alex's dip timing would have to be impeccable lest he risk losing an appendage.

"Bad Thing?" his mother said. "I could think of a few related to work. How about when I got home? Cigarette butts all over the backyard. It appears there was quite the shindig."

Bracing himself for the bomb drop, Alex swallowed his meat a bit prematurely and had to rush to the glass of milk to ease it down.

"All of you can go out there and clean it up. Tonight. George Taylor's coming this weekend. The last thing I want him to see is hoodlum detritus. Bawrence, that means you."

"What the hell for? I wasn't there."

"Quit your God damned cussing, Bawrence," Frank said.

"And my New Thing is that I'm grounding Alexander for the entire weekend."

"Yes, Alexan-*dor*. It is our understanding, based on a recent conversation with John-n-n-n, that you and he engaged in a, shall we say, pas de deux. Which apparently resulted in you throwing him into the stagnant water congregating by the garage."

Alex recovered nicely from gulping the meat and calmly inserted the next piece into the bubbling, spitting stew. "Does anyone know why I was in the backyard in the first place? It wasn't so John could come out. He actually wasn't, you know, invited. No, I invited my friends. My bandmates. And a bunch of other musicians. We had a bake sale."

"Ah." Frank's eyes lit up, but Faith's glower wasn't going anywhere.

"Not sure if John mentioned that little detail. But yeah. Brownies. Meredith, she's our drummer. She baked them. She's really good at that. Jonathan and Louis were awesome. They helped me sell them."

"Four hundred bucks, bitch!" Jonathan and Louis high-fived.

"Four hundred dollars?" Frank's jaw practically fell on his fondue fork. "My God. And what, may I ask, will you do with all those funds?"

"Music camp. With my friends. Because I made it happen. With the help of friends. And family. So that's my Good Thing." He withdrew the meat and took a bite. His bangs were shutting out most of the stares, but he relished them all the same. "I guess my Bad Thing is that I'm grounded. But just for the weekend. Which is good in a way. See, Frank? I'm being philosophical. And my New Thing? Is that the Glyphs auditioned for the RV dance. We were the only ones from Holbein. New because it's the first time we've ever auditioned for a high school dance. And we rocked. Literally and figuratively."

"I ever tell you about my high school days, playing for school dances, playing in clubs even? Of course, our music was jazz."

Except for going to the bathroom or getting something to eat, Alex was not allowed out of his room over the weekend. He was the only one who used the amp in the music room with any regularity, but with his and John's room directly above the living room, hauling it upstairs was out of the question. No matter, he could still practice without it. Better yet, late Saturday morning, Jonathan stopped by on his way to an outing in the Pine Barrens. In his hands was Alex's glistening red bass. He also handed over a thick wad of cash.

"Took fifty out, yo. More than I told you, but consider it a lesson learned for what you did to John. Shit, man, I wouldn't even do that to Barry."

Not even being grounded could nudge him from his cloud nine. He had his bass back, and the Glyphs would be together this summer. That meant a summer away from this place. His creative juices, stagnant for days, started flowing anew. Alex grabbed the music camp brochure and parked himself on the lower bunk. He'd looked at this brochure a million times, but another perusal wouldn't hurt. The facilities and equipment really did look fantastic. The musician instructors looked professional yet cool, like people you wanted to hang out with as well as learn from. The names of the workshops were amazing, yet mysterious. Consider: "Bass: The

Fourth Dimension." Or: "Down with Poser Bands: An Introduction to Putting Your Heart into It." And then there was: "Music to Make You Sweat and Make You Smarter." Alex started rocking on the edge of the bed as images flashed through his well-feathered head of him and Meredith and the dudes having an awesome time jamming and learning to be a true professional band.

"So are you totally fucking bored out of your mind right now?" Meredith said.

"Hey. Guess what? My bass. I got it back."

"What the hell did we rent one for?"

"And I have more than enough money for this summer."

"What's it like to sit in your room and do nothing?"

"You know what would be really cool? Like, super rad?"

"More pot brownies?"

"If you snuck over here. Tonight. As in, climbed up the tree. The one with all the branches. It's easy. Louis has done it. And so did that kid down the street who lived across from the castle and used to sneak in all the time to play with our Christmas lights."

She swished the long phone cord around like a jump rope. "Whatever, moron."

At some point in the early afternoon, Alex pondered calling his father. The old man would probably be suspicious as to why his boy was phoning on a Saturday afternoon.

He got up and walked over to the two windows facing Broad Street and the tree he'd mentioned to Meredith. A sloppy stack of *Batman* comics threatened to topple. Would John get pissed if he read one? He imagined Meredith climbing the tree. She loathed physical exertion in all its forms. The two times a year they had to run a mile for gym class saw her among that group of pale introverts who didn't even try and got lapped by the overachievers.

"What are you smiling at?" The smell of vinegar hit him as he turned to find Dan holding a brown paper bag and a soda, shades perched on his thick blond hair. Sporting an accidentally bleached Orioles T-shirt and army-green shorts with torn and dangling threads at the hem, hairy tanned legs ending at flip-flops, he sipped from the soda. "It's freaking me out. I'm not used to you smiling. Here. Me and Louis stopped at the Wawa. Italian hoagie with everything. Sour cream and onion chips. Now you don't have to worry about going downstairs. I've been grounded before, I get it."

Was this some sort of prank? Stuffed at an awkward angle to accommodate its length was a hoagie wrapped in oil-and-vinegar-logged paper with a green bag of chips crunched against the side.

"Oh, and we're going to be out on the roof."

"What up, motherfuck?" Louis called with his trademark chuckle as he flip-flopped up the stairs. He took the beach theme even further with a yellow sleeveless shirt. When he noticed Alex's deadpan bemusement at the cavorting tuxedoed pigs on the shirt's front, he said with all seriousness: "Hogs, baby. Super Bowl XVII. Remember that? First night here?" He headed back out and up the stairs. "We got towels up here?"

"Why hogs though?" Alex said. "They're called the Redskins."

"Because they're fucking massive," Dan said. "Best blockers in football."

Louis flip-flopped back down with bright towels and his boom box and poked a Copenhagen-stained finger into Alex's chest. "Blocking and tackling are the key. The key to winning at football. The key to winning at life."

In addition to those two windows facing Broad, the room had a window facing Hogg's house. The roof on that side may not have abutted any climber-friendly trees, but the lack of shade was exactly why it was better for getting some sun. Louis tuned his box to the local rap station while Dan lathered himself in baby oil.

Alex made short work of the hoagie. As he reorganized his thoughts into a more logical order, something Dan had said struck him as odd. He poked his head out the window. The brothers lay perfectly still on their backs. Dan had his sunglasses on while Louis kept his eyes shut. "Question for you, sir. Earlier you mentioned you were grounded."

"We both had our asses grounded," Louis said.

"Back in Kensington."

"I see. But it's still kind of strange. Frank hasn't grounded anyone here. Not even Barry. Which is surprising."

Louis chuckled. "My father would never ground us. My real father, I mean. He knows there's no fucking point to it."

"You must be pissed," Dan said. "Barry wets his bed all the time and gets no punishment."

"Jonathan's a fucking criminal. Nothing."

"That is kind of amazing," Alex said.

"Turn that shit down," Dan said as the Fat Boys began beatboxing. "It's not amazing if you think about it. Jonathan's his son. His real son. I wet my bed, you think he'd put up with it?"

"Or grew pot?"

"What's it like to share a room?" Alex said. "With Stephen?"

Louis picked his nose and wiped it on a shingle. "When we first started sharing that room, I was afraid he'd stab me in my sleep. I still am."

Alex ended up reading several issues of *Batman*, but he only half paid attention to the narratives. At some point he nodded off and dreamed about Monday morning. He got to school early because he wanted to catch Meredith before homeroom. She wasn't at her locker. He bided his time in the cafeteria, far enough away to enjoy the direct line of sight to her locker without her spotting him. The anticipation was so palpable he could barely breathe.

Finally there she was, looking awesome as always, this time in black jeans. She didn't notice him until he was right in front of her. And that's when he did the dance. He wasn't sure what kind of dance he was doing just exactly. Like all dreams, only so many details registered. He knew it involved a lot of hopping from one leg to the other while turning. He pulled it off without a single misstep. Meredith exploded with laughter. Boy, she had a great smile, didn't she?

Clayton appeared out of nowhere. "Dude, what the *fuck*?"

"But she likes it, dude! She likes it! Move!"

"What are you doing?"

"Move!" Clayton wouldn't budge, which only seemed to feed Meredith's hysterics. She was bending over in tears as Alex exaggerated his limb movements so she could still watch him from the other side of this dickhead. "I fucking hate you, dude."

"Fuck you!"

Alex swung a fist that landed squarely in his guitarist's jaw.

A sweaty Alex woke with a start at the pang shooting up his arm. He'd just punched John.

Alex had been lying on the lower bunk with an open *Batman* comic on his chest. His kid brother stood several feet away with a hand to his jaw and shock on his face. Alex swallowed to lubricate his cotton-dry throat while he thought of how best to articulate an apology and explanation, but the fuse had already been lit. John launched a kick at the dangling leg and nailed it right on the shin. Alex could barely get out the agonized grunt before John started kicking him repeatedly, spewing profanity with every thrust.

"God damn it!" Faith threw open the door and let it crash against the wobbly spring stopper.

"He punched me!"

"Not even Bawrence and Jonathan fight this much."

"But Mom—"

"Keep up this bullshit and I'll ground both of you for a fucking month." She bored holes in their heads with her eyes before spinning around and thumping back down the hall.

"All is well?" said Frank as he came up the stairs. "Ah!" His eyes lit up when he saw the *Batman* comic. "I ever tell you I used to own the very first *Mad* magazine? I was, let's see. Twelve, thirteen? Obviously I had no idea how huge it was going to be. And then when I moved to Houston, I threw it out. You believe that?"

"That's not too terrible," John said. "Now if it had been the first *Playboy*..." They cracked up.

Alex shook his head in wonderment. The old man was a natural. He hopped out of bed, collected the rest of the comics from the floor, and placed them neatly atop the precarious pile.

He buried his head in algebra, flipping backward, reliving the mathematical memories of the past school year, while John and Frank moved on to Frank's dating adventures. At some point John said all this girl talk reminded him that he was late for Tara's. They were due for the date kids went on when they either didn't know what else to do or couldn't drive yet: Lumberton Plaza for a movie and King of Pizza. John chucked the *Batman* comic onto his desk and walked out without another word or another kick.

When Alex dialed his father, his stepmom answered with music blaring in the background. "Hello? I'm sorry, who is this?"

"Oh. Hey. Hey, Jen. It's Alexander." He recognized the Mamas & the Papas. The Glyphs had actually tried their hand once or twice at "California Dreamin'." If they did land the dance gig, maybe they could add that to the playlist.

"Who *is* this?"

"It's Alex. Alexander. Hello?"

The music turned down just in time for Alex to hear his father say, "...said turn it down! That counterculture crap is going to drive you deaf as well as insane."

"Thirty minutes a night! We agreed!"

Ford paused before saying, much more calmly, "Hang up, please, Jennifer." Another pause to allow for the louder-than-necessary click. "Ford here."

"Hey, Dad."

"Who is this?"

"Alexander. Hey."

As his father said something else, the Mamas and the Papas started blasting again. Apparently Jen had missed the cradle when body-slamming the phone. Ford erupted in more profanity before slamming his own phone against the dark wood of that two-shelf bookcase in his study where he kept that old-fashioned black phone he'd had since college. The march of his cowboy boots, which he only wore when working, faded from one phone and into the orbit of another as he read his wife the riot act. After Jen's line was cut off, the boots returned with purpose. "I'm very busy. Explain yourself immediately."

"Dad."

"Johnny!"

"Alexander."

After the most pregnant pause Alex had ever experienced: "Alex!" Ford hadn't said his name loud enough to warrant the exclamation mark, but I put it there because of Alex's optimism. "You wouldn't believe those bastards I work with."

"Doesn't sound very rad, whatever it is."

"You have a mind to make a career out of mathematics, don't forget the why. That's all I have to say on that subject. Bastards. I wasn't getting fleeced for child support, and I'm saying support in quotes since I know Faith doesn't need all of it, then I'd have enough financial security to quit these warmongering Republicans and go into work for myself. Maybe teach a little."

"Well, you know. I'm sorry John and I are getting in the way of, you know, your grand plans."

"Jen's losing it. Just completely. Last weekend I thought I would take her bowling. One of our first dates was bowling. I don't know, call me a nostalgic softie hiding behind the horned rims of a scholar trying to better humanity. Only this time? Oh the humanity. Jen has some bad luck early on, bowls a couple of gutter balls. You can tell she's trying so hard. But then you know what? Off the deep end. Into a pool with nary a drop. She starts bowling gutters intentionally and cackles like a maniac. Makes a total scene. Ah hell. Her company still beats the tail fire out of those of some of my colleagues. You've never met such a collection of nitwits. Where are you?"

"My room."

"When you visit, bring that rain with you. We're having a drought."

"School's almost done. But, you know, not quite."

"By my calculations, it is approximately thirty-seven minutes past seven o'clock in the p.m. on your side of the world. And this being a Saturday night, I surmise you are home with nothing to do while my little Johnny, the ladies' man of Boulder, is taking a pretty girl out for movies and dinner. Kid's only eleven, and he outclasses them all."

"He's got a powerful kick. I just found that out."

"What are you saying, child?"

"Have you spoken with him recently?"

"Depends what you mean by recently. Different people have different notions of time. John would understand that."

"So in the past twenty-four Earth hours, John hasn't, you know, called?"

"No, sir."

"I'm grounded. That's why I called you. And I'm bored. I've done everything else. You're the only game left in town. As Frank would say."

"I'm working with grounded missiles. Want to know why they're grounded? Because Reagan and Gorbachev have convinced themselves they don't need them, even though they do need them. Which reminds me of something far more important than futile defense shields and nuclear holocausts: That dumb dog of yours. Gorbachev. That mutt still among the living?"

"Purebred, Dad. Lhasa apso. He's cute. But, you know, I just wish he wouldn't shit in the house."

"I sing every time he does that."

"I beat up John."

"That must be a mistake. Remember how it was in Colorado? John was five, you were eight. He could kick your tail from here to Central City. Remember that? You were famous for fighting like a girl. Everyone talked about it. They still do."

"I threw him into the lake. Well, puddle. But it's a huge puddle."

Ford guffawed.

"Too bad you're not here or I'd offer you a pot brownie. It just pissed me off. He's very private with his friends. Like Donald. He always keeps Donald to himself. That's how I knew Donald didn't steal the money. Because, you know, that would mean John also stole it. But my point is, it's not fair."

Something crashed in the background. Jen shouted epithets. "Oh Saint Peter, give me strength or take me now."

"You said you would move this!"

"It's an idol worshipped by the indigenous peoples of Maui. It is very rare and therefore very expensive. What did you do to it?" Ford's boots receded into the depths of the bottomless tin can. "Just because it was given to me on my thirty-ninth birthday by my ex... You always find fault with it no matter where I set it up to shake the hula hoop."

"AHHHHHH!"

Alex fell off his chair with a start.

When he regained his feet and hung up the phone, he caught the lanky silhouette through the window by the tree.

"What the hell, you jerk!"

A voice mumbled from somewhere outside.

"Hey. Meredith. Hey. Mer. So. What's going on out here? Looks like more brownies you got there. All right. Pretty rad."

"You asshole. It's Mom's leftover casserole. I'm just trying to be nice, but I didn't think you'd have a bum guarding you."

Alex craned his neck and just managed to hide his bewilderment at the sight of Stephen sitting outside his bank of windows. He was nursing a diet soda in a glass with lots of ice and rubbing Gorbie's belly. Next to him lay his mangled trumpet. "Hey. Hey, Stephen. Rad moon."

As Alex helped Meredith climb in, Stephen said, "I ever tell you about how Barry's mom tried to ground me?"

"She tried, huh?"

Stephen stabbed the air with his finger. "But she didn't succeed."

"You think I should've said something to my mom?"

"Can I be honest? I'm not the biggest fan of your mom." He continued stabbing the air for emphasis. "However! She is a much smarter woman than Joanne. Or Joan. Or whatever she calls herself now. Faith might be evil incarnate, but she's smart. Joanne's mean and an idiot. So there you go, Alexander. There's a lesson there."

"This is getting cold," Meredith said. After she closed the window: "What is the deal with that dude?"

Alex didn't realize how hungry he was until he took the Tupperware off her hands. "We need to nuke it. That's a problem."

"You don't know how to use a microwave? Jesus."

"It's downstairs. In the kitchen. That's a problem. Because I can't, you know, go there."

She snatched the Tupperware from his hands and headed out the door and skipped down the stairs. Alex stood by the door and listened as Meredith interacted with someone whose voice was too low to recognize. Eventually the microwave beeped. She said something else to the mystery kitchen TV watcher before laughing on her way down the hall. When she reappeared, she was bearing warmed-up casserole, Soft Batch cookies, and sodas. "The cookies are for both of us. Who else sleeps here? Are those your socks, you fucking slob?"

They sat facing each other on the bottom bunk. The casserole was positively divine, and Alex didn't mind telling her even though he predicted her response from a mile away.

"Fuck you, you're just saying that because you're hungry."

After they stuffed themselves, Meredith sat back against the wall with her socked feet dangling over the edge. Her cutoff jean shorts only concealed the upper half of her thigh. Sure, her deodorant had worn off on this humid night. That she was wearing a Phillies tank top didn't exactly help matters, but if anything, her BO was consistent with her no-bullshit nature. Apparently, his glances at her gams weren't furtive enough.

"Admit it, you think my legs are hideous. I'm leaving."

"Want to hump again?"

"Are you seriously using that word?"

He went for her neck.

"What the hell?"

"I hope this doesn't, you know, get in the way of our band."

"You could've warned me first."

He took another heavy-lidded look at her neck. Some of his spit was still there. When he tried to wipe it off, she slapped his hand away.

"I said warn me first!"

"Okay. So. This is a warning. I'm about to give you a hickey. Which might lead to, you know, other things."

"Jesus, whatever."

Nothing could compromise their concentration, not *Conan* down the hall, Baltimore in the other direction, Oscar Peterson directly below, Beethoven across from that, or the Olympics in the poolroom. Better yet, Meredith anticipated his moves.

"You really think we'll win?" she asked afterward as they lay side by side. "Are you coming to school? I can't face rejection alone."

He burped up some of the casserole and swallowed it back down. "Two meals for the price of one. Awesome."

"Asshole."

Minutes before the end of eighth period on Monday, gym for Alex and Bruce, the principal blared on the PA that four of Holbein's very own would be playing at RV's end-of-year dance. Bruce was ahead of Alex during the mile run. Upon the announcement, he turned around and tackled him. "Oh get a room," several people said.

After school, Alex and Meredith made out at the top of the Mount.

Afterward, studying the leaves floating above, she asked, "You think any of your brothers will come?"

"I hadn't thought of that. But yes. Louis and Jonathan will most likely be there. Which could be a problem."

"Why?"

"Because they might pull me off the stage and, you know, beat the shit out of me." They heard voices crossing the boundaries of the Mount somewhere below.

"How long do you think we can keep this a secret?"

"Who were you talking to in the kitchen? The other night?"

"Your mom. She was watching this old repeat of *Carol Burnett*."

"That makes no sense. She's usually in her little room."

"She's so nice. At first I thought that show was stupid, but she was like, 'Just watch. You'll see.' And I was like, 'Wow, that's fucking hilarious.' And she didn't even mind me cussing. You never told me your mom was so cool. Or that she could rock the piano."

He was getting a headache.

She turned on her side to face him. "So how long? Do you think?"

The voices were getting closer. Worse, Alex knew exactly to whom they belonged. "For about five more minutes. Six. If I was a gambling man. Which I am most definitely not."

10

STEPHEN

RIGHT-WING MING AND AHNULD MOTHERNATOR

"*The Great Gatsby* proves that Republicans are right and Commie Liberals are wrong."

Stephen tried not to smile too much at the dead-silent classroom, but it was tough. The intense focus required made his pits drip.

"Commie Liberals think the government needs to be in everyone's business. A good example in the nineteen twenties was Prohibition. Prohibition did nothing good for this country. It created an underground economy for people to get rich. One small problem with an underground economy: it's illegal. This created gangs, and that led to a lot of people getting killed. This included innocent people who had nothing to do with bootlegging. In *The Great Gatsby*, Myrtle is a good example. She is run over by Gatsby, who is a bootlegger. And so that is how this book shows it's best if Commie Liberals go home and let Republicans run the country. Republicans know better than to get in the way of the people, and that the best economy is a free market economy."

He paused and took his time swallowing to allow for questions or, as happened during his presentation about how *Macbeth* proved all women were genetically predisposed to mental instability, protests and profanity and thrown objects. But the classroom remained perfectly still. That should have been a good thing, yet for some reason a thin film of sweat was coating his forehead.

"Another way *The Great Gatsby* shows the right is always right is in how it depicts the community of West Egg. West Egg is a beautiful community with lots of big, beautiful houses. It really is paradise. Unfortunately, it is impossible to have a paradise like West Egg anymore. Why, you ask? One word: taxes. Taxes represent another way the Commie Liberals get in everyone's way. There was a time when no one paid taxes. And it was easy to have a house like the ones in West Egg. We will never see those houses again. And I find this to be sad. That is why *The Great Gatsby* is a tragedy."

Reining in that Nicholsonian grin was getting harder than ever. His jaw muscles trembled, and his mouth only grew drier despite long pulls of water. He cleared his throat. Almost there.

"The third and final way *The Great Gatsby* shows why Republicans are the good guys and Commie Liberals are the bad guys is with the character of Daisy. Daisy starts out as a good model for women: an obedient wife who spends all her time in the house and does everything her husband tells her to do. *The Great Gatsby* takes place in the nineteen twenties, right after women got the right to vote. I believe the right to vote was a bad thing for women. It makes them think they're smarter than they really are. This leads them to make decisions that get them into trouble and ruin their marriage. When Daisy cheats on Tom with Gatsby, everything goes wrong. She would not have done this if women weren't given the same rights as men."

"What the hell?"

"Quiet, Marnie," said Miss Wallace.

"Daisy and Myrtle show that women are genetically predisposed toward mental instability. I know there are some of you here who don't know what that means. That means it's easy for women to go from sane to insane. I have a lot of experience with mentally disturbed women. My mother is mentally disturbed. So is my step-mother. My stepmother threw a can of peas at my brother's head. It is my opinion that she should be committed. F. Scott Fitzgerald married a woman named Zelda. She was crazy too. That's why he had her committed. Because women are predisposed to mental sickness, I believe they should no longer be allowed to vote or be allowed to work."

A pen flew past him and smacked the chalkboard.

"In conclusion, *The Great Gatsby* makes a solid case that Commie Liberals are not supposed to be in power. They get in the way of freedom. They take all our money. And they give women too many rights. The end."

"So hold up." One of the girls raised her hand. "You against women having a right to an education?"

"I have *two* answers to that," Stephen said with a stab of his finger. "In an ideal world, meaning a Conservative Republican world, women should not be educated past a certain grade level. Let's say eighth grade. Because we want you to read and write."

"Who's we? Racist white folks?"

"My second answer reflects the realist that I am. Realistically, I believe women are entitled to a high school education so long as they focus on home economics."

"Maybe you're the one who's crazy," another girl said.

"And your stepmom?" Miss Wallace asked.

Stephen looked around. "Did someone say Satan?"

"How are her home ec skills?"

"That is a loaded question."

"You're not the only Roggebusch I've taught. I've heard she's great at math and science. I'm willing to bet she's not so good in the kitchen. I suppose the can of peas proves my point."

Stabbing the air so hard his shoulder popped: "*That* is the exception that proves the rule." Stephen knew this was the time to focus on his breathing, but he was too pissed off at Miss Wallace. Look at her. Look at that smug smile teasing the corner of that bright red mouth.

"Thank you for presenting, Stephen. At least you know what you believe, and you back it up and stand by it. Your evidence, however, is a bit faulty in some cases by lack of attention to detail. It's not Gatsby who runs over Myrtle. He confesses to it, everyone thinks it's him, including, tragically, Myrtle's husband George. Also, your comments about West Egg assume it's a real place." The class cracked up. Someone threw their *Gatsby* and nailed him in the face.

"You see?" His face was getting hot. "Unstable, irrational behavior."

"That wasn't a girl who threw that!"

After school, Stephen hopped into Faith's Rabbit and drove to Miss Wallace's house in Medford Lakes to have a roll in the hay. Afterward, she rested her head on his chest and dozed. Some kids rode by on their bikes on the otherwise tranquil street. The surrounding forest created one of the more peaceful enclaves in Burlington County. "Any blacks live here?"

"No idea."

"I thought you were supposed to be a Liberal champion of the minority underclasses."

"Can we please not talk about politics? Please?"

"I'm not talking about politics. I'm talking about what you say versus how you live."

"If you go to the prom, and black people are there, will you turn around and leave?"

"You didn't say if *we* go to the prom. I take it you've made your decision?"

She turned her head to face the sealed blinds. "My needle is trending toward no."

"Trending toward no. Trending a lot? How much trending are we talking about?"

"You don't think about anyone but yourself. It might be fun for you to take the teacher to the prom. But you know what? Next year? You're in college. Deriding all the black kids in North Philly. I'll be here. People will whisper in the back of the class when I'm trying to teach them how to think critically about what they read."

"I don't believe that's accurate. That I only think about myself. I would like to dispute that."

"I don't blame you. Whenever I see a kid all wrapped up in

himself, thinking the sun, moon, and stars revolve around him, I says to myself, I says, 'His parents made that happen.'"

"I also contest the, how shall I say, *Scarlet Letter* scenario. Just to remind you, I'm covering all expenses: your dress, dinner, the limo."

"Now what kind of situation would we call this in class?"

"I do not think about school when I am not in it. It is anathema to my nature."

"Hey, question for yas. Who brought you into this world? Who cleaned you and fed you when you were a helpless little nose picker? Your father? According to you, he was out sleeping with his neighbor. That only leaves one person."

"Everyone who will be at the senior prom, by definition of being seniors, won't be at RV next year to whisper in the back of class. Now I grant you some will bring dates who are underclassmen. Those underclassmen, by definition, will be back next year. But I contest the assumption that they'll be whispering in the back of class. For one thing, that assumes they will all be in your class, which of course is impossible."

"Kids remember everything. Speaking of which..." She got out of bed and wrapped the sheet around her on her way out. Then she whipped her head back into the room, her blond hair swishing to one side. "I have to take a shower and wash my sheets or they'll smell that someone was here. And they'll remember. And then they'll tell their father. And anyone else who'll listen. For years, if not the rest of their lives."

"And that matters... why? You're divorced. He's remarried..."

She headed out. "Unless it involves the Berenstain Bears, I don't have the fucking energy to tell stories to my kids."

Louis and John switching rooms was supposed to have been a good thing. As far as anyone knew, John didn't possess any proclivities for destroying musical equipment. But he did possess puberty. When Stephen got home, John and Tara were in the room with the door closed, their hushed tones punctuated by the odd burst of laughter.

While Stephen pondered whether or not to pounce, he heard his father getting out of the steam room shower up on the third floor. No, he just wasn't in the mood for this family right now. He went back down to the poolroom, dug out his calculus from his cubby, and took shelter in the music room. Chances were decent, even with his luck recently, that he wouldn't be bothered here. Almost everyone at 48 Broad played an instrument, but most either practiced right after school or at night.

During dinner (Dad whipped up a masterpiece of T-bones and rosemary potatoes), Stephen put on the best show of faux cordiality perhaps ever. He only made fun of Barry a little bit and otherwise laughed at all of Daniel and Louis's jokes while fantasizing about knocking both of them unconscious with a sledgehammer for all those times they made fun of his weight in Kensington. Speaking of knockouts, when it was his turn for Good Thing Bad Thing New Thing, he celebrated what he considered a knockout job on *Gatsby*.

After dinner, while Daniel dove into the dishes and Frank and Faith headed into the music room for a piano duet, Stephen's urge to get away from these people burned hotter than ever. Because he was too lazy to do something like go for a walk or maybe drive to the Seven Heaven, his method of getting away was to climb to the top of the house. The only way to do that was to use the roof right outside the master bedroom. As he climbed out with Gorbie tucked under one arm, the sunlight was already getting lost behind the big tree in Hogg's yard that protruded over here. Once out on the roof, he reached back in for his mangled trumpet before gingerly sliding the window shut. With a chuck of the pooch followed by the brass, Stephen used George Taylor's stepladder to achieve the crown. The breeze always made the effort worth it.

Gorbie's opinion seemed to be on the other side of the pole. Poochie didn't budge from where he'd landed, inches from the gutter. Taking a page from his namesake, this little Lhasa opted for modesty, stability, and security over pushing his luck with forces beyond his control. Stephen scooped him up as well as the trumpet and easily negotiated the inclines. The crest of the back half of the house collided perpendicularly with that of the roof that spanned the width of the front half of the house, forming the A-frame over Barry and Jonathan's rooms on either side. Stephen parked himself on the comparatively flatter, if shorter, crest of the little A-frame that encased the Broad-facing window of Barry's room. To his immediate left was the chimney leading to the walled-up fireplace in the music room.

"How's life been treating you, little guy?" He leaned to the side and peeled off a monster fart courtesy of the sloppy joe he'd had for lunch. "Too bad Joanne's not up here. Or I'd push her off." He farted again and laughed. "I love you, Gorbachev, but you're a sissy. Just like the real Gorbachev. They should've named you the Terminator. That would've been just the ticket for your self-confidence, man."

A couple of cars passed along Broad in both directions. The view wasn't spectacular just exactly, but he still felt a sense of power hardening his muscles and gut. Not power in that he could do whatever he wanted and get away with it. It was the feeling that whatever was happening down there didn't affect him. People drove by with their mufflers coughing up petty problems, they walked by spatting and spitting, kids screamed and complained, parents fumed and cussed, old folks scorned the world... Not a jot of it mattered up here.

"What do you think I should play?" He tested and tuned his trumpet. Because it was damaged, of course it didn't sound like it should have. Stephen didn't care. He needed to play it like he needed to breathe. "Good choice. 'Piña Colada' it is." About halfway through the song, a thought invaded his brain that would not be turned away or willed into oblivion: he hadn't called his mom in over a month. They'd never been on regular speaking terms, not like her and Jonathan and not remotely like the Sunday-night ritual with Barry and Joanne. Still, the last thing he needed was her to call him and guilt him into thinking he was a neglectful ingrate.

Stephen dropped Gorbie onto the roof outside the master bedroom before negotiating the stepladder. As soon as he and the pooch were inside, he heard his father down the hall.

"Baw-*rence*! Have you seen your oldest brother?"

"Which oldest brother?"

"The one actually related to you."

"I don't know."

"I see. So Stephen ran in the opposite direction of you, which makes the most sense. Some life-forms repel, others attract." The old man was already tipsy on the scotch, but that didn't hide that he was miffed. The thumping noises indicated he was heading down to the first floor. "Jona-*than*! Stay right there and don't fucking move. I'm not letting this night end until your brother is found."

Stephen's gut, which just seconds ago made him feel impervious to the world, melted into lumpy knots. At least he could take advantage of his father's voice filling up the house to conceal any noise he might've made placing the stepladder back inside the master closet. He'd been gripping the trumpet so firmly in his sweaty fingers that he forgot it was there as he descended the stairs. "Father!"

"Ste-*van*!" Frank thumped down the hallway with the most purpose Stephen had ever seen from the old man this late at night. "Come, let's adjourn to the living room where your brother has been patiently waiting."

"Where the fuck you been, man?"

"Quit your goddamned cussing, Jonathan."

Frank didn't sit in his recliner so much as throw his full weight into it. He reached for his floss on the adjacent bookshelf to clean out the steak between his teeth. Jonathan sat in Faith's high-back blue leather chair. Stephen was going to sit in the cushioned rocking chair closest to the hallway, but he didn't want to let himself get too comfortable.

"I brought the both of you here to talk about your mother," Frank said. He finished flossing and discarded the white threads with their little dark clumps into the Super Fresh paper bag he used as his personal wastebasket.

Stephen shot a look at Jonathan, who shrugged.

After a healthy slurp of nectar, their father said, "Mary has done something so profoundly disturbing I think it's safe to say I've never been so pissed off the way I am pissed off at this very instant." He looked back and forth between them with an inscrutable look.

"And why's that?" Stephen surprised himself with the softball question, but if he took his usual tack of trying to provoke, it would only keep him here that much longer.

"That's an interesting question! I'm not entirely sure I know all the background, but I do know enough to say that if she were here? Right now? I would kill her."

After allowing for some silence, Stephen said, "Should I ask again?"

Frank cleared his throat, took a quicker-than-usual gander at all his books, then turned back to them while folding his hands on his belly. "Gentlemen. The following has transpired. About a half hour ago, I phoned your mother. Now, lest you get confused, this was not a social call. I called to check on the college fund I set up for the two of you. Stephen is starting college in the fall, and while he's been accepted to Temple and will most likely go to Temple, there's always the possibility he'll chose another college. Barring that, while Temple's tuition is free, Stephen will have other expenses to contend with. Books. Residency, if he decides to live there. If he lives here and commutes, he'll have gas mileage. Maintenance and upkeep of his vehicle. All of those things cost money, far more than your allowance could keep up with. Further, Jonathan will be attending college in three years' time. You may think that's a long time from now, but it's not. Trust me."

"So I don't have to go to Temple is what you're saying," Jonathan said.

Frank cleared the nothing in his throat and considered the war tomes right next to him. "I have been depositing money into your college fund since shortly after you were born. Every month. Every. Single. Fucking. Month. At first your mother was not depositing anything because she was unemployed."

"That's not true," Jonathan said. "She was a secretary at the FBI. You told us that."

"That was in the sixties. Once we were married and had the two of you, she quit. Such was the custom among women. After our divorce, your mother went back to work. And per our agreement, she contributes to the fund, same as I." He slurped his scotch. "But then, in the mail today, I received the quarterly statement regarding this fund. Now. Even if your math is, you know, kind of shaky? You could probably surmise that a fund, or a bank account, or your piggy bank would contain more money than it did the same time last year. You follow? It could be a lot more, a little more, moderately more. But if you have two people depositing money into it consistently, at a set cadence, it should be appreciably more, year over year."

"That depends on how you define appreciably," Stephen said with a finger jab. He had no idea why he said that. Perhaps if his father knew at least one other person in the room could think as critically as him, he'd relax a little. Or he might blow up.

With a pronounced finger jab of his own, Frank said, "If defined as a million dollars, then the difference between your college fund last year and this year would not be appreciable. If, however, you define appreciable as a hundred or a thousand or more than a thousand, the difference between last year and this year is appreciable. At least it should be appreciable." He considered his boys in turn. "Which leads me to why I called you here. Upon reading over the statement, I was startled to find that it was not only less than this time last year, it was less than last quarter. And I would say it was appreciably less. Thousands of dollars less. Now, since this is an investment, it is not impossible for a fund to depreciate. It depends somewhat on the market. Market's bad? It might go down. Bad enough? It could drop significantly. But the economy is strong. Reagan has the right idea about the Russians. All signs point to funds appreciating in value. So you can imagine my surprise when I read the statement. In fact, I thought I was reading it wrong." After another slurp, he stabbed the air. "Question: What happened to the money?" He glared back and forth between them.

Stephen's head was hurting. Jonathan seemed to feel the same, judging by his blank, openmouthed look.

"Gentlemen. Let me introduce you to a concept called Occam's razor. Occam's razor says that when you're trying to figure out how something happened, of all the possible explanations, the simplest tends to be the right one. Now sometimes it takes the greatest effort to arrive at the simplest explanation. That's called a paradox. Your mother?" He glared. "Stole the money. She withdrew five thousand dollars from your college fund. And then she took out another five hundred to pay the tax on that. They tax you if you take money out of a fund before you're supposed to. Like a 401(k)."

"Why'd she take money out of it?"

Stabbing the air: "Another example of Occam's razor. Your mother claimed, quite passionately, I might add, that she needed the money for a variety of needs and expenses that could no longer be delayed or deferred. If she didn't service these debts, so she said, there would ensue a calamity even worse than the act of taking money from her children. Now." Another sip. "Might I propose a simpler explanation?" Frank leaned forward and stabbed the air yet again. Had the air been a person, it would've been a gruesome scene. "Your mother is an unspeakably evil human being."

"What if she really needed the money, Dad?"

"Jonathan, your mother is a crook. She may even be a sociopath."

"What the fuck?"

Frank sat back and thumb-scratched his scalp. "I know your allegiance tends to lean toward your mother. I don't know why that is. I may never know why."

Jonathan guffawed. "Because your crazy bitch wife threw a can of peas at my head and you didn't do shit about it. How's that for your stupid fucking razor theory? Know what Mom said when I told her? That if she'd been here, she'd've had Faith arrested. That's child abuse."

"I have not the slightest interest in Faith's methods of defending herself against people twice her size, however unorthodox those methods may be. Your allegiance is with your mother? Fine. Bawrence is more loyal to his mother? Fine."

"I don't think that's it," Stephen said. This must've been what professional tightrope walkers felt like: balance that was true yet with a lethal drop just a hair's breadth to either side.

"You don't think what's it?"

"I don't think Jonathan's hypothesis comes from an alliance with our mom. Although I should point out that I do agree with his stance on the can of peas incident. And I'm usually the last person in the world to defend him. But since you proffered his point of view as you understand it, I feel it's only proper that I reciprocate. Fair enough?"

With his hands already clasped, Frank crossed his feet. "Okay, sure."

"Defending or allying with our mother may have been his secondary point, granted, but I believe his main point was to find a simpler explanation."

"For why she would steal her children's money, you mean."

"I choose not to use the word steal."

"Maliciously and vindictively."

"I believe his main point was to find a sharper Occam's razor."

"So you're saying she needed it for credit card debt?"

"Wouldn't debt be a simpler explanation?"

"How often do you talk to her? Every week? Every other week?"

Stephen shrugged.

"Twice a month? Twenty-four times a year?"

"Sounds like a lot."

"Twenty times a year. That's once a month, plus a bonus call every other month or so. Now I don't know about you, but if you are keeping in touch with that kind of consistency, and she suffers some kind of financial calamity or misfortune that is so severe her only recourse is to pilfer five thousand fucking dollars from your college fund, she would most likely let you know about said calamity or misfortune."

Stephen raised a finger and tried to keep the smile small. "Your premise is false. Mother and I speak, on average, once a month, occasionally skipping a month, for an average of eight times a year. With an average call lasting ten minutes, that means we speak, on average, eighty minutes in any given year. However, I do agree that if something critical had occurred in her life, not only would she have shared it with Jonathan, Jonathan would have been the very first to know." While he maintained a mostly equable demeanor on the outside, inside Stephen was dancing on his brother's grave. The look on Jonathan's face alone was worth the confetti.

"So we're agreed," Frank said. "Your mother is a shameless crook." He wiped the froth off his mustache. Thumps came down the hall. "Speaking of taking what doesn't belong to you: Baw-*rence!*"

Jonathan leaped up the stairs two at a time, then stopped and said, "Yo, Barry. Dad were a decent guy, you wouldn't exist. How does that make you feel?"

Barry turned and disappeared down the hall.

"Ste-*van.*"

"Father."

"Your mother is a crook."

"If you say so."

"I know you're not fond of Joanne. You say she mistreated you during your summers in Kensington. I'm still not entirely sure what that means, but in any event, I look at it like this: Whatever her flaws and deficiencies, Joanne would never do to me what your mother has done." Frank slurped and considered his son. "I don't expect any of this to change your view of the world, but I thought you should at least know my view of the world. That's fair, right? You love your mother. Of course you do. She's your mother after all. But what she did was wrong. Just plain, fucking wrong. I would rather not take her to court, but if she doesn't return the money, things will get ugly."

"Okay." He'd survived the stunt. Now how the hell could he escape this circus tent?

"You're almost done with high school!"

"I look forward to it. On many levels."

Frank smiled with sleepy eyes. "Hey! This is a big, fucking God damned deal. You know why it's a big, fucking God damned deal?"

"I give up. Why is it a big deal?"

"Because you're graduating high school!"

"Ah!"

"The end of school. Not forever. You're going to Temple. But that's a different kind of school. In a good way. For me, high school meant putting up with unremitting asshole teachers who tried to fuck me over by sending me to a Quaker college. But then I started at GW, and things got better. Oh I keep meaning to ask: Are you going to the prom?"

"A very good question."

Frank peered closely at his tumbler until his nose was inside it. When he looked up, he was wearing another sleepy smile. "I'm going to pour another scotch. And put on some jazz that I will turn up as loud as humanly fucking possible."

At school the next day, reading one of his sci-fi pulp novels in the library during lunch, Stephen hit upon an idea that brought a smile to his mug like few others could. He was still smiling after dinner when he acted on it. With a Tab and a bowl of ice cream, he took shelter in Faith's wardrobe closet. His father and Faith's classical piano duets filled the house.

"Are you watching your soaps?"

"You just missed your aunts."

"Would you like to hear how your ex-husband yelled at Jonathan and me?" By the time he finished recounting last night's tongue thrashing, his mother was thrashing a tongue of her own. In her own way, that is. Her Southern hospitality seemed to preclude four-letter words.

"So the womanizer was upset, was he? He has nerve, I tell you what. How galling. Poor innocent children."

"Did something happen to you?"

"Beg pardon?"

"Why do you need the money?"

"Stephen, hon, I don't want to get sore at you. You haven't done anything wrong."

"No, you did. That was Dad's point."

"Your mama doesn't exactly earn the big bucks, okay? And I don't have wealthy friends in high places overpaying me for cushy work-from-home jobs that help me pay off my mortgage in less than a year."

"That would imply Dad has all of those things."

"Baby, you remember that man? What's his name? He and your

daddy have known each other since GW. Got a private jet and everything. We had him and his now ex over when we were living in
Washington."

"What does he have to do with Dad's mortgage?"

"The mortgage in that house you're living in? Sweetie, your
daddy's already paid it off. Know how long it usually takes to pay off a
mortgage?"

Stephen took his glasses off and rubbed his eyes. Suddenly he
wanted more than anything in the world to hang up, but his mother
seemed to be divulging something that could prove useful against the
old man. "Still not seeing the relevance, Mother."

"Soon as your daddy dumped that hussy and married the math
whiz, his rich college buddy hires them to work for his company.
Doing what, I haven't the foggiest, but after he got that job, your
daddy paid off that mortgage in a jiffy. He bragged about it."

"That how he's been able to keep up with the huge alimony?"

"Beg pardon?"

"He says the monthly payments are huge. Maybe he needed the
extra work to keep up with you."

Mary was silent for what seemed like forever. "That man talk
about anything else but his money?"

"He says you're a crook."

"I swear to holy Jesus I'm going to fly up there right now and ring
that man's neck."

"I should tell Jonathan about Dad's rich friend. We hardly see that
guy anymore."

"Know how your daddy bought his first house? House we moved
into when we came back from Houston right after you were born?
That was his daddy. Show me something he bought with his own
money because every house he's ever lived in wouldn't count."

"So you're not going to tell me?"

"I could fly up there right now. I'm this close."

"Why'd you steal money from your kids?"

"Sweetheart..."

"Hey, I don't care. You have a shopping problem? Gambling problem? Whatever. Temple's free. Jonathan probably won't go to college at all. Unless it's a college for drug dealers."

"I'm coming up there."

"To tell us why you stole our money?"

"I'm so beside myself I could scream!"

"You kind of are screaming, Mother."

"Baby, I'm not mad at you, I swear. Or Jonathan."

"Oh don't worry, Jonathan knows he's your favorite."

"Come again?"

"I have calculus to do. Finals are coming up. And then I'm graduating. But I know you won't come up for that since you're saving your money for when Jonathan graduates."

"Oh hush, you know why I'm not coming."

Stephen wasn't lying. He really did have a ton of calc to do for tomorrow and more to study for next week's exam hell, Mr. Giacomo's sadistic system that inflicted one quiz a day for the week leading up to the final. That bald, rotund, needle-nosed sweat sack was on a roll the next day. Most RV teachers were low-key on Fridays. Maybe they'd put on a filmstrip about a teenager learning a hard life lesson (but not too hard). Or maybe they'd declare it study hour. You also had teachers who turned their classrooms into a political pulpit to declaim for or against Reaganomics. Stephen had no reason to fear any of those things, for Mr. Giacomo lashed his kids with every impossible equation.

After a day like this, Stephen didn't have the energy to head up to the roof. As it was, he could barely keep up with Good Thing Bad Thing New Thing. After dinner, he popped some corn, grabbed a Tab, and ran upstairs for some *Conan the Destroyer*. By the time Arnold recruited Grace Jones, he was out for the count.

When he awoke the next morning with popcorn on his chest, John told him they were going up to the library lot to play football. "Soon as Dan gets back from getting his tux and Alex gets back from band practice."

Stephen straightened his specs and polished off the warm Tab.

His head felt heavy with the grogginess of too much sleep. "How about we debate whether I should play?"

Louis stuck his head in the room. "Suit the fuck up, fatty!"

"But I don't want to be on your team!" Barry protested to Louis. The brothers were walking up Buttonwood. "You always yell at me!"

"Barry, quit your bitching," Dan said.

"The other team already has four players, you retard. It's you and me and Stephen. And Stephen sucks almost as bad as you do."

"Hey, I can catch." Stephen's smile was genuine. He'd decided it was hard to find a Saturday more satisfying than watching his father's other offspring, adopted or from another mother or otherwise, go at each other like raging, rabid wildebeests. "Who made that awesome catch last time?"

"Your dorky ass made a lucky catch," Jonathan spat.

"All right, let's do this! Our team has fewer players, so we get the ball first."

"Tackle?" Dan asked with mock innocence as they started for opposite ends of the field.

Looking like a true criminal with his sleeveless gold Redskins Hogs tee, cutoff jeans, and wraparound shades, all Louis had to do to send Dan into hysterics was point at him.

Stephen mock stopped abruptly and pretended that what he'd been bursting to tell Jonathan since last night had only just occurred to him. "I called Mom and told her about Dad getting all pissed." His smile morphed into a garbled chuckle.

Jonathan's freckles didn't so much as twitch. "What'd she say?"

"She got so pissed, man. It was beautiful. She kept threatening to come up here."

"She always does that."

"She would tell us why she stole our money, but she won't because she's not mad at us." He laughed at his brother's nonplussed look. "Anyway, good luck!" One of the first plays was Louis fake handing off to Stephen before giving the ball to Barry, who got pulverized, and by Alex of all people. "Oh shucks, Bawrence Barney." Stephen helped him up. "If only you could run as fast as Dad ran from your mom." A few possessions later, Jonathan ran a fancy out pattern that was too clever for Dan's bullet spiral. "Geez, Double, you didn't get a return on your investment. What good is being Mom's favorite if you're not going to learn from her thievery?"

Stephen being Stephen and his thug of a brother being a thug of a brother, it was only a matter of time before the former's faux jocularity crumbled in the face of the latter's effortless provocations. Only this time it would be a battle royal for the ages.

The moment came when Dan threw a duck twenty yards over the heads of everyone except Jonathan. The pot kingpin still had to haul ass for it. As that duck wobbled something fierce, he stretched those lanky, freckly arms like a blond, mop-headed Mr. Fantastic with a maniacal laugh. His fingertips clutched the tip of the pigskin just before it touched the grass. He caught it!

Or did he?

Jonathan spiked the ball. He and his teammates celebrated while Stephen led Louis and Barry in a chorus of protests. "Bullshit!"

"The fuck you say?"

"That wasn't a catch and you know it!"

"Come on, Dan," Louis said. "Third down."

"I didn't really see it because you and Stephen were burying me in the grass."

"He caught it!" John said.

Alex, his deadpan tone sounding completely alien in this setting, added, "I saw it too. I believe this is where Frank would say touchdown six points. Or is it seven? Or three maybe?"

"Bullshit. Incomplete pass. Third down."

"You're a cheater! You missed it!"

"Barry, shut the fuck up before I throw a touchdown spiral with you."

"No fucking way that's a touchdown, yo," Louis said. "It touched the grass."

"I had control."

Maybe it was the fat jokes (why did they still do it even though he'd dropped all that tonnage?). Or maybe it was their mother. Or their father. Or some hot mixture of the above plus more he couldn't name. Whatever the reason, Stephen's head was suddenly so full of steam that he didn't realize he was approaching his brother until Jonathan jabbed the football in his gut. "Why do you need to cheat to win?"

"Back the fuck off, man."

"Third down."

"Alexan-*dor*," Louis said with a spot-on impersonation of Frank. "You're an honest kid. I know you don't give a flying fuck if your team wins or loses. Can you tell us honestly—because if I find out you're lying, I'll kick your goofy ass—if Jonathan caught the ball and had control before the ball touched the grass?"

"In my estimation, and based on my powers of observation, Jonathan successfully made the catch. For eight points. Or is it ten?"

Before Stephen could fully analyze the wisdom of his words, they came spewing forth like a rogue well choking on boiling black stuff. "Hey, Jonathan, when you're done doing the black people shuffle, I have something to tell you. Know why Mom likes you better? Because you cheat and pretend you don't."

"Get the fuck back there, man. We're kicking off."

"You didn't catch it! It touched the grass! I saw it! You didn't have control!" When Jonathan just looked at him, his mouth hanging open with the hint of a smile teasing one side of those freckles, Stephen breathed and willed himself not to take the bait.

"Fuck it, yo," Louis said. "Let them have it."

Stephen's chest burned. Of all the people to throw in the towel, he never would've expected it from the kid who destroyed his music equipment in the dead of night. Was Louis ceding the touchdown out of lingering guilt from stabbing Jonathan? "Bullshit. He didn't have control. I saw the whole thing."

"Cheater!" Barry squeaked from behind the protective barrier of Louis.

"Yeah, Stephen," Jonathan said. "Stop cheating. You'll never be as good at cheating as Dad. That man's a master. Ask Mom. Or Joanne."

"But he admits it. Fucking admit you didn't have control."

"Come on, guys." Dan started to make his way toward the other side of the field. "We're kicking off. Stephen? Suck it in, fatty. Double's a better player than you. But that's okay. You have your virtues too. See? Frank taught me that. Everyone has their own strengths."

Stephen's innards boiled with a type of acid he hadn't felt since those summers in Kensington. Jonathan, John, and Alex were walking past him to follow Dan. Through the blood-red hue of his vision, Stephen caught sight of Jonathan's freckled smirk. "Fine, let the PUSSIES have it!" And on "pussies," he whipped his arm around and slapped Jonathan square on the back with a firecracker sound. Judging by his Jedi-like reflex in spinning around to return the blow, Jonathan had anticipated it.

And with that, these two Florida-bred gators launched at each other.

Stephen wouldn't remember the details surrounding most of this fight. Over the years, as he and his siblings recounted what became one of the most famous scuffles in 48 Broad history, Stephen would form an image of this fight from a third-person perspective. He and Jonathan traded slaps to the head and punches to the arms and chest, and as they did so, their shuffling and dodging and backstepping and fore stepping added up to a full circuit around the perimeter of the library lot.

The fight began on the same side of the field as the alley leading out to Buttonwood. From there, the frothing behemoths slapped and jabbed their way around to the other side where a smattering of trees shielded the lot from the Victorian library building, then up along the edge of those trees (Dan would later say that he expected Stephen to bolt for the library to grab some books and throw them at Jonathan, for what better way for a nerd to defend himself?). Eventually they reached the other end zone, punching and slapping along the fence and rounding the corner as their energy dissipated along the backs of the houses that fronted Buttonwood.

As for the first-person perspective, what always stood out in Stephen's mind were the cheers. At first, when he and Jonathan were still over by the trees near the library, he assumed they were cheering for Jonathan. Stephen may have had his father's ego, but he also had his father's clear-eyed honesty about how liked he was, or wasn't, in any given setting. Like his father, he assumed the majority of every grouping wouldn't like him because he was smarter than them, at least in the erudite sense.

By the time they were coming full circle, Stephen finally figured out that they weren't cheering for one or the other but simply at the spectacle and for the spectacle not to stop. Yet stop it did, as all spectacles must. The gators stumbled and fumbled to a gradual cessation, faces beet red, lungs gasping for air, saliva dangling from their lower lips.

"Someone's watching you, dudes!" John called.

"Gentlemen, you have an audience!" Dan called in perfect Frank style.

With a hand pressed to his dagger-cramped midsection, Stephen straightened up and followed their gaze toward the alley.

"I should've known I'd find you two fighting. And your daddy's nowhere in sight. Shame on that shameless philanderer!"

To say that Stephen's heart stopped, breath stopped, blood curdled, and every follicle on his head and neck sprang erect would've been selling grossly short what he felt as his eyes beheld, against their will, the carrot-topped, freckle-faced, perpetually sneering older female version of Jonathan. That ridiculously large and loud purse may have blended in at those Gulf Coast beaches, but up here it stood out like a veined, mottled malignancy. Then you've got her blinding, deafening floral peachwear. And that perfume, reeking of dead roses and boiled caramel, could only just camouflage the booze-flecked aura.

"Well? Aren't you going to give your mama a hug?"

Jonathan, that criminal who struck terror in the hearts of the masses, giggled like a little boy as he picked up his mother and rocked her in a bear hug.

"Oh good lord, you smell like cigarettes! Mm-wah!" She pecked him on the forehead.

"I promise I'll quit, Mama."

"How long are you staying? When did you get here?"

Mary and Jonathan cracked up. Their laughs were two hideous halves of the same dark humor. "And what on earth has happened to you? My firstborn catch the flu?"

"Sounds like you're dying, man."

Stephen massaged his tongue against the roof of his mouth in a futile attempt to revive the well. His face heated like a 48 Broad furnace. It hurt to breathe. The daggers in his midsection only multiplied.

"Heavens to Betsy, Stephen Roggebusch." Mary dug into her purse. When her spindly fingers finally reemerged, they clutched a flask. "Helluva way to greet your mama. Take some inspiration from that."

This wasn't Stephen's debut with whiskey. A couple of Christmases ago, during a visit to North Fort Myers, his mother had gotten her claws on a well-aged bottle of Tennessee whiskey from one of her sisters, Stephen's stark raving lunatic, pit bull-loving Aunt Anne. Then as now, the molten gold liquid scorched his esophagus on its way to blasting open a hole clear through his innards. He had to hand it to her though. It did the trick. "I'd known you were coming up, Mother, I'd've dressed more appropriately."

"Horse pucky."

"That whiskey?" Louis asked. "Can I grab a sip?"

"Hi, I'm John." John ran forward with a smooth smile and a firm grip. Stephen would've given anything to punch him out right then and there. "Pleasure to meet you."

"Aren't you adorable? Now where do you fit in this mess?"

"Faith's younger son from her first marriage. Alex is my brother."

With a perfunctory wave and his trademark lack of emotion, Alex said, through a curtain of hair that concealed his face: "What's up, homie?"

"I feel a migraine coming on." Mary turned to Louis as if she only just heard his whiskey question. Then she squinted at Daniel. "Oh good lord, I do declare. Last time I saw you two, you were small as my daddy's chopped-up stumps. Look at you! Daniel, you're a stalk! And Louis. Looking at you, I reckon you play sports."

"They don't let him play anymore because he fails all his classes," Stephen said. He'd've gladly surrendered a limb if it meant Conan would gallop to the rescue and whisk him away. After chopping off his mom's head, of course.

Mary's squint didn't land on Barry so much as trip over him. "Little Bawrence!"

"My name's Barry."

"Sweetheart, you were no bigger than a ripe tomato last I saw you. Mable almost ate you. Oh my, what's happened to your face?"

"It broke," Stephen said. "Mother, what are you doing here?"

"Take some inspiration, Louis, but don't go plum crazy. It's supposed to last me through the trip."

Mary was staying at the Howard Johnson's on 541 next to the turnpike, right down from the Burlington Center. As she explained to her two kids during the drive to HoJo's in her rented hatchback, she and Frank had already had a heart-to-heart about their college trust fund. The result of the conversation was still nebulous to Stephen by the time they sat down for lunch in the HoJo's diner. He stuck with tomato soup and crackers while his brother and mother, as if taunting and tempting him to fall back to his wayward, carb-monster ways, ordered club sandwiches and a small mountain of waffle fries.

"I reckon I could've gone to the bank. I don't know. But I'm not sure I would've qualified, know what I mean? And the interest, well. Y'all understand anything about that?"

"I do. Jonathan doesn't."

"Fuck off."

"Jonathan Monroe Roggebusch, you know better."

"Algebra is my strongest class, Mama. I'm getting a B."

"It probably wasn't the smartest thing to do."

"Did I just hear that?" Stephen said. "You're actually admitting a mistake?"

"I didn't tell anyone because I was going to fix it before anyone was the wiser."

"Why'd you need the money?"

"Honey, who are you taking to the prom?"

"Mother?"

"We've all got debts, Stephen. Maybe you don't because you're perfect."

"Debts don't just appear. Who are you in debt to? And if you don't have money, how did you afford to fly up here and rent a car and stay here? More debt?"

"You really caught your daddy's sass, didn't you? Are you eating enough?"

Mary and Jonathan spent the rest of Saturday at Great Adventure while Sunday saw them at Springfield. Stephen spent his Sunday hanging out with Barry. They watched *Goonies* and *Christine* and played games on the Commodore. Stephen set a new record by not uttering a single mean-spirited syllable in Barry's general direction during the whole course of the day.

Another first: He welcomed Monday with open arms, and that included calculus. The she-demon couldn't get to him here. With the sun approaching solstice, the light started playing new tricks on Mr. Giacomo's glossy pate. Stephen struggled mightily to keep pace with those tricks simultaneous with that rapid-fire South Jersey Italian accent blitzing through quiz results.

"Roggebusch!"

Stephen practically fell out of his chair. Mr. Giacomo, his chubby mitten brandishing stubby chalk against a backdrop of matted pits, glared at him with heavy eyes. "But I got a hundred on my quiz, Mr. Giacomo."

The other students laughed, but Mr. Giacomo's guffaw rose above them all. "My smart friend, you have a visitor." He nodded at Miss Wallace standing at the door. "I value English above all else. It's the language that helped my grandparents thrive when they were new to our shores. But still, make it quick, eh?"

"If I didn't have morals, I'd flunk your ultraconservative ass right now and make it my mission for you to repeat senior year." Miss Wallace had barely closed the door behind Stephen when she pounced. The cavernous fluorescent hallway was empty save for one kid shuffling way down yonder. Was that Jonathan? "Look at me, Stephen. Or should I call you Mama's Boy?"

"What is this? Are you having your monthly?" He remembered the term from an old novel they'd read earlier in the year.

"Getting your mother to get you out of going to the prom with me? Even for you..."

That same crypt-cold chill returned with a vengeance to grip his spine and paralyze him. He couldn't even feel his tongue, so that when he spoke, he sounded deranged. "You saw my mother?"

She was about to spit venom when Laz turned the corner, yukking it up with Louis. After they passed, she lowered her voice. "When I was in college, I dated a guy just like you. Couldn't stand being wrong. I used to let him win arguments sometimes because otherwise he wouldn't talk to me for days. You were scared I was going to say no. And if I had, you would've sulked for a week. So instead of being on the losing end, you go ahead and 'change' your mind and get the jump on me. And to rub it in, you get your fucking mom to storm in during my class. Have you completely lost your mind?"

He put a hand to his mouth to stop what he thought would be a vomiting fit. When nothing came up, he stroked his chin to play it off. And yet another first: never in his life had he been at such a complete loss for words. He stared at the lockers and would've gladly traded places with any of the inanimate objects inside them, even if it was a book by or about Jimmy Carter.

"Always putting women in our place, right? I'm an independent woman. I have a career. I take care of myself. And yes, one time I had an abortion. And it drives you God damned crazy." She stepped back and considered him. Stephen felt like she'd jammed a knife halfway in and was now contemplating whether to pull it out or ram it to the hilt.

"I didn't know." Christ, did he sound pathetic or what? It was like puberty never happened. "Go with me. I didn't know. Honest."

Those hard eyes probed his for another agonizing moment before she turned and threw open the stairwell doors and inflicted a kind of pain on the stairs that she probably wanted to let loose on him.

Stephen didn't hear a word Mr. Giacomo said for the rest of the class. When the two twenty-nine bell rang, he stayed fused to the chair the way the chair's metal neck was fused to the desk.

"Love it so much you can't leave, eh, Roggebusch? As Uncle Mickey used to say, 'Get outta your head, son. You'll catch something.' He-he!" He poked a porky finger on Stephen's forehead. Stephen would've jerked away if his whole body hadn't felt so leaden. Instead, Mr. Giacomo was the one who jerked away, wiping his finger on his shirt. "Maybe you should see the nurse, Roggebusch. We can talk later."

"Talk?"

"Just wanted a quick word, but if you're sick, it can wait."

"Having a quick word now versus later will have no effect on whether I am sick now versus later, nor will it impact my ability to talk if I am indeed sick now, as you suggest. Moreover, with school winding down, and with it my high school career, your window of opportunity for a quick word grows ever narrower."

"Your ma came to see me this morning."

"I gather she's been making the rounds."

"Technically, it's supposed to be planned ahead of time if it's not part of the PTA cadence, but hey, I'm flexible like that."

"She tell you to flunk me no matter what? Make sure I don't graduate?"

"She's a sweet gal. We had a super talk, a super one."

"Fascinating."

"So sweet I asked her out on a date. Know what she said? It's me you're talking to. Of course she said hell yes."

"Signore, your advice to seek care from the nurse was more sage than even your vast intellect can appreciate, for I am about to become violently ill."

Stephen bent every fiber of his will toward finding that little Lhasa as soon as he stormed into the house to the sight of Barry and John playing *G.I. Joe* on the Commodore, the sound of Louis and

Tanisha laughing at the TV in the living room, and the racket of Alex's bass in the music room. "Gorbie! Gorbachev! Gorbashay!"

He hadn't stalked the land with such single-minded purpose since that trip to the 7-Eleven for a Whatchamacallit. Where the hell was that ball-tonguing serial shitter? If he wasn't sleeping on the couch by the Buttonwood window or under the poolroom couch or on any of the living room furniture, and no one was taking him for a walk...

Sure enough, the little fur ball was curled up, oblivious to the world, under the master bed. No sooner did he summon Gorbie than a cannonball voice blasted out of the nook and knocked him on his ass.

"What the hell's going on out there?"

"Get over here, Gorbie. Come on... OW! Fucking mutt!"

"He's a purebred. Show some respect. His parents were champion show dogs in Canada."

"I've never shown respect to Canadians, and I won't start now." Only now did Stephen see that Gorbie hadn't been asleep but had been gnawing on what was left of a haunch bone. Having grown up with a certain floppy-eared Mable in North Fort Myers, he knew rule number one about dogs was not to go near them while they were feasting on gourmet. At the moment, though, he had no time for rules, just like he had no time for his stepmother's vitriol. He pretended the little bastard's teeth didn't hurt like mad while pulling him out by his forelegs.

He bundled the pooch under one arm and shuffled down the hall to his room and slammed the door. You could always count on Gorbie having a short memory. In no time at all, he was so comfortable on the bed that he turned over on his back so Stephen could massage his belly. The therapy worked. Or rather, it would've. Stephen had just nodded off when Jonathan thudded down the stairs with what sounded like a customer. They stopped to talk about payment before continuing to the first floor. When he heard his brother thumping back up, Stephen jumped out of bed and threw open the door. "Where's Mom going with Mr. Giacomo?" When

Jonathan answered with a blank look, he related what his calculus teacher told him.

"That doesn't make sense. Mom hates Italians."

"I don't think she wants to marry him. She just wants to get laid."

"Aw come on, man!"

"Where are they going?"

"The fuck should I know?"

"Ask her."

"Fuck you, you ask her."

"You really think she'd tell me?"

"What's in it for me?"

"The potential for sadistic satisfaction derived from sabotaging our mother's happiness."

"That's fucked up, man."

"Fine. Money."

"I've got enough dough. How about you be my chauffeur for a week?"

"I can't tell if you're joking."

"You're the one with a driver's license, bitch. I would ask Dan, but he'd actually have fun doing it."

"Could I pick a week during summer break?"

"You bet your ice cream-loving ass. I don't want anything else getting in the way. You're going wherever I tell you. Philly. New York. Fucking Amish country. Deal?"

"Sounds great." Stephen stabbed the air. "To compromise!"

Jonathan guffawed. "Dumb shit. I already knew about Mom and Mr. Giacomo. He's taking her to the Burlington Center." He guffawed again. "You're going to look so rad in a chauffer's hat."

It was during the drive to the Burlington Center that the full impact of what his mother had done to his prospects with Miss Wallace began to sink in. By the time Stephen pulled into the lot, he could barely breathe for the blood boiling inside him. If they weren't at the food court, the prospect of storming around both levels of the mall and bellowing their names, knocking over anyone who got in his way, preferably down the escalator and into the *Jungle Book* fountain, didn't seem so unreasonable.

It didn't take him long to spot them at the food court. As he made his way over, Stephen's mouth once again shriveled up. He detoured to the hot dog counter, got a large diet soda, and sucked half of it down before making a move toward the giggling couple.

"What did you say to Miss Wallace?"

"Sweetheart! Rocco and I were just talking about you. He's been telling me what a star student you are."

"He's a bit eccentric now," Mr. Giacomo said. He swallowed the rest of his egg roll and picked his teeth with a pinky. "Sometimes a bit too quiet when I know he's got the answer."

"Mother..."

"Can this wait, baby? Rocco and I were thinking of going to High Street for dessert."

Stephen sat down, not because his legs were tired, but because it was the only way to resist the pulsating urge to pick up the chair and body-slam it on his mother's flaming red hair. "Mother. What did you say?"

"Your English teacher, honestly. Rocco, what do you think? You're an intelligent man."

"Thanks, Ms. Miller, I appreciate that."

"Oh please. Mary. We're past that."

"I'm so used to the whole PTA bullshit, having to be all superpolite when all's I really want to do is cuss those bitches out. They don't get what it's like. No one does."

She gripped his hand. "You and I are of one mind."

"Mother..."

"Stephen, I don't think it's healthy for you to date your English teacher. You know what it does? It sets a bad precedent. Rocco?"

"What are you up to, Roggebusch? You're a smart kid. A little weird, sure. So maybe you like to draw puppy dogs in the margins. We've all got our quirks, am I right? But banging the teacher? Even a hot one like Miss Wallace?"

"You said I should go to the prom. That I was obligated."

"Baby, I figured it was implied you'd go with another student."

"I took a freshman," Mr. Giacomo said. "Gorgeous gal. Huge tits."

"Oh Rocco!" Mary covered her mouth and giggled as her face went beet red.

"Who's the man now, Mary? 'Course, then I knocked her up, married her, she left, took everything I had, and fuck you very much." He jabbed his chopsticks at Stephen. "Heed that shit, my friend."

Stephen stabbed the air. "Allow me to spell this out in terms even a drooling mental midget could grasp. Mother. I advise you to replace the money in your children's college fund. And stop getting back at your ex by ruining my life." In spite of the promise to himself that he wouldn't cry, a hot tear or two did escape. "I love her, you bitch." Stephen shot up, not knowing what he'd do next.

Mr. Giacomo belied his girth by leaping to his feet and gripping Stephen's arms from behind. "Breathe, my friend. Breathe. That's it."

To slip his calculus teacher's full nelson, Stephen copied the maneuver Louis used to escape Jonathan during the odd tug-of-war with Barry. It included popping Mr. Giacomo square on the nose.

"Aw fuck me."

Stephen grabbed the half-eaten egg roll from his mother's Styrofoam plate and crammed it into her mouth. And then, for the first time in his life, he lost time. In a blink, Mr. Giacomo was walking with him and patting him on the shoulder. They stopped at the escalator. Below, the little boy riding the elephant was aiming his gleeful, blinding laugh directly at him while the never-ending water squirted out of the trunk.

"All good? Just keep breathing."

"She tell you why she's here?"

"The woman can't get laid in Florida apparently. Jersey boys, we're easy."

"She tell you she's a thief and a liar?"

"Anyone told you there isn't a woman alive who isn't?"

They considered the fountain. "I've never read *The Jungle Book*. Can I call you Rocco?"

"Not if you want to graduate."

"How long were you married to the freshman?"

"Stop changing the subject. The prom sucks, Roggebusch. You're not missing anything."

"I appreciate the sage wisdom."

"No offense and all? But I'm not convinced you love Miss Wallace. You might think you do."

"I really wanted to take her."

"The whole goddam thing is a stupid charade. Look it, you want to spend all your dough on a tux, flowers, limo, all that shit?"

"I had a relationship with her."

"Shit like that's hot in porno movies. But in real life? Messy, my friend, messy."

"If I can look past a woman being a Commie Liberal, wouldn't that be love?"

"You think I don't get she's hot? I've been around this very same block, my friend. Look it here. A woman smart as her? And that young? Scares the shit out of me, know what I'm saying? But maybe your ma didn't really get it."

"Of course she did." He stabbed the air. "What the Great Satan did was among the lowest forms of human behavior I've ever witnessed. I'm not saying choking her with an egg roll was right, only that you understand why I did it. I'll never forgive her."

"I can't wait till you can drink, my friend." They considered the fountain again. "I'm guessing you won't go to the end-of-year dance? I hear some band from Holbein won the gig."

"I could probably think of a thousand legitimate reasons not to go. Absent those? A thousand illegitimate ones."

"Check this out. I've got two super God damned legitimate reasons you should go. I bet you'll never guess what they are. Go on, guess."

Stephen locked eyes with the kid. He knew it was impossible, but the smile seemed wider. "Before I die, I want to ride an elephant."

"It'd sure last longer than sex." They yukked that one up. "Get the hell outta here, ya bum. Let me finish my chow mein so I can do the nasty with your ma."

The drive home allowed Stephen to absorb everything Mr. Giacomo had said. By the time he pulled up to the Queen Anne, he knew what he had to do.

Stephen was far from the only senior at RV's end-of-year dance. As soon as he walked into the gymnasium, with Alex and his Glyphs doing a fairly solid rendition of "You Spin Me Round (Like a Record)," he spotted a cluster of seniors, some from calculus, grouped over by the punch table. That girl with the giant glasses who sat up front and never said hello to anybody made eye contact with him and nodded in his direction. He was so taken by the simple gesture that he nodded back and grinned before he knew what he was doing. On his way to the food table, he ran into a girl he recognized as one of the juniors who had gym the same time he did, third period. Every gym period featured a class from all four grade levels. This being high school, it was anathema to socialize with anyone from any of the other classes, especially if you were a senior. This being a dance, though, and with school and all its unspoken rules about to take a two-month breather, Stephen didn't think twice about chewing the fat with her. When she apologized for his not going to the prom, he channeled Rocco the Wise and Good in declaring it overrated. Her red-faced giggling dissolved some of the burn in his chest. Her name was Christina. When her two friends came back from the dance floor, Stephen said it was nice meeting her and moved on to the food table where he ran into another student from calculus.

Louis and Tanisha and a bunch of other students from the Gardens stood in a roughly hewn circle toward the center of the dance floor. Once in a while, when the Glyphs hit upon the right kind of song, Louis and Tanisha separated themselves from the group to get into the groove. Jonathan, meantime, stood over against the wall with one foot up against it. Now and again a student or teacher would walk by and say something to him without looking at him, to which he would respond while looking in the opposite direction.

With his siblings too preoccupied to mock his diet or history of weight issues, Stephen felt free to gorge himself on the pasta and baby pizzas. He was about to head back for thirds when he literally bumped into Christina.

"Hi again!" Mistaking his trying to swallow for trying to remember her name, she squeaked, "Christina!"

"You try this yet? It's quite rad." This launched Christina into a diatribe about how much she hated her mom's cooking. That led to a discussion about great restaurants. The only decent restaurant that came to Stephen's mind was that one in Wheaton Plaza near Kensington where Joanne used to take them for dinner on those nights when Frank was "working late." Restaurants led Christina to talking about driving patterns and how her mom drove her and her friends to school too slowly for their taste and that she'd be better off junking their beat-up seventies boat.

"My dad drives a Caravan," Stephen said. She made a face that suggested unfamiliarity. "It's one of those newfangled types of vans. They're vans, but they're smaller. Minivans!" He stabbed the air.

"Radical! See? That's what we need! And you can drive it and stuff since you're a senior and all."

"Maybe if I lived farther away. But I'm right down the street. You know Broad and Buttonwood?"

"I *love* that house! Oh my God, you don't understand. I totally tell my mom all. The time. How I wished we lived there. That is the coolest-looking house, like, ever!"

"I don't think you're thinking of the right house." He explained it again, but she only grew more stoked.

"That is the most radical thing I've ever heard, Stevie. Oh my God, I just called you Stevie!"

"I've been living there for three and a half years. Not once has it ever occurred to me that living there should be viewed as a positive experience. Christina? I believe you are teaching me objectivity."

"Amazing!"

"Hey. Stephen. Dude."

Stephen recognized the voice but at first didn't have a clue who this guy with the ponytail was. He'd never seen Alexander with his hair tied back.

"I can see you're perplexed. By my hair. It's making my head hot. And sweaty. That makes my scalp, you know, itch. So that's why I scratch it. See? God damn it. I don't know why I tied my hair back. I guess I thought it would help. But I don't know why I thought that."

"This is one of my brothers. Only he isn't. I'll explain later."

"Hey, man. Thanks so much. For coming here. Sorry for speaking. In short sentences. Even for me. Out of breath. Voice dying. Maybe dead. Already."

"Here!" Christina fetched Alexander a tall cup of punch. He downed the whole thing in a single pull and took several gasps of air before talking again.

"Rad. Thanks. So you must be Stephen's date. You must not be a senior. Because if you were, ya know, you'd be at the senior prom. Of course, Stephen is a senior, and that's the only requirement for you to go to the senior prom. So you still could've gone. If you were with Stephen."

Only now did it occur to Stephen that music was still playing even though the stage was empty. "Who's playing that seventies crap?"

"The DJ over there. You might've missed him because he looks like a student. That's because he is a student."

Stephen spotted the skinny kid with the narrow head bob back and forth in time to the music with a giant pair of headphones that, from this distance, gave him Princess Leia earmuffs. Just behind the DJ he caught sight of Jonathan slipping out.

"It's important to rest between sets. And drink fluids. And preferably suck on lemons. Because otherwise, your voice will become shot."

"That's a really rad guitar."

"Bass. I hope you start going steady with Stephen. Because if you do, that means Stephen will, ya know, have a girlfriend. And you're a nice person. Hopefully, once you start going steady, you'll come over to our house."

Christina gasped.

"You've been a true intellectual addition to the conversation, Alexander."

"Because the thing is? The sad fact? Is that we normally don't get nice people at our house. Except maybe her. See her? That's Tanisha. She dates Louis. She's really cool. Really rad at math."

"You seem rad. Stevie seems super rad."

"Stevie." Alexander squinted ever so slightly. "Oh. Yeah. She means you. I disagree. He's not very nice. Stevie. But that's okay. Because I'm not very nice. My stepdad, his real dad, is supersmart and wise. But is he nice? Jonathan is definitely not."

"God, you are such a fucking dork, I hate you!" Meredith threw her arms around Alexander from behind.

"And this young lady here? She likes to cuss a lot, but she's still nice. And a rad drummer."

"Come on, asswipe. Time for the second set."

"It was nice to meet you. And Stevie?"

"Never call me that again."

Stephen watched Alexander and Meredith—was his hand on her ass?—hurry back up to the stage and high-five their fellow Glyphs before diving into Yazoo's "Don't Go." Stephen had really wanted to say something else to his stepbrother, but now he had no idea what that would've been. His head was spinning. The swirling colored lights, the music, all these damned jibber-jabbering teenagers...

"He seems rad. You must have really rad brothers."

He mumbled some excuse for having to step away and huffed and puffed toward the exit. Not until he was outside did he notice the sweat coating his forehead and matting his pits. Had he been in North Fort Myers right now, he'd grab a bunch of comic books and a Whatchamacallit and a Tab and head out to the porch swing. He had no idea how long he stood there, the Glyphs' riffs frolicking with the cricket chirps, when he heard another sound, beyond the crickets: Jonathan.

Jonathan and the police officer were both wearing dark clothing, so they weren't obvious at first even if they were dead ahead in the end zone on the far side of the football field.

"What do you think, I'm just a retard with a gun?"

"Ask Garrett. He's inside. Go ask him."

"So you came here not because of all the potential sales, but because you wanted to ask your buddy about going to the Burlington Center."

"No."

"What?"

"You didn't let me finish."

"Jesus Christ, where are my fucking manners?"

"Cherry Hill Mall. But we don't have a car, and Garrett's brother's got a pickup. How do you think we get to the Pine Barrens, man?"

Officer Douglas flattened the impeccably mown grass with his black boots as he closed the distance between them. "Every lie is an insult, you know that, right?"

"What the fuck is your problem?"

"I have given you so many chances, Roggebusch, it's sick. Why shouldn't I confiscate your weed right now and toss your ass in the clink?"

"But then Tara would get all pissed because she's dating my brother. Then our families would be like Romeo and Juliet and shit."

"Don't ever say my daughter's name again, you fucking truant."

Jonathan tried to maintain a tough look that, in the face of the behemoth before him, came out looking so pathetic it was all Stephen could do not to blow up in hysterics.

The cop took a step back. "Know what your problem is? Seriously? You think too short-term. You probably think a week in jail wouldn't be so bad. But it goes on your record, dumbass. And what would your father say?"

Jonathan blurted a guffaw. "You think he'd give a shit? My stepmom threw a fucking can of peas at my head, he didn't do shit. Put me in jail right now, he probably wouldn't notice."

"You're breaking my heart, junior. Let me know when you get to the part where the evil stepmom stole your common sense."

"Jonathan! Jonathan!"

Stephen's heart stopped as he whipped around to behold the flame-topped she-goblin barreling down the football field. He didn't move. Did she even notice him?

"My word!" Mary was bending over and panting as if she'd just returned a kickoff for a touchdown.

The cop stepped up to her and offered a hand, maintaining his steely countenance. "Officer James Douglas, ma'am, Mount Holly Police Department."

"Jonathan... What...?"

Stephen took a step back. Could it be that he'd slip away without anyone being the wiser?

"Stephen!"

Since when was he that lucky?

"You one of the brothers?"

"Depends how you look at it," Stephen said as he and Officer Douglas shook hands. "You could say I'm his only brother. Or one of six." He stabbed the air. "It's all about perspective, as our father likes to say."

"Baby, what's going on? Why are you talking to this pig?"

"Beg your pardon, ma'am?"

"Nice one, Mother."

Jonathan guffawed.

"Stephen, you are pathetic. You should be at the prom with a pretty girl. What kind of role model do you expect to be for your baby brother? Pardon my candor, officer, but what is your mission for this evening? I didn't see too many black children in there."

"Everyone, meet my mother! Mother, you're in New Jersey now. The mores of the Deep South didn't really make it up here after that whole Civil War thing."

"Officer Douglas is here for me, Ma. He's arresting me."

"Baby, that's not funny. Oh you two will be the death of me."

"Ma!"

"Heavens to Betsy, what has gotten into you?"

"I want him to arrest me. I broke the law. You won't acknowledge it now, but maybe watching him lead me away in cuffs will wake you up. You and Dad, man. I don't know how you two survived together. Both of you, it's like you don't want to see what's real, what's right in fucking front of you."

Mary closed her mouth and let the words on her tongue slide down her throat like a bad oyster shot. She checked her watch, then considered her firstborn. Stephen squinted at her with a cackle ready to launch. The Glyphs grew louder. Stephen imagined the notes pouring out of Alex's bass like they did Louis's chuckle. Twin streams of notes flowed and meandered out of the gym and collected into pools above their heads.

"Fuck it. Here." Jonathan dug a squished baggie out of his pocket and slapped it in the palm of Officer Douglas. "Already sold most of it to some punk sophomores who think they're hot shit just because they're sophomores. Subpar shit that'll char their throats before it gets them high." He offered his wrists.

All trace of Mary's joviality went the way of the sophomores' throats. "Stephen!"

"All sophomores think they're hot shit," Officer Douglas said as he clicked the cuffs into place. Stephen noticed he left them a bit loose. "You can survive freshman year, you can survive anything."

"Stephen! Jonathan!"

"Double high five, bitch!"

"Your aunts would be beside themselves if they could see the pair of you now."

"Hey, Jonathan, you care what crazy bitches think?"

"I've got enough of them to deal with up here."

"Mother?" Instead of stabbing the air, Stephen glided his open palm through it with a slow, thick motion like a warm knife through cake. "Your sisters are out of their minds."

"Move it, Roggebusch." Officer Douglas led Jonathan away.

"Hey, Jonathan. Why do you think Faith took the blame for Barry?"

Jonathan looked back at him and said something that was drowned out by the Glyphs' cover of Outfield's "Your Love."

"Frank's own son by that cow took his money?" Mary hooted and hollered. "If that ain't poetic justice, darlin'!"

Stephen had no idea how long he stood there after Jonathan and Officer Douglas left. What would Gorbie be doing right now?

Snoring on top of the couch by the windowsill? Eventually his mother yanked him back down to earth with:

"That reminds me, baby. You might want to know she's here." When he looked at her, she added, "The cow."

The world started to precess like a disturbed top, faster and faster. Stephen collapsed into a cross-legged position on the moist grass. The Glyphs were hammering nails into his head. His mother's fiery mane glowed against the black sky, a vision ripped from the pages of a Victorian horror novel.

Mary cackled. "Joanne Barney Roggebusch. I know she saw me. That bitch. That scheming devil. I smiled at her. And she just got in her car and drove away."

"Joan." Breathing was next to impossible. Stephen snatched at thick gobs of the stubborn, humid air. "Purvis. Her mother's maiden name."

"Beg pardon? Stephen, what are you doing down there?"

"Her new name's Joan Purvis." And I have to see her.

Stephen had very little memory of the drive to the Howard Johnson's. After throwing himself into Faith's Rabbit, the next thing that registered was jumping out of his crooked parking job and stomping up to the first cleaning lady he saw, a stout middle-aged woman with enough gravity in her face to dim the patio bulbs above her. "Joan Purvis. Joanne Roggebusch."

"No names, hon." She held up a crumpled sheet of lined paper and jabbed it with a stubby finger that was being strangled by an old bronze ring. "Room numbers."

A man in an AC/DC shirt appeared out of nowhere. What with the old stretched freckles, the thinning, darkening blond hair, and scruffy goatee, this could be Jonathan in twenty years. "We don't give out guests' names, dude." Those glassy, bloodshot eyes had called it a day some time ago.

"Her son's dying."

"Christ on a Popsicle stick, what's the name?"

"I think it's Joan Purvis now."

AC/DC scratched his forehead and spat phlegm as he lumbered into the office.

Stephen hurried across the parking lot and stopped a foot or so shy of the highway and looked in both directions. A station wagon zipped by close enough to make his loose-hanging button shirt flap against his midsection. Suddenly he was aware of his weight. When was the last time he stepped on a scale? Was he starting to gain back some of that prepubescent girth? Was that why Daniel and Louis were making fun of his past weight struggles more frequently?

"You might want to get away from there."

"You mean get away from New Jersey?"

"She's gone, dude."

Stephen turned to him but stayed near the highway. "Where?"

"Plans must've changed. She was supposed to stay here a few more days."

"Until the graduation."

"I remember her. She comes barging in, all frazzled and shit. You know how chicks get. She's got to go now. No reason, no explanation. I was like, 'Hey, man, how 'bout paying me for one more night?' You know, that's the honorable thing to do, am I right?"

"She say where she was going?"

"The fuck you keep asking that?"

"What kind of car did she drive?"

AC/DC shrugged and raised those tired-looking arms. His droopy eyes looked like they really wanted to widen to convey his surprise that he'd be expected to know that detail.

"What room did she stay in?"

"Sir, you know..." He closed his eyes as if a wave of pain or oblivion was washing over him.

Stephen looked up and saw the cleaning lady unlocking a room. He was running up the stairs when AC/DC yelled out, "Hyundai! I think it was red!"

As soon as Stephen stepped inside, he knew this was the room. He'd forgotten about her penchant for slapping Jergens aloe on her hands every day, but now the redolence triggered a flood of memories, not all bad. Indeed, it was only now, with the scent swirling around him and those familiar bobby pins atop the TV (she always managed to misplace a few), did he grasp that, in the end, she was the only one in that house on Soward Drive who had made any effort to cater to his idiosyncrasies. Exhibit A: the soup.

Stephen didn't realize he was walking farther into the room until he was just a couple of feet from the sheer white vanity. What he thought was someone in his peripheral vision turned out to be a reflection of himself in the body mirror glued to the bathroom door, open at just the right angle to show an infinite number of Stephens in the vanity mirror. He didn't think he looked too fat, but it was impossible to tell without someone like Jonathan or Daniel next to him.

A sky-blue shower cap clung to the knob. Was that the same cap from the Kensington days? If so, that she left it in a motel off the New Jersey Turnpike suddenly became sadder than he could handle right now. He distracted himself with the cleaning lady, who at the moment was changing the two queens. "How long was she here?"

"What was that, hon?"

"The woman. Joan Purvis."

"A week maybe? She was nice."

"A full week?" His chest started burning. He spotted a couple more bobby pins on top of the nightstand.

"Sweet lady. Can I help you with something?"

"Twice now you've pointed out how nice she was."

"She gave me a tip."

"A tip?" That came out all wrong, but Stephen had never heard of such a thing. The Roggebusch family had made its fair share of vacations together, including the (in)famous 1980 trip, and never once had he seen his father leave a tip for housekeeping. He picked up the phone. "Barry! How's it going, buddy?"

"Fine."

"Playing the Commodore?"

"I don't know."

"That Dad talking?"

"We're watching TV. It's about the Nazis."

"Ah, the Nazis. Any good?"

"I don't know."

"Faith there?"

"I don't know."

"Upstairs probably? In her private sanctum?"

"I don't know."

"Was anyone there earlier? Any guests?"

"I don't know."

His brother's voice sounded so puny and helpless. His mother had just come up here, the mother he'd barely spent any of his life with, and he had no idea. He was sitting there in the cushioned rocking chair, his father buzzed on scotch and blowing hot air about this or that plan by Eisenhower or Patton, Gorbie slobbering his nuts. A pang flared in the center of his chest. "What was that?"

"Daddy said are you at the dance?"

"Yeah. You know, taking a break. I'll see you soon."

Stephen had no idea how late it was but apparently late enough for this stretch of 541 to see a minute or so of peace between cars. He knew how ridiculous he looked, but it didn't matter. The swelling in his breast mandated this be done. He stood dead center in the middle of the highway facing Mount Holly. Forty-Eight Broad was barely three miles away, yet it may as well have been someplace past Pluto. He wasn't entirely sure what he said, only that it was loud, contained more profanity in a minute than he'd spewed in the past year, and left his throat feeling shredded.

As he huffed back over to the parking lot, he grabbed the fascinated manager by the arm, yanked him into the office, and made him give up the room number of Mary Miller. As soon as the cleaning lady let him in, Stephen scanned the room just like Arnold in *The Terminator*. Only, Stephen's Sarah Connor turned out to be a hair dryer, a Walkman, and some blouses on a rack. After stomping on those first two items until they were flattened shadows of their former selves, he tossed the blouses in the tub, squirted them with the various squirtables, and blasted the water. For the gravy, he grabbed the motel stationary and scribbled a message that was as aggressive as he could make it while still staying true to his hero: "You have been terminated." He left it on the toilet seat.

The next day, after he and his father picked up Jonathan from jail, Frank told them on the drive back that Mary had agreed to restore their college trust fund.

As soon as they got home, the two boys walked without a word into the poolroom to play the Summer Olympics on the Commodore. Neither got very upset when the other scored higher, not even when Jonathan nailed a perfect ten at diving.

"Dudes." Alexander was standing behind the couch, popping some Pop Rocks. "What a show last night, huh? I saw both of you. At one point. Or, for that matter, at many points. Stephen, that girl you were with looked fetching. And that's a word I don't get to use very often."

"Nine point eight! Suck on that, bitch!"

"Did you really go to jail, Double? Again?"

"I only came last night to do some business." Jonathan mimed rubbing dollar bills between his fingers.

"So if I told you we had a rad time at Meredith's last night, ya know, getting stoned on pot brownies, you'd probably say I was an asshole. Ya know, for rubbing your face in it."

"Pretty rad, man."

"But I'm thinking that'll be the last time. For me and pot."

"Scared straight already?"

"We got away with it last night. But that doesn't mean we will every time. See, I'm a numbers guy. Like my mom. Numbers flow in my blood. Sooner or later I'll get busted. It's what they call a statistical probability. So Frank says. Mom calls it common fucking sense."

"Yeah, man," Jonathan said as he lost in the long jump. "You'll always get busted in the end."

"Alexan-*dor*?" Stephen turned to his stepbrother for the first time since he walked into the room. He must've washed his hair this morning. It seemed fluffier and even longer than last night. It took a second to locate the eyes. "Given that this is the first and last time Jonathan will ever provide advice to anyone that makes any sense, my advice to you? Is to listen."

At dinner that night, Daniel said his Bad Thing was that his mother wouldn't be able to make it to the graduation.

"Oh that's too bad," Frank said with a note of emotion that caught Stephen off guard.

"Can't get away from work, apparently."

"What do you expect?" Louis said as he stabbed his blue-cheesed salad. "She works two jobs, UNC and The Family Doctor. Right, Barry? Sometimes when we go down there, it's like, what's the point? She even works weekends."

Stephen kept his eyes on his plate as he calmly carved the Cornish game hen, buttered his wild rice, spooned the snow peas aside, ignored the salad, and emoted nary a jot.

Frank's Good Thing saw him go on at great length about how happy he was that the dispute with Mary had ended amicably, or as he put it, "As amicably as can be reasonably expected when dealing with Cujo. Never in my life have I been that upset."

"We get it, love."

"Not even the so-called teachers at Sidwell Friends were so nasty, and what they did to sabotage my academic career could fill up a binder. I ever tell you they tried to send me to a Quaker college?"

"And Daddy Dearest swooped in to save the day." Jonathan chuckled. Stephen couldn't help following suit.

"Now for my Bad Thing? I'd like to stay with Mary's side of the family, in particular her children." Stephen and Jonathan stopped midchew. "Sort of a dual Bad Thing. I can do that, right? Stephen, my Bad Thing for you is you didn't go to the prom."

"You didn't miss much," Daniel said. "Food was terrible."

"And my Bad Thing for Jonathan is that he went to jail for selling pot at the school dance." Faith kept her eyes on her giant bowl of peas while the kids, led by Stephen, applauded with a hearty bravissimo times three.

"And look at that, he's already out," John said. "Just like in the movies. Bad guys never stay in jail."

"Very astute observation, John-n-n-n."

"That's why the solution is always to kill them," Alexander said. "Blow them away. Not that, ya know, I would wish that on you, Double. That would suck."

"And for my New Thing, I have something very interesting to announce. Next Sunday, Bawrence and I are going to meet with Leo Stringfellow. You might remember him visiting not too long ago. His sister Bunny was a student here. In fact, Leo will bring his great-granddaughter, who's around Bawrence's age. Her name is also Bunny."

"Bunny's really rad!" Barry exclaimed.

Jonathan almost chuckled the milk out of his mouth.

"She *is* rad?" Alexander said.

"She was playing a lot of rad music when she died."

"Bawrence, name something by Beethoven," Faith said while shoveling peas into her mouth.

Normally, Stephen would shout "Bawrence Barney!" in mock indignation to rub Barry's face in it, but now, for the first time ever, he was rooting for him to win. That's why, when Barry answered, it made Stephen's legs itch to jump up.

"Violin Concerto in D Major! That's opus 61. That means it was the sixty-first thing he wrote. Because opus is Latin for work."

Frank set his knife and fork down, crossed his hands, and considered his youngest. "That is correct, Bawrence."

"It's got a lot of high notes," Barry went on.

"What?" Alexander said.

Stephen couldn't help the smile itching the corner of his mouth. Every eye was on Barry but not for the usual reasons.

"What do you mean, high notes?"

"What do you *think* it means, Alexan-*dor*?" Barry said with a lean of his head across the table. "It also has three movements. But then again, most have three movements. Fast, slow, fast."

"Yes, that last point is obvious," Faith said. "Although I'm not so sure that's such an obvious piece by Beethoven." She cleared her throat loudly to punctuate her point before sipping her ice water.

"Actually," Frank said. "Opus 61 is not only an obvious piece by Beethoven, it's considered a gold standard of the repertoire. My mother were here, she'd read us chapter and verse on this point."

"And Tchaikovsky! His first name was Peter. He did D major too. But his was opus 35. And you're supposed to play the second and third parts without stopping ever. It's really hard."

"Dude." John stopped his fork midsalad stab. "You for real?"

"You feed him all this?" Faith glared at her man with furrowed brows that resembled a bird of prey midflight.

"I have not discussed this topic with Bawrence, no."

"Mendelssohn's first name was Fred."

"Felix!" Faith snapped.

"And his song's called E Minor, and it was opus 64. This one's really different because Bunny, I mean, the violin player gets to play all by herself at first."

"Bawrence..." Faith failed to suppress a titter. "I can cite twenty violin concertos right now that start with a soloist."

Frank cleared his throat. "I believe what Bawrence is referring to is how Mendelssohn's concerto was innovative in the context of its day. Before Mendelssohn, as my father could tell you, you always started with the orchestra."

"There's also a bridge!"

"Between which movements?"

"All of them!"

Faith guffawed with peas in her mouth.

"Bawrence is half-right," Frank said. "The bridge is between the second and third movements. And as my mother could explain, as this piece is one of her favorite to play, the three movements aren't so obviously defined from each other. The first kind of flows into the second. I don't know why you're shaking your head, lovey. Next time my parents come up, I'll ask Mother to perform it for you. She'll be tickled you made the request."

Faith switched from shoveling her peas to stabbing them. "Still seems odd that he would go from knowing absolutely nothing about classical music or music in general to suddenly having insight on bridging passages."

"I know how he knows," Jonathan said.

"Bawrence?" Faith cleared her throat and slammed her fork down. "How would you describe the note pattern of a concerto by Mozart versus, say, Brahms?"

"Note pattern?" Stephen said.

"I'm not sure even I could describe the note pattern of Mozart versus Brahms," Frank said.

"Maybe you should call your parents."

"What is the point of your question?"

Stephen saw the wave of dread rippling across Barry's countenance. "Bawrence Barney? Hey, man. That was awesome."

"Next time Frank's parents are up, I'm going to have to, ya know, talk to them," Alexander said. "The Glyphs could use a violinist. That would be pretty rad."

"Bawrence, what can you tell me..."

"Faith, wait." Frank waved his hands as if wiping away a film of crap. "What is the point of the question?"

"Do you want me to die?"

Everyone suddenly found fascination with the contents of their plates. Stephen used his peripheral vision to keep tabs on who'd be the first to lift their head. Once again, his heart went aflutter at the winner.

"Stop complaining!" Barry reciprocated Faith's laser-beam glare with a look of disgust that twisted the healthy side of his face. "Whenever I complain, everyone gets mad at me. But how come you get to complain? That's not fair! Dummy Stupid Shut up, that's Faith!"

Sometime after dinner, when he heard Barry stomp out of Faith's wardrobe closet following his Sunday-night chat with his mother, Stephen stopped him at the stairs to see if he wanted to go with him to take Gorbie for a walk. After staring at his older brother like he was the proof of alien life we've all been waiting for, Barry finally jerked his head in the affirmative.

Stephen decided the 7-Eleven route would be best. He even let his little brother hold the leash. "Moms suck, don't they?" he said when they were on their way back.

His brother was showing that Coke-Mountain Dew Slurpee who was boss. When he finally came up for air: "I don't know."

When they reached Garden Street, Stephen had them go right instead of left. "Let's go the long way. Past the schools. It's my last year at RV, your last at Folwell. Going to miss it?"

"I don't know."

They took a left on Clover, followed by the soft right onto Jacksonville Road. As they came up to Ridgeway, Stephen considered the Folwell campus. It didn't have too many exterior lights. Perhaps the utter emptiness of the grounds added to the darkness. It only just occurred to him that he'd never seen the inside of that school. Now that Barry was wrapping it up, he'd never see what it was like inside, never have a clue what Barry's life had been like for the past three and a half years.

RV didn't have Folwell's lighting problem. The lights along both Jacksonville and Ridgeway, as well as those in the parking lot, were more than enough to make those pillars glow.

When they were on their way down Ridgeway, Barry chomped down on his Zero.

"I think moms suck. When we moved up here, your mom moved in the opposite direction."

"I like North Carolina. It's fun."

"She ran away. Daniel and Louis are too stupid to see that. She's not coming up for the graduation. And she doesn't want you living with her."

"She has to finish her classes and stuff. So she can have enough money."

"She's a coward. But don't feel bad. My mom sucks too. But you know who's not our mom? Faith. We win!" They exploded in laughter and were still laughing when they made the left onto Buttonwood.

The day after graduation was the lunch date with Leo and Bunny. Since first mentioning it the previous Sunday, more people decided they wanted to go. When would they get another chance to meet living history? Or so Frank put it. Only when Jonathan said he wanted to go did Stephen cave to groupthink and throw his name in.

Lunch was to be at a classy two-story restaurant in Burlington. Frank had reserved a table on the second floor, overlooking the river. Everyone started congregating on the first floor toward eleven.

As Stephen came downstairs, he was greeted to the right by the tinkling sounds of his father teasing the ivories. He was playing his theme song, "Moonglow" meets *Picnic*. To the left, Faith's crisp enunciation oozed from the poolroom like lava. Louis, John, and Jonathan were scrunched together on the couch while Daniel and Alexander took to the floor to grab a last bit of Commodore action. Their (step)mother loomed and spewed a warning to be sure they remained on their best behavior, kept their volume in check, and otherwise comported themselves in a totally opposite manner from last night at Charlie's Other Brother. Stephen parked himself on the couch by the Buttonwood door to rub Gorbie's belly.

Barry thumped downstairs in that god-awful pair of blue pants that defied categorization. He stomped into the music room and continued saying "Daddy!" in a whine until Frank paused, took a breath, then belted out a rapid-fire hook. Only then did he stop to hear his son's concern about finding a shirt that matched.

"All right, team!" the old man said as he marched into the hall. "Everybody read-yyyyy? Gorbachev, you have the house. Try not to party."

"You're a pain in my ass," Barry spat at Jonathan after the latter guffawed at those ridiculous pants. Double messed up his baby brother's hair and yanked him in for a one-armed hug.

"Ste-*van*! Be sure to lock the door behind us please."

The kids jostled and fussed and laughed their way out the door while the church on High Street tolled eleven.

Somewhere upstairs, someone was making a momentous decision.

ABOUT TOM

Tom Lady is the author of the collection *48 Broad: Stories* and the forthcoming novel *Son of Slut*.

In the real world he lives in Burbank, California. In the virtual world you can find him at 48broad.com.

Be social with Tom at facebook.com/tomladyscribbler and insta-gram.com/thomaslady.

Got a question for Tom or just want to say hey? Hit him up at barry@48broad.com.

Made in the USA
San Bernardino, CA
13 December 2018